Hope Springs

Books 1–3

Not Until Forever
Not Until This Moment
Not Until You

Valerie M. Bodden

Hope Springs Books 1–3 © 2019 by Valerie M. Bodden.

NOT UNTIL FOREVER
NOT UNTIL THIS MOMENT
NOT UNTIL YOU

Not Until Forever Copyright © 2019 by Valerie M. Bodden. All Rights Reserved.
Not Until This Moment Copyright © 2019 by Valerie M. Bodden. All Rights Reserved.
Not Until You Copyright © 2019 by Valerie M. Bodden. All Rights Reserved.

Scriptures taken from the Holy Bible, New International Version®, NIV®. Copyright © 1973, 1978, 1984, 2011 by Biblica, Inc.™ Used by permission of Zondervan. All rights reserved worldwide. www.zondervan.com The "NIV" and "New International Version" are trademarks registered in the United States Patent and Trademark Office by Biblica, Inc.™

All rights reserved. No part of this book may be reproduced in any form or by any electronic or mechanical means including information storage and retrieval systems, without permission in writing from the author. The only exception is by a reviewer, who may quote short excerpts in a review.

This book is a work of fiction. Names, characters, places, and incidents either are products of the author's imagination or are used fictitiously. Any resemblance to actual persons, living or dead, events, or locales is entirely coincidental.

Cover design: Ideal Book Covers

Valerie M. Bodden
Visit me at www.valeriembodden.com

Hope Springs Series

Hope Springs Box Set 1–3
includes
Not Until Forever
Not Until This Moment
Not Until You

Hope Springs Box Set 4–6
includes
Not Until Us
Not Until Christmas Morning
Not Until This Day

Hope Springs Book 7
Not Until Someday

Hop Springs Book 8
Not Until Now

River Falls Series

Pieces of Forever

Contents

Hope Springs 1
Hope Springs Series 1
River Falls Series 1
Contents 2
A Gift for You 7
Not Until Forever 9
Prologue 11
Chapter 1 16
Chapter 2 29
Chapter 3 37
Chapter 4 43
Chapter 5 52
Chapter 6 61
Chapter 7 66
Chapter 8 76
Chapter 9 82
Chapter 10 90
Chapter 11 100
Chapter 12 112
Chapter 13 122
Chapter 14 131
Chapter 15 136
Chapter 16 139

Chapter 17 149

Chapter 18 159

Chapter 19 168

Chapter 20 177

Chapter 21 184

Chapter 22 191

Chapter 23 196

Chapter 24 204

Chapter 25 211

Chapter 26 218

Chapter 27 224

Chapter 28 234

Chapter 29 237

Chapter 30 242

Chapter 31 246

Chapter 32 254

Chapter 33 261

Chapter 34 265

Not Until This Moment 271

Chapter 1 273

Chapter 2 278

Chapter 3 283

Chapter 4 295

Chapter 5 299

Chapter 6 309

Chapter 7 315

Chapter 8 320

Chapter 9 324
Chapter 10 327
Chapter 11 331
Chapter 12 338
Chapter 13 349
Chapter 14 355
Chapter 15 358
Chapter 16 362
Chapter 17 368
Chapter 18 375
Not Until You 379
Chapter 1 381
Chapter 2 386
Chapter 3 389
Chapter 4 399
Chapter 5 409
Chapter 6 418
Chapter 7 426
Chapter 8 439
Chapter 9 451
Chapter 10 458
Chapter 11 469
Chapter 12 485
Chapter 13 496
Chapter 14 507
Chapter 15 515
Chapter 16 521

Chapter 17 529
Chapter 18 534
Chapter 19 542
Chapter 20 554
Chapter 21 563
Chapter 22 574
Chapter 23 587
Chapter 24 592
Chapter 25 602
Chapter 26 610
Chapter 27 619
Chapter 28 626
Chapter 29 637
Chapter 30 645
Chapter 31 653
Chapter 32 663
Chapter 33 668
Chapter 34 677
Chapter 35 685
Chapter 36 696
Chapter 37 699
Chapter 38 702
Chapter 39 705
Chapter 40 709
Chapter 41 717
Chapter 42 721
Chapter 43 726

Chapter 44	730
Chapter 45	738
Epilogue	743
A preview of Not Until Us	751
More Hope Springs Books	754
And Don't Miss the River Falls Series	755
Acknowledgements	756
About the Author	758

A Gift for You . . .

Members of my Reader's Club get a FREE story, available exclusively to my subscribers. When you sign up, you'll also be the first to know about new releases, book deals, and giveaways. Visit www.valeriembodden.com/gift to join.

Not Until Forever

-Hope Springs Book 1-

But when the kindness and love of God our Savior appeared, he saved us, not because of righteous things we had done, but because of his mercy.
—Titus 3:4-5

Prologue

Five Years Earlier

Spencer paced behind the park bench, tipping his head toward the gray clouds swirling above him. His nerves swirled faster. He patted at the pocket of his hoodie for the eighth time, letting the solidity of the little box there reassure him. Even if some parts of his life were falling apart right now, this was the one thing he was sure of.

He squinted toward the parking lot, watching for the flash of Sophie's bright red Camaro. But the lot was empty, aside from his battered pickup truck, already packed with the few things he needed from his apartment. It was hard to believe he was going to walk away without his degree with less than a semester to go. But this was what he had to do. His family needed him.

He scrubbed a hand over his face and made himself sit down. He should be on his way already. But he couldn't leave without doing this. Without telling Sophie what he wanted for the future. Their future.

Finally, the rumble of the Camaro's engine caught his ears. Spencer fumbled at his pocket again as Sophie whipped into the parking lot. The wind unfurled her golden hair behind her as she stepped out of the car. Spencer shoved a hand roughly through his own hair and swallowed hard. What had he been thinking, doing this here?

He should have picked somewhere more romantic. More elegant. More Sophie. But this park had been their place since their first date three years ago. It was where they came to talk, to laugh, to share everything. Doing this here, now, felt right. Spencer forced himself to take a slow breath as Sophie hurried toward him, her strides long and sure in her heels and slim black skirt.

Just the sight of her lightened his heart. He had no idea what a woman like her saw in a man like him, but he'd learned not to question it. For whatever reason, they worked. And for that, he thanked God.

Spencer sank his face into her hair as his arms tugged her closer. This was what he'd needed. Whatever he was facing, holding Sophie made everything right in the world.

She pulled back a few inches and slid her fingers over his unshaven cheek. "You look tired. You sure you want to make the drive back to Hope Springs yet tonight?"

Not now that he was with her, he didn't. But he nodded. "I have to, Soph."

He'd only been home a couple of days—just long enough to sit with Mom through the worst of the waiting at the hospital. Through the hours of not knowing if Dad would make it.

Sophie looked away, but not before he caught the flash of disappointment in her eyes. "How's your dad?"

Spencer disentangled from her embrace and grabbed her hand, leading her around the muddy patches toward their favorite spot at the edge of the park's little pond. A family of ducks quacked at them and shuffled out of the way.

"He's stable. Should be out of the hospital in a few days, but he's not going to be back in the orchard anytime soon." He couldn't push away the image of Dad's gray face. His slow movements. How could a heart attack have transformed his powerhouse of a dad so drastically?

Sophie bit her lip in that way that made it almost impossible to resist kissing her. "It's just so close to graduation. It seems like a waste to throw away everything you've worked for."

Spencer sighed. He'd had this argument with himself all the way here. But he couldn't see any way around it.

"The work won't wait, Soph. The seasons keep changing, no matter what's going on in our lives." He squeezed her hand. "Anyway, it's not like if I don't finish my degree now I can't ever do it. I have my whole life." *Our whole life.* But he was getting ahead of himself.

"I know." Sophie offered a half-hearted smile. "I just hate the idea of saying goodbye sooner than we planned."

He pulled her to a stop next to the bench they'd spent so many hours on. "Me too. That's actually why I asked you to come here."

He gestured for her to sit, and she did, giving him a curious look as he remained on his feet. He drew in a shaky breath. He'd been so busy thinking about everything else that he hadn't prepared what to say.

"There's something I have to ask you."

A wind gust blew her hair in front of her face, and she swept it behind her ear as he dropped to one knee. Hands shaking, he pulled the ring box from his pocket, opened it, and held the small diamond solitaire toward her.

Sophie gasped, lifting a hand to her mouth. "Spencer, don't—"

"Sophie, will you—" Spencer stopped as her words slammed into him. "What?"

Sophie sprang to her feet and practically leaped over the bench, as if trying to construct a physical barrier between them. "You're emotional right now. You're not thinking clearly."

Spencer pushed slowly to his feet and moved closer to the bench, reaching for Sophie's hand across its back. "I'm not doing this because I'm emotional. I already had the ring. I was planning to wait until graduation, but with everything going on, I wanted you to know that I want a future with you."

He squeezed her hand and tried to pull her around the bench so he could try again and this time do it properly. Leave it to him to screw up the proposal the first time.

But Sophie pulled out of his grasp and looked past him, toward the pond.

Spencer's heart crumbled. She didn't want to marry him.

"I'm leaving for Chicago in two months, Spencer. You know I can't pass up this job offer."

He wanted to tell her it didn't matter. That he'd go with her. Or he'd find her a job that was just as good closer to home. Anything.

But admitting his need would only lead to more hurt. Would only remind him that he'd never be worthy of her.

"I'm sorry," Sophie whispered.

And then she turned and walked away.

And he let her.

Chapter 1

Five Years Later

Sophie stepped off the L, deftly dodging the enormous puddles on the sidewalk from last night's rain so she wouldn't ruin her new Jimmy Choo heels. She inhaled deeply, trying to catch a hint of spring. But spring in Chicago smelled nothing like spring at home in Hope Springs. There, the season carried the heady scents of ice melt and earth and fruit blossoms. Here, all she could smell were exhaust fumes and the overripe garbage bins that had been set out on the sidewalk for pickup.

It didn't matter—she'd likely be inside all day and long into the night anyway. This new development was the biggest deal she'd worked on yet, and with any luck, it was the one that would secure her promotion as the firm's youngest VP. It didn't matter how much time she had to spend indoors or how many hours it took. She'd make it happen.

She pushed through the doors of the sleek glass tower on North Clark and hurried across the lobby, relishing the sharp click of her heels against the polished marble floor. She still couldn't believe sometimes that she'd landed a position with Heartland, one of the most prestigious development firms in the country.

"Good morning, Sophie," the white-haired security guard greeted her as he did every morning.

"Morning," Sophie mumbled as she hurried past and jabbed at the elevator's up button.

At the twenty-eighth floor, she stepped out into the posh lobby of Heartland and made her way to her office. As always, her eyes were drawn immediately to the breathtaking view of the city and the Lake Michigan shoreline. There was a slight chop on the water today, though the waves winked in the sun.

Not that she had time to stand here and admire the view. Sophie settled into her leather chair and grabbed the project she'd been working on for two weeks. She leafed through the papers. This was her first project as lead developer, and she had a lot riding on it. But if she could pull off the purchase and development of the combination apartment, shopping, and entertainment complex she'd envisioned . . .

One step at a time, Sophie. When you get ahead of yourself, you get sloppy. How many times had her mom used that reprimand on her growing up? It seemed to apply to everything from math tests to ballet recitals. Somehow, nothing she did had ever been good enough for her parents.

She shook herself. She'd never earn her promotion if she focused on the past instead of the task at hand. She pulled out the latest renderings from the architect and dove in.

An hour later, a rap on her door made her jump.

"Staff meeting, three minutes." Her assistant Tina passed her a fresh cup of coffee.

"Ah, thanks." Sophie smoothed her hair and shuffled the papers she'd spread across her desk into a neat pile. Then she gathered the whole bunch and hurried to the conference room.

The firm's six other developers were already gathered around the room's large mahogany table. This room was definitely the most intimidating in the office, with its oversize table and chairs that seemed to swallow her, but Sophie kept her chin up as she entered the room and grabbed a seat next to Chase. He gave her a warm smile and a subtle wink.

She ducked her head to hide her blush. Not that it was a big secret that the two had been casually dating. But Sophie felt awkward when he acted like that at work—especially in front of his father, who also happened to be one of the partners.

"Glad you could make it, Sophie." Mr. Davis's joke barely masked a hard edge of irritation.

"Sorry, I got caught up in the Hudson project."

Mr. Sanders, who'd always been the friendlier of the two partners, turned to her. "How does it look? Everything on track?"

Sophie patted the folder in front of her. "I think so. But—"

"Excuse me." All eyes swiveled to Tina as she poked her head into the room.

Sophie gestured for her to step back outside. Heartland had a strict policy about interruptions during meetings. As in, you didn't do it. Ever.

"I'm sorry." Tina motioned to Sophie. "You have a phone call. It's your grandmother."

"My grandmother?" She hadn't talked to Nana in months—and never at work. A slice of fear cut through her. It must be an emergency. Her mouth went dry, but she pushed her chair back and mumbled an apology, not sure if her words were audible.

Once she was out of the conference room, she sped across the common area to her office.

She lunged for her phone and snatched it off the desk, hitting the flashing button. "Nana?" The word came out breathless, as if she'd just finished a marathon cardio Pilates session.

"There's my Sophie." Her grandmother's voice rasped through the phone.

"Nana, is everything okay? Of course it's not okay or you wouldn't be calling me at work in the middle of the day. Is it Mom? Or Dad?" What if it was both of them—a car accident, maybe, on one of the rare occasions they were actually together.

"I knew you'd make time for me." Nana's words sounded garbled, and Sophie felt as if she'd been dropped into the middle of a foreign movie.

"Make time for you? Nana, what's the emergency?"

"I just wanted to hear your voice."

Sophie held the phone away from her ear and gave it an incredulous stare. Nana had interrupted her meeting to hear her voice? She rubbed at her temple as she pulled the phone back to her ear. "It's so good to hear from you, Nana, but I'm actually in the middle of a meeting." She glanced at the clock above her door. "I'll call you back in an hour or so, okay?"

She was met with silence.

"Nana?"

"Do me a favor, Sophie."

Sophie drummed her fingers on her desk. Now wasn't the best time for favors. "You got it, Nana. Whatever it is, I'm on it. Just as soon as my meeting is over. I'll—"

"Remember that I love you and so does God." Nana's voice was getting fainter, as if she was holding the phone too far from her mouth. Sophie strained to hear. "If you remember that, then I've done my job. Okay, Sophie?"

"Okay, Nana." Sophie didn't really have time for Nana's philosophical musings right now. "I have to go. I'll call you—"

"That's okay, Sophie. You don't have to call back. I just wanted to hear your voice one more time before I go."

"Go?" A brainstorm about the Hudson project hit Sophie, and she reached for a pen and a sticky note to jot it down. "Are you taking a trip?"

Nana was always going somewhere or other.

"I'm going home, Sophie."

"Hmm." Sophie finished her note. "Where are you now?" Probably the Mediterranean or somewhere in East Asia. She'd probably forgotten the time difference.

"I'm in the hospital, dear."

Sophie dropped her pen and straightened. Nana had been battling cancer for a couple years and had ended up in the hospital more than once in that time. Still, Sophie knew how much she hated being cooped up.

"But you get to go home soon? That's good news."

"Not that home, dear." Nana's voice was overly gentle, like it had been the first time Sophie came to her with a broken heart.

"What do you mean, 'not that home'? What other home do you have?" Sophie frowned. She hadn't noticed any decline in Nana's mental ability, but much as she hated to face it, Nana *was* getting older.

"I mean, I don't think I'll see that home again. I'm going to my true home."

"True home?" This conversation was making less sense by the minute.

Nana sighed, and Sophie felt like she'd missed something important, but she couldn't for the life of her think what it could be.

"Heaven, dear. I'm going home to heaven."

Sophie's head jerked up as she sat hard in her desk chair. She opened and closed her mouth a few times before she could get any words out. "You don't know that, Nana. I'm sure you have lots of time left. You—"

"You can't argue my way out of this, Sophie." Nana's chuckle grated against Sophie's nerves. How could she deliver news like this and then laugh?

"How long—?" Sophie swallowed the boulder that had lodged in her throat.

"A couple of days, the doctors think. Maybe a week."

"I'm sorry, Nana." Her voice was barely a whisper. She fought off the sharp sting gathering behind her eyes. If she didn't cry, she wouldn't feel. It was a skill she'd perfected over the years.

"Don't you be sorry for me, child." Nana's voice was firm. "I know where I'm going. And I got to say goodbye to my Sophie. That's all I asked. God is good."

Sophie chewed her lip. A phone call was no way to say goodbye to the woman who'd been almost a mother to her. Who had loved her unconditionally her whole life, even when her own parents hadn't.

"I'll be on my way in ten minutes. Do you think you could—" Sophie sucked in a breath. "Could you wait for me? Before you—" But she refused to finish that sentence.

"It's in God's hands, dear."

It wasn't the guarantee Sophie had been hoping for, but it would have to do. She hung up and took a minute to steel herself. Then she pushed slowly to her feet and walked to Mr. Sanders's office, taking a steadying breath before she knocked on his door.

Chase was already in with his father, but Mr. Sanders invited her in as well.

She waited for one of them to say something about the phone call, but when neither did, she pushed forward. "I need to request a few days off. That was my grandmother who called—" Sophie cut herself off. No need to remind them of the interruption to the meeting. "Anyway, she's not doing well. The doctors only give her a few days." She didn't let herself dwell on the words. "I'd like to go home. To say goodbye."

Chase toed the floor, not meeting her eyes.

"Are you close to your grandmother?" Mr. Sanders's voice was neither compassionate nor judgmental. It was a solid neutral.

"I am. Or, well, I was. I haven't been to visit her in a while . . ." Sophie cleared her throat.

"You understand how important this project is? To the firm as well as to your career?" Mr. Sanders folded his hands in front of him on the desk.

Sophie bit her lip, nodding.

"Then—" Mr. Sanders stood, and Sophie understood the move as a dismissal. "I'll leave it up to you. If you stay, you keep the project. If you go, I'm going to put Chase on it. We can't afford to lose out on this one, and if you can't dedicate yourself to it one hundred percent . . ."

Sophie blinked at the unfairness. He was going to make her choose between her family and her career?

She ducked out of her office, her insides roiling. How was she supposed to make a decision like this?

Halfway across the lobby, Chase caught up with her. "Sophie, wait. What are you going to do?" She couldn't tell if that was eagerness in his voice or compassion.

"I guess I'm going to—" The word stay almost came out. It's what she should do. For her own good. But the image of Nana, alone in her hospital bed, pushed into her head. Could she really forgive herself if she let Nana die alone like that? "I'm going to go. I'll get you the plans."

To his credit, Chase didn't gloat or even smile. "For what it's worth, Sophie, I'm sorry. I know how much you wanted this project."

She shrugged. "There'll be others." Of course, she could kiss that VP position goodbye. If Chase hadn't been a shoo-in before, he certainly would be after this.

She stepped around him and into her office, grabbing the stack of plans for the Hudson project off her desk. She passed it to Chase. "I should get going."

He gave her hand a quick squeeze. "Don't be gone too long. Maybe you can help me put the finishing touches on the project plan."

Sophie nodded and stepped out of the office toward the bank of elevators.

She had no intention of staying in Hope Springs a moment longer than she had to.

The lowering sun lit the water on fire as Sophie crested the hill above Hope Springs five hours later.

She pulled down the Camaro's sun visor and rubbed at her weary eyes.

As the road dropped into the town, she slowed, letting herself take in sights she hadn't seen in more than five years.

It was odd how everything looked the same and yet different. It wasn't yet tourist season, so most of the shops were closed for the evening, and the streets were mostly empty, aside from the occasional local walking their dog.

Memories piled up and slammed into her as she passed the Hidden Cafe. The Chocolate Chicken. The post office. Sophie tried to beat them back. She wasn't here to reminisce. She was here to say goodbye to Nana and then get back to her real life.

She accelerated, trying to leave the memories behind as she passed out of town. Her stomach tightened into double knots as she pulled into the long, winding driveway that led up the highest bluff overlooking the lake. Bare trees pressed in on her from all sides, until her parents' over-large house finally came into view, all hard lines and sharp angles.

She parked in the large section of the driveway her parents reserved for guests and sat for a minute, gazing toward the now-dark waters of the lake. Was this really the same lake she'd been looking at hours ago from her office in Chicago? It was the one thing that connected her two lives. That and the memories. But those she tried not to think about.

She forced herself to push her car door open. To grab her suitcase out of the trunk. To follow the slate path to the front door.

She reached for the doorknob but then thought better of it and pressed her finger to the doorbell.

When no one answered after a minute, she let herself in. "Hello?" She felt oddly like an intruder as her voice echoed around her childhood home.

"In here." Mom's voice carried from the kitchen.

Sophie left her suitcase in the foyer and followed the sound.

Mom was seated at the long granite breakfast counter, poring over a design magazine. She barely glanced up when Sophie entered. "I told you, you didn't have to come."

"I wanted to come." Sophie gave her mother an obligatory kiss on the cheek.

She knew better than to ask where her father was. If her mother was home, her father was likely at the club. The two had barely been in the same room together, aside from at church and when brokering real estate deals, in the past fifteen years.

"How's Nana?" Sophie went to the refrigerator and grabbed a bottle of water.

"Call her grandmother." Sophie's mom gave an exaggerated huff. "You know I hate when you call her Nana. Sounds like that dog from that movie."

"Peter Pan?" Sophie wrinkled her nose. She'd been calling her grandmother Nana since she was seven. She wasn't about to stop now. "Have you been to see her?"

"I called earlier. There's no change." Mom flipped the page of her magazine. "I don't know what you think being here is going to accomplish. You should have stayed at work."

Sophie took another sip of her water to keep from striking back. It was the same old story. Her parents would never be satisfied with anything she did.

"I wanted to say goodbye." She focused on keeping an even tone.

Her mother nodded, eyes fixed on her magazine. "I'm thinking about redoing the kitchen. What do you think of these cabinets?"

Sophie set her water on the counter and walked out of the room without looking at the magazine. "They're nice, Mom."

She grabbed her suitcase and trudged up the staircase before her mother could infuriate her any more. Not that Mom had ever been emotionally available, but planning to redecorate the kitchen while her own mother was dying was too much even for her.

At the end of the hallway, Sophie pushed open the door to her old room. It'd been completely redone as a guest room almost the moment she left for college. All her old posters had been stripped from the walls. The poppy orange she'd painted the room when she was fifteen had been replaced by a soft lilac. She had to admit that the room was more to her taste now, but seeing it stripped of her former self stung.

Oh, well. It's not like she could ever go back to who she used to be.

Sophie hefted her suitcase onto the overstuffed chair in the corner and collapsed on the king-size bed. That was new, too. She longed for the twin-size canopy bed she'd gotten from her grandmother—it'd been the one place that always felt cozy in the cold house.

After a few minutes, she grew restless. She'd had way too much coffee on the way up. She wouldn't be able to sleep for hours yet, but the thought of returning to the kitchen and doing another round with Mom turned her stomach. She crossed to the room's built-in bookshelf. When she'd lived here, it'd overflowed with books. Mysteries, mostly. Romance. Some classics.

Now, it held mostly knickknacks, but a few books were sprinkled here and there. She ran her fingers over the spines until they landed on *Pride and Prejudice*. Had this really been her favorite book once? Had she really believed that two people who were so different, who came from such different backgrounds, could make a life together? Well, Jane Austen may have been that naive, but she wasn't. Not anymore.

Still, she couldn't resist pulling the worn copy off the shelf. A bookmark stuck out about a third of the way through the book.

As she flipped to the page, something small and white fluttered out and drifted to the floor.

She bent to pick it up, and her breath caught.

It was a pressed cherry blossom, in pristine condition.

From Spencer. When he gave it to her, he said it reminded him of her—strong and delicate at the same time.

She gently lifted the blossom to her face. A faint scent of spring lingered on it. Or maybe that was just wishful thinking.

She replaced the blossom in the book and stuck it on the shelf. That part of her life was over.

Besides, Spencer likely had a wife and family of his own by now.

A pang sliced through her belly. What if she ran into him while she was home? Worse, what if she ran into his new family? Could she handle seeing him with another woman?

She shook her head and flopped onto the bed. She was being ridiculous. It wouldn't matter if she saw him and his family or not.

She had a highly successful career, an upscale apartment, a casual boyfriend who didn't expect anything long-term from her. She had everything she had ever wanted.

Which didn't explain the hollow feeling that had taken up residence in her chest.

Chapter 2

Spencer grabbed a cherry branch and pulled it closer to his face. The wood that had appeared barren from a distance showed little signs of new life all along its length, tiny buds just barely poking out from the bark.

Spencer ran his fingers over them. They were no guarantee that the tree would actually blossom and fruit, but it was a good sign.

A sign they needed right now.

He stepped back to survey the tree, choosing the branches he'd prune. He needed to choose carefully. Last year, a late season frost had destroyed their entire crop. If they hadn't had his woodworking to fall back on, the farm probably would have gone under entirely.

But cherries were the lifeblood of the peninsula, drawing tourists from all over the state. If the crop failed this year—

He couldn't think about that.

He grabbed his pruning saw and lifted it to a dead branch. With a practiced rhythm, his saw bit into the wood until the branch came off clean in his fist. He slathered sealant on the fresh wood underneath to prevent disease, then selected another branch to prune. Spencer let himself fall into the familiar routine of spring on the orchard as he shaped the tree, ensuring maximum air flow and sunlight to the branches. When he'd finished, he gathered his fallen branches and dragged them toward the trailer he and Dad had been filling all morning.

Dad was taking the lopping shears to a tree near the pile. Spencer still had to think about each cut he made, consider the tree before choosing a branch to trim, but for his father, it was second nature. He never hesitated, just snipped branch after branch until the trees were shaped perfectly.

"Slow down, Dad. You're making me look bad."

Dad grunted and lowered his shears, rubbing at the left side of his chest. He shifted to lean his weight heavily against the tree trunk.

"Dad?" Spencer moved closer. "You okay?"

Sweat gleamed on Dad's face, despite the chill breeze that blew in off the lake. He waved Spencer off. "Fine. Just need a break for a second." He pushed off the trunk and set back to work.

Spencer studied him. Since he could remember, Dad had always been the first to work and the last to quit. But he'd slowed down some in the years since his heart attack. "Why don't you go back to the house for a bit? I've got this. Give me a chance to catch up."

His father kept clipping. "Stop coddling me. I get enough of that from your mother." He lowered the shears again to roll out his left shoulder, then lifted it to the next branch.

"I'm not coddling, Dad. But you know Mom would never forgive me if—"

"You let me worry about your mother. I don't need a break, and I'm not going to take one. In case you've forgotten, we've got a whole orchard to get ready. We don't have time to stand here arguing."

He wasn't wrong about that. Last year's lost crop meant they didn't have the money to hire on any seasonal help this year. Dad bent and gathered his discarded branches. Spencer reached to help him.

"I said I can do it." His father's voice held the sharp edge of warning Spencer recognized from his childhood.

"All right, Dad." Spencer raised his hands and moved to the other side of the row to trim the next tree. Arguing would only make it worse.

Spencer's phone rang, overly loud in the silent orchard, and he pulled it out of his pocket, answering as he examined the tree.

"What's up, Dave?"

Their neighbor from the next farm over huffed into the phone, and Spencer waited for him to catch his breath. Dave was older than Dad, but he still insisted on doing all his work himself. Spencer always worried that one of these days it would kill him.

"Having an issue with Old Bessie over here," Dave puffed. "She's bottomed out pretty good. Think you could come over and help me push her out?"

Spencer's shoulders tightened. Helping Dave with the tractor would put him back at least an hour. And this orchard wasn't going to prune itself. But if the situation were reversed, Dave would be over in a second. And if his father had taught him anything, it was that neighbors were a farmer's lifeline. "Yeah, Dave. I'll be right over."

He jabbed his phone into his pocket and stalked toward the ATV he and Dad had ridden out to the orchard. He unhitched the trailer from it and lowered it to the ground.

"Gotta go help Dave with Old Bessie," he called to his father.

Dad waved to acknowledge he'd heard but kept working his saw. Spencer almost asked one more time if he was okay but bit the question back. Having his head torn off twice in one day wasn't worth it. He jumped on the ATV and took off toward the field that bordered Dave's farm. Mud from the rains that had saturated the ground the last few weeks shot up at him, but he pushed the machine harder. He had too much to do today to worry about getting a little dirty.

Ten minutes later, he found Dave knee-deep in mud, slogging around his old, beat-up tractor.

The ground sucked at Spencer's feet as he jumped off the ATV.

"Gonna need to invest in a new tractor one of these days," he called to Dave.

Dave grunted. "Not ready to give up on Old Bessie yet."

Spencer pulled out the chains he kept in the ATV's storage compartment. He passed one end to Dave. When everything was secure, he jumped on the machine and gunned it. He gritted his teeth and squinted against the mud spraying up around him, throttling up higher.

But after half an hour, the old beast remained stuck.

Spencer switched off the ATV. No sense killing it, too. He pulled out his phone. "Gonna have to call in the old man for reinforcements," he called to Dave.

He scrolled to Dad's number. But the phone rang until it went to voice mail.

Spencer frowned and dialed again. He clenched his teeth as the rings added up. Voice mail again.

Something heavy dropped in Spencer's stomach. He shouldn't have left Dad alone. He'd promised Mom. It didn't matter that Dad had been in perfect health for the past five years. Didn't matter that his mood had made it easier for Spencer to walk away. If something had happened to him—

Spencer reined in his thoughts.

Just because Dad wasn't answering his phone didn't mean anything bad had happened. He probably didn't have his phone on him. He was forever leaving it at home or in the shed.

But Spencer couldn't stop picturing how Dad had been rubbing at his chest, rolling his shoulder, sweating. Weren't those exactly the signs he was supposed to watch for?

With a sudden decisiveness, Spencer jumped off the ATV and worked to free it from the chains.

"What's up?" Dave called.

"Dad's not answering. I'm going to go check on him. I'll be—"

But Dave was at his side, a hand on his shoulder. "Let me do this."

Spencer didn't stop to think. Just dropped the chains his shaking hands had been unable to unhitch and jumped on the ATV, bringing it roaring to life. The moment Dave said "go," he shot off.

The machine whined as he pushed it to its limits, barely noticing the branches that whipped at his face as he raced the ATV through the thin stand of trees between their farm and Dave's.

Please let me get there in time. He repeated the prayer over and over as he maneuvered the ATV closer. Why couldn't the machine go any faster?

Finally, he reached the orchard. He jumped off the ATV, swiveling his head toward the spot Dad was working last. But the orchard was empty.

He probably went back to the house for a break, like you told him to.

But Spencer knew in his gut Dad wouldn't have taken that advice.

"Dad?" He ran down the long line of trees, trying not to let the panic that clawed at him take over. How far could Dad have gotten?

"Dad?" When he'd gone a hundred yards or so, he stopped. None of these trees showed any signs of having been pruned.

He made his way back toward the ATV, more slowly this time, eyes trained on the ground, just in case.

Please not that.

As he approached the trailer, his eye caught on something sticking out from the far side. Was that a foot?

He sprinted to close the distance. "Dad?"

A groan.

Spencer's heart lurched.

He jumped over the trailer's tongue.

Dad was half-sitting, half-leaning against the trailer, his hands pressed against his chest.

"Dad?" Spencer dropped to the ground next to him. "What is it?"

But he already knew. Already had his phone in his hand. Was already dialing 911.

"I'm fine—" Dad's face contorted, and he closed his eyes, his hands tightening into fists.

"You're not—" Spencer cut off as the dispatcher answered.

He had to push aside the fear gripping his own heart to speak. "I think my father's having a heart attack."

"I'm not—"

Spencer ignored him and gave the dispatcher their location, then shoved his phone into his pocket.

"Okay, Dad, we need to get you to the house. They aren't going to be able to get an ambulance back here."

"I'm not going in any ambulance." Dad sounded stronger now. "It's just indigestion. We have work to do." He pushed to his feet, and a moment of doubt hit Spencer. Was he overreacting?

But the second Dad was upright, he sagged. Spencer reached out a quick arm to help him to his feet. "You're not fine." Spencer's voice was firm. "You're getting on this ATV with me. And then you're getting into that ambulance and going to the hospital."

"Don't tell—" Dad stopped and doubled over, bracing his hands on his knees. His breath came in short gasps.

"This time I am telling you what to do, and you're going to do it." Spencer steered his father toward the ATV. "Get on."

To his relief, Dad obeyed.

Spencer climbed on and eased the ATV into gear. He wanted to push it as hard as it could go, but he wasn't sure Dad was strong enough to hold on through that.

But driving slowly gave him too much time to think. He should have recognized the signs earlier. Should have insisted that Dad take a break. Should have told Dave he couldn't help. *Should have. Should have. Should have.*

Finally, the farm's long driveway came into view. Spencer dared to throttle up a shred more. Behind him, Dad's arms went slack. His full weight slumped against Spencer.

In the distance, the wail of sirens split the air.

Spencer prayed for them to come faster.

Chapter 3

Sophie smoothed her fingers over the translucent skin of Nana's hand.

She'd come to the hospital first thing this morning, but the nurses said Nana had been in and out because of the morphine.

So far today, she'd only been out.

Sophie had considered talking to Nana while she slept, but every time she tried, she stopped. It felt too awkward. So she'd settled for holding her hand instead. When had Nana's skin become so thin and wrinkled?

Growing up, Sophie had never thought of Nana as old. She wore jeans and kept her white hair long and burst with energy. When they'd biked together, Sophie had struggled to keep up.

But now.

Now, the skin on her face was folded into wrinkles and stained with age spots. The little hair she had was thin and stuck up in wisps around her head. Tubes and monitors ran into and out of her body.

Sophie rubbed at her eyes. As a kid, she couldn't have imagined going a week without seeing her grandma. Now, she couldn't even remember the last time she'd visited Nana. It must have been way back in undergrad. Christmas of her freshman year, maybe? Before she'd started making excuses not to come home.

How had she cut Nana completely out of her life? The woman who had taken her out on the lake every weekend as a kid when her parents were too busy signing deals to notice her. The one who had made cookies and cocoa with her on winter weekends as they sat up together late into the night. The only person she'd confided in when the boy she had a crush on in middle school liked someone else.

Nana had always been there for her.

And when Nana had needed her, when she'd been diagnosed with cancer, Sophie had been nowhere in sight. She'd been too wrapped up in her own career to call more than once or twice.

Sophie swallowed against the ache in her throat.

She needed some coffee or something. But she couldn't convince herself to leave Nana's side. What if she woke up and Sophie wasn't there? What if it was the last time she ever woke up and Sophie missed her chance to say goodbye?

Then again, the thought of going through with that goodbye made her want to run screaming from the room. Maybe it'd be better to let Nana go like this.

Sophie pushed to her feet. Mom had been right. She shouldn't have come.

She'd taken two steps toward the door when a soft sigh from behind stopped her.

She hesitated a second, indecision pulling her in two directions at once.

"Sophie?"

Hearing Nana's voice made the decision for her.

Her feet kicked into a run, adrenaline pushing her toward the elevator at the end of the hall. Ignoring the calls of the nurses behind her, she slipped through the door as it slid closed.

Inside the elevator, she heaved in a breath and jabbed blindly at the lowest button on the panel. As the elevator descended, she tried to get a grip on her emotions.

It wasn't like her to lose control like this.

Slowly, her breathing calmed. Her heart rate came back into normal range. She'd been foolish to run like that. That much she could admit. But it didn't mean she was ready to go back up there.

She wasn't sure she ever would be.

The moment the elevator doors opened, she barreled through them.

Right into someone solid.

Coffee sloshed onto the floor at her feet, and Sophie sidestepped to avoid it.

"Oh, I'm sorry, I—" But her voice failed the moment she lifted her eyes.

"Sophie?"

The heart rate she'd finally gotten under control took off again. Every rational thought fled her head.

Except his name. "Spencer." It came out as an exhale.

Patches of mud caked his clothes, joined by a spreading coffee stain on his t-shirt. His hair was tousled, and his cheeks sported at least a day's worth of stubble. But somehow, he looked better than ever.

He moved a step closer, raising his arms slightly as if to give her a hug, and Sophie's stomach swooped. But half a step in, he seemed to think better of it and stepped back.

"What are you doing here?" Spencer used the crumpled napkin in his hand to wipe futilely at his shirt.

"I came to see my grandma." And had utterly failed at it. She looked away, blinking furiously. If she had to run into Spencer during this trip, it wasn't going to be while she was showing her own weakness.

"Oh, hey, it's okay." This time Spencer did pull her in for a hug.

Everything in her stiffened, then relaxed at the familiar press of his arms around her. He smelled sort of woodsy and . . . Spencer-y. She managed a shaky breath.

After a second, he cleared his throat and released her, taking a not-so-subtle step backward.

"Thanks." Sophie picked at a nonexistent piece of lint on her shirt. She couldn't look at him. If she did, it'd be too hard to remember that he wasn't part of her life anymore.

"Is your grandma okay?" Spencer's voice was guarded, yet compassionate.

Sophie shook her head, swallowing hard. "Not really. The doctors don't think it will be long." Her breath hitched. "I wanted to say goodbye, but . . ." She shook her head again. What kind of person ran out on her dying grandmother?

"But you never were good at goodbyes." Spencer said the words simply. Sophie searched his eyes but didn't find any signs of bitterness there.

"No, I guess I'm not. I just—" She didn't know how to explain it.

"I know." Spencer moved a fraction closer. "But, Soph, if you woke up tomorrow and your grandma was gone, wouldn't you regret not talking to her today? Even if it's hard."

In spite of herself, Sophie nodded. Of course Spencer was right. Then again, he'd always been way better at the emotional stuff than she was. For him, saying *I love you* had always come naturally; for her, it was a constant struggle to get the words past her lips, even though she loved him. *Did love him*, she reminded herself. *Past tense.*

Spencer gestured toward the elevator. "Come on. I'll ride up with you. I was going that way anyway."

Sophie froze. How had she been so dense? Obviously Spencer didn't just happen to be at the hospital when she needed him. For all she knew, his wife was upstairs ready to give birth to their first baby. Or their second. A lot could have happened in five years.

She forced the words out. "What are you doing here anyway?"

Spencer seemed to wilt right in front of her, and he suddenly looked exhausted. "My dad had another heart attack this morning."

Sophie inhaled sharply. "I'm sorry. Is he— I mean, will he—" Her tongue felt all tangled up. How could she ask him that?

Spencer rescued her. "He's in surgery. The doctors don't know—" He looked away and rubbed at his already tousled hair. The move was achingly familiar. It had always been his tell for when he was upset.

She laid a hand on his arm without thinking. His poor family had already been through this once.

"Anyway." Spencer pressed the button for the elevator. "If you wouldn't mind praying for him, I'd appreciate it."

"Of course." Sophie stepped into the elevator ahead of him. No sense letting him know it'd been so long since she'd prayed that God had probably forgotten who she was by now. Her prayers wouldn't do his dad much good.

The elevator door closed behind Spencer, and they rode up in silence. The weight of everything they hadn't said seemed to fill the small space, sucking out all the air.

When the doors finally opened on the third floor, Sophie's feelings were so knotted that she wasn't sure if she was relieved or disappointed.

Spencer gave her arm a gentle squeeze. "You can do this."

Sophie nodded and stepped out of the elevator. She forced her feet to carry her down the hall toward Nana's room. It took all of her willpower not to turn around for one last look at Spencer.

Finally, she couldn't resist any longer.

But when she turned back, the elevator doors were closed.

Chapter 4

Spencer stepped off the elevator on the fourth floor, feeling like he was moving through water. Or maybe a dream.

When Sophie had walked away from him five years ago, he'd been sure that'd be the last time he'd ever see her. Seeing her again—it was surreal.

She looked almost the same—same flowing blond hair, same sleek figure, same dark, fitted business suit. But the worry in her eyes. The fear. That was new, and he'd wanted so badly to take it away. To make things better for her.

He stopped his thoughts right there. That wasn't his role anymore. He couldn't let himself go down that path again. He couldn't handle having his heart smashed by her a second time.

And based on the way his heart was acting right now, that's exactly what would happen.

Mom was still pacing the waiting room when Spencer walked back in. He knew better than to tell her to sit down. He'd already tried half a dozen times—and she'd been on her feet again within a minute each time. It was what had driven him in search of coffee. And a few minutes of peace.

Too bad he had neither to show for his trip to the lobby. Running into Sophie had only left him in more turmoil than ever.

"Any word?" He had to put his focus back on what was important. On being here for Mom. On praying for Dad. On holding their family together.

Mom shook her head, then stopped short. "What happened to you?"

"What?" Spencer followed her gaze to his shirt. "Oh. Someone bumped into me."

She nodded absently, as if she'd already forgotten her question, and resumed pacing.

"It was Sophie, actually." He'd promised himself he wouldn't say anything, but the words shot out of him anyway.

"Sophie?" Mom's voice jumped, and the slightest hint of a smile touched her eyes. "I'm so glad you asked her to come. Where is she?" She peered around him as if he might be hiding his ex-girlfriend in his back pocket.

He shook his head. "She came to see her grandma. It's—" He saw again that haunted look in her eyes as she'd told him the news. "It's near the end."

Concern furrowed Mom's forehead. "Oh, I'm sorry to hear that."

Not for the first time, Spencer marveled at his mother's compassion. Here she was, pacing a waiting room, not knowing if her husband would survive, and she was worried about someone else. Not just anyone else, but the woman who had walked away from him, who had never been willing to meet his family, let alone become part of it.

"Tell her I'll keep her family in my prayers." Mom pressed a hand to her heart.

Spencer eyed Mom. Tell her? When did she think he was going to see Sophie again? "Mom, I'm not—"

She lifted a finger in warning. He may be an adult, but the gesture still had the power to silence him. "Since the moment you two broke up, I've told you God has his ways of bringing people together when the time is right."

"I wouldn't start planning the wedding just yet," Spencer said dryly. He believed in God's power as much as the next person, but he was pretty sure that wasn't what was at play here. It was just a coincidence. One that would pass over soon enough. Until then, he'd just have to do his best to avoid Sophie.

And to keep Mom from getting her hopes up.

"Tyler hasn't called yet?" A stab of guilt jabbed him at the cheap tactic to change the subject. But it worked.

Mom's face fell. "He's busy. I'm sure he'll be here soon."

Spencer held back his snort. When his brother had taken off ten years ago, he'd made it clear he had no intention of ever returning. Hadn't bothered to visit for even a day last time Dad was in the hospital. As usual, he'd left everything to Spencer to take care of.

If they were really lucky this time, Tyler would call to send his love.

Love, his foot. In Spencer's book, love meant being there for people.

A weight pressed on his chest. Who was he to talk? Dad had always been there for him. But where had he been when Dad needed him this morning?

"Mom?" His voice came out scratchy. "I'm sorry."

She paused and really looked at him, then crossed the room and had her arms around him in a second flat. Her head only came halfway up his chest, but that didn't matter. He felt safe here.

"This is not your fault." Her voice was firm and sure.

He nodded. But that didn't stop the tears that dripped from his chin into her hair.

Sophie had been standing outside Nana's room for ten minutes, trying to work up the courage to step over the threshold. It felt like taking that step would mark a turning point in her life—one she wasn't sure she was ready for.

But Spencer was right. She'd never be able to live with herself if she didn't say goodbye. Even if it was the hardest thing she'd ever had to do.

She pulled in a quick breath and stepped into the room, her heels clicking against the floor tiles.

"Nana?" She sounded like a little girl who wasn't sure if she was in trouble. Which was exactly how she felt.

Nana's eyes had been closed, but she opened them and turned her head toward the door. Her smile made the wrinkles on her face stand into ridges. Sophie moved closer to the bed and took Nana's outstretched hand.

"I'm glad you came back."

Sophie sniffed and dropped her gaze to the floor. "I'm sorry about before."

But Nana pulled her closer and smoothed a hand over her cheek. Sophie closed her eyes. She was supposed to be here to comfort Nana, and here Nana was the one offering comfort, just as she always had.

"No worries, my Sophie. This is easier for me than it is for you."

Sophie gave a weak laugh. Somehow, she didn't think dying was the easier option.

Nana grimaced as she shifted in the bed.

"You're uncomfortable. Do you need more morphine?" Sophie reached for the button the nurses had showed her and held it out to Nana.

"Not right now. I want to be awake to talk to my Sophie. Anyway, I can handle a little pain in my life. Soon I'll be going where there's no more pain." She said it matter-of-factly, as if she were commenting on the weather.

Sophie winced. "Please don't talk like that, Nana."

"And why not, dear? You don't want me to go to heaven?" Nana's eyes held that glint they always took on when she was teasing.

But it wasn't funny. "Not yet, no."

Nana let out a half-laugh, half-cough. "That's my Sophie. Same stubborn tone you used to give me when I told you to go to bed and you wanted to stay up. It didn't work then, and it's not going to work now. I'm ready to go home to heaven, and whenever Jesus is ready to call me, there's nothing you can do about it, so you might as well accept it."

Sophie gazed toward the window, unwilling to meet Nana's eyes. She didn't accept it. Not by a long shot. But it was better to appease her grandma, just like she'd done as a kid, going into her room but lying up reading for hours into the night.

Nana patted her hand. "Tell me about your life in Chicago."

Sophie breathed easier. This, at least, was a safe topic. "I'm at Heartland, one of the biggest real estate developers in the country. I'm on track to become VP in record time."

Nana waved a hand through the air. "I'm proud of you for that. But I didn't ask about your job. I asked about your *life*. What do you do with yourself when you're not working?"

Sophie shrugged. "Not much. I'm pretty much working all the time."

Nana's wrinkles deepened. "Are you happy?"

Sophie was ready to toss off a flippant yes. Of course she was happy. She had a prestigious job, an apartment to die for, everything she'd worked so hard to achieve since she was a little girl.

But that empty feeling from last night pressed on her chest. She pushed it away. "Don't worry, Nana. I'm happy."

She ignored the niggling doubt that squirmed into her thoughts.

Nana's gaze cut through her. "Don't forget that life isn't all about achievements. They're nice in their way. But they're never going to fill you up. They'll never replace love. Don't go through life alone, Sophie. You'll miss so much."

Sophie shifted in her seat. Nana was wrong. Being alone was the only way to guarantee you never disappointed anyone. Never failed to live up to their expectations.

"I'm fine, Nana," she finally said.

Nana gave her a hard look. "Good. But just in case you need a reminder, I want you to have this." She slid the amethyst ring from her left hand and held it out to Sophie.

But Sophie shook her head and lifted her hands, as if fending it off. "No, Nana. I couldn't." That ring was as much a part of Nana as her hair or her voice. Sophie couldn't remember ever seeing her without it.

Nana thrust the ring closer. "I'm not going to need this where I'm going. It'd make me happy to know you had it."

Sophie's hands fell. How could she resist that? She reluctantly slid the ring onto her finger. The stone seemed to pull in and give off light at the same time.

"Did I ever tell you about that ring?" Nana closed her eyes and shifted against her pillow, letting out a soft moan.

"Can I get you anything?" Sophie's heart twisted to see Nana suffering. She picked up the morphine button and held it out, but Nana waved it off.

"It was from your grandfather. The ring."

Sophie held her breath. Her grandfather had died long before she was born, and Nana almost never spoke about him.

"He didn't have money for a wedding ring when we were first married, but he bought that for me a few years later. He called it a forever ring." The creases of pain around her lips were replaced by a soft smile. "I was so mad at him for so long. He promised me forever, but then he left me a few years later."

"But—"

Nana lifted a feeble hand. "It wasn't his choice. I know that. But when you're grieving, nothing makes much sense."

Sophie nodded. That's how she felt already, and Nana was still here with her.

"I don't think I handled my grief very well. Especially with your mother. She wanted to talk about her father, but it hurt me too much, so I didn't let her. And then after Jordan—"

Sophie choked on a sharp gasp at her older brother's name, but Nana kept talking as if she hadn't noticed. "I didn't talk to her about that, either. And I watched as she shut her heart down." She clutched at Sophie's hand. "I don't want that for you."

"I'm not— I won't—" But shutting down her heart. That was the only way she'd survived so far. Was the only way she'd survive Nana's death, too.

"Anyway." Nana released her grip. "Now I get to go home and see them." She closed her eyes, and her hand fell limp. Sophie's heart clambered up her throat. Surely she didn't mean this moment? Holding her breath, she leaned toward her grandmother.

Nana's eyes sprang open, and Sophie jumped back, pressing a hand to her chest.

Thank goodness.

"Promise me—" Nana wrapped Sophie's hands in both of hers. "Whenever you look at that ring, you remember that forever is real. Not here. But after, in heaven. And you keep your heart open. To

God. And to the people he puts into your life to love you. For however long they're part of it."

Sophie stared at her smooth hands planted in Nana's wrinkled ones. "I promise."

It was a promise she was pretty sure she couldn't keep. But she'd try. For Nana's sake.

Nana closed her eyes again, and Sophie sat watching her, trying to memorize every feature. After a few minutes, Nana spoke again. "I'm glad you found your way home, Sophie."

Sophie nodded, her throat too full to answer.

She may be home, but she felt more lost than ever.

Chapter 5

Spencer swiped at the sweat on his brow. He'd been pruning like mad all morning, trying to outrun the images of Sophie that insisted on pushing into his thoughts. The way she tipped her chin up when she laughed. The way her hand had always fit perfectly in his. The way she was just the right height that when he wrapped his arms around her, he could rest his chin on her head.

Stop.

He gave the pruning saw another thrust. It'd taken him years to stop thinking about Sophie every day. And seeing her for only a few minutes yesterday had undone all of that.

Spencer clipped one last branch, then stood back to survey the orchard. A ragged sigh escaped him. There were so many trees left. And who knew how long Dad would be out of commission. Which meant it was all up to him. Again.

Much as he loved the farm, the weight of its responsibility pressed on him right now. How would his life have been different if he'd been like Tyler and left and never come back? Would he and Sophie still be together? Married?

Spencer scrubbed at his face. He couldn't go down this what-if road. He'd made his choice—and Sophie had made hers.

His phone pealed, and he tore it out of his pocket, inexplicably hoping his thoughts of Sophie had conjured a call from her. Which was ridiculous. She'd probably already left town. The Sophie he'd known wouldn't have stuck around any longer than necessary, especially not when things got emotional.

He grimaced as he caught the number on the phone. "About time."

"How is he?" Tyler's voice was raw and cracked.

"So you do care?" The words were out before Spencer could stop himself.

"Don't be a jerk." But Tyler's voice lacked the older-brother authority Spencer was used to hearing from him.

"That's rich. You're the one who waited nearly twenty-four hours to even bother to call, and I'm the jerk?" Spencer bent to stack the branches he'd cut, jamming his phone between his shoulder and his ear.

"Knock it off, Spence. Is Dad okay?"

Spencer relented. He'd never heard his brother plead like that before. "He was in surgery most of the day yesterday. They said two of his arteries were almost completely blocked. They put in stents, but—" He really didn't want to deliver this kind of news over the phone.

"But?" Tyler's voice was hoarse.

"His heart was pretty damaged. If he has another heart attack . . ." Did he really have to say this? "They're not sure what the outcome would be." The words left a bitter taste in his mouth.

Spencer waited. This was the part where Tyler would say he sent his love and then hang up.

"Do you think—" Tyler broke off as a small voice started to wail in the background. The phone rustled, and Spencer caught the low murmur of Tyler talking to someone on the other end. The words were too quiet to catch.

After a moment, the wailing stopped. "Sorry." Tyler sounded as weary as Spencer felt. "The boys won't stop crying for Julia."

Spencer tried to picture his twin nephews, but he'd only seen a picture of them in last year's Christmas card—two chubby toddlers with Tyler's bright blue eyes and Julia's dark hair.

"Julia working today?"

Tyler was silent so long that Spencer pulled his phone away from his ear to make sure the call hadn't dropped.

"Tyler, you there?"

"Yeah." That raw edge had returned to his voice. "Julia's not—" Tyler's voice broke. "She left."

Spencer dropped the bundle of branches he'd been hauling.

"What do you mean she left?" Spencer had always thought of Tyler and Julia as the definition of soul mates—same interests, same taste in music, even the same corny sense of humor.

"She packed a bag, took one of the credit cards, and walked out the door."

"When?"

"Yesterday. I spent the day trying to get her to stay and then trying to figure out how to make the boys stop crying. I didn't realize my phone had died, otherwise . . ."

Spencer rubbed at his forehead. He'd assumed the worst of his brother. And here Tyler had been going through his own crisis. "I'm sorry, Ty." What else could he say? "Maybe she'll come back."

"She won't." Tyler's voice was dull. "There's someone else."

A white heat surged through Spencer. He and Tyler may not be close anymore, but once upon a time, they'd been each other's staunchest defenders, and that instinct came rushing back now.

"I mean, I have no idea how to take care of two boys on my own." Tyler's voice went up. "Julia was the one who was good at that. How am I supposed to—"

"Look, why don't you and the boys come to visit. Mom and Dad have been dying to meet their grandsons." He winced at the word choice, but it was too late to change it.

"You think they would want to see me after—" Tyler's swallow sounded through the phone.

"I know they do. Kind of annoying how much they want to see you, actually, considering I'm right here." Spencer tried to play it off as a joke, but the truth was, he'd always felt a little bit like the older brother in the parable of the prodigal son.

"Yeah. Maybe." High-pitched cries cut through the background. "Jonah, no." Tyler's exasperated yell made Spencer smile. He'd wondered what kind of father Tyler made.

His brother came back on the line. "I gotta go. Jonah got into the markers."

The line went dead, and Spencer lowered the phone slowly. That was not at all how he'd expected that conversation to go.

He restacked his dropped bundle of branches.

If Julia could leave Tyler after six years of marriage, what guarantee did anyone have that love could be forever?

Apparently there was none.

In which case, maybe it was best Sophie had left him when she did—think how much worse it would have hurt if they'd already built a life together.

Sophie bent over the rows of colorful tulips that bobbed in the early morning sun. With deft movements, she snipped flowers here and there, careful to spread out her selections as their gardener Alex had taught her years ago.

The garden had always been her favorite place on the entire property. She'd spent hours crawling around in the dirt out here, until Mom had told her she was too old to go around with ragged nails and dirt-stained knuckles.

But being out here, savoring the rustle of the breeze in her hair, the soft baking of the sun on her back—it almost made her, not happy, exactly, but at peace with being home.

A song Nana used to sing popped into her head, and she hummed the tune as she clipped. She couldn't remember all the words, but she thought it had something to do with "Savior's arms."

But thinking of arms made her think of Spencer's arms. Of the flippy thing her stomach had done when he wrapped them around her. Force of habit, certainly, but it had been disconcerting nonetheless. And nice. She couldn't deny that.

But she had to.

She shoved the thought away and straightened, cutting off her humming mid-song.

She carried her armful of flowers into the house and surveyed the collection of ornate vases Alex would fill with fresh flowers throughout the summer. She reached past them to grab a simple, straight one that was more to Nana's style. On a whim, she grabbed a second one just like it and placed half the bouquet in each.

All the way to the hospital, she debated with herself.

Bringing flowers to Spencer's father would probably mean running into Spencer again. And she should be doing everything possible to avoid him—it would be better for both of them that way.

But she couldn't pretend she didn't want to see him again.

Badly.

By the time she got to the hospital, her mind was made up.

She strode to the information desk and asked for the room number for Marcus Weston.

"I'm not seeing . . ." The man trailed off, typing again.

A sudden fear clutched at her stomach. What if he hadn't made it? Her pulse quickened as the volunteer at the desk typed something into the computer and scanned the screen, then typed some more.

She should have stayed with Spencer. Should have been there for him. Shouldn't have let him go through this alone.

"Ah, there he is." The volunteer scribbled on a slip of paper as Sophie leaned heavily into the counter. Her hand shook as she took the paper from him.

"Thank you," she managed to get out as she grabbed the vases and spun away from the desk.

She navigated to room 421.

The door was slightly ajar, but she didn't feel right just walking in, so she tapped softly on the frame.

"Come in," a woman's voice called a moment later.

Sophie pressed hesitantly on the door and stepped inside. Unlike Nana's private room, this room had two beds. The far bed held a man who must be closer to Nana's age, judging from the silver wisps and wrinkles. In the closer bed, a man with the same broad forehead and defined jaw as Spencer was half-propped, talking to a petite woman perched on the edge of the bed.

Sophie stepped into the room, her heels sounding too loud on the tile floor. She stopped halfway to the bed. "I'm looking for Mr. Weston." She sounded like a timid child rather than the fiery developer who had left grown contractors quaking for missing a deadline.

"You found him." The man even sounded like Spencer, though his voice was a touch deeper. "What can I do for you?"

Sophie laughed, the man managing to put her instantly at ease. "Absolutely nothing. Actually, I stopped by to give you these."

She held one of the vases of tulips out, and Mrs. Weston took it from her, her eyebrows raised at her husband.

"Well, now, you're going to get me in trouble with my wife." Mr. Weston winked at her. "She doesn't like when I get flowers from pretty young ladies."

Mrs. Weston snorted. "I'm not worried." But she set the flowers on the side table, then leaned down to kiss the top of her husband's head.

Something in Sophie jumped, and she averted her eyes. She didn't want to intrude on their tender moment.

"Not that I don't enjoy getting flowers from mysterious strangers," Mr. Weston said. "But maybe you'd like to tell me your name so I know who to thank."

Sophie felt her cheeks warm. She hadn't even introduced herself.

"I'm sorry. I'm Sophie Olsen. Spencer and I—" She caught herself.

"Oh, Sophie." Spencer's mother jumped to her feet and wrapped her in an unexpected hug. "It's so nice to meet you at last. Spencer mentioned that he'd run into you yesterday. I added you and your grandmother to my prayers last night."

"Thank you." Sophie's arms circled the woman tentatively, and her head spun. Spencer had wanted her to meet his parents so many times, but she'd always resisted. Which apparently hadn't stopped him from telling them about her. So why was this woman greeting her so kindly?

"Is Spencer, um— I mean, did he step out for a coffee again?" Sophie felt ridiculous asking, but her desire to see him was stronger than her embarrassment.

"No, he had some work to do on the farm. Boy never stops working," Mr. Weston said. "Trying to chase off demons, if you ask me. Not that I'm complaining. He keeps that place running." Pride laced his every word about his son.

A pang hit Sophie right in the center of her chest. What would it be like to hear her parents talk about her like that?

"I wouldn't think you'd complain." Spencer's mom poured water into a plastic cup and passed it to her husband. "If he hadn't had the sense to call 911 when you said you were fine, you wouldn't be here today." She turned to Sophie. "Men tend to let their pride get in the way of their common sense sometimes, if you haven't noticed."

Sophie suspected she was talking about more than her husband, but she let it pass.

"You should go out to the farm," Mr. Weston said. "I'm sure he could use a break."

"Oh, I'm sure he's busy." Sophie rubbed a petal of one of the tulips. "Anyway, I should get to my grandma. Just tell him—" Just tell him what? That she wanted to see him? The full extent of how ridiculous she'd been to come searching for him hit her.

His life was here.

Hers was in Chicago.

"Just tell him I said goodbye."

Chapter 6

The sun was low in the sky, casting a kaleidoscope of colors onto Lake Michigan, by the time Sophie left the hospital. Although Nana had slept through most of the afternoon, it had been comforting just to be near her.

But sitting all day had left her with pent-up energy she needed to burn off. The thought of going back to her parents' wasn't exactly appealing. She wished for the hundredth time that her parents had a relationship more like that of Spencer's parents. Sitting in Nana's room with nothing to do but think, her mind kept drifting to the way Mrs. Weston had kissed her husband and poured him a glass of water before he even asked for one. No wonder Spencer had believed in true love. He apparently had a view of it every day. But Sophie knew better. Even if a couple seemed to be in love, all of that could change in a single, devastating moment.

But still, the way Spencer's parents had looked at each other—she couldn't shake that image. Only two people in her life had ever looked at her like that. One of them was dying.

But the other—he was right down the road.

Sophie chewed her lip. She couldn't do this again. But maybe Spencer's dad was right. Maybe Spencer did need a break. He'd always been a workaholic. More so when he was worried. And he didn't worry about anything more than he did his family.

Before she could second-guess herself, she directed her car toward Hidden Blossom Farms. She'd driven past it a hundred times in her life. But she'd never so much as turned down the driveway. Hadn't even known Spencer, who'd gone to school in the next town over, lived there until he was assigned as her friend Cade's roommate in college.

But today, this moment, she felt almost compelled to see it. To see the life she'd said no to when she'd walked away from Spencer. To convince herself she'd done the right thing in leaving him.

The big farmhouse near the road was dark, but warm light spilled from the open garage door of a large pole shed near the end of the driveway. Hesitating only a second, Sophie pressed her foot to the gas. She'd come this far already.

As she pulled to a stop in front of the shed, her eyes picked out a modest ranch home beyond it. Through the twilight, she could just see the large open meadow behind the house. Early season wildflowers added a spark of color against the darkening grass.

Sophie's heels sank into the soft gravel as soon as she stepped out of the car, but she picked her way to the shed door.

Blinking against the bright lights inside, she peered around the large space. A tractor and an assortment of what Sophie assumed was farming equipment filled one half of the shed. But the other half was set up as a woodworking shop. Several large tools dominated the space: what she thought was a table saw and a workbench covered with buckets of paint and stain. But her eyes slipped past the rest of the tools to the finished products scattered around the space. There was a rocking chair with gracefully curved arms, an elegant console table, and—

Sophie's breath caught, and she moved into the shed as if pulled.

When she reached it, she stopped. The seat was covered with boxes, and a dirty towel hung over the back, but she recognized it.

The bench was a perfect replica of the one in the park where Spencer had proposed to her.

She ran her fingers across the wood and let the memories submerge her. They'd talked on that park bench. Laughed on that bench. Kissed on that bench.

"Hey, there."

Sophie jumped and yanked her hand off the bench. Her face flamed and her heart set up a staccato rhythm as she whirled to catch Spencer watching her. How long had he been standing there?

"Sorry, I—" She felt as if she'd been caught prying into his private life. "This is beautiful." She touched the bench one last time, then shuffled away from it.

"Thanks." Spencer tilted his head, staring at her as if he'd never seen her before.

He looked at home here in his worn jeans and faded flannel. Even the scruff on his chin seemed to belong in these rugged surroundings.

She glanced down at her tailored navy pants suit. She, on the other hand, did not belong.

"What are you doing here, Soph?" Spencer's voice was gentle but guarded.

Sophie stared at him. She had completely forgotten why she'd thought it would be a good idea to come.

"I just—" She licked her dry lips. "I just wanted to thank you."

He raised his eyebrows. "Thank me?"

"For talking me into not running away from seeing my grandma yesterday. You were right."

"You're welcome." Spencer shuffled his feet. An awkward silence fell.

Finally, Spencer sighed. "Was there anything else you needed?" She hated the formality in his tone, as if he didn't know her better than anyone else in the world.

What had she been thinking, coming here? Of course he didn't want to see her. "Nothing else." She tried to apply the same detachment to her voice and found with relief that it was easier than she'd expected. She picked her way across the shed toward the door.

She paused when she was even with him. "Bye, Spencer." The words fell from her lips and hovered in the air between them.

Jaw tight, he nodded. She waited another beat, then continued toward her car, pushing down the sting at the back of her throat. She was being ridiculous and overly emotional after her day with Nana. What had she expected? That he'd pull her into his arms and say he'd missed her and couldn't live without her? It's not like she wanted that.

"Soph?"

She froze, gripping the car door, an unexpected hope tugging at a place deep in her heart.

"Yeah?" She couldn't look at him. Couldn't bear to have that hope punctured. Not today.

"Do you want some dinner?"

Chapter 7

He was the biggest fool on the planet. Spencer knew that with certainty the moment the words were out of his mouth.

But a warmth he hadn't felt in years spread through him as he watched Sophie turn toward him, the moonlight spinning her hair into a river of light. He was seized with the urge to gather her in his arms and run his fingers through it.

Yep, definitely an idiot.

He was only setting himself up for heartbreak. And the worst part was, he didn't care.

"Dinner sounds nice." Sophie smiled. He'd missed that smile. The way the left side of her mouth lifted a fraction higher than the right.

"I was going to order in pizza tonight, but—" He eyed her sharp suit. She was used to better than Jerry's Pizza. "We can do something else, if you want."

"Pizza sounds great." She started toward him, but her heel snagged on a rock, and she stumbled. He lunged forward just in time to grab her before she face-planted.

As soon as she was steady on her feet, he snatched his hands back and shoved them into his pockets.

"Thanks." Sophie sounded breathless.

He took stock of her three-inch heels. "You're never going to make it across the yard in those. It's a swamp from all the rain."

Sophie glanced from the yard to her heels, then kicked off her shoes, standing on the gravel in her bare feet. "There."

Spencer's mouth fell open as she stooped to retrieve her shoes. He'd only ever seen hints of this spontaneous version of Sophie.

But she winced as she took one step and then another.

Before he could think what he was doing, Spencer positioned himself with his back to her. "Hop on."

She gave a disbelieving laugh. "I'm not going to ride on your back."

"Seriously, Soph, just get on." It's not like it'd be the first time he'd given her a piggyback ride.

"Seriously, Spencer, no."

"Suit yourself." Good to know her stubborn streak hadn't changed. He walked purposefully toward the house. Behind him, he heard Sophie's sharp inhales with every step. But he kept going. Two could play the stubborn game.

By the time he'd crossed the yard and reached the front door, she was only halfway across the driveway. She eyed her shoes.

"Don't put those on," Spencer called. "You'll break an ankle."

Sophie's exasperated huff made him chuckle. "You sure you don't want a piggyback ride? Last offer."

The moonlight played over her features, and Spencer could pick out the moment her hesitation gave way to resignation. He jogged back across the yard, ignoring the squish of water in his shoes from the saturated grass.

When he reached her, he gave a slight bow. "M'lady. Your chariot."

She rolled her eyes, but a smile tugged her lips up.

He let his own lips tip into a grin, then turned and stood braced for her to climb onto his back.

He tensed as her hands fell on his shoulders. Oh yeah, this had been a big mistake. But he couldn't exactly dump her back onto the ground now.

Gritting his teeth and willing himself not to notice the feel of her against him, he charged across the yard. She gasped and tightened her grip around his neck.

The moment they made it to the porch, he deposited her on the bottom step. Working hard to keep from brushing against her, he reached around her to open the door and gestured for her to enter in front of him. Once she was inside, he took a moment to collect his thoughts before he lost his mind altogether.

"I'll call for pizza." He pulled out his phone and dialed as she wandered around his living room, pausing now and then to look at a photo. He'd always considered his home comfortable, but now he saw it through her eyes: the well-worn couch and faded curtains. The anything-but-elegant wooden coffee table he'd made as a kid—one of his first woodworking projects. The lamp he'd found on the side of the road and rewired.

Was she thinking about how she'd escaped a life so beneath her standards when she walked away from him?

He finished placing the order and hung up the phone, then immediately wished he hadn't. Now what were they going to do? What did you talk about with the woman who'd shredded your heart five years ago?

Probably not that.

"You have a nice place." Sophie settled into his favorite easy chair. "It's so cozy."

Spencer laughed a little. Sophie had always been diplomatic. "Thanks."

He sat at the end of the couch farthest from her chair. That way he couldn't do anything stupid. Like act on his impulse to grab her hand.

"So how long are you in town?" There. That should put a damper on his thoughts. Bring him back to reality.

Sophie's sigh was weighted. "I don't know. My boss wants me back as soon as possible. But—" She chewed her lip as she'd always done when she was uncertain. "I feel like it's important to stay with Nana until the end. I know it won't make a difference, but—"

Spencer shifted a fraction toward her. "It *will* make a difference."

Her eyes held his. "You think so?"

He nodded. "Having people you love around you for those life-changing moments? That's important."

Sophie's lips parted.

There were so many things he could say right now. So many things he shouldn't say.

Spencer jumped to his feet. "Drinks! You want something to drink?"

Sophie startled at his abrupt movement, but he needed to put at least one wall between them for a minute.

He was already on his way to the kitchen. "I have water, soda, milk. I don't think I have any wine, but—"

"Water is good."

"Water it is then." In the kitchen, Spencer braced his arms against the counter and took a few slow breaths. He had to get himself together. He was catching up with an old friend. That was all.

His feelings in check, he pushed off the counter and grabbed two glasses out of the cupboard.

"So," he called toward the living room as he grabbed the water jug out of the fridge, "where are you these days?" How strange that he didn't know where she lived, let alone what her life was like. Or if she was with someone.

The sucker punch of the thought drew him up short, and he jerked his arm. Water cascaded onto the counter.

"Shoot!" He yanked the jug upright.

"Everything okay in there?" Sophie's voice drifted into the room.

"Fine. Just a little spill." He gritted his teeth as he yanked a towel out of the drawer and sopped up the mess.

"Here, let me help." Sophie glided into the room, still barefoot, and moved the water glasses to a dry spot on the counter. She reached past him to grab the jug. Her arm grazed the hairs on his, and he shifted away.

"I still live in Chicago." She took the towel from him and wiped the outside of the glasses, then passed him one.

He took a long drink, watching her over the top of his glass. Did she always have to be so self-assured and in control? Wasn't her heart bouncing all over the place the way his was? Then again, there was no reason for it to be. She clearly adored her new life.

"And what do you do there?" Whatever it was, he had no doubt she'd made a success of it. She'd never known how to fail.

"I work for a real estate development firm. On my way to VP, actually."

Spencer's grip tightened on his glass. "That's great, Soph." He was happy she was successful, but there was no love lost between him and real estate developers. The parasites came sniffing after his parents' farm every few years, looking for an opportunity to snatch it up.

Before he could think of something else to say, the doorbell rang. He escaped to grab the pizza.

When he returned, Sophie had the table set with plates she must have rummaged through the kitchen to find. It warmed him from the inside to think of her making herself at home here.

You are being a supreme idiot.

She had just told him she lived in Chicago. That she was happy there. Making herself at home here was the farthest thing from her mind.

He held the pizza box out to her as he slid into the chair across from her. He grabbed his own slice and set it on his plate before folding his hands and bowing his head. Across from him, he heard

Sophie shuffle a napkin and sigh. He peeked up without raising his head, just in time to see her fold her hands, too. His mind went blank. He and Sophie had prayed over their meals together so many times, but it suddenly felt too intimate.

"Thank you for this food, Lord," he finally managed. "And thank you for old—" His mind scrambled for a safe word. "For old friends."

"Amen," Sophie murmured.

"Amen." He grabbed his water glass and guzzled down half its contents in one gulp.

When he lowered the glass, he dove into his pizza. It'd been a long day, and he was famished. And if his mouth was full, he would have an excuse not to talk. Not to say something stupid.

He was grabbing another piece when Sophie finally broke the silence. "Tell me about the farm."

Spencer stopped with the pizza slice halfway to his mouth. In the three years they'd been together, Sophie had never once asked about the farm.

"What do you want to know?"

She dabbed at her lips with a napkin, looking thoughtful. "How long has it been in your family?"

He did some quick math. "About a hundred and twenty years? My great-great grandfather planted a small cherry orchard, and each generation has expanded it over the years. We have about fifty acres now, with a few thousand trees."

"That's— Wow." Sophie sat back in her chair, laying her napkin on her plate. "That's a lot."

His face warmed. If he didn't know better, he'd think she was impressed.

He pushed back his chair. "The cherries should be in bloom in a day or two. You should come see them. They're pretty spectacular."

Great. Now he was inviting rejection.

But that smile lit her face again. "I'd like that."

He carried their plates to the dishwasher, avoiding her eyes. Did she even know what she was doing to him?

"What about the woodworking?" She stood and brought their empty glasses to him.

He lifted a shoulder. "Just a side gig I do in the winter when things are slower on the farm. Brings in a little extra income." Income they desperately needed after last year's failed crop. Which was why he had so many half-completed projects in the shop. He'd taken on way more than he could handle this winter to try to make ends meet.

"You're very talented, Spencer." Sophie kept her gaze directed at the dishwasher, but her cheeks pinked.

Her comment pleased him more than it should. He slammed the dishwasher closed harder than he meant to. "Thanks."

He turned to make his escape to a less confined room, but she was right there.

She took a step back to avoid getting run over.

"I should get going." But she didn't move. Something hovered in her words, and for a moment Spencer let himself think she wanted him to ask her to stay.

He dried his hands on his pants. "Yeah. I'll walk you out."

Sophie could feel Spencer's presence behind her as he shepherded her to the door. Dinner had been nice. Better than nice, actually. It'd been the best night she'd had in a long time.

Which was why she had to get out of here.

Sooner rather than later.

She scooped up her shoes from the rug in front of the door, then let Spencer reach past her to open it. Still a gentleman.

"You should visit Violet while you're back." Spencer followed her onto the porch.

She froze. "I don't think she'd want to see me." If Sophie had one regret about how she'd handled things after she and Spencer broke up, it was cutting her best friend out of her life. But at the time, it had seemed easiest to cut every last tie to Hope Springs. She hadn't come back for Violet and Cade's wedding. Or for Cade's funeral two years ago. The memory of the text from her mom saying Cade had died slammed into her. She and Vi and Cade had been a trio since grade school. Cade was like a brother to her. And the thought that he was gone—it had been too much to deal with. She couldn't face saying goodbye to him. Couldn't face seeing Vi's grief.

So she'd sent a card and told herself it would be enough. And then she'd buried herself even deeper in her work.

"She'd want to see you." Spencer's eyes were too gentle, too understanding.

"How is she?" Sophie managed to keep her voice steady, not to betray the roil of emotions churning in her stomach at the thought of what her friend had gone through without her. Of course, that didn't mean Spencer couldn't see them.

He reached for her arm but dropped his hand before it made contact. "She's doing okay, I guess. She and Cade had an antique store that she's kept going. But she's not the same person she used to be." He gripped the porch railing but turned his head toward her. "Losing someone does that to a person."

The moment Sophie's eyes landed on his, lined in silver in the moonlight, they skipped away. What she saw in his—that wasn't something she was prepared to deal with.

"Thanks for tonight." She rushed down the steps, ignoring the cold sting of the concrete on her bare feet, the cold squish of the mud between her toes as she stepped into the grass.

By the time she'd reached the driveway, her feet were so numb she barely felt the stab of the jagged rocks. Too bad the ache in her heart wasn't as easily dimmed.

Chapter 8

Sophie stared down the doors of the church as a warm breeze lifted the hair off her neck. Her parents had already gone inside, but she couldn't quite bring herself to step through the doors. The relentless pounding of the Lake Michigan surf below seemed to take the place of her heartbeat. She didn't know what she was doing here. Not really.

She hadn't been inside a church anywhere in years. But Nana had barely woken at all yesterday, and she felt out of options. Maybe if she put in some time at church, God would listen to her prayers.

Anyway, in one of Nana's few lucid moments, she'd made Sophie promise to come.

Sophie steeled her shoulders. If she could face angry contractors and disgruntled buyers, she could handle an hour of church.

She pulled the door open and strode inside, letting her eyes travel the space. She hadn't been in here since her senior year of high school. And yet so little had changed. To the left was the same oversize fireplace surrounded by several leather couches. Above, the same high, white wooden beams gave the room an open, airy feel. Scattered groups of people talked and laughed together.

Everyone seemed so at home here. Had she really felt that way once, too?

She tried to wind her way through the clusters of people without drawing attention to herself.

But just before she reached the entrance to the sanctuary, she lifted her eyes, and they fell on Spencer. She stopped abruptly, barely noticing when someone ran into her from behind.

"Sorry," she mumbled. But her eyes were locked on Spencer's, and she couldn't tear them away, no matter how much she wanted to.

She'd spent most of the day yesterday convincing herself that the things she'd felt the other night at his house were only nostalgia—a reminder of the time before there were careers and apartments and dying grandmothers to worry about.

But with his eyes on her, the strength of her arguments crumbled at her feet.

Spencer's expression remained neutral, but he waved her over.

It was only then that she noticed the others standing around him. A couple who looked vaguely familiar and two women, one of whom Sophie recognized immediately, even from the back. Those dark curls could only belong to her former best friend.

Her heart jumped as Vi spotted her, gave her a gigantic smile, and broke away from the group to charge across the lobby. She threw her arms around Sophie and engulfed her in a hug that left Sophie gasping for air.

Sophie clung to her former best friend, even as she scrunched her eyes against the wave of emotion.

"Spencer said you were back. It's so good to see you." Vi was still squeezing her tight.

"You, too." Sophie's voice was too full. She didn't deserve a welcome like this. Not after she'd abandoned the one person she'd promised to be there for forever.

She pulled back, gripping her friend's shoulders. "I'm so sorry about Cade."

Vi nodded and blinked a few times. Her eyes lacked the bright spark and easy smile that had led her to be voted "friendliest senior" in high school. "Thanks, I—"

But the rest of the group reached them. Vi gestured to the couple that Sophie thought she knew but couldn't place. "Soph, do you remember Ethan and Ariana? They graduated a year ahead of us." The couple unwound their arms from around each other and each held out a hand to Sophie. Now that Vi said their names, she recognized them. Ethan had always been a star athlete, but his whole family had been killed in an accident. Sophie always wondered how someone recovered from something like that. It was hard enough to lose one person.

"And this is Emma." Violet gestured to a tall, pretty blond standing close to Spencer.

Very close.

The woman scrutinized her with a hard look but held out a hand.

Sophie forced her hand forward even as her shoulders tensed. Her eyes shot to the woman's left hand. Ring free.

Not that it matters.

"And, of course, you know Spencer." What was that look Vi gave her? Could she read the swirl of Sophie's thoughts at seeing her ex with another woman?

Spencer offered a tight smile.

"I didn't know you came to church here." Sophie directed her words to Spencer. "I thought you always went over in Silver Bay." It'd been the only reason she'd even considered coming here this morning.

"We started coming here to be with Vi after Cade's death." The blond woman—Emma—answered for him.

Sophie nodded stiffly.

Of course they had. They'd been here for Vi when she hadn't.

Ethan glanced at his watch, then fiddled with a pager on his hip. "We should probably go grab a seat."

Sophie scanned the nearly empty lobby. Her parents had probably long since taken their customary spot in the second row from the front.

Vi nudged her. "Sit with us?"

Sitting with Spencer and his new girlfriend for an hour sounded like absolutely the last thing Sophie wanted to do. But the church was full, and she didn't exactly feel like parading to the front to join her parents.

She followed the group as they filed into a half-full row near the back. Her whole body tensed as she realized she'd be sandwiched right between Vi and Spencer. She squeezed as close to Vi as she could in the cramped space and bowed her head, trying to recall the words of the prayers Nana had taught her as a little girl, but her mind drew a blank.

Panic welled low in her stomach. Had it really been that long since she'd prayed? What right did she even have to be here?

Her legs itched with the need to get away. But she'd have to climb over Spencer and Emma to escape, and she wasn't about to attempt that. She tried to direct her attention to Pastor Zelner. But she was too aware of every shift in Spencer's position, every accidental brush of his arm against hers. His familiar scent of spicy woodland and warm cinnamon wafted over her.

By the time church was over, Sophie was ready to bolt.

"It was so nice to see you again." She leaned over to hug Vi, then pushed to her feet.

"Wait. Where do you think you're going?" Vi latched onto her arm, as if afraid she'd sneak away. "We always grab some lunch after church. You have to come."

Sophie scanned the church, searching for her parents. They were standing on opposite sides of the sanctuary, each deep in conversation. Hopefully they wouldn't be long.

"Sorry, Vi. I'd love to, but I caught a ride with my parents, so . . ."

Vi's face fell. "I can give you a ride to the restaurant, but I have to rush off afterward."

"I'll give you a ride home." Spencer's voice was low but definitely directed at her.

Sophie's gaze darted to Emma, whose jaw had hardened. "Oh, you don't have to—"

"That settles it then." Vi tightened her grip on Sophie's arm and steered her toward the lobby. "You're coming with us."

Sophie opened her mouth to protest, but the pleading look in Vi's eyes stopped her. After five years of not being there for her friend, she owed her at least a lunch. "Where to?"

Chapter 9

"Don't even say it." Spencer held up a hand as he jumped out of his truck and met Emma and the others outside the Hidden Cafe to wait for Violet and Sophie.

"Say what?" Emma's voice was all innocence, but Spencer knew her better than that.

"You were about to lecture me about not falling for Sophie again. But trust me. I've got that covered."

"Yeah, volunteering to drive her home is a good way to keep yourself from getting too close again. I hope you realize I'll be coming with you." She knotted her blond hair—so similar to Sophie's—into a bun at the nape of her neck.

Spencer rolled his eyes. "That won't be necessary."

He'd only known Emma a few years, but sometimes she acted more like a mother than a friend. Then again, he'd been a mess when they'd met, and she'd been the only one he could confide in about how broken Sophie's rejection had left him. The one who had helped him pick up the pieces and move on with his life. He was grateful that she didn't want him to go through that again.

But he didn't need her protection. "For your information, I offered to drive her for Violet's sake." It wasn't entirely a lie. He knew how much seeing Sophie again meant to Violet. Emma didn't need to know how much it meant to him, too.

He smoothed a hand over his hair as Violet's car pulled into the parking lot, Sophie gazing out the passenger window.

Emma snorted. "Look at you, preening for her."

"I'm not preening." But he dropped his hand to his side.

Emma gestured to Ethan and Ariana, who'd been watching them with matching amused grins. "Do you see this?"

Ethan gave Spencer a helpless shrug, and Ariana sent him a sympathetic look.

"I think it's sweet." Ariana smoothed Ethan's hair. "Some people could take a lesson from you."

"You know you like my hair messy." Ethan grinned at her and re-mussed his hair.

Emma huffed out a breath. "You two lovebirds are no help. It's not sweet. We're talking about the woman who ripped his heart out of his chest, ran it through a wood chipper, and then left him to pick up the pieces and stuff them back in."

"Hey." Spencer held up a hand to stop her, but she wasn't far from the truth. In fact, he may have once used those words to describe how he felt when Sophie walked away.

"And—" Emma pointed a finger at his chest. "Don't think I didn't notice the way you two were mooning over each other in church."

Spencer scoffed. "Now I know you're crazy." He'd used every ounce of his willpower to avoid looking at Sophie during church. And when he'd failed and sneaked a glance, her eyes were nowhere near him.

"I'm serious, Spencer." Emma's brow puckered, and she rested a hand on his arm. "You need to be careful."

He relented at Emma's worry.

Maybe she was right.

Maybe he was being too unguarded with his heart.

Sophie opened her car door, and his pulse kicked into overdrive. Apparently, he was about to find out.

Sophie couldn't believe she'd made it through the meal. Thankfully, Vi had kept her occupied, asking about her life in Chicago and telling her about the antique store. Talking about everything except Spencer and his new girlfriend.

Whose chair was practically on top of Spencer's. And who kept finding excuses to touch him.

Sophie got the message already.

Spencer was taken.

It'd be nice if Emma didn't feel the need to rub it in her face every second.

But that wasn't fair. Of course Emma wanted to touch him. She was in love with him. And she had every right to be.

Sophie had given up her claim to Spencer years ago.

And it had been the right decision.

She knew it had.

She had no doubts.

Or at least none she was willing to examine closely.

She had never wanted to get married and have children. Never fantasized about walking down the aisle or cuddling a baby. It just wasn't her.

The stab she felt every time Emma covered Spencer's hand with her own was only because the last few days had been so difficult.

Nothing else.

She tore her eyes off the spot where Emma's shoulder pressed against Spencer's and focused her attention on Vi. "So, who helps you with the store now—" She broke off abruptly. How could she ever get used to saying that Cade was dead?

"It's just me now." Vi wiped her mouth and pushed her chair back. Apparently not a topic she wanted to talk about.

Sophie and the others pushed their chairs back as well. Sophie swept the check off the table. "This one's on me." The others sent up a stream of protests, and Spencer shot her a hard look. He'd always accused her of trying to buy people's approval.

But that wasn't what this was about. And, anyway, he didn't have a say in what she did anymore.

The others filed out the door as she approached the counter to pay. She appreciated the moment to herself.

But the cashier was too efficient, and after a minute she was outside with everyone else.

She said her goodbyes to the others, promising to see them again before she returned to Chicago. Before she was ready, Vi, Ariana, and Ethan were gone, and she was left standing with Spencer and Emma. She looked back and forth between them, unsure if it would be more awkward if Emma did or didn't come with them.

"I'll see you later," Spencer told Emma.

She pursed her lips but nodded. "Call me." She lifted onto her toes to kiss his cheek.

Sophie looked away.

"Ready?" Spencer's voice sounded strained.

She bobbed her head and followed him. If her parents didn't live five miles out of town and she weren't wearing heels, she'd walk. Actually, walking might be preferable anyway.

But she let Spencer lead her to his black truck. He opened the door for her and held out a hand to help her up.

She wasn't prepared for the jolt that surged up her arm as his hand closed around hers.

She trained her focus on getting into the vehicle, looking at anything but him.

Spencer closed her door, and she tried to slow her revving heart as she fastened her seat belt. Her thoughts skipped over all the things she could say when he got in, but nothing seemed right.

Spencer opened his door and hopped onto his seat in one easy movement.

"Emma seems nice," Sophie blurted. She clamped her mouth shut the moment the words were out. Did she really want to go there?

"Yeah. She is." Spencer's smile crinkled his eyes. Was that the same smile he used to wear when he talked about her?

She swallowed and forced herself to go on. "How long have you two known each other?"

Spencer frowned in thought. "Four years? Maybe five? She bought the horse farm down the road from Hidden Blossom shortly after I moved back. I thought she was crazy at the time. That place was falling apart. But she's really made something of it."

Sophie turned toward the window. A smear of trees blurred past. Emma was a farmer. A much better fit for him than a Chicago developer.

"How's your grandma doing?" Spencer's question brought her back to what really mattered. She shouldn't be worrying about her own lonely life when Nana was dying.

A heavy sigh escaped her. "Not well. She's only been awake for a few minutes at a time. Same old Nana when she is though." She gave a short laugh. "Even managed to talk me into going to church."

Spencer's gaze cut to her. "I'm glad you came."

Sophie shrugged. "I'm not sure it did any good. I haven't been to church in—" But she couldn't even remember the last time. "Years. God has no reason to listen to me."

She ran a knuckle across the cool window, trying not to notice Spencer studying her.

"You know it doesn't work that way, Soph. You don't have to do something for God so he'll listen to you. He loves you."

She shrugged again. If he wanted to believe that, that was fine. But in her experience, nothing ever came without conditions.

Not happiness. Not forgiveness. And definitely not love.

Outside, the trees along the road grew denser as they reached her parents' driveway. Only a few more yards and she'd be free to make her escape.

"How's your dad?"

His forehead creased, the way it always had when he was worried. "He's doing better. But it's hard to see him like this." His jaw jumped. "He's been larger than life to me forever. And now . . ."

He seemed lost in thought, and Sophie waited quietly in case he wanted to continue.

Spencer cleared his throat. "He says thanks for the flowers, by the way."

Sophie's hands stilled. "It's no big deal. I was cutting some for Nana anyway, and I just thought—" What had she thought? It had been a stupid, impetuous move. One Spencer's girlfriend probably didn't appreciate.

"It was a big deal, Soph. Why didn't you tell me you'd been to see him?" Spencer's voice held a thread of gratitude and something else she couldn't place.

She shrugged. It'd been on the tip of her tongue a few times the other night, but she hadn't wanted to overstep her bounds.

"Anyway, he hasn't stopped talking about it." Spencer's lips lifted, and she let herself smile back.

"It was nice to meet him. He reminded me of you."

Spencer's eyes darted to her and then away, and a hint of pink tinged his cheeks. "Well, it meant a lot to him." He cleared his throat again. "And to—"

But he broke off as they rounded the last curve of the driveway. She followed his gaze to the black BMW parked near the house, a man in a sharp suit leaning against the trunk, facing the lake.

Sophie's stomach dropped. She knew only one person who dressed like that on weekends.

"You know him?" Spencer's voice had taken on a funny, raspy quality.

Sophie nodded dumbly, trying to process. "He's my . . ." But her brain had closed up shop. What did she call Chase? And what was he doing here?

"Ah." The single syllable said everything Spencer was thinking. She opened her mouth to correct him, but what difference did it make? He was with Emma anyway, so he couldn't care less if she was with someone else.

"Thanks for the ride." She fumbled for the door handle, her eyes fixed on Chase, who marched toward the truck with his long, confident strides and Armani suit that was so out of place here.

"You're welcome." Spencer hit the unlock button, and she shoved out the door and slammed it behind her before Chase reached them. There was no need for these two to meet.

The moment she took a step away from the truck, the tires crunched over the blacktop.

"Surprise!" Chase dropped a quick kiss on her lips. She took a step back and glanced over her shoulder, but Spencer's truck was already retreating down the driveway.

She tried to infuse something close to enthusiasm into her voice. "Chase! What are you doing here?"

Chapter 10

Spencer's knuckles stood out white against the steering wheel. He had only himself to blame for letting his heart go where it wasn't supposed to go. Served him right for offering to drive Sophie home. For admiring the way her hair fell in a curtain around her face when she ducked her head in embarrassment. For basking in every little smile she sent his way. For thinking that she'd felt the same familiar spark he had the other night.

He unclenched one fist, lifted it from the wheel, then slammed it back into place. Emma had been right. When it came to Sophie, he had no common sense.

Case in point: He'd forbidden himself from looking in the rearview mirror as he'd left Sophie's parents' house. But his resolve had lasted all of three seconds. He'd glanced into the mirror just in time to see that man—that good-looking, well-dressed, BMW-driving man—kiss her.

Spencer stretched his ear toward his shoulder, trying to release the tension that had seized his neck.

He had to face it. The man Sophie was with now—that was the kind of man she deserved to be with. Someone who could give her the kind of life she'd always had. The kind of life she'd always wanted. The kind of life he could never offer.

Sure, he'd been good enough for a college boyfriend. Good enough for someone to hang out with. But when she'd had to consider the kind of man she wanted to spend the rest of her life with, he hadn't measured up.

Spencer shook himself. He'd already gotten over Sophie. There was no reason to get so worked up over the fact that she'd found someone else. It's not like he hadn't imagined a thousand times the kind of man she'd end up with. A man just like the one with her right now.

He pulled into Hidden Blossom's driveway, slowing to examine the rambling farmhouse he'd grown up in. The paint had been peeling since before he was born. But now it was in desperate need of repainting. Shingles were peeling up in several places as well. But with Dad's new medical expenses, both things would have to wait.

Spencer was plenty used to doing without, but it hurt to see his parents still struggling after all these years. It seemed life on the farm never got easier.

Another reason it was best he stopped dreaming about Sophie. He had to give all his attention to helping his family.

Speaking of—

Spencer leaned forward as he approached his house. An unfamiliar car was parked in front of the shed. His eyes traveled past the car to his front lawn.

The old farm dog Buck must have followed the car to the house and was now trying to sniff two small boys, who kept running away.

Their shrieks cut through Spencer's window, and he grinned as he caught sight of his brother chasing the boys. Every time Tyler caught one of them, the other ran off, screaming even louder. Buck chased along, apparently finding the whole thing one big game.

Spencer was tempted to stop the truck right here so he could just sit watching his brother and nephews. The weight that had been pressing on him lightened. He hadn't realized how much he missed his brother until this moment, seeing him again. And the boys reminded him of himself and Tyler when they were younger.

He pulled into the driveway next to Tyler's car. The moment his big brother's eyes fell on him, relief took over his face.

Spencer shoved his door open and jumped from the truck, calling the dog to him.

He ordered Buck to heel and led him slowly into the yard. He told the dog to sit. Buck obeyed, his tongue lolling to the side, and gave Spencer a pleading look as if to ask, "Can we play again?"

"Stay," Spencer commanded. Then he crouched at Buck's side. He patted the dog's head with one hand and held out his other hand to the boy latched to Tyler's leg. "See, he's a nice doggy." As if to prove the point, Buck swiped his tongue down Spencer's cheek.

The little boy laughed and took a small step closer.

"This is Buck. You can pet him," Spencer said. "Maybe he'll give you a kiss, too."

The boy giggled again and toddled closer. His brother watched from Tyler's arms, letting out an occasional cry.

As soon as the closer twin was within reach, Buck stuck his snout forward to sniff. The boy let out another scream and almost toppled over backward, but Spencer grabbed his hand. It was sticky and a little wet but warm, and it made something pull in Spencer's gut. This was his nephew.

"It's okay," he soothed. "The doggy just wants to sniff you. That's how doggies say hi."

The boy looked from Spencer to the dog, then took a tiny step forward. This time when Buck sniffed him, he giggled. "It tickles."

Spencer laughed and the boy stepped right up to Buck, petting the dog's ear. Buck used the opportunity to lick the boy's nose. The twin giggled harder, and from behind him, his brother joined in.

Soon, both boys were petting the dog and taking turns getting dog kisses.

Spencer pushed to his feet and met his brother's eyes. Tyler held out a tentative hand, but Spencer pulled him in for a quick hug. "It's good to see you, man. I'm glad you came."

Tyler slapped Spencer's back. "Thank goodness you showed up when you did. I was about ready to throw the boys back in the car and take off. And I'm not sure I could have handled another ten-hour drive with these two. Julia always—" His voice cracked, and he scanned the farm, face gathered into a frown. "Gotta say, I never thought I'd be back here again."

Spencer clapped his brother's shoulder. "Ah, it's not so bad here. You might even find you like it."

At his feet, the twins were fighting over who got the next "Bucky kiss." Spencer bent to scoop one twin up in each of his arms, relishing their heft. "Enough love for the dog. What about your uncle Spencer? He's way cooler than a dog. And he can give kisses, too." He flicked his tongue at the twins, who squealed and tried to squirm away.

But Spencer pulled them closer, and they wrapped their little arms around his neck, letting him carry them inside.

Sophie massaged her temples, trying to ease the splitting headache that had kicked in right around the time she found Chase outside her parents' house. Apparently, he'd already arranged everything with her mother and would be spending the night here. The second guest room was being prepared for him.

"You really didn't have to come," she said for at least the eighth time as she sat stiffly on the straight-backed chair in the formal living room.

"I told you, I missed you." Chase leaned forward and reached to squeeze her hand. She tried to squeeze back, quashing down the guilt at the fact that she had barely thought of him since she'd left Chicago.

"So what's there to do around here?" Chase's eyes fell on the picture windows overlooking the lake. "You must have a boat, right? Should we take her out for a ride?"

Sophie frowned at him. It was already way past the time she should be at Nana's. "I was planning to spend the day at the hospital." She gestured toward the window. "But you're welcome to check out the lake. There's a great public pier next to the marina downtown."

Chase sighed, not bothering to hide his pout. "No, that's okay. I'll go with you."

Don't do me any favors.

But Sophie gave him a tight smile. "That sounds nice."

She led the way to the front closet and grabbed a light jacket. Chase plucked it from her grip and held it up to help her into it. Sophie gritted her teeth, then forced herself to relax.

Why was she so annoyed with everything he did right now? He was only trying to be thoughtful. He'd driven all the way from Chicago, after all. He wouldn't have had to do that.

She tried to ignore the fact that he hadn't asked about her grandmother. Hadn't apologized for dropping in on her unexpectedly. Hadn't really seemed to think of her at all.

Still, she resolved to give Chase the benefit of the doubt.

She opened the front door but stopped short at the sight of Mom standing on the top step, staring out toward the lake. "Mom?"

Mom jumped and spun toward her. "Oh, Sophie, you startled me." Her eyes fell on Chase, and her smile warmed. "I hope you have everything you need."

Chase gave her the suave smile that had helped him close plenty of deals. "And then some."

"Good." Mom stepped to the door as Sophie and Chase started down the steps. "Where are you kids off to?"

"To visit Nana."

"Sophie." Her mother's tone held the familiar reprimand. "You two should go and do something fun. Nana won't mind."

Sophie bit her tongue to keep from asking how Mom would know what Nana would or wouldn't mind, when she hadn't been to visit her once since she'd been in the hospital.

"I promised Nana," she said simply.

"Well at least go out to dinner afterward." Mom stepped into the house. "Take him to Alessandro's." She turned to Chase. "It's divine."

Sophie puffed out an irritated breath as Mom closed the door. "Sorry about her."

But Chase had pulled out his phone and was lifting it to his ear.

"What are you doing?"

Chase waved a hand to shush her. "Making reservations." He gave his attention to someone on the other end of the phone.

Sophie rolled her eyes and led the way to her car. It was going to be a long afternoon.

Chase got off the phone as Sophie directed the car toward town. For the next ten minutes, he filled her in on the latest details on the Hudson project. She tried to bring her thoughts into focus on what he was saying. It would give her a leg up when she got back to the office.

But her mind refused to cooperate. It kept rewinding to earlier that afternoon. To the way Spencer had thanked her for visiting his dad. To the way he'd tensed when he saw Chase.

She signaled and turned onto Hope Street. Early-season tourists were out in full force today, and Sophie craned her neck to spot Vi's antique shop.

There.

Tucked right next to the fudge shop.

"Well, this is quaint." Chase didn't bother to mask his derision. Clearly, to him quaint meant backward.

Sophie tightened her hands on the wheel but then forced them to relax. After all, she'd thought of her hometown that way more than once. Since she'd been back, though, quaint had started to seem like a good thing.

She shook herself. Quaint might be fine for a visit. But her life was in the city.

With Chase.

Not here. Not with Spencer, who even now refused to exit her thoughts.

That had to stop.

She pulled into the hospital parking lot and turned to Chase. "Thanks for—"

But his phone rang, and he shifted his attention to the screen.

"Sorry, I have to take this." Chase answered the call before she could respond.

She sighed and stepped out of the car, waiting for Chase to join her. Even though he was on the phone and had no idea where they were going, he took the lead. She sped up to match his long strides, occasionally pointing to keep him going in the right direction.

By the time they reached Nana's room, he still wasn't off the phone. Sophie waited a few minutes, but when he didn't show any sign of wrapping up the call, she entered the room alone.

"Hi, Nana." She'd finally gotten used to talking to her grandmother when she was sleeping. Nana's form seemed to have shrunk since yesterday so that she looked almost like the toothpick figure Sophie had once constructed for a school project.

Sophie crossed the room to open the curtains. Streamers of white-gold light speckled the floor. "It's nice out today. The lake was so glassy this morning. Made me think of that time we went over to Strawberry Island. Remember? The water was so flat you said we should try walking on it." She paused, gazing out the window. "So I tried. But I couldn't, obviously. And then you held me up, so I'd feel like I really was walking on the water. And you told me—" Sophie swallowed and crossed the room to Nana's bedside. She brushed at the wispy strands of hair that poked up from Nana's head. "You told me that you'd always try to hold me up, but when you couldn't God would still be there, holding me." She settled into the chair next to Nana's bed and blew out a slow breath. A shadow of the truth had been nagging at her for the past couple days, and being in church this morning had only given it substance. "But, Nana." Her voice came out as little more than a whisper. "I've pushed God away. I'm not sure he's holding me anymore."

She tried to shove down the confusion that had overcome her this week. She wasn't used to being so unsure. She willed Nana to wake up. To tell her how to fix this. But Nana didn't stir.

"Glad that's taken care of." Chase's over-loud voice ricocheted around the room. Sophie cringed and held a finger to her lips.

"Oh, sorry." Chase lowered his voice. His face had paled, and his eyes darted around the room, as if searching for a safe place to land.

"Here." Sophie moved to bring the other chair in the room closer, but Chase shook his head.

"I'm good." He anchored himself on the narrow windowsill.

"Okay then." Sophie's eyes flicked from Chase to Nana. "Nana, this is Chase. He's my—" She fumbled. "We work together. Chase, this is my grandmother."

Chase gave a quick nod but didn't look at Nana.

"It's okay." Sophie hadn't pegged him for squeamish. "You can talk to her."

Chase gave her a blank stare. "She's out."

"I know." Sophie moved back to her chair. "You get used to it."

Chase nodded again but didn't say anything.

Sophie chewed her lip. Having him here made her self-conscious about talking to Nana, too.

So she just sat, holding Nana's hand.

Out of the corner of her eye, she saw Chase pull out his phone. After a quick glance, he heaved a noticeable sigh and clicked it off.

Five minutes later, he did the same thing.

And five minutes after that.

Finally, Sophie couldn't take it anymore. "Why don't you go check out the pier? It's a few blocks to the north. I'll meet you there in a bit."

The relief that passed over Chase's face was almost comical. "You sure?"

But he was already striding toward the door.

She tensed as he detoured to drop a kiss onto her cheek.

The door clicked, and an overwhelming peace settled over the room.

Sophie squeezed Nana's hand. "Now, where were we?"

Chapter 11

Spencer wanted to yank the hair out of his head.

He had been listening to two screaming boys for an hour and a half, and he was pretty sure he was going to lose his mind if it didn't stop soon.

"Let's try the bears again," he yelled to his brother over the screams.

Tyler nodded, his jaw tense, as he pulled Jonah to him.

Spencer grabbed Jeremiah and tried to give him the stuffed bear he'd dug out of an old box in his parents' attic. But the toddler chucked it into the wall on the other side of the room. Kid had a surprisingly good arm. Maybe he'd play football someday.

If they all survived this night.

On the other side of the room, Tyler was having no better luck. Little Jonah was stomping on his bear's head.

"I give up." Tyler set Jonah down and dropped into the unpainted rocking chair Spencer had brought in from the shed.

He buried his face in his hands. "They want their mommy." His voice was muffled through his fingers, but Spencer heard the pain in it. "I want her, too."

Spencer retrieved the two bears and set them on the dresser.

He glanced at the window. It was so dark outside. Maybe the boys needed a night-light.

Not that he had any of those lying around. But maybe—

"Hold on." He jogged out of the room as the twins resumed their screaming behind him.

He pushed out the front door and jogged down the porch steps and across the yard to the workshop.

He'd brought a small reading lamp out here a few weeks ago to help him see the fine details better in the dark space.

As he crossed the workshop, his eyes fell on the bench he'd made for Sophie months before proposing to her. It was supposed to be a wedding present.

How had he been so sure she'd say yes? How had he been so wrong about their relationship?

And now, all these years later, he still couldn't bring himself to get rid of it. Maybe he should sell it. Make a few bucks off it, at least.

But getting rid of it felt too permanent. Like he was giving up all hope of ever being with Sophie.

Not that there's anything to hope for anyway. You saw her kissing another man. What more proof that she's over you do you need? An invitation to their wedding?

Spencer yanked the lamp off his workbench with a snarl at himself. He was being stupid, thinking about Sophie, when he had two screaming nephews and a heartbroken brother to take care of.

He grabbed the lamp and sprinted to the house without another glance at the bench.

If possible, the volume of the wailing had increased. Both boys were in the portable cribs Tyler had brought along, standing with their hands gripping the sides. Streaks of tears and dirt clung to their splotchy cheeks, and snot dripped toward their mouths. If he hadn't seen much worse helping Emma deliver horses, Spencer would be disgusted.

Tyler stood between the two cribs, shoulders hunched, arms hanging limply at his sides.

"Here we go." Spencer tried the soothing voice he used with Emma's horses whenever they were spooked. He clicked on the reading lamp, then turned off the overhead light.

The boys went silent for a moment, and Spencer held his breath. Had he really solved the problem?

He was a hero.

Super Uncle.

Spencer the Great.

He was—

The wailing started again.

Spencer groaned.

Tyler spun his back to them, fists on his forehead. "How am I ever going to do this?"

Spencer crossed to his brother and wrapped an arm around his shoulder, leading him toward the door. "Go. Take a walk or something. I'll handle this."

Tyler shook his head. "You'll handle it?"

I always do. But Spencer bit back the words. Now was not the time.

Tyler opened his mouth again, then nodded once and left the room.

A second later, the front door banged shut.

"There, now it's just you and me, boys." Spencer moved into the rocking chair. "Tell you what. I'm going to sit here and listen to you two scream. And when you tire yourselves out with that, you can lay down and go to sleep, okay?"

But the twins had more willpower than Spencer had given them credit for. After twenty minutes, he considered joining in the screaming. Anything would be better than listening to it.

He needed backup.

But his mom had been staying at the hospital with his dad, and he didn't want to wake her in case she was actually managing to get some sleep.

He'd always assumed that when he got to the point of dealing with screaming children, it'd be with Sophie at his side as they made their own family memories. But if she was going to be taking care of kids with anyone, it was with Mr. BMW.

What about Emma? She took care of baby horses all the time. Maybe she'd know what to do with baby humans, too.

He sent her a quick, desperate text.

A few seconds later, she texted him back. *Try this. Helps me sleep.*

There was a link attached. Spencer clicked it, and it took him to a video. Relaxing Horse Galloping Sound Effects.

Spencer stared at it, then shrugged and hit play. He was willing to try anything at this point.

It took the boys a few seconds to notice the sounds of horse hooves and waves, but as they did, they quieted to listen.

Spencer turned up the volume on his phone a notch.

The boys yawned and rubbed their eyes.

Ten minutes later, both laid down.

Spencer closed his own eyes, letting the sound of their soft breathing mingle with the horse hoofbeats.

Maybe this was what peace felt like.

"Finally," Chase breathed into Sophie's ear as they entered Alessandro's. "Somewhere civilized."

Sophie's hands clenched. *Only a few more hours.*

Then she could go to bed. And escape Chase. At least until morning.

She caught herself before she groaned out loud.

Whatever it was about him that had appealed to her in Chicago had lost its luster in her hometown. There, he seemed confident and in control. Here, it was more like pompous and overbearing.

Earlier, when she'd rejoined him at the pier after her visit with Nana, he'd lunged at her in relief, as if she'd abandoned him in the wild for days.

"Glad that's over with." He'd given her his deprecating smile. "You would not believe how many little brats have taken over this pier in the past hour."

Sophie hadn't bothered to point out that it had only been half an hour. That she'd cut her time with Nana short because she'd known he'd be getting impatient.

It had been too early for their reservation, though, so she'd driven him to see the sights the peninsula was known for—the farmer's market, the giant sunfish statue, the Old Lighthouse. His reaction to each had been the same: indifference.

Finally, she'd given up and they'd come to Alessandro's early. At least Chase would be content waiting here. In his element.

The maître d' took their name and ushered them to an elegant lounge with high chandeliers and plush carpeting to wait.

"I'll get us some drinks." Chase disappeared without asking what she'd like.

Sophie scrutinized the space as she sank into a supple leather chair. Her parents had brought her here for countless birthdays, even when all she'd wanted was a simple party at home. She'd always felt like she was on display here, her parents showing her off to all their country club friends. And those friends boasting of their own children's achievements, which always outshone hers, until, by the end of the night, she could feel her parents' disappointment radiating off them.

Her eyes fell on Evelyn and Andrew Carter, and she sent up a small plea. Maybe they wouldn't notice her.

But as if drawn by the thought, Evelyn's eyes landed right on her. The woman's diamond tennis bracelet sparked in the light as she tapped her husband's shoulder and pointed at Sophie, then gave an exaggerated wave.

Sophie gritted her teeth but raised her hand in a small wave. The Carters were already on their way toward her.

Sophie pushed her lips into a painful smile as they reached her. "Mr. And Mrs. Carter. It's so nice to see you."

"And you, dear." Mrs. Carter leaned in to give Sophie a kiss on each cheek. "How are your parents?"

"They're fine." Sophie kept her answer short. Maybe once the pleasantries were over, the Carters would move on.

"And what brings you back to Hope Springs, dear? Our Myla is so busy she never makes it home. She's a resident now, you know. Neurosurgery."

Sophie grimaced. She had no interest in knowing what her oldest rival was up to—though the two girls probably never would have become rivals if their parents hadn't constantly pitted them against each other.

"My grandma is ill." Sophie kept her tone civil but hoped the Carters would get the hint that she was done talking.

"Oh, I did hear that. Myla's grandmother died last year, but she was so busy she couldn't make it back. We all understood, though. You're lucky your job is so much less demanding." Evelyn's eyes traveled down Sophie's simple black dress. "What is it you do now, dear?" If the woman were any more patronizing, she'd pat Sophie on the head and hand her a lollipop.

Before Sophie could answer, she spotted Chase. She'd never been so grateful to see him. "I'll let you go. I should get back to my—" She gestured toward Chase.

"Oh, yes, I see." Evelyn's sharp laugh punched through the air and Sophie winced. "Poor Myla hasn't found herself a man yet. But she has time, of course. I'm always telling her to get her career off the ground first and then—" She broke off as Chase reached them.

He passed Sophie a glass of wine and held out a hand to Evelyn. "I don't believe we've met. I'm Chase."

Evelyn's eyes flicked to Chase's tailored suit and handmade patent leather shoes. She looked mildly impressed. "Evelyn Carter. The Olsens are good friends of ours. Aren't they dear?" She gestured to her husband, who had yet to say a word.

The hostess approached the group. "Table for two for Sanders."

"That's us." Sophie barely masked her relief.

"Well, it was lovely seeing you, dear." Evelyn held out a hand to Chase again. "And delightful to meet you. I'm sure we'll be seeing plenty more of you. Be sure to invite us to the wedding."

That was enough of that. Sophie practically shoved Chase toward the hostess.

"Evelyn seemed nice," Chase said once they were seated. "Your family is close to theirs?"

Sophie shook her head. She didn't really want to talk about the Carters. But she couldn't think of anything else to talk about. "They've been friends with my parents since before I was born. They have a daughter my age. Myla." Even the name left a bad taste in her mouth.

Chase snickered. "What's so bad about Myla?"

Sophie wrinkled her nose. "Nothing."

"Come on." Chase nudged her leg with his under the table. "Let me dislike her with you."

Sophie couldn't help but laugh. "Well, she was always super-competitive, for one. Constantly trying to one-up me. And her parents encouraged it." As did Sophie's. She could still picture her parents' expressions when they'd learned she'd be graduating second in her class, behind Myla. "And she couldn't let an argument go. Always had to have the last word. And—"

But, no. She was a bigger person than this. She was successful now. She didn't have to compare herself to Myla or anyone else.

Chase raised an eyebrow at her, waiting.

Fine.

"And she was so— So driven. Nothing mattered to her but being the best." And making Sophie feel the sting of her own inferiority.

Chase's eyebrow remained hiked. "So she was basically you?"

Sophie opened her mouth to argue. She was nothing like Myla.

Except maybe she was.

The thought slammed back and forth in her head. Was that really who she was? Someone who thought only about her own achievements, about the next thing she needed to do to get ahead?

Her jaw snapped shut.

"So, anyway, the Hudson project..." Chase picked up the subject as if he hadn't just blindsided her with his comment.

She grabbed her wine glass with shaky hands. Was Chase the only one who saw her this way, or did everyone?

Did Spencer?

But she already knew the answer. She swallowed the bitter drink and pretended to listen to Chase for the rest of the meal, interjecting the occasional "yes" or "uh-huh." If Chase noticed she wasn't giving him her full attention—or even a tenth of it—he didn't seem to mind.

"Now what?" Chase asked as he finally pushed his plate to the side.

Sophie lifted a last bite of duck confit to her mouth. Even as the rich flavor coated her tongue, all she could think about was how much she could go for a pizza.

"We could take a walk." Fresh air would do her good. "The beach is always pretty at night. There are these amazing sand dunes."

Chase frowned. "In these shoes? And you're wearing your favorite Manolo Blahniks."

She shrugged. "We could take them off. Go barefoot." It seemed to be a thing with her lately anyway.

He wrinkled his nose. "I was thinking a little more upscale. Any clubs around here?"

Sophie laughed. "Not exactly. This town pretty much shuts down by ten. Actually, I kind of have a headache. Do you mind if we go back to my parents' place?"

Chase gave a heavy sigh. "Yeah, okay."

She was unmoved by his pouty act.

The drive to her parents' house was blissfully silent, and Sophie spent the time dreaming of snuggling into her favorite pajamas and curling up with a book before going to sleep.

When they reached the house, Sophie led the way upstairs to the guest bedrooms. She paused at her bedroom door. "Goodnight, Chase. Thanks for dinner."

Instead of passing her to move to his own room, he stopped, too. His eyes traveled to the spot where her dress strap slipped from her shoulder.

Before she realized what he was doing, he'd moved in and pressed his lips to hers, his hands coming to her arms.

Sophie stiffened and pulled her head back, shoving a hand against his chest.

"What's wrong?" He grabbed her hand and tugged her closer.

"Chase—"

He didn't let go of her, but he did stop trying to pull her to him. "What is it?"

She couldn't tell if it was hurt in his expression or petulance.

She didn't want to make things awkward. But she had to be honest. "I don't think our relationship is a good idea."

He held up a hand. "You're worried about your job. I get it. But I've already spoken to my father about this. It's not like I'm going to pursue a relationship that could destroy my career."

How sweet.

But he was still talking. "I explained to my father that our relationship is like a business partnership with benefits." He brought his mouth closer to hers. "Like this."

She swiveled her head so that his lips landed on her cheek.

She reached behind her and fumbled for the doorknob. "It's not going to work, Chase."

"But Sophie—" His voice grew hard. He was used to getting his way.

"I'm sorry, Chase." Her hand connected with the knob, and she shoved the door open. "I think you should go home in the morning."

Chase's face reddened. But Sophie stepped into her room and pushed the door closed behind her.

A few seconds later, she heard the door to Chase's room next door close hard.

She crossed the room and laid on her bed, fully clothed.

A business partnership? Is that really the kind of relationship Chase thought she wanted?

Then again, why wouldn't he think that? Almost the only thing the two of them had in common was work. And most of their dates centered on talk of the latest projects. What else would he think?

She stared at the ceiling, wrapping her arms around her middle. Something big and empty had opened inside her. Even though she could hear Chase in the next room, all she could see was Spencer.

The relationship he'd offered her once hadn't been a business partnership. It'd been one based on joy in being together. On a commitment to the same values. On love.

She squeezed her arms tighter.

She'd been so sure then that she didn't want what he was offering. Didn't want love and family.

But it turned out he'd been offering her everything she needed.

And she hadn't realized it until this moment.

When it was too late.

Chapter 12

Sophie stabbed at a piece of cantaloupe and brought it to her mouth mechanically. Chase had left before she'd gotten up this morning, without so much as a goodbye. Which meant things would be worse than awkward when she got back to Chicago. But that was a problem for another day. What was it Nana had always said? "Each day has enough trouble of its own." That was from the Bible, if Sophie remembered her Sunday school lessons correctly.

A sharp click of heels on the floor announced Mom's arrival. Sophie tensed and sat up straighter. She'd promised herself she'd have this conversation with Mom, but she wasn't eager to do it.

"Morning." Mom went straight for the coffee.

Sophie took a deep breath, but Mom spoke first. "Where's your boyfriend?"

Sophie blinked. "Boyfriend? Oh, Chase? We weren't really— I mean, we went on a few dates, but—" Why did it matter to her what Mom thought about this? "Anyway, he left early this morning."

Her mother frowned. "So soon? He just got here."

"Yeah, well, I asked him to leave."

Mom lowered her coffee cup. "Why would you do that?"

Sophie shrugged. She and Mom had never talked about this kind of stuff. Nana had always been the one Sophie confided in. "We aren't right for each other."

Mom snorted. "Yeah, successful businessmen who also happen to be the son of the owner always make the worst matches."

Sophie gawked at her mother. Did she really expect Sophie to be in a relationship to further her career?

"I'm going to visit Nana. I think you should come with me."

Mom drained her coffee cup and turned to the sink to rinse it. Then she grabbed the rag and wiped at the already-clean counter.

Sophie opened her mouth to repeat her request even though she knew Mom had heard her the first time.

But Mom beat her to it. "I'm not going."

Exactly what Sophie had expected. But she was ready for it. "I know it's hard for you, after Jordan." Her mother's shoulders hardened, but Sophie pressed on. "It's hard for me, too."

"I'm not going—" Mom's voice was too calm, too quiet.

"But, Nana—"

"I said no."

Sophie bit her lip. If it were about anything else, she'd retreat. But she couldn't this time. It was too important. If Mom didn't say goodbye to Nana, she'd be left with regrets the rest of her life.

"You know what I think, Mom?" Sophie moved closer and laid a hand tentatively on Mom's arm.

Mom looked from Sophie's face to the spot where Sophie's hand rested on her arm. Then she very deliberately took a step away.

She spun on her heel and strode from the room.

Sophie sighed.

She'd longed so many times for a relationship with her mother. But it looked like that was just one more thing she couldn't have.

Spencer's arms throbbed with the weight of his nephew, but he wasn't about to put the boy down. He'd been dragging his brother and the twins around town to show them the sights all morning. It was a good way to distract them from missing Julia. And to show them off, if he was honest.

They'd already visited the pier, the toy store, and the fudge shop, where Ariana cooed over the boys and plied them with too much fudge.

Jonah rubbed his chocolate-streaked face against Spencer's shirt.

"Hey." Spencer tickled the boy, eliciting a contagious giggle.

"You up for one more stop?" Spencer asked his brother.

"Lead the way." Tyler's eyes had grown brighter throughout the morning, his gait more sure.

"Good. Violet would never forgive me if I didn't bring these two to meet her." He stopped outside the antique shop.

Tyler's forehead crinkled. "You want to bring them into a store full of breakables?"

Spencer eyed the store, then his nephews, whose eyelids were starting to droop after the long morning. "They'll be fine."

Tyler shook his head as Spencer pulled the door open and gestured for him to enter. "I hope you have your credit card ready."

"Relax. It'll be—"

But the moment he followed his brother into the shop, he rethought his assessment.

Not because of the breakables.

But because of the person standing at the counter talking to Violet.

Sophie.

His eyes flicked around the store. If Sophie was here, her boyfriend must be, too. His grip on Jonah tightened. He couldn't deal with this right now. The urge to flee seized him. Was it too late to back quietly through the door?

But Violet had already spotted Tyler and was headed toward them.

"And who are these two?" she asked with a wide smile.

Sophie turned then, too.

She did a double-take as her eyes fell on Spencer. Jonah had lain his head on Spencer's shoulder. The boy's soft breaths puffed onto Spencer's neck. It was oddly reassuring.

"Violet. Sophie. This is my brother Tyler. And these little terrors"—he gestured with his chin toward Jeremiah, whose head dropped against Tyler's chest—"are my nephews Jeremiah and Jonah."

Violet crossed the space to shake Tyler's hand. "Yeah, they look like real terrors, about to fall asleep in your arms."

"That's because they're so exhausted from screaming all night." The hair on the back of Spencer's neck lifted at the thought of going through all that again tonight.

Violet laughed. "It couldn't have been that bad."

Spencer groaned. "Worse. Thank goodness for Emma. She had this horse hoofbeat soundtrack, and it put them right to sleep."

Across the room, Sophie's head jerked up, but she didn't make eye contact.

Violet turned to Tyler. "So how long will you be staying in Hope Springs?"

Tyler's eyes widened, and he looked for all the world like the raccoon Buck had treed last fall. "I'm not sure yet."

"You married Julia, right?" Violet pressed on, apparently oblivious to the fact that her signature hospitality was killing his brother. "How's she doing?"

Tyler opened and closed his mouth. "Uh—"

Spencer jumped in. "Where's your friend?" he shot at Sophie. "How long's he staying?" He shouldn't have said it. He didn't want to know the answer.

"He's not—" Sophie started, but her phone gave a sharp blast that made her jump. The moment she looked at the screen, her brows drew together, and she lifted the phone to her ear.

"This is she," she said after a second.

As she listened to the caller, her face went white and she pressed her lips together, drawing her hand to her forehead as if shielding her eyes from the sunlight.

Spencer was moving before he realized it, passing Jonah to Tyler and crossing the store to stand at Sophie's elbow.

She didn't look at him.

After a moment she spoke into the phone. "Thank you for letting me know. I'll be right there."

She hung up the phone but stood staring at it. Her ragged breaths tugged Spencer closer.

"Sophie?" He reached toward her.

"That was, um—" She licked her lips and swallowed. "That was the hospital. It's my grandma. She's gone."

Spencer didn't think. He just leaned over and wrapped his arms around her, pulling her into him.

She didn't resist. Her arms went around his back, and she buried her face in his neck.

Spencer could feel his heart slipping.

But he didn't care.

Right now it wasn't his own heart he was worried about.

Right now, he would give anything to heal the pain in hers.

Sophie clutched Nana's cold hand, swallowing over and over to keep the tears at bay.

Seeing her grandmother like this made her feel like the first time she'd ever been on a boat—wobbly all over, as if the laws of physics no longer applied to standing still.

She swayed, but a firm arm wrapped around her from behind and held her up.

"It's okay." Spencer's voice was low, steady. Reassuring.

Sophie took in a couple of deep breaths, letting his presence calm her.

"She looks so—" Sophie couldn't think of the word to describe how Nana looked.

"Gone, I guess," she finished.

Spencer's hand moved in small circles on her back. He'd sent Tyler and the twins home in his truck and insisted on driving her to the hospital.

A flood of memories threatened to drown her. Nana standing at the helm of her boat, the sun hat she'd perched on her head flying off in the breeze. Or pulling a fresh batch of cookies from the oven, a dusting of flour on her nose. Bandaging yet another scraped knee Sophie had managed to get roller skating because she could never get her gangly legs under control.

Nana was in heaven now, like she'd wanted. She'd been ready.

But Sophie wasn't.

A light tap on the door was followed by soft footsteps. "Doing okay in here?" It was the nurse who had led them into the room half an hour earlier. She'd become Sophie's favorite in the last few days. Always attentive. Always seeming to know when Sophie needed to talk and when she needed to be left alone with her thoughts.

Sophie nodded. She couldn't find her voice.

"Take your time." The nurse laid a small canvas bag on the table near the bed. "Feel free to use this to pack up your grandmother's things. Or we can do that for you if you'd prefer."

Sophie shook her head and shot a desperate look at Spencer.

"We'll do it," he told the nurse.

The nurse patted Sophie's shoulder on her way past. "I'm sorry for your loss. Your grandma was a special lady." She paused in the doorway, as if deliberating. "When she first came in, she talked to me a lot. I'd fallen away in my faith because of—" She waved a hand. "Well, for a lot of reasons. But your grandma helped me see God again." The woman ducked her head. When she lifted it, her eyes were shining. "She made a big difference in my life."

Sophie pressed her lips together. Why couldn't she have gotten here sooner, so she could have had more of those conversations with Nana? She hadn't even realized she needed to talk about those things until she'd come home. And now that she wanted to talk, she had no one to talk to.

Spencer gave her arm a gentle squeeze. "I'll pack up this stuff."

As he stepped around the bed, she was seized with the urge to grab him and pull him back toward her. Having him here was the only thing getting her through this. But he'd only come because he was a good man. He had a girlfriend, his own life, to get back to.

She moved Nana's arm and settled onto the bed next to her motionless form. "I'll miss you, Nana."

On the other side of the room, Spencer quietly emptied the chest of drawers that held Nana's possessions. Sophie kept talking to Nana. It wasn't weird with Spencer here, the way it had been with Chase.

"Uh, Soph?" Spencer interjected when she fell silent.

She lifted her head. Spencer was standing over the chest of drawers, holding a thick leather journal. "I think you should see this." He crossed the room and held it out to her.

Sophie's hand closed around the leather, and her breath caught. Embossed in gold on the cover were the words "Sophie's Wisdom."

"What is this?" She lifted the cover carefully as if the book were a rare treasure. Inside, the first page was covered with Nana's familiar, small handwriting. Sophie fanned through the rest of the book. Nearly every page was filled. She flipped back to the beginning and read out loud.

"My dearest Sophia. You were born today, and what a precious child you are. I am starting this journal for you to share the things I've learned in my life that you may not be ready to learn for a long time. But when you are, they will be here for you, even if I'm not."

Sophie cut off, swallowing down the sobs that threatened to overtake her. From the day she was born, Nana had been thinking about what she'd need for her future. And what had Sophie done for Nana?

Left her.

Ignored her.

She turned back to the page, but the words blurred.

A gentle hand lifted the book from hers. "Your name means wisdom." Spencer's voice was low and sure as he read. "It's a fitting name. My prayer for you, on the day of your birth, is that you would turn away from the wisdom of this world. From a desire for fame and glory and achievement. For recognition from people. That wisdom is too fleeting, too easily lost. I pray that you seek instead the wisdom from above. The wisdom that tells you that you are loved unconditionally by your heavenly father. And by me."

Spencer stopped reading and wrapped an arm around her shoulders, pulling her in close.

"I don't deserve that," she choked out.

Spencer's laugh was gentle. "That's why they call it unconditional."

Sophie pressed her face into his chest and let him hold her. Just for today, she'd let herself believe that was true. It was better than admitting she hadn't come close to living up to Nana's expectations.

Chapter 13

Sophie's whole body felt like a spring that had been coiled beyond the breaking point.

She rubbed her heavy eyes, relieved for the break in the receiving line. She knew it was a testament to how many lives Nana had touched that the line had stretched to the back of the church for the past hour, but if she had to accept one more person's condolences, she was going to lose her hold on the emotions that had hovered at the back of her throat for the three days since Nana's death. Three days that she'd spent holed up in her room, reading Nana's journal. Though its words brought her comfort, they also scraped at her already raw heart.

Sophie glanced at her parents, one on each side of her. She longed for them to grab her hands, to squish her between them the way they had after Jordan's death. But neither even seemed to care that she was there.

"I'll be right back." She said the words to both—or neither, she wasn't sure. "I need some water."

In the lobby, Sophie let out a long breath, then forced herself to inhale for a ten-count.

Now that she was out here, she realized she needed fresh air more than water. She pushed through the lobby doors.

Outside, a thick fog had rolled in, cloaking everything in a gray mantle. She caught the scent of the lake.

What if she . . .

Before she could complete the thought, she'd kicked her shoes off and dashed to the steps that ran alongside the church and down to the beach below.

The cool sand curled over her toes.

She dropped her shoes and made her way to the spot where the waves licked the shore.

The sharp cold of the water sent pinpricks up her feet.

"What do you want from me?" The words ripped out of her as she peered into the nothingness of the fog. She didn't know who her question was directed to, only that she was desperate for an answer. "How am I supposed to get through this?"

A lone sea gull's scream was the only answer.

"You're sure you'll be okay?" Spencer's fingers fumbled to fasten the tie at his neck as he stepped past a screaming Jonah. He tried to ignore the knot of panic in his stomach. The funeral started in half an hour, but how could he leave his brother alone with the twins, who'd been in a howling fit all morning?

"I'll be fine." Tyler bent to scoop a toy car out of Jeremiah's mouth, setting up another round of yells. "I'm their father. I have to learn to do this on my own at some point."

Tyler shoved Spencer's hands away from the tie, taking over for him. "I'm more worried about you."

"Me?" Spencer pretended not to know what his brother was talking about.

"Seriously, Spencer. You've always worn your heart on your sleeve. Just don't hand it over too easily. I know you care for this woman."

Spencer opened his mouth to argue, but Tyler cut him off. "If you didn't, you wouldn't have spent last night telling me every detail of every time you've seen her since she's been back."

Yeah, Spencer had known that would come back to bite him.

"I'm just saying—" Tyler cinched the knot around Spencer's neck. "Be there for her, but not *too* there. Her feelings are probably all mixed up right now. What might seem like affection is probably just her dealing with her own stuff from her grandma's death."

Spencer nodded. Tyler was right. He knew he was. But that didn't change the fact that he was determined to help Sophie through this. It's what friends did for each other.

With a last glance over his shoulder at the screaming twins, Spencer dashed out the front door.

Fog clung to him as he jogged to his truck. He'd be pushing it to get there in time.

He leaned forward in his seat to peer through the fog and spent the drive praying that he'd know how to offer Sophie the comfort she needed. She'd managed to hold back her tears at her grandma's bedside the other day, just as she always had, but he knew how much she must be hurting. It shredded him to think of her suffering like that alone. But that was Sophie. Even when they were dating, she'd never let him in completely.

He'd spent nearly every moment of the three days since her grandmother died fighting down the urge to call her, to burst into her parents' house and be there for her. He'd had to remind himself about a billion times that it wasn't his role anymore. But no matter how many times he repeated it to himself, he couldn't simply stop caring about her. Couldn't shut off the way his heart ached to be there for her.

Well, you have to.

Sophie wasn't his anymore. She had a new life. A new boyfriend. A new support system.

She'd only let Spencer comfort her the other day because he was the only one there.

The fog grew thicker as he got closer to the water, and Spencer had to slow almost to a crawl. But his thoughts were clearer than they'd been since Sophie returned. He pulled into the church parking lot with a new resolve. He'd go to the service, pay his respects, and then say goodbye and not think about Sophie again.

His plan steeled his steps as he exited the truck and strode toward the church. He could do this.

Inside, Sophie's parents stood at the front of the church, receiving the last few people waiting to offer their condolences. Spencer's eyes roved the crowded church, but he couldn't pick out Sophie's golden hair. He spotted Violet sitting near the back.

He moved to her and leaned down to whisper, "Where's Sophie?"

"I don't know." Violet shifted to make room for him. "I haven't seen her yet. Her mom said she went to get some water, but that was a while ago." Worry hovered in her eyes. "Maybe I should go find her."

Spencer stood. "I'll help."

As they opened the doors to step into the lobby, the pianist began to play "How Great Thou Art."

"We have to hurry." Violet pushed him into the lobby. "Sophie wouldn't want to miss this."

Actually, Spencer was pretty sure that's exactly what Sophie wanted. Whenever things became emotionally difficult, she ran.

"You check the bathrooms." He was already striding toward the long hallway off the lobby. "I'll see if she's in one of the conference rooms."

Violet nodded and sped in the opposite direction.

Spencer's thoughts skipped over all the places Sophie might have found to take refuge from her feelings. But as he passed a side exit, his eyes tracked to the beach, barely visible through the fog, and he knew.

He shoved out the door and charged down the rickety stairs that led to the beach below. He found her abandoned shoes at the bottom and scanned the sand in both directions. A smudged figure stood at the edge of the water a hundred yards down the beach. Spencer kicked off his shoes and set off toward her at a run. But he'd only covered half the distance between them when he started to question himself. Wasn't this exactly the kind of thing he'd just promised himself not to do? He slowed to a walk. She hadn't noticed him yet. He could turn around and walk away. Let her grieve in peace. Deal with things in her own way. It was what she'd want anyway.

He stopped, a collision of indecision, longing, and fear making it impossible to move.

At that moment, she glanced over her shoulder. Her hair swept around her face, making her look young and vulnerable. But it was the bleakness in her eyes that made his decision for him.

His steps devoured the distance between them, and he crushed her to him. She stiffened for a second, then sank into him. He breathed in the strawberry scent of her hair. He could stand like this forever.

But they didn't have forever.

After a few seconds, he moved his hands to her arms and gently nudged her back a step. "What are you doing out here, Soph? The service is about to start."

As if on cue, the church bells began to ring behind him.

Sophie winced and turned toward the smear of water and sky. In the fog, it was impossible to tell where one started and the other ended.

"I can't do it again." Her lips barely moved as she spoke.

Understanding washed over Spencer. How had he not realized it earlier?

All of this must be bringing back so many memories. "Jordan?"

She flinched at his name. In all the years he'd known Sophie, she'd only talked about her brother a handful of times.

"I feel like the day we—" She bit her lip, and he was afraid she'd shut him out as she had so many times before.

But after a second, she continued. "The day we buried him, something broke in our family. My dad kind of checked out. And my mom—" A shiver shook her frame, and Spencer shrugged out of his suit coat and draped it over her shoulders. She pulled it tighter around herself but didn't look at him. "She was so angry. I think she turned off her feelings that day. And I'm afraid—" A wisp of hair fluttered onto her cheek, and Spencer automatically reached to tuck it behind her ear. She closed her eyes for a second, and he jerked his hand away. What was he thinking?

"You're afraid?" His voice came out hoarse.

Sophie sighed deep and long, the sound mimicking the brush of the waves against the beach. "I'm afraid maybe I turned off my feelings, too. And now, with all of this—" She gestured toward the church. "It's like they're trying to turn back on and—"

Spencer waited, barely breathing. She'd never been this open with him before.

"And it hurts," she finished in a whisper.

"Ah, Soph." It wrecked him to see her like this. But maybe it was what she needed. "It's not bad to feel." She opened her mouth—surely ready to protest—but he didn't let her get a word in. "I'm not saying it's always pleasant. But that hurt you feel? That's only because you felt so much love for her." The same reason he'd been so destroyed when Sophie had left him. He pushed the thought aside. "And if you let yourself feel that hurt now, it will get better someday. You'll be able to heal. But if you don't—if you keep trying to run from those feelings, they'll catch up with you eventually. And it will be so much harder."

Her eyebrows lowered, and she opened her mouth, looking ready for a fight. Spencer held up his hands to fend off the tirade. But instead of an argument, a strangled sob escaped her. She covered her mouth and turned away from him. But in a second, he'd spun her back around and pulled her close.

"It's okay." He stroked her hair. "You can cry. It's okay."

The sobs rocked her body, and all he could do was hold on and repeat that it was okay, that he was there.

When her tears finally slowed, he leaned back a fraction.

"I don't think your grandma would have wanted you out here, alone, thinking about how sad you are. She'd want you to be in there, celebrating that she's in heaven."

"Now you sound like her." A slight smile lifted the edges of Sophie's lips, and it was all he could do not to lean down and kiss them.

He dropped his arms. "Should we go inside?"

She blew out a long breath. "Will you stay with me?"

The gash in Spencer's heart deepened.

There was no way he could say no.

He held out a hand, and she grasped it, letting him lead her toward the stairs. As they stopped to put on their shoes, she studied him.

Her eyes were clouded, and he had no idea what she was thinking. "What?"

"Just— Thanks." She ducked her head and swiped at her eyes again. They were darker now, as if letting out all her feelings had deepened them. "That's the second time that you've come after me when I tried to run away."

Spencer wanted to say, "You're welcome," but his throat had closed off. He may have come after her these two times, but they couldn't make up for the one time he'd let her go.

Chapter 14

Sophie clutched Spencer's hand as he opened the church door. The final strains of a hymn faded, and Sophie had to resist the urge to turn around and run. Spencer squeezed her hand and offered an encouraging smile. She drew in a breath and stepped through the doorway, Spencer right behind her. What would she do without him right now? And how had she come to rely on him so thoroughly when she'd promised herself that would never happen again?

"Oof." Sophie gasped as she was tackled in a hug.

"Oh, thank goodness." Vi gave her another squeeze, then released her. "You okay?" Her eyes traveled to where Sophie's hand was locked with Spencer's. Sophie gave a short nod and followed Vi to a seat near the back of the church, ignoring the curious looks directed her way. She clung tighter to Spencer's hand as they sat.

Pastor Zelner was just standing to deliver his message. "I knew Alice Harris almost my entire life. Whenever there was a potluck, I made sure she was going to be there. She made the best cakes." He patted his rounded stomach, and there was a smattering of laughter in the congregation. "Alice was an accomplished pianist. An avid boater. She was kind. Generous almost to a fault. She donated that beautiful playground we have outside. When she was younger, she gave her time to mission trips in Thailand. And when she couldn't physically make those journeys anymore, she provided funding so that others could." Pastor Zelner paused, letting his eyes travel the congregation.

Sophie's heart swelled with pride at all Nana had accomplished. She'd been a remarkable lady. Sophie only hoped she could accomplish half as much in her life.

"But—" Pastor Zelner picked up, and Sophie's eyes trained on him. "None of that matters."

Sophie shifted, ready to flee again. She wasn't going to sit here and listen to Pastor Zelner tear down everything Nana had done. Treat it as worthless.

But Spencer squeezed her hand and gave her a significant look.

Fine.

Back stiff, she focused her attention on Pastor Zelner, who continued, "And Alice would have been the first one to tell you that life wasn't about anything she was or anything she did or anything she achieved or gave. She knew that without Jesus, we are all worthless in God's sight."

Out of the corner of her eye, Sophie could see Spencer nodding. But she wanted to stand up and argue. If her achievements were worthless, what was the point of anything she'd done?

"But here's the thing Alice knew." Pastor Zelner's gaze roamed the church until it fell on her. Sophie stared back, daring him to go on.

"She knew her worth was in Christ alone." He shot her a gentle smile, then moved toward the other side of the church, letting his eyes sweep over the people. "The last time I met with Alice, she knew the end was near. And though she was sad to leave her family behind, she knew with absolute certainty where she was going. She told me there was one thing she wanted me to tell you all at her funeral. And if you knew Alice, you know that if she asked you to do something, you were going to do it." Sophie couldn't help but smile a little. He was right about that.

"So here's her message: You will never be enough on your own." Pastor Zelner's eyes locked right on hers—this time she was sure of it. Nana had probably orchestrated that. "But that's okay. Because you don't need to be enough. God doesn't care what you've accomplished. He loves you without condition. When you look to Christ, you will triumph. You will have everything. You will have the victory." He paused. "Just like Alice."

Sophie stood mechanically with the rest of the congregation, joined in singing the next song, bowed her head for prayer, but in the back of her mind, she kept hearing those words: *Look to Christ. Victory.*

Was it really that simple?

"Soph?" Spencer nudged her. "The service is over."

Sophie shook herself and glanced around. The church had largely emptied already.

She let Spencer pull her to her feet and lead her to the lobby, Vi following behind with a hand on Sophie's back.

In the lobby, Vi engulfed her in another hug. "I have to get back to the store, but let's get together before you leave."

Sophie startled. She hadn't even thought about returning to Chicago over the last few days. But there was really no reason to stay now. She nodded to Vi.

Seeming satisfied, Vi walked toward the doors but then looked back. "I mean it, Soph. Don't leave without telling me." Under the teasing note, Sophie heard the fear. She wouldn't do that to her friend again.

Sophie scanned the lobby, feeling lost. She was supposed to go bury Nana now, but she wasn't sure she could face that. Not alone.

She leaned toward Spencer to ask if he'd come with her. He'd already given her more than she deserved. She knew that. But she wasn't sure how else she could get through it.

"Hey, Spencer."

The eyes that fell on her were warm and open, and she stumbled. "I know I have no right to ask, but—"

"There you are." Her mother's call pulled their gazes across the lobby. Sophie turned in time to watch her close the last few feet to reach them, her lips set in a thin line, eyes dry, makeup perfect.

How could the woman be so composed when she was about to bury her own mother?

Mom's mouth tipped into a frown as her eyes fell on Spencer. Sophie could almost see her cataloging him: off-the-rack suit, bargain shoes, worn tie. The frown deepened as her eyes landed on their linked hands.

Instinctively, Sophie drew hers back. She couldn't deal with both Spencer and her mother right now. And this was the easiest solution. Even if the hurt in Spencer's eyes made her feel sick.

"Mom." She tried to keep her voice steady. "This is Spencer. We—" Oh, boy. How did she finish that sentence? "We went to college together."

Next to her, Spencer stiffened, but he held out a hand to her mother. "I'm sorry for your loss, Mrs. Olsen."

Her mother accepted his handshake about as eagerly as she would have taken a dried fish.

The moment she dropped it, she turned to Sophie. "The limousine is waiting to take us to the cemetery."

"Oh." She hadn't known there'd be a limo. Being confined in a car—no matter how luxurious—with her parents was the last thing she could handle right now. "Actually, I was just about to ask Spencer if he could—"

"It's okay, Soph." Spencer's voice was detached, and he refused to meet her eyes. "I should get back to help Tyler with the boys. And you should be with your family."

A crack opened right in her middle, and she wrapped her arms around her shoulders to keep her feelings from spilling out all over the floor. "Of course." She wasn't sure if the words actually came out or if she only thought them.

"Goodbye, Soph." With a last look she couldn't read, he disappeared through the doors.

And she wondered: Was this how he'd felt when she'd walked away?

Chapter 15

Even the twins' giggles as they zigzagged between the trees couldn't touch the cold spot in Spencer's core that refused to thaw despite the sweat trickling down the front of his shirt.

"Uncle Spencer, can't get us," Jonah taunted from behind him.

Spencer shot the boys a half-hearted smile and made a vague gesture as if to chase them, but the twins weren't buying it. He didn't blame them. He wasn't buying it either.

"Un-cle Spen-cer." Jeremiah had sure perfected the art of whining.

"Leave your Uncle Spencer alone." Tyler wrestled a dead branch out of the tree they'd been pruning. "He's a grumpy pants today." Behind the funny voice, Spencer detected the note of I-told-you-so.

"Sorry, boys." He shook himself. "I'm not a grumpy pants. Just thinking."

About how Sophie had dropped his hand in front of her Mom yesterday. How she'd introduced him as a college classmate. She'd apparently never told her parents about their relationship.

He'd always suspected she'd rejected his proposal because she was ashamed of him.

Now he knew.

That's her problem.

He had plenty of other things to worry about. Like getting the rest of these trees pruned before they reached full bloom. And helping his brother move on with his life. And keeping his nephews entertained.

He set his clippers down. "Watch out, the tickle monster is coming." He wiggled his fingers at them and roared. The laugh that burst out of him as his nephews shrieked surprised even him.

He let himself forget everything else as he chased the boys, catching first one and then the other and tickling them until they were overcome with deep belly giggles. Finally, Tyler joined in and tackled him. Spencer struggled to escape his brother's pin as the boys set to tickling him.

Jeremiah got a hand in Spencer's armpit, and Spencer's howl set them all to laughing.

Spencer's heart swelled. This was what he'd longed for when he'd come back to the farm. Family. Warmth. Fun.

Over the last few years, the financial hits, the constant work and worry, had taken their toll, but if that's what it had taken to get to this point, it had all been worth it.

A strange sound cut through their fun, and they all paused.

"What's that?" Jonah's eyes were wide.

The noise sounded again. "It sounds like it's coming from under you." Tyler pointed through Spencer.

"It's my phone." Spencer tried to roll to the side. "Get off me, you oaf." He gave his brother a shove, then reached to grab his phone out of his back pocket.

"What's up, Violet?" With Cade gone, he'd become the one she relied on when she needed to move big pieces to her shop floor.

"Hey, I was just thinking—"

Spencer held back a sigh. Violet's "just thinking" usually ended up with him on a terrible blind date with someone she'd met who would be "perfect" for him. Problem was, he'd already met the woman who was perfect for him—only she didn't want anything to do with him.

"Sophie's leaving tomorrow after church," Violet continued, "and I thought it'd be fun if we all got together before she goes. We're going to meet at Sylvester's, okay? Seven o'clock. You have to come." She crammed it all into one breath, probably knowing he'd interrupt her to say no if she gave him even a split second.

Spencer hated to say no to Violet, no matter what she asked. Which is how he'd ended up on so many awful blind dates. But this was asking too much. Seeing Sophie when he knew he couldn't be with her. Knowing how she really felt about him. Saying goodbye to her all over again.

"I'm sorry, Violet, I don't think—"

"Please, Spencer." Her voice went up. "I need her to know she's welcome to come back. In the future. I don't want her to stay away five years again. Or longer. I've missed her."

So did he. Too much. Which is why he should say no and hang up right now.

But his traitorous mouth made the decision for him. "Fine. I'll see you at seven."

Chapter 16

Sophie groaned as she pushed her plate away.

Across the table, Vi grinned at her. "Yeah, the Hidden Cafe has a way of making you eat way too much."

That was an understatement. The pile of fries on her plate had been stacked taller than her burger. And she'd eaten every last one.

But even better than the food had been the chance to reconnect with Vi. She'd done the right thing, giving in to Vi's plea that she stay for the weekend and head back to Chicago tomorrow afternoon.

She sighed. "This was great, but I should get back to my parents' to pack."

Vi tossed her napkin on the table and rummaged in her purse. "Oh, no, you don't. You're mine for the night, remember? We're going to Sylvester's."

"Sylvester's?" She couldn't hold back the surprised laugh. "Aren't we a little old for mini golf?"

Vi brushed off her argument and dropped some money on the table, then led the way to the door. "Never too old for mini golf. Anyway, we used to go all the time in college, if you remember."

But remembering was what Sophie was afraid of. All those trips to the mini golf course just blocks from campus. The way she'd pretended not to know how to putt, so Spencer would put his arms around her and help her. How they'd been mini golfing when he'd first asked if she'd consider going on a date with him. The way he'd ducked his head as he'd asked but then couldn't resist giving her a hug when she said yes.

"I'm sorry, Vi, but—"

"Nope," Vi cut in, steering her to the car. "You disappeared on me for five years. Tonight I get to decide what we do."

"Fine." Sophie let her head fall onto the headrest of the passenger seat. "But that's the last time you get to play that card tonight."

"Deal." For the one hundredth time, Sophie was overcome with gratitude at how easily her friend had forgiven her—she'd welcomed Sophie back into her life as if Sophie hadn't completely abandoned her for nearly half a decade.

As they got closer to Sylvester's, Vi tapped her finger against the wheel. Then she started bouncing her left leg. When she began to shoot surreptitious glances her way, Sophie threw up her hands. "What's going on, Vi?"

"Don't be mad." Vi's fingers drummed like mad on the steering wheel.

"Why would I be mad?" Sophie shifted in her seat to face her friend.

"There might be a few other people meeting us there."

"That's fine. You know—" But the realization hit her hard in the center of the chest. "Vi, no. I can't."

"Please." Vi turned down the street leading to Sylvester's. "You've been gone—"

Sophie held up a hand to stop her. "You just promised not to play that card again."

Vi laughed. "Fine. I won't." But she pulled into the driveway of the mini golf course and jumped out of her seat as if the matter had already been decided.

Sophie twisted Nana's ring around her finger. Either she sat in the car and looked like an idiot, or she got out and acted like an adult who could handle seeing her ex without going to pieces.

The first option seemed better all the time. But just when she'd decided to stay put, a familiar truck pulled into the space next to her.

Spencer gave her a grim not-quite-smile as he pushed open his door and climbed out. Before she knew what he was doing, he'd opened her car door, too.

She sat frozen for a moment, feeling suddenly exposed, as if he could read every thought of longing she'd had for him since he walked away yesterday.

"You coming?" Spencer's voice was bland, emotionless.

Fine. If he could do this, so could she.

They joined Vi in front of her car.

"Who else is coming?" Sophie tried to keep her voice even, despite the fact that standing so close to Spencer had set her stomach flip flopping.

"Ariana and Ethan are hoping to come, but she texted a little while ago to say we should start without them. Ethan got called to an accident, and it's hard to say when he'll be back." Vi linked her arm through Sophie's.

"What about Emma?" Not that she really wanted to know.

"She teaches riding lessons on Saturday nights." Spencer ran a hand over his face.

So it was just going to be the three of them. Sophie swallowed. That was fine. As long as she had Vi, everything would be fine. She wouldn't be tempted to do anything stupid. Like reach over to brush at the errant lock of hair that had fallen onto Spencer's forehead.

Sophie forced herself to look away as they got into line.

But she could feel Spencer behind her, and nothing could block out the welcoming, woodsy scent that always clung to him, as if he'd spent his whole day among the trees.

Which he probably had.

Sophie tried to take short, shallow breaths so she wouldn't become intoxicated from being so close to him. As soon as they had their clubs, she burst through the door leading to the course, leaving Vi and Spencer to grab the balls and scorecards. She sucked in a lungful of the popcorn-tinged air.

There, that was better.

Her head was clearer now.

"You okay?" Vi held out a ball and scorecard as she approached.

Sophie nodded. She was fine.

Absolutely fine.

But then Spencer came out of the building, his white button-down shirt failing to hide his broad shoulders, and she had to admit it. She was far from fine.

"We ready?" He didn't look at either of them.

"Yep." Vi's voice was overly cheerful as her eyes darted from Spencer to Sophie and back again. Obviously, things were not going according to her plans.

Well, serves her right.

Vi may have been responsible for getting them together in college, but that was a long time ago. Things had changed, and even Vi's matchmaking talents weren't up to this task.

They moved toward the first hole, but before they reached it, Vi's phone rang. Relief crossed her face as she pulled it out of her pocket. "It's Ariana. I'm sure they're on their way." She lifted the phone to her ear. "Hey, Ari. What's up?" She listened for a second. "Just a sec. I have terrible reception." She pulled the phone down and turned to Sophie and Spencer. "I'll be right back. You guys go ahead and play."

"We can wait for you. Actually, I'll come with you." No way was Sophie going to stay here alone with Spencer. That would be far too dangerous for her heart.

But Vi waved her away. "No. Go ahead. Otherwise we'll get stuck behind all these people." She pointed to the crowd that was starting to gather behind them. "Seriously, I'll be right back."

"Fine." Spencer shrugged and dropped his ball on the first green.

Sophie pressed down the welling panic as Vi walked away. If she didn't know better, she'd think her friend shot her a parting grin.

"Your stroke." Spencer's voice from behind made her jump.

Get it together.

She dropped her ball onto the artificial grass and surveyed the obstacles. There was a mini construction gate, complete with a

"Caution" sign, about halfway down the course. She had to grimace at the irony.

"A little to the left." Spencer crouched at the other end of the green, studying the angle of her ball.

She shifted automatically, realigning her shot.

"Little more."

She shifted again.

"Just a tad more."

Sophie huffed and whacked the ball without moving again.

It sped toward the caution sign and hit it with a sharp thwack, ricocheting off and coming to a stop an inch from where it had started.

To his credit, Spencer didn't say anything.

He just tapped his ball into the hole and then waited silently as Sophie took three more strokes to get past the gate.

"Six," she said as the ball at last dropped into the hole.

"Not bad." Spencer's politeness irked her. Once upon a time, he'd have teased her for her lack of coordination, made fun of her impatience. As much as she'd always pretended to hate the teasing, she'd take it any day over this stiff formality.

She bent to pick up her ball, then jogged to catch up with Spencer, who was already halfway to the next hole. Vi had better get back soon. The two of them obviously couldn't handle being alone together much longer.

Thankfully, Vi reappeared just then. "Sorry about that. Ariana is having car trouble, so I told her I'd go pick her up."

Relief and disappointment washed over Sophie in equal measure. This might be the last time she ever saw Spencer, and she wasn't ready to say goodbye. And yet, spending more time together was clearly going to be unbearable.

She picked up the ball she'd been about to putt. "Let's go."

But Vi shook her head. "No, no. You two keep playing. I'll go get Ari."

"But Vi—"

But Vi had already done a quick pirouette and was bustling toward the exit. "We already paid," she called over her shoulder. "And you guys already started. Just keep going."

She disappeared into the crowd swarming outside the clubhouse. A second later, Sophie's eyes tracked her as she emerged on the other side of the building and practically ran through the parking lot to her car.

Behind her Spencer let out an exasperated laugh. "Classic Violet."

"What?" Sophie turned her gaze to him.

His brows were drawn low over his eyes, but the ghost of a smile hovered on his lips. "Remember the first time I asked you out?"

Of course she remembered.

They'd been at the mini golf course near campus, the three of them, and Vi had left to pick up Cade, who'd run out of gas and—

Oh.

"You don't really think she'd . . ."

But it didn't take his emphatic nod to tell her what she already knew. Of course she would. Just like she had that first time. She hadn't admitted until a year later that Cade hadn't run out of gas—that he was actually waiting for her down the block.

"She seems to like to play bad romantic comedy with our lives." Spencer twirled his golf club in his hands, and Sophie couldn't help the laugh that escaped. At least he was talking to her like a friend again. Not like the cold stranger who'd been filling in for him since he said goodbye at Nana's funeral yesterday.

But Vi's matchmaking still didn't make sense. "Why, though? I mean, it seemed like she and Emma are friends."

Spencer's eyebrows dropped into a V, and his forehead wrinkled. "They are. What does that have to do with anything?"

She hesitated. Maybe it'd hit a nerve, hearing his old girlfriend ask about his new one. "Well, I mean—"

"Excuse me?" A teen from the large group behind them cut in. "Are you going to play?"

"Why don't you putt through?" Spencer offered, stepping off the green and grabbing Sophie's elbow to tug her to the side with him. Now, more than ever, she had to ignore the jolt his touch sent through her.

"You were saying?" Spencer watched the group of teens, but his comment was definitely directed to her.

He was really going to make her say it.

Fine.

She kept her gaze directed at the teens, too. One of the boys was talking earnestly to a girl, who moved in closer, her eyes never leaving his face. Had that been them once?

"Well, I just think it'd be weird for Vi to recreate our setup when she likes Emma, and you two are clearly—" Did she really have to say the rest?

But Spencer was watching her now, his forehead even more creased. "Are clearly what?"

"Are clearly happy together." And in love. But she couldn't say that part.

She twisted her hands together, picking out the spots where her fingers interlocked.

Spencer's abrupt laugh made her head jerk up. "I guess we're as happy as two friends can be. But we're not together."

The pressure on Sophie's chest eased, but Spencer's look grew darker. "Of course, that doesn't excuse Vi for trying to set us up when you have a boyfriend."

Sophie stopped him with a hand on his arm. Suddenly it seemed important to set the record straight. "Chase isn't my boyfriend. He's a colleague."

Spencer's jaw relaxed.

But she wanted to be completely honest with him. "We did date a few times—"

Under her hand, Spencer's arm muscles went taut.

"But—" She forced herself to meet his eyes. "He wasn't right for me. I told him it was over when he was here."

"Yeah." Spencer shuffled away, and she let her hand fall to her side. "I hear women hate those good-looking, wealthy types."

"They may make good business partners, Spencer. But not—" She pushed the words out in a rush. "But not good life partners."

Spencer's eyes locked on hers. She could read the question in them. What kind of man would make a good life partner?

You.

But she didn't have a right to tell him that. She'd given up that right when she walked out on him.

The silence stretched between them, but neither looked away. "Soph—" Spencer's voice was quiet, tender.

"You guys can play now."

Sophie jumped, and Spencer's eyes flicked from hers to the kid who had interrupted them.

"Uh, we're done, so . . ." The kid scurried away at Spencer's scowl.

Spencer ran a hand through his hair, making it stick up on one side. A second ago, Sophie wouldn't have hesitated to smooth it. But now—

Now the spell had been broken.

And it was probably for the best.

"Should we golf?" Spencer gestured to the green, and Sophie shrugged. Vi had already paid for it. And she and Ariana should be here any minute.

Surely she could guard her heart until then.

Chapter 17

"Eight." Spencer smirked as he jotted the number on Sophie's scorecard, and she shoved his shoulder playfully. Dark had fallen twenty minutes ago, and with it, everything that stood between them seemed to have fallen away as well. They were acting like the teens in front of them, trading teasing barbs and the occasional good-natured swat. It was like, while they were here at Sylvester's, the rest of the world, the rest of time, didn't exist. Life was simple, as it had been once. Neither of them had other responsibilities, other lives to get back to. All they had to worry about was this moment.

"Last one." Spencer led the way to the final hole, with the waterfall it was almost impossible to putt through. But going around took twice as many putts on a good day.

"Already?" The surprise in Sophie's voice delighted him. "I wonder what ever happened to Vi and Ariana."

Spencer gaped at her. He'd been having so much fun he'd forgotten that Violet and Ariana were supposed to join them. Hopefully they were okay.

But Sophie had pulled out her phone and was laughing.

"What?"

"Let's just say you were right. Definitely a setup." She passed him the phone, which was open to a text from Violet.

Have fun! Below that was a picture of Violet and Ariana waving—from Violet's kitchen.

"Those stinkers." He'd wanted to wring Violet's neck when she'd first pulled her disappearing act, but now he was ready to pick her up and twirl her around to thank her.

He passed the phone back to Sophie. "So how do you want to play this?"

Sophie studied him, apparently weighing his meaning. Finally, she shook her head. "You first." She gestured to the hole.

Okay. He could go along with that. Pretend there hadn't been more than the game behind his words.

He dropped his ball to the green and nudged it into position with his toe. He lined up his shot, and the ball banked off the wall, in perfect position to go around the waterfall on his next shot.

He gave a mock bow, but Sophie raised an eyebrow. "Playing it safe?"

"Sometimes that's the best way to get to your goal." Something it had taken him a long time to learn.

He took his next two shots, then sunk the ball in the hole on the fourth. He waited as Sophie lined up her shot. Her hair hung in her face, and she paused to grab a rubber band off her wrist and pull it into a ponytail. The casual hair, combined with the pink shirt, slim jeans, and tennis shoes, made her look like a softer version of herself, more open. More kissable.

The thought popped into his head, and once it was there, he couldn't erase it.

Didn't want to, really.

Sophie lifted her eyes at that moment and caught him staring at her. He should look away, pretend he hadn't been watching her. But he didn't.

She gave him a slow smile, and he was pretty sure his heart stopped for a beat.

She tucked a loose hair behind her ear, then dropped her head, swung the putter, and gave the ball a sound whack.

"And sometimes you have to take a risk." Her eyes followed the ball as it sailed toward the waterfall. It hit the wall of spray with a thud, and Sophie ran to his side to watch as it sailed through the waterfall. The momentum of the spin pulled it toward the hole.

Sophie clutched his arm. "Keep going. Keep going." She bounced on her toes.

With a clatter, the ball dropped into the hole.

"Yes!" Before he could react, she had thrown her arms around him.

All the air whooshed out of him in surprise, but his arms rose to her back of their own accord.

She felt so good.

He could get used to this again. He could—

No you can't.

Gently, he let go.

After a second, Sophie seemed to come to her senses and let go, too.

"Sorry." But her cheeks were flushed an adorable pink, and her eyes held a light he hadn't seen the whole time she was home. "That was fun."

He nodded as he led the way to the clubhouse. It had been fun, and he hated that it was over. He wanted to live in this time warp forever. But that wasn't how life worked.

Inside, they placed their clubs on the counter and turned to leave, but the clerk stopped them. "Don't you want to play the second round your friend paid for?"

Spencer's eyes met Sophie's, and he was pretty sure his own face mirrored the grin on hers. Maybe, just for tonight, they could stay in this time bubble.

An hour later, Spencer's cheeks hurt from smiling so much. A small price to pay for such a fantastic evening.

He hadn't had such a good time since—

Well, since he and Sophie had been together.

"I really think I improved my score that time." Sophie bent to grab her ball out of the final cup. Spencer snorted, and she stood to elbow him. "Except for the last hole."

He snorted again. It'd taken her fifteen strokes on the final hole this time. The ball had bounced off the waterfall on the first fourteen attempts, but she'd insisted it would be more satisfying to go through the obstacle than to go around it. Spencer had to give her credit for that.

But not for her final score. He finished tallying. "So, your first round, you had one hundred eight. And this round . . ." He left a dramatic pause, enjoying the anticipation in her eyes too much. "One hundred thirty-six."

The laugh that burst out of her was the most delicious sound he'd ever heard.

"Oh, yeah, Mr. Showoff? And what was your score?"

"Fifty-one," he deadpanned.

She plucked the scorecard out of his hand and reviewed it. "Well, then it looks like you get to buy me ice cream."

He snorted again. But any excuse to spend more time with her was fine by him.

They dropped their equipment off, and he opened his truck door for her, still caught in the time trap of mini golf. How many times had he held a door for her, ushered her into his truck, taken her for ice cream?

The drive was quiet. But it wasn't the uncomfortable silence of earlier. It was the kind of pleasant quiet that flowed from knowing a person so well there was no need for words.

He had to park several blocks from the Chocolate Chicken. That's what happened when it was the only place on the peninsula open after ten. He jumped out of the truck and crossed to open her door. A sense of déjà vu overtook him as they walked next to each other. The only difference was they weren't holding hands this time. He resisted the urge.

Inside, Sophie leaned toward him. "I think we might be the old folks here."

Spencer surveyed the shop. Sure enough, it overflowed with young people in groups and couples. They appeared to be the oldest ones in the place. Apparently time had marched on after all. The room was warm and bright, the buzz of voices loud. "Want to take this to the gazebo?" Spencer passed her the double scoop of triple chocolate in a waffle cone.

Sophie nodded as she took her first lick. Spencer had eaten ice cream with her so many times before that he knew to watch for it—the way her eyes closed as she savored the first taste.

She gave him a sheepish grin as she opened her eyes again, then led the way to the door.

A cool breeze blew in off the lake as they made their way to the public gardens on the hillside above the marina.

A gust played with a strand of hair that had come loose from Sophie's ponytail, sweeping it across her face—and into her ice cream. She groaned.

"Just a sec." They'd passed his truck half a block ago, and Spencer jogged back to it. He grabbed a stack of napkins from the glove box, then, in a flash of inspiration, reached into the backseat to grab the blanket he always kept for emergencies.

A second later, he was at Sophie's side.

"You think of everything." She took the napkin he held out to her and wiped at the chocolate streak in her hair.

"You missed a little." Spencer pointed to the ice cream dripping off a strand of hair, careful not to get too close. Sophie swiped toward the spot with her napkin.

"That wasn't even close." He couldn't help the laugh.

"Well, then help me." Sophie thrust the napkin at him.

He swallowed, the laughter dying on his lips. To help her, he'd have to touch her, and if he touched her—

His pulse jumped at the thought.

"It's right"—he tried to do a more accurate job of pointing—"there."

But Sophie shook the napkin at him. He licked his suddenly too-dry lips and took it, passing her his ice cream.

The moment his hand fell on her silky hair, a flood of memories overtook him. Sitting on the park bench, letting her teach him to braid her hair. Absently combing through it with his fingers as they watched a movie. Sliding his hands into it as he kissed her.

His eyes darted to her lips, glistening with a faint trace of ice cream. He yanked his gaze back to her hair and concentrated on wiping at the sticky ice cream coating the strands.

"There." He forced himself to lower his hands. To take his ice cream. To act as if his heart hadn't just jumped out of his chest and thrown itself to the ground at her feet, ready for her to cradle it or stomp on it, as she pleased.

They strolled onto the path that led through the public garden toward the gazebo. Old-fashioned streetlamps that could be straight out of a Dickens novel lined the path, casting patches of light and shadow on the tulips that had closed their petals for the night. The damp scent of the lake carried on the wind.

Next to him, Sophie sighed. "I didn't realize how much I missed this place."

"Yeah?" Her words hooked right into his heart, tugging at it.

They stepped into the gazebo and settled on a bench facing the water. He spread the blanket across both their laps. Sophie burrowed into it, pulling the worn fabric to her shoulders.

"I miss the gazebo. The ice cream. The lake." She hesitated, eyes directed toward the water. "The people."

He froze. *What people?*

But he didn't have the courage to ask.

Besides—

"Correct me if I'm wrong, but you have the same lake in Chicago."

Her eyes slid to him, and she stiffened.

"Come on, Soph, someone had to bring it up."

What are you doing to me here? his heart screamed. *If you hadn't brought it up—*

What? His common sense got the better of him. *She'd have forgotten she lives in Chicago and has her own life?*

Spencer tried to ignore the internal argument and forced his attention back to Sophie.

"It's not the same lake there," she was saying, her expression earnest. "I mean, technically, it's the same lake. But it's not the same, you know?"

He nodded. He did know. It was like how cherry trees that weren't part of Hidden Blossom were still cherry trees, but they weren't the same. Or how Sophie was the same as she'd been when she was his but not the same.

"Anyway." Sophie licked the last bits of ice cream from her fingers. "I almost never get out on the lake there. I'm always working."

Spencer could relate. "But you love what you're doing?"

She shrugged. "I'm up for a big promotion."

"That's great, Soph." But something between them had shifted when he'd brought up Chicago. He might as well deliver the final blow. "You go back tomorrow?"

Did a shadow of regret pass over her eyes, or was he only imagining it? "I head out after church."

He'd already known the answer, but his whole body tensed. What was he doing here, with the woman who'd already shattered him once? Who would only shatter him again when she drove away tomorrow?

But that wasn't fair. She hadn't come to Hope Springs to see him. She'd come to say goodbye to her grandma. She didn't owe him anything.

He couldn't take the way she was looking at him. "It's too bad you didn't get a chance to see the cherries blossom," he said, just to fill the silence. "They're starting to open."

"Maybe next time."

He nodded. But he knew there wouldn't be a next time. Once she left . . .

It'd likely be the last time he ever saw her.

"Spencer." His whispery-soft name on her lips almost undid him.

He let himself slide toward her. Let the soft dance of the moonlight on her lips beckon him closer.

He had dreamed of this moment for the past five years. But he'd never expected that dream to come to life.

And once it did, then what?

Who cared? He'd deal with that tomorrow. For now, all he wanted was this moment.

He slid a fraction closer, his eyes never leaving hers. He could read it there—she wanted the same thing.

But he couldn't shake the thought of her leaving.

He straightened and cleared his throat. "We should probably go. You have a long drive tomorrow." The words clawed their way out, leaving behind a raw trail that burned up his throat.

Sophie's eyes stayed on his a moment longer—long enough for him to glimpse the hurt there before a hood dropped over her expression.

"You're right." She got up in a quick motion that yanked the blanket off his lap.

But the sudden chill that cut through him had nothing to do with the cold air.

Sophie gathered the blanket into a ball, then took off down the garden path, leaving him to catch up.

Chapter 18

The burning behind Sophie's eyes was nothing to the burning in her heart. She'd been reading Nana's journal for the past two hours, unable—or maybe unwilling was the better word—to turn out the lights and go to sleep. She was afraid of whose face would haunt her dreams if she did. Afraid she'd see the way he'd pulled back when she'd said she was leaving tomorrow. Afraid she'd feel the too-gentle squeeze he'd given her hand when he dropped her off at her parents'. Afraid she'd remember her own desire to kiss him—a desire that had almost overcome her common sense.

She shook her head. Here she was thinking about it again.

She turned back to Nana's journal. Reading Nana's words over the last days had filled her heart in a way nothing else ever had. Her grandmother had had an incredible faith—a faith that had survived through the death of her husband and grandson, through her daughter's rejection, through her granddaughter's abandonment. Through it all, Nana had never shown anything less than love for them all—and even more, for God. Her journal was full of Scripture verses Sophie had known once but hadn't thought about in years. Her favorite so far was from Romans: "But God demonstrates his own love for us in this. While we were still sinners, Christ died for us."

The sheer magnitude of that kind of unconditional love took Sophie's breath away. Christ had died for her while she was still a sinner. She hadn't done anything to earn or deserve his approval, and yet he approved her anyway because of Jesus.

It had gotten her thinking about Pastor Zelner's comments at Nana's funeral—about finding her worth in Christ. If God approved of her, what did it matter if she ever won the approval of her parents or her boss or even Spencer?

A giant yawn overtook her, and she closed her eyes, the journal still open on the bed next to her.

A strange heaviness clung to Sophie as she packed, making her movements lethargic.

She clicked on her phone to check the time.

Noon.

She should be on the road. Church had been done for an hour already.

She'd said her goodbyes to Vi and Ariana and Ethan there. Spencer had been conspicuously absent from the service, and she couldn't help but feel it was her fault. That he didn't want to see her one last time before she left.

As she clicked the phone off, she pretended not to notice the swoop of disappointment that he hadn't called or texted. She'd let herself half-hope he'd try to convince her to stay. But he hadn't the first time, so why should he now?

And anyway, it's not like she'd really consider staying. She couldn't. Her job, her life, was in Chicago.

Even if, over the past week and a half, it was like someone had taken all the appeal she'd felt for Chicago and flipped it to Hope Springs. Which was ridiculous. She hadn't been able to wait to escape this place.

But being back, seeing family, seeing friends, and, fine, seeing Spencer had reminded her what she'd given up when she left.

Finally, her suitcase was packed, and she had no more excuses to stall. She surveyed the room. Better not forget anything. Who knew when she'd be back.

Her eyes fell on the worn copy of *Pride and Prejudice* on the nightstand. She grabbed the book and flipped it open to the page with the cherry blossom. Her fingers traced the paper-thin petals.

She should leave it here. Then there'd be nothing to tempt her to think about Spencer.

Yeah, nothing but her memories. Ones she'd thought she'd buried long ago but that had fought their way to the front of her thoughts and refused to leave.

She snapped the book shut and tucked it into the front of her suitcase, then pulled the suitcase off the bed and wheeled it into the hall. The thought of talking to her parents was suddenly too much, but she couldn't just walk out without saying goodbye. A search of the kitchen, formal dining room, and living room came up empty. They'd come home with her after church, but apparently they'd taken off again. She suppressed a sigh. Why should she be surprised that they hadn't stuck around to see her off? Anyway, this would make things easier. Which didn't explain the pit in her stomach. Did they really care that little about her?

Whatever. She was done worrying about what they thought of her.

She forced her chin up and wheeled her suitcase toward the front door.

But as she passed the den, she paused. She could have sworn she heard a rustling sound from inside. But that didn't make sense.

Neither of her parents had been in that room in years, as far as she knew. Heart thundering, she crept to the doorway and peeked cautiously inside.

"Mom?" In her surprise, the word came out louder than she intended, and her mother's head jerked up. She lifted a quick hand to swipe at her eyes but not before Sophie saw the moisture hovering on her lashes. An old photo box sat open in front of Mom, but she dropped the picture she'd been examining and yanked the cover onto the box.

Shock coursed through Sophie, but she wasn't sure what startled her more—seeing Mom crying or seeing the photo box. She recognized it immediately.

"Are those—?" She stepped gingerly into the room, easing toward Mom.

"They're nothing." Mom twisted to stash the box in its spot under an unused stack of books on the built-in shelves, but Sophie intercepted her. With something approaching reverence, she lifted the cover off the box. After Jordan died, she'd pored through this box so many times, until Mom caught her and told her it was off limits. She said Sophie needed to move on and that dwelling on her brother would only hold her back from her own life.

Sophie only wished she'd understood then that Mom's way of dealing with grief was unhealthy, that ignoring your feelings wasn't an answer. She picked up the photo Mom had thrown on top of the pile.

It was one of her and Jordan, playing together in the lake. Mom had snapped the picture right as Jordan sent a huge splash of water careening toward Sophie. She was smiling in this picture, but the moment after, she'd been crying and screaming at Jordan.

What she wouldn't give to have moments like that again. "I miss him."

Mom's head swung toward her, and Sophie covered her mouth. She hadn't meant to say it out loud. She knew Mom wouldn't talk about him.

But Mom gave a tight nod. "Heading out?"

"You know, I think Nana managed to get a picture of me screaming at him after this. When she showed it to me, I asked if she was going to throw it away." Sophie kept talking as Mom moved toward the doorway. "She said we should keep it because it was important to remember all the moments—not just the good ones—because it's all the moments that make us who we are." Sophie had thought then that Nana was crazy, but now she was starting to understand what Nana had meant.

Sophie lifted her head. If Mom could only see, too. But Mom had disappeared down the hallway.

Sophie shook her head at herself. Why did she bother?

But for some reason she couldn't explain, she felt compelled to follow Mom to the kitchen.

She stood at the counter, waiting for Mom to pour herself a cup of coffee. The sag to Mom's shoulders unnerved Sophie almost as much as seeing her cry had. Since the day of Jordan's funeral, she'd never seen her mother anything less than one hundred percent put together.

She longed to step around the counter, hug Mom, and tell her they could mourn Jordan and Nana together. But they'd never had that kind of relationship.

She bit her lip, trying to figure out how to say goodbye.

But Mom beat her to it. "You should get going."

Sophie nodded and opened her mouth to agree, but instead, what came out was, "I could stay a little longer if you wanted."

Mom's eyes flicked to hers. "Why would I want you to stay?"

All the air seeped out of Sophie, like a balloon with a small hole that widens as it deflates. "Never mind," she mumbled. "Just thought you might need help cleaning out Nana's house." She reached for the handle of her suitcase.

"I called a service to do that. They should have everything out of there by the end of the week."

Sophie let go of the suitcase, wincing as it crashed to the floor. "What will they do with it all?"

Her mother took a slow sip of coffee. "What do you mean what will they do with it? They'll donate the furniture and stuff. Toss the rest."

Sophie pressed a fist to her stomach. Could her mother really let some strangers throw everything of her grandmother's away?

"Don't you want to keep anything?" Her voice sounded high and little-girlish, but she suddenly felt like a little girl.

"Of your grandmother's?" Mom may as well have rolled her eyes for how well she hid the scoff in her voice. "She decorated her house with garage sale bits and pieces. There's nothing worth anything there."

"What about her personal stuff? Jewelry, pictures?"

Sophie's mother drained her cup. "Your grandmother wore costume jewelry and took terrible pictures. None of it's worth keeping. It's just stuff. Junk."

Sophie supposed it was true that it was just stuff. But stuff could have meaning, couldn't it? Memories?

"What if I clean out the house?" The words came out before Sophie could think them through. "Or we could do it together."

Her mother studied her with the closest thing to compassion Sophie had seen from her in a long time. She didn't dare to breathe. Was Mom really going to say yes? But Mom's careful, neutral expression snapped back into place. "You have to get back to work. And I have better things to do with my time than sort through your grandmother's clutter."

Mom was right, of course. She did have to get back to Chicago. But the thought of every memory she'd made with Nana being thrown into the trash was too much. And besides, the moment the idea had popped into her head, she'd been overcome with a peace she hadn't known in a long time. She didn't know why exactly she felt the need to stay, but she did.

"It'll only take a few days. I haven't taken a single vacation in the five years I've been with the firm. I have plenty coming to me. I'll just call Chase and let him know."

Her mother raised an eyebrow. "Chase, the man who was here the other day?"

Sophie nodded warily. Here came another lecture.

"Good, and while you're talking, make sure you patch up whatever went wrong the other day. He certainly suits you better than that farmhand you sat with at your grandmother's funeral."

Sophie's chest burned, and she fought every instinct to lash back. Spencer wasn't a farmhand. He was running that farm. And whatever he chose to do with his life, he was the best man she'd ever known.

But there was no point in defending Spencer to her mother. It's not like she'd ever be with him again anyway.

"So you're okay with me cleaning out Nana's house?"

"If you can get it done in a week. I want to get that house on the market before tourist season is in swing. Lots of potential buyers then."

"Deal." Sophie snatched her suitcase and headed for her room to unpack, her footsteps lighter than they'd been since Nana died.

She dialed Chase's number, more than a little relieved when he didn't answer, and left a message that she needed to sort some things out and would be staying another week. She promised to make it up to him by dealing with their least favorite architect on every project for a year.

As she passed through the kitchen, she asked Mom one more time to come with her. Apparently, she was a glutton for punishment.

But at least her expectations were realistic enough that she wasn't crushed when Mom repeated her no.

On the way to the car, Sophie pulled out her phone.

Her finger hovered over the number for only a second before she pressed it. This time her expectations were too high. But she couldn't bring herself to dampen them.

Chapter 19

Spencer slammed the stack of financial statements to the kitchen table and snatched at his ringing phone. He scowled at the unfamiliar number on the screen. He couldn't shake the bad mood that had clung to him all morning as he pictured Sophie on the road back to Chicago. It didn't help that since the moment he'd gotten home from church he'd been trying to deal with the farm bills that had piled up while Dad was in the hospital. Managing the books was his least favorite part of life on the farm, especially when a look at their financial standing left him wondering how they'd make it to harvest without going bankrupt.

"What?" he snarled into the phone. He was in no mood to be polite to telemarketers today.

"Spencer?"

Spencer closed his eyes, all the pent-up frustration leaking from him. In its place he was left with something even harder to handle.

Hope.

He tried to tamp it down.

"Hey, Soph. Is everything okay?" Maybe she'd gotten a flat tire or something on her way out of town.

"Yeah, everything's fine. I don't know why I called, actually. Well, I mean, I do, but I'm not sure why I thought you— I mean, I wanted to—"

Spencer couldn't help his grin. Sophie was always so certain, and yet, on the rare occasion when she wasn't, she babbled like a fool.

A very cute fool.

"What's up, Soph?"

He heard a quick intake of breath. "You weren't in church this morning."

He tapped his pen against the table in a sharp rhythm. "I went to church in Silver Bay this morning."

"Oh." How could she put so much meaning into one syllable?

"It's closer and—"

"Yeah, of course." Sophie brushed off his lame excuse. "Anyway, I was just calling to ask if your invitation to see the cherry blossoms was still good."

Spencer dropped the pen. "Aren't you going back to Chicago?"

"No. I mean, yes." Another quick breath. "I mean, I am, but not for a few more days. I'm staying to help clean out Nana's house first."

Spencer fought to control the way his heart surged. She was staying for a few more days. Not forever.

"So does it?" She sounded tentative, unsure, and he wanted to reassure her, tell her of course it did—whatever "it" was, but he couldn't for the life of him remember her question.

"Does it what?"

Her sparkling laugh reached right through the phone and wrapped itself around his heart. "Does the invite to see the cherries still stand?"

"Yeah." He pushed the words out past the snag of emotions. "It still stands."

"Great." Relief and something deeper mingled in her voice, but Spencer refused to let himself put a name to it. "I need to get a start at Nana's first, but how about I come around four?"

"Four sounds perfect." Spencer hung up and tried to focus on the paperwork in front of him. But it was hopeless. He shoved the papers aside and jammed his feet into his work boots. He needed to move.

On the way out the door, he almost bowled Tyler and the twins over.

"Hey." He swept Jonah up into a hug. "How's Grandpa?"

"Good." Jonah squirmed free and ran into the house, followed by Jeremiah.

Spencer looked to Tyler, waiting for his assessment.

"They're planning to release him later today." A giant smile overspread Tyler's face. "Our old man's one tough guy."

A relieved laugh made its way up from Spencer's core, and he pulled his brother in for a quick hug. "Thank the Lord." If Dad was coming home, then everything would be fine. He'd take over the paperwork, get everything squared away.

"By the way, Mom wants to have a celebration dinner tonight." Tyler gave him one last clap on the back and released him.

"Tonight?"

Tyler gave him a playful shove. "Yeah. Why, you have plans?"

Spencer shoved back. "Maybe."

Tyler's eyebrows shot up. "Really? I didn't think you'd get over Sophie that quickly. I *am* good."

Tyler may have been awake when Spencer got home last night. And Spencer may have poured his heart out to him. And Tyler may have helped him see that Sophie's leaving before he got his heart in any deeper was a good thing.

Spencer kicked one boot into the other. "Actually, the plans are kind of with Sophie. She called to say she's staying a couple more days to clean out her grandma's house. And she wanted to come see the cherry blossoms."

"Spencer, she's—"

Spencer held up a hand. "I know. She's going to leave. And I'm prepared for that."

"Really?" Tyler's eyebrows were so high they almost got lost in his hairline. "Is that why you about stuffed Jeremiah into the trash when he asked for a piggyback ride this morning?"

"I didn't—" But Spencer couldn't deny that he'd let his mood affect his interaction with his nephews this morning. "I'll go apologize."

Tyler grabbed his arm. "There's no need. He thought it was funny. It's just—"

Tyler peered past Spencer toward the orchard, but Spencer got the impression he was seeing farther, into the past. "I know how much it hurts to be left. And I may not have been there for you the first time. But I'm here now. And I don't want you to get hurt."

Spencer clapped a hand to his brother's shoulder. "I know what I'm doing. You don't have to worry about me."

Tyler rubbed at his forehead. "I'm the big brother. It's my job to worry."

Spencer didn't have the heart to remind him that for most of their adult lives he'd been the one to take on the big brother role. He appreciated Tyler's genuine concern.

"So anyway," Spencer said after a moment. "Do you think Mom and Dad will mind if I bring Sophie?"

"No." Tyler huffed. "You know Mom. Always the romantic. The last thing she told me when I left was to make sure you didn't let Sophie go this time."

Spencer spluttered. "Let her—? But she— I—"

Tyler lifted his arms and stepped into the house. "Take it up with Mom. She seems to think you two are meant to be together. Of course, she still watches fairy tales, too, so . . ."

Spencer joined his brother's laugh as he bounded down the steps and headed toward the workshop. But the truth was, he was beginning to agree with Mom.

If only Sophie was, too.

Anticipation coursed through Sophie as she turned into the driveway of Hidden Blossom Farms. It was because of the cherry blossoms, she told herself. It had nothing to do with the almost visceral need she'd felt to see Spencer again.

He was leaning against the shed when she pulled up, looking like he belonged in some outdoor magazine in his faded jeans and white t-shirt, hands perched easily in his pockets, dark hair rumpling slightly in the breeze. Sophie's grip on the wheel tightened, and her mouth went dry. This was a bad idea. Being here with him was only going to confuse her more. Make her want something she couldn't have.

But she couldn't hold back the smile that stretched her lips as soon as she stepped out of the car.

"Hey, Soph." She'd always loved the way he said her name. The way he lingered a moment on the "o."

"Hey, yourself." She drew in a deep breath of the blossom-tinted air. This was the scent of spring she'd been craving. A warm breeze lifted her hair, and she brushed it back. "It's so peaceful out here."

Spencer smiled and crossed the driveway to stand next to her. "How was your grandma's?"

"It was—" She paused before the word "fine" could slip out. She was determined to be completely open with him. "It was sad but good." Going through Nana's stuff had brought back wave after wave of memories. And even though it hurt that she wouldn't be able to make new memories with Nana, it had been comforting to think about all the memories she'd already collected.

"Actually." She opened the rear door of the car and leaned inside, reaching around Nana's favorite cookie jar—an ugly thing in the shape of a tree stump with a squirrel on top—that she couldn't bear to part with.

"This reminded me of you." She pulled her head out of the car and passed him the ship in a bottle that used to sit on top of Nana's bookshelf.

"Wow," Spencer breathed, lifting the tiny bottle to examine the intricate ship inside.

"I was thinking about that time we went to the museum, remember? And you stood and looked at that ship in a bottle for like twenty minutes."

He met her eyes. "I remember that day. It was the first time—"

He dropped his eyes back to the bottle. But he didn't need to say it. She remembered their first kiss, too.

It'd been dark by the time they'd emerged from the museum, and they'd been laughing about something stupid—Sophie couldn't remember what anymore. But when they stopped laughing, the air had seemed to shift around them. Spencer had grazed a hand lightly over her cheek, then leaned down and brushed the softest kiss onto her lips. When he'd pulled back, she'd tugged him closer for another, deeper kiss.

Sophie touched two fingers to her lips, remembering how it had been different from any other kiss she'd ever had. It had felt real. True. Life-changing.

She looked up at him now, and when their eyes met, she could almost pretend that the last five years had fallen away, that they were still together. That he still loved her.

But of course the years had happened. They weren't still together. He didn't still love her.

And she didn't still love him.

Obviously.

"See that?" Spencer pointed to something inside the bottle, and Sophie closed the space between them to get a better look.

"There." Spencer shifted so that his shoulder was pressed against hers. "See that fine detail, the carved dragon on the helm. Isn't it amazing?"

Sophie nodded, but the only details she could concentrate on were his hands, curved around the glass; his eyes, crinkling as he squinted at the ship; his arm, brushing against hers. And his scent—that fresh clean smell she'd missed so much.

"Anyway." Spencer held the bottle out to her. "Thanks for showing me this."

She shook her head and pushed it back to him. He'd always been so terrible at accepting gifts. "I want you to have it."

He gave her another doubtful look but closed his hand around it. "Why?"

"Because you like it. Because it makes you happy. Because I—" She broke off in confusion. She couldn't say the words that were about to roll off her tongue too easily. "I just want you to have it."

Spencer's eyes seemed to slip right past her defenses, see right into her heart.

He took a step back, clearing his throat. "Thank you. Let me put this in the house, and then I'll give you the tour."

As soon as he disappeared inside, Sophie pulled in a few deep breaths.

She had to be more careful.

NOT UNTIL FOREVER

She wasn't staying indefinitely, and she was determined not to break his heart this time.

Even if it meant breaking her own.

Chapter 20

Spencer set the ship in a bottle on a high shelf in the living room. As long as the twins didn't scale the shelf—which he couldn't entirely rule out—it would be safe.

He should get back out to Sophie, but he needed to collect himself. He couldn't read too much into the fact that she'd given him a gift from her grandma's house. Or the fact that she'd stayed in Hope Springs a few extra days. That she'd sought him out.

A burst of noise from outside pulled him to the door. He shoved it open as he caught sight of the chaos in the yard. The twins were chasing each other around Sophie's legs as Tyler tried to talk to her over their squeals. So much for peaceful.

"Jonah! Jeremiah!" he jogged across the lawn. "Here comes the tickle monster." If he caught their attention, hopefully they'd leave Sophie alone.

But they weren't interested in him.

"Boo!" Jonah waved his hands at Jeremiah as he took off around Sophie again.

Spencer scooped to pluck first Jonah then Jeremiah off the ground. The boys wiggled, but he firmed his grip, chancing a glance at Sophie. Amusement sparkled in her eyes, and a smirk played on her lips. Something inside him eased. She'd never hidden the fact that she didn't want children, but the way she was looking at these two . . .

Whoa, there, buddy. Where you going with that thought?
Right.
Enough of that.

"Now, boys, this is how we greet a lady." He shifted them to the ground and crouched beside them. "You hold out your right hand, like this." He stuck his hand out, waiting for the boys to mimic him.

"Good. Then you take her hand in yours, and you shake it, like this." He grasped Sophie's hand, ignoring the rough rhythm his heart took up. He pumped her hand gently twice, but he couldn't bear to let go quite yet. "And then"—he winked at the boys—"if you really want to be a gentleman and you really like her, you kiss her hand." He flipped Sophie's hand over in his and brought it gently toward his lips.

Behind him, Tyler cleared his throat. Loudly.

Spencer jumped and dropped Sophie's hand. He kept his head down.

"Now you try it." He gave Jonah a gentle push in front of him, practically using the boy as a shield.

Jonah shyly held out a hand, and Sophie crouched to take it. "It's nice to meet you." She shook Jonah's hand, but her eyes were locked on Spencer. He could feel it even though he hid his own gaze in Jonah's hair.

"Nice meet you," Jonah repeated woodenly, and they all laughed.

"Do you want to kiss her hand?" Spencer murmured to his nephew.

"Ew." Jonah wiggled away, but Jeremiah pushed into his spot. "Me turn."

He grabbed Sophie's hand and yanked it toward him, knocking her off balance.

Spencer's hand shot out to steady her, but Jeremiah kept pulling until her hand was at his mouth.

Instead of the quick peck Spencer had been about to demonstrate, Jeremiah dropped a big, juicy kiss right in the middle of Sophie's open palm.

Spencer flinched, but Sophie's laugh washed over them. "I see you have your uncle Spencer's way with women."

Spencer ignored Tyler's hearty guffaw at that.

"Hey, come here," Sophie whispered to Jeremiah. He shuffled a few steps closer, and she leaned over and dropped a quick kiss on his cheek. "You're quite the charmer."

He giggled, then ran off in the direction Jonah had gone, screaming that he was the kiss monster.

"Guess they learned a new game." Spencer straightened, pulling Sophie up with him.

"Great." But Tyler's eyes were directed pointedly at the spot where Spencer still gripped Sophie's elbow.

Spencer let go and crossed his arms in front of him.

Sophie turned to Tyler. "You have lovely boys."

Tyler groaned as the twins disappeared behind the house. "Not sure lovely is the word I'd use." But he took off after them with a smile.

"He's a good dad." Spencer couldn't help but be impressed with how well Tyler had adjusted to caring for the twins.

"I can tell." Sophie dropped a casual hand onto his arm. "He said your dad's coming home from the hospital today. That's such great news."

"Yeah." Spencer was caught up in the way her eyes gleamed. She was genuinely happy for his family, he could tell.

"I'm sure you want to be with him for that. We can do this another day." Sophie took a step toward her car.

He grabbed her arm to stop her. "He won't be home until later this afternoon. Actually, we're having a little celebration tonight—"

"Oh. Of course. I'm sure he'll—" She tried to pull away again.

"Soph." He didn't mean to sound so exasperated, but couldn't she see he was trying to tell her something? "I'd like it if you came to that. With me."

Her lips parted a little, and he had to fight down the temptation to kiss her right then and there.

"With you?"

He slid his hand down her arm to grasp her hand. "With me."

Hesitation hovered in her eyes.

"Please? For my dad? He won't stop talking about the lovely girl who brought him flowers. I mean, he knows your name, but he calls you that anyway. Lovely girl." And Spencer could see why. She *was* lovely. In every way.

She laughed. "Fine. I'll come." She squeezed his hand. "But only for your dad." The sun played tricks with her eyes, transforming them from brown to gold and back again.

The urge to kiss her was stronger than ever.

He had to stop this.

He let go of her hand and strode in front of her to the shed. "Let's go see the blossoms."

"Uh, Spencer?"

"Yeah?" He kept walking.

Distance.

He needed distance.

"Isn't the orchard that way?"

He didn't need to look to know she was pointing east, to where the cherry blossoms hovered like puffs of pink cloud above the earth. "Yep."

"So then why—?"

He pressed the keypad to open the shed's garage door and waited for the realization to dawn on her.

"Oh."

Behind the door sat the mud-caked ATV he hadn't had a chance to clean off. Spencer glanced over his shoulder, eyeing Sophie's clothes. She looked relaxed in a pair of jeans and a soft lilac shirt. In place of her usual heels, she wore a pair of running shoes. He grinned. Apparently, she'd learned from her first trip across his yard. He liked when she went casual like this.

No, make that loved it.

His gaze traveled to her eyes, which were comically wide.

"You up for this?"

Her throat bobbed as she swallowed, but she nodded.

"All right, then—hop on!" He swung a leg over the seat and watched as determination settled over her.

She strode to the machine, gave it one last apprehensive glance, and threw her leg over it behind him.

"That's my girl!" He caught himself. "I mean—"

But she was laughing, and she'd wrapped her arms around him, and he forgot whatever he'd been planning to say.

"You ready?" He managed to croak.

"Let's do this." Sophie's arms tightened around him as he throttled the ATV up slowly.

His heart on the other hand—that shot from zero to past all hope of recovery in half a second flat.

Spencer's fist overflowed with the petals he'd offered to carry for Sophie when her collection had become too large for her hands.

They'd left the ATV at the edge of the orchard and had been walking and talking for he didn't know how long.

Being out here, seeing the trees through her eyes, was refreshing. She exclaimed over every blossom-covered tree, stopped to examine a patch of grass or the occasional mushroom. At one point, she stopped to show him a spot where the petals had fallen to the ground in a near-perfect heart shape.

She listened as he explained the work they did to maintain the orchard through the seasons.

"Isn't it hard, though?" she asked now. "I mean, there are so many things you can't control."

He sighed and ran a hand over the top of his head. "Yeah, it's hard. And there are days I wonder if it's worth it. If we can keep the place afloat much longer. But then there are days like this . . ."

Perfect days.

She moved closer and nudged him with her shoulder. She felt it, too, didn't she? How right it was for them to be together. To be here.

His phone dinged with a text, and he stopped to fish it out of his pocket as Sophie kept walking, her face tipped toward the sky, hair dangling low down her back. It took an incredible force of will to take his eyes off her and check his phone.

The text was from Tyler. *ETA one hour.*

Spencer tucked the phone into his pocket. That meant they had to get back to the real world soon.

A gust of wind sent a torrent of blossoms dancing through the air. Ahead of him, Sophie began to twirl in the midst of them, her arms lifted to her sides. She spun faster and faster, until she collapsed to the ground in a heap of giggles.

Something in Spencer broke loose.

He didn't want to resist how he felt anymore. Was powerless to, anyway.

His footsteps were certain as he walked to her side and reached to help her up. "Come on, I want to show you something."

Chapter 21

"Where are we going?" Sophie leaned into Spencer and yelled to make herself heard over the rumble of the ATV's engine. It was the tenth time she'd asked, and for the tenth time, Spencer shot her a mysterious look over his shoulder but didn't say anything.

"Hold on!" he yelled now.

"What?" She was already holding on. Never wanted to let go, if she was being honest.

"Hold—"

A spray of cold water sloshed over her. She let out an involuntary shriek and looked up in time to see they'd driven into a fast-flowing creek.

A wet, thick blob landed on her cheek, and she shrieked again. Water flowed into her shoes.

She tucked her head into Spencer's back, her arms instinctively tightening around his waist.

"Almost across," Spencer called, and a second later, she felt the front of the ATV lift, as if they were climbing a bank.

She waited a second to make sure she wasn't going to get wet again, then lifted her head. The bank was steep, but Spencer handled the ATV with a sure hand.

When they reached the top, he throttled down and brought the machine to a stop.

"Soph, I'm so sorry. I haven't been over here much this year, and I didn't realize—" But he broke off as he swiveled on the seat to face her.

His eyes widened, and his lips lifted a fraction as he fought to keep a straight face. And if she looked anything like he did, she didn't blame him. Mud speckled his hair, a glob stuck under his left eye, and his shirt had gone from white to brown more effectively than if it'd been dyed.

She felt her own lips lift into a smile. And then she was laughing.

A moment later, she was laughing so hard she was crying.

"What?" Spencer tried to deadpan but failed to hold back his own grin. "Did I get a little muddy?" He dabbed daintily at his face, and Sophie broke into another round of laughter. This time, he couldn't fight it. His deep laugh joined hers, and the sheer joy of sharing this moment made Sophie laugh even harder.

When their laughter finally subsided, Spencer became suddenly serious. "I am sorry I ruined your clothes, though."

Sophie glanced down. Both her jeans and her shirt were dotted with mud. But she didn't care. "They can be washed."

"And your face."

"You ruined my face?"

Spencer's eyes landed on hers, locked in place. "Nothing could ruin your face. It's perfect."

"Oh." She didn't mean to sigh at that, but how could she help it? Somehow, he always knew the right thing to say.

"But—" His gaze shifted to her cheek. "You do have a little something here." His fingers grazed her skin, brushed at her cheek.

She resisted the urge to close her eyes and lean into his hand.

She had sensed it growing all afternoon, this thing between them. But she had to be the strong one, the one who resisted the pull—for Spencer's sake.

"Should we—" Her voice came out too soft, and she tried again. "Should we keep going?"

Spencer swallowed. Nodded. Withdrew his hand slowly.

"So, where are we going?" She tried to channel some of the playfulness from before, but Spencer shook his head and throttled up the ATV.

For the rest of the ride, Sophie concentrated on making as little contact with him as possible without falling off the machine.

By the time he slowed the ATV, her shoulders were in knots from the effort.

"Here we are." Spencer waited for her to climb off, and she did, careful to grab his shoulder for only a second, just long enough to keep her balance.

"And where exactly is here?" Sophie spun in a slow circle, taking in the cornfield on one side, the edge of what appeared to be a small woodland on the other.

The sun had fallen low in the sky so that it just sparked on the treetops.

"It's beautiful," she breathed.

"It is." Spencer's eyes seemed to trace the edges of her face, and she turned away. If he looked at her like that one more time, she wouldn't be responsible for anything her lips may choose to do.

"But—" Spencer grabbed her hand and tugged her toward the trees. "This isn't what we're here for."

He pulled her into the stand of trees, and she let their earthy scent—the same scent she always associated with Spencer—wash over her. He led her on a weaving path through the trees, and she tightened her grip on his hand—only because her eyes hadn't adjusted to the low light in here yet. The dark must be the reason her blood thrummed in her ears, too.

Finally, Spencer drew to a stop. He turned toward her expectantly. She gazed around. All she saw was more trees.

"It's a forest." She didn't want to insult him, but if he wanted to show her trees, they could have saved themselves the walk.

"Close your eyes."

"What?"

He moved behind her and reached to cover her eyes. "Take ten steps forward." His breath tickled her ear.

"What?" She remained planted.

"Just trust me, Soph. Ten steps forward."

She wanted to remind him that she didn't do well with surprises, but she shuffled dutifully forward.

"Bigger steps." Amusement colored Spencer's voice. It sounded good on him.

"I don't want to crash and get hurt."

"I'd never let that happen." His voice—it was so soft, so sincere, she wanted to spin right there in his arms. One of his hands moved to her waist, and the other shifted to cover both eyes.

She widened her steps as he'd instructed.

"Seriously, Spencer, what is this about?"

But instead of answering, he nudged her a fraction forward. "Open your eyes."

Spencer didn't know why he should be so nervous. He wasn't the one who'd been walking with his eyes closed. Even if it felt like that's exactly what he was doing, bringing Sophie here, to this spot that held so much of his family's history. That he hoped might hold so much of its future.

He pulled his hand slowly away from Sophie's eyes, then shifted to stand next to her so he could watch her discover his favorite place on the whole farm.

He knew the moment she noticed the knotted old cherry tree in the center by the way her eyes widened. She moved toward it without saying anything. He walked next to her, feeling an odd sense of pride in the old tree and its blossom-rich branches.

"This is the tree the farm is named for. The hidden blossom tree. It's part of the original orchard planted by my great-great grandfather when he first settled here. The rest of the trees in this section were wiped out by disease long ago. But this one has stood through disease, storms, drought, you name it."

Up close, the fragrance of the tree's blossoms enveloped them.

"It's amazing." Sophie ran her fingers along a blossom-covered branch. On impulse, Spencer plucked a flower and tucked it behind her ear.

She lifted her hand to cover his.

He froze. Met her eyes. "You know, this spot is sort of part of a family tradition."

"Mmm?" The silk of her hair slid against his hand every time she moved a fraction.

"My great-grandparents got married in front of this tree, my grandpa proposed to my grandma here, and my parents had their first kiss under these branches."

"Wow," Sophie whispered, or maybe it was just a breath. He couldn't tell. Her eyes were too entrancing for him to think about anything else.

"Yeah, and—"

But he couldn't say anything else because Sophie's lips were suddenly pressed to his. Spencer's hand slid further into her hair as his lips responded. Her arms circled his neck, and she pulled him in closer.

Her lips were so familiar, and yet there was something new in her kiss, something he'd never felt before, something more open, more real, than anything between them had ever been before.

Somewhere in the back of his mind, a warning bell with a voice suspiciously like Tyler's sounded. Spencer tried to push it aside, but it was annoyingly persistent.

Gently, he moved his hands to Sophie's shoulders and pulled his head back.

At the look on her face—the combined contentment and confusion—he almost leaned in again.

But Tyler was right. He couldn't go through this again.

"I'm sorry," Sophie half-gasped. "I shouldn't—"

But he shook his head. "I'm glad you did." He couldn't deny that. "But we should get back." He pulled out his phone.

Sure enough, three new texts from Tyler:

We're back.

Dinner's about ready. Where are you?

Starting without you. You better not be doing anything stupid right now.

Spencer clicked off the phone. He wasn't doing anything stupid. Unless you counted kissing your ex-girlfriend as stupid. Your ex-girlfriend who was going back to Chicago. Your ex-girlfriend who was going back to Chicago, who you were still madly in love with.

Okay, maybe he was doing something a little stupid.

Chapter 22

Sophie focused on keeping at least two feet of empty space between herself and Spencer as they walked through the trees toward the ATV. It meant she kept stumbling over roots and getting slapped in the face by branches she didn't notice until the last minute, but it was safer than getting too close to Spencer. Otherwise, she might give in to the temptation to kiss him again.

She couldn't quite bring herself to regret that kiss, even if it hadn't been fair to him.

She worked to take her thoughts off the soft brush of his lips against hers. They were so warm and—

She had to stop. "So do you think you'll stay on the farm your whole life? Or do you ever think about going back to school and finishing your degree?" She tried to ask it casually, to pretend there was nothing behind the question.

Spencer didn't slow his pace. "Yeah, I've thought about it. Especially after last year, when we almost lost everything. But Soph—" He stopped without warning, and she had to pull herself up short to keep from breaking her two-feet-of-space rule. "Sometimes it feels like this is what I was born to do. You know?"

Sophie nodded, even as her heart slid down through her feet and into the ground. He'd never consider the plan that had taken hold of her this afternoon. She'd thought maybe they could be together, maybe he'd be willing to move to Chicago with her, get his degree, get a job there.

But he was clearly more attached to this land than he was to her.

They walked the rest of the way to the ATV in silence. It wasn't until she was settling in behind him on the machine that he spoke again. "What about you? Do you think you'll be in Chicago forever? Or will you ever come home to Hope Springs?"

The question caught her so off guard that she opened her mouth to answer, then snapped it shut. She'd been so sure all her life that she'd never be willing to live here again. But—

"Right." In front of her, Spencer's back stiffened. The ATV roared to life, and Sophie had to make a mad grab for Spencer's shirt to keep from falling off backward as they took off.

She couldn't keep two feet between them on the cramped seat, but as they crossed the fields, she concentrated on making only as much contact as necessary to keep herself on the ATV. Which meant she got even wetter when they crossed the creek the second time.

By the time they parked in the shed, her teeth were chattering, and her legs were stiff. She swung gingerly off the machine, rubbing her hands up and down her arms.

All she wanted was a nice warm bath and a chance to snuggle under her blankets to wallow in thoughts of the man she couldn't have.

But she'd promised that man she'd have dinner with his family.

Spencer swung off the ATV, frowning at her. "You're drenched and cold. Let's get you inside."

He was soaked, too, but somehow he managed to pull off the mud-caked look. Just one more sign that he belonged here.

She should argue. Tell him she'd be fine. But she couldn't make her teeth stop chattering long enough.

As he led her inside, the warmth of the house embraced her. It wasn't only the temperature. It was the whole feel of the place. She'd noticed it the first time she was here and hadn't been able to stop thinking about it since. The house may not be fancy, and its decor might be lacking a certain sophistication. But this was a *home*. The word stuck in her head even as a violent shiver racked her frame.

"Here." Spencer slid past her and disappeared into a room down the hallway.

He emerged a few seconds later, holding out a sweatshirt. "You can change into this. The bathroom's down the hall, first door on the left."

Sophie eyed the sweatshirt. She should say no to wearing his clothes. It was too familiar. But the idea of being warm and dry was too tempting.

In the bathroom, she pulled off her sodden, mud-stained shirt and slipped the soft sweatshirt over her head. She pushed up the sleeves that reached well past her hands and pulled down the hem that hit her at mid-thigh.

The big UW loomed at her from the mirror, backward in its reflection, but Sophie recognized the shirt. It was the same one she'd worn countless times before. She'd claimed it from Spencer almost the moment they started dating, when she got cold at a football game, and he took it off to give it to her. She hadn't given it back until she'd packed up her apartment after graduation. Then she'd stuck it in a box with all his other stuff, except the plush giraffe she couldn't bear to part with, and mailed it to him here. She pictured him getting the box, opening it, finding the sweatshirt, and shame washed over her.

It was a miracle he'd even talked to her when they'd run into each other at the hospital, let alone stood by her through Nana's funeral and taken her to the orchard today. And returned her kiss.

The kiss that never should have happened, she reminded herself as she stepped out of the bathroom.

Spencer was setting a mug of coffee at the table when she walked into the kitchen. He stared at her in the sweatshirt as she settled onto the chair, a half-smile lifting his lips. "Remember when you spilled ketchup on that shirt?"

Sophie chortled. "How could I forget. I was afraid you'd break up with me. You were so mad."

Spencer held up a hand. "I wasn't mad, I was—" He shook his head. "Okay. I was mad. But only because I couldn't afford to buy another one, and I was afraid you'd leave me for some other guy who had a clean sweatshirt you could wear."

A laugh burst out of her just as she was about to take a sip of coffee. "I told you it would come out."

Spencer snorted. "That's only because we washed it like nine times. That's how it got so faded."

Sophie ran a hand down the faded letters. Truth was, she liked it this way. It made it feel familiar, like it had always been a part of her. A part of them.

She glanced up to find Spencer watching her. He cleared his throat. "I'd better go get changed so we can get to my parents' before there's no food left."

As he disappeared, Sophie wrapped her fingers around the mug, letting its warmth seep into her stiff knuckles. Her eyes fell on a stack of papers on the table, and she slid it closer. Maybe reading would keep her mind off Spencer.

But as she scanned the pages, her thoughts shifted to concern. If these pages told the farm's full financial story, it was in trouble.

Serious trouble.

Footsteps sounded in the hallway, and Sophie pushed the papers aside. She had no business going through Spencer's financial statements.

"Ready?" Spencer stopped in the kitchen doorway. He'd changed into a pair of dark jeans, and a blue button down that magnified the color of his eyes.

She pushed to her feet, stealing one last glimpse of the papers on the table to keep from staring at him.

Looked like the farm's finances weren't the only thing in trouble.

Her heart might be, too.

Chapter 23

Spencer pressed his hand lightly to the small of Sophie's back, steering her out the front door of his house. Outside, the night's chill washed over him. Maybe that would clear his head of all the ridiculous thoughts swirling there. Force some common sense in.

All the way back on the ATV, the whole time he was making Sophie's coffee, all the while he'd been changing, he'd been turning over Sophie's question about staying on the farm forever.

He'd thought he sensed something under the question. Was she asking because she wanted to know if he'd leave the farm to be with her?

And if that's what she was asking, would he consider it?

It's not like living on the farm forever had been part of his original plan. He'd always intended to finish his degree and get a real job someday. But then he'd been here, and it'd been—not easy, but familiar. And he loved the land, loved its rhythms, loved working with his hands.

But he loved Sophie, too.

There was no point in trying to deny that anymore. At least not to himself.

So would he be willing to give this place up for her?

"Spencer?" Sophie's voice cut into his thoughts, and he realized she'd said something to him.

"I'm sorry. What was that?"

"I was just asking if your family will be upset we're late."

Spencer chuckled. If Mom knew he'd spent the afternoon with Sophie—which she probably did, thanks to Tyler—she'd be calling Pastor Zelner right about now to schedule the wedding. "They won't mind."

Except for Tyler. He'd sent another text while Spencer was making the coffee.

Seriously, Spencer, not worth getting your heart broken again.

But maybe he didn't have to get his heart broken. Maybe things could work out.

He could move to Chicago, or better yet, she could come back to Hope Springs.

And be a farmer's wife? The voice of reason cut through as his eyes fell on his parents' house, a fraction of the size of the home Sophie had grown up in. They walked down the short jog in the driveway that led to the tired-looking garage.

And anyway, hadn't her silence when he'd asked if she'd consider coming back said everything he needed to know?

She may have kissed him, but when it came down to it, she'd never pick him before her career or her accustomed lifestyle. It was why she'd said no to his proposal in the first place.

"Everything okay?" Sophie grazed his hand tentatively as they reached the front steps. "You're quiet."

He forced a smile she'd see through in a second. "Just thinking."

He opened the door, and a wall of sound from inside hit them. His smile became genuine as Dad's booming laugh carried to the door.

He couldn't worry about the future right now. He needed to take the time to celebrate this moment with his family.

He steered Sophie through the living room to the kitchen. Everyone was already at the table, one twin on Tyler's lap, the other on his mother's. Both boys were throwing more food than they were putting in their mouths. While Tyler was trying to make them stop, Dad's laugh boomed out again.

"Don't encourage them." But Tyler was smiling, too.

Oh, boy. What had he brought Sophie into? He was sure meals at her house never descended into chaos like this.

"I'm sorry, I—" But one glance at Sophie and his apology died on his lips.

Delight danced in her eyes, and her smile lit up her whole face. "This is wonderful," she whispered, leaning toward him.

He nodded, heart full. It was pretty wonderful. His family, all together in one place for the first time in years. And there was no one he'd rather experience this with.

He led her to the table and pulled out a chair. She gave him a look, but he just smiled and waited for her to sit, then kissed his mom on the cheek and clapped his dad on the back before taking the seat next to Sophie.

"You look good, Mr. Weston." Sophie took the bowls his mother started passing the moment they sat.

Spencer grinned as his father ducked his head and put on a gruff act. "Not back to full strength yet."

Spencer scooped some corn onto his plate. "Give it time, Dad. You'll get there." He leaned over to whisper to Sophie in a mock-conspiratorial tone, "Dad hates to sit still."

"Well, what's a man good for, if not to work?" Dad speared a piece of chicken. "I've felt worthless in that hospital room for the past week."

"You'll be back out there soon enough." Spencer pointed his fork at Dad. "Before harvest, for sure."

And once Dad was on his feet again, Spencer could start to think about his own life. About what he really wanted. Whether he could leave the farm for Sophie—assuming she wanted to be with him, of course.

"Actually." Mom set down her fork and gave Dad a significant look. "He won't be."

Spencer stopped with a forkful of chicken halfway to his mouth. "Well, maybe a little longer then, but—" He broke off at Mom's pointed stare.

His head swiveled to Dad, who was shredding a napkin.

"Your father," Mom began, but Dad interrupted.

"I'll tell them, Mary."

Now everyone's eyes swiveled to him. "But first I want to say something."

They all waited, everyone's forks still. A churning started in Spencer's gut. He felt like he had at the hospital—like he was waiting for bad news.

"I just wanted to say—" Dad's hands shoveled the shredded napkin pieces into a pile. "Thank you to all of you."

"There's nothing—" Spencer started to say, but his father held up a hand to stop him.

"No, I mean it. I know I haven't always been a perfect father, but I'm proud of the way I raised my sons. When I needed you, you both came through. Spencer—" When Dad's eyes lifted to him, Spencer felt the need to both sit up straighter and duck under the table. "You saved my life. And you've kept this farm running."

Spencer clenched his teeth together and blinked rapidly at the table with a short nod. Sophie's hand covered his, and she squeezed.

"And Tyler." Their father turned to Tyler, who held the twins on his lap—both now miraculously quiet as they munched on cookies. "I know we've had our rough patches. But when I needed you, you came home. And you brought me two of the greatest gifts I could imagine."

"You can keep them if you want," Tyler muttered, and they all laughed as Jonah shoved a mushy piece of cookie into his father's mouth. Tyler spluttered but grinned.

"And Sophie—"

Sophie's head shot up, and it was Spencer's turn to squeeze her hand. She looked utterly—and adorably—startled that Dad had singled her out.

"You brought me flowers. And you make my son happy. What more could I ask for?"

Spencer choked on his water. "Dad, we're not—"

Sophie laid a hand on his arm, and he stopped. "It's the least I could do."

Spencer studied her, but she pulled her hand away and refused to meet his eyes. Her cheeks had a slight glow to them.

"Alan," Spencer's mother said from next to him.

"Oh, yes, and my beautiful wife. Who hasn't left my side once in the past week and who has stood by me for thirty-five years." He grabbed her hand and brought it to his lips.

"You're welcome," Mom said, "but you know that's not what I meant." She gave him a stern look and twisted her hand to lace her fingers through his. Spencer had seen that look before. Something big was up.

His father stared at the table. "There's something else." He cleared his throat as they all waited. "This second heart attack has been kind of a wake-up call. Guess the first one didn't take." He plucked a piece of shredded napkin off the pile in front of him and set it off to the side. "But I want to be around to see my grandchildren grow up. Which means I need to take care of myself. Avoid stress." He blew out a long, slow breath. "That's why I've— We've—" He looked at Mom, who gave an encouraging nod. "We've decided to sell the farm."

Spencer dropped his fork but didn't bother to pick it up. "But you just said you feel worthless when you're not working."

Dad give him a long, hard look, and Spencer struggled not to squirm under the scrutiny. He knew that look. It was the one Dad always gave when he was waiting for Spencer to catch on to something on his own. But he couldn't for the life of him figure out what it was.

"*Feel* worthless Spencer. Feel worthless. But I know I'm not worthless. I have worth to God—"

"And to us—" Mom piped up.

"And to my family," Dad agreed. "No matter what I do or don't do. No matter how I feel. So, I'm going to rely on that."

"Besides—" Tyler picked up a crying Jonah, who had banged his head on the table, and passed him to Dad. "Your job now is full-time grandpa." He glanced around the table. "We're going to stay in Hope Springs, if that's okay with everyone."

Next to Tyler, Mom burst into tears. "Ah, Mom." Tyler leaned over to give her a hug. He shot a look at Spencer, whose mind had gone completely blank. Dad was selling the farm. Which meant he wouldn't have to feel guilty if he left. But the thought of losing his family's legacy left him with a hollow feeling right in his middle.

"Sorry." Mom waved a hand in front of her eyes. "It's an answered prayer."

"Mary." Dad's voice held a note of warning. "We promised we wouldn't pressure them."

"I know. I know." She wiped at her eyes with a napkin. "Either way, I'm just glad I'll be near my grandbabies."

"Either way what? Pressure who?" Spencer was missing something. Mom sometimes forgot they weren't mind readers.

"I'd like to give you boys first option to buy the farm. Either alone or together. I'd give you a good price, of course, and we could work out fair terms. And . . ." He fell silent, and Spencer wondered if he was waiting for them to jump in. But he couldn't open his mouth, and even if he could, he wasn't sure what would come out.

Tyler looked equally dumbstruck. A fleeting moment of disappointment and maybe sadness flashed in Dad's eyes but then was gone. "Anyway." He stood and picked up his plate, but Mom plucked it out of his hands and pushed him gently back into the chair. Spencer didn't miss the concerned twist to her mouth.

"You don't have to decide right now," Dad continued. "Take some time to think about it. But please know this is your choice. I don't want either of you to feel obligated."

On his other side, Sophie shifted, and he made himself look at her, much as he dreaded seeing her reaction to his dad's offer. She was staring into her lap, where her fingers were twisting a purple ring.

Spencer turned back to Dad. He'd never hesitated to call this man his hero, so somehow he hadn't noticed until this very moment that he did look older, more fragile.

A fierce ache started in his gut at the thought that someday Dad wouldn't be around.

If selling the farm meant Dad would be with them longer, then that's what Dad should do. Even if it put Spencer into the position of deciding between his family and a future with Sophie.

Again.

"Yeah." He dragged a hand over his face. "I'm going to need some time to think about it."

Chapter 24

"Thank you for dinner," Sophie said quietly to Spencer's family as she filed out the door Spencer held open for her.

His dad's announcement had put a damper on the celebration, and Spencer seemed in a hurry to leave. But once they were out the door, he shuffled toward his own house, barely seeming to notice Sophie was at his side.

The temperature had dropped enough that Sophie shivered and pulled her hands deeper into the sleeves of Spencer's sweatshirt.

Finally, she couldn't stand the silence any longer. "Are you going to buy it?"

Spencer pushed a hand through his hair and sighed so deeply she thought it would never end. "I don't know."

She gnawed her lip. She should keep her opinion to herself.

But the numbers on that financial statement haunted her. This place was barely staying afloat. One more bad year, and it would go under. She didn't want that for Spencer.

"Spencer." She reached for his arm, dragging him to a stop.

The tenderness in his eyes when he looked at her was its own kind of torture. What she was about to say might erase it for good.

But if she cared about him—and there was really no way she could pretend not to after their day together—she had to.

Cold air ripped at her lungs. "I saw the financial statements on your table."

He opened his mouth, but she jumped in. "I shouldn't have looked. I'm sorry. But—" She sucked in a sharp breath. "I have to tell you that in my professional opinion, it's not a good investment."

Spencer's eyes roved her face, and she wondered what he was searching for.

Instead of the anger she expected, he sounded defeated. "I know it's not. We were barely holding on, and then, after last year—" He tipped his head back and stared at the sky. There was only a sliver of moon tonight, and Sophie couldn't read his expression in the dark.

"But it's my home. My family's legacy." His Adam's apple bobbed. "I always imagined that one day I'd be picking cherries out here with my kids and then my grandkids. I just never really thought about owning the place. I guess I took it for granted that my dad would always be here."

Sophie nodded, even though his head was still tipped skyward and there was no way he could see her.

"Do you ever feel like a star?" His question came out of nowhere.

She wrinkled her nose. "Like a movie star?"

A gentle chuckle. "No." He pointed toward the sky. "A *star* star."

She leaned her head back, too. Thousands of stars created a tapestry of the night sky, and she drew in a stunned breath. When was the last time she'd let herself just look at the sky?

"How do you mean? Burning bright? Twinkling?" She tried to lighten the dark mood he'd fallen into. "You definitely sparkle, Spencer, if that's what you mean."

He offered a half-hearted smile. "I guess I was thinking about how many stars there are. How it seems to make each one insignificant."

Without thinking, Sophie closed the space between them and grabbed his arms. He pulled his gaze away from the sky, toward her. The doubt in his eyes—had that always been there, or was that her fault?

"You are not insignificant, Spencer. Didn't you hear your Dad in there? You saved his life. You've kept this place going. You matter. To your family. To God." It felt strange to be giving spiritual advice, given that she'd only just started thinking about God again herself, but she knew it was true. Spencer mattered to God. And so did she. The knowledge gave her courage to keep going. "And you matter to me, for the record."

For a moment, Spencer just watched her. Then he lowered his head toward her so slowly she thought time must have stopped.

When his lips finally met hers, the sigh that escaped her said everything she hadn't been able to put into words.

Sophie woke up with a smile on her face. She could still taste Spencer's lips on hers. Still feel the gentle kiss he'd given her in the middle of Hidden Blossom's driveway and the one he'd given her when they reached her car—deeper, longer, more certain. It was a kiss that said she wasn't the only one with lingering feelings.

And with his dad's plan to sell the farm, Spencer was no longer tied here. He could leave—come to Chicago with her—without an ounce of guilt. It was perfect timing. Surely he had to see that, too. Otherwise, he wouldn't have asked her to dinner again tonight.

She felt light on her feet as she sped through getting dressed. She had plenty to do at Nana's before she could think about tonight. She'd better load up on coffee if she was going to get everything done.

But the argument that carried from the kitchen drew her up short in the hallway.

"I told you the bid was too low." Irritation snapped from Mom's voice.

Maybe Sophie didn't need coffee after all.

"It was a fair bid." Dad's retort was hard and firm. "If you want to make a profit, you can't go throwing money at people because you love the view."

"The view is what sells," Mom spat back.

The urge to flee, to run and climb under her blankets and cover her ears as she had when she was a child almost overpowered Sophie.

But she was an adult now. And a skilled negotiator to boot. She pulled her shoulders back and marched into the kitchen.

"Morning." She tried to keep her voice cheerful. "Everything okay in here?"

Mom and Dad were on opposite sides of the room—Dad seated at the table with a cup of coffee, Mom standing at the counter pressing buttons on the coffee maker. With a pang, Sophie remembered the way they used to huddle around their old coffee machine together, Dad sneaking a kiss the moment Mom turned to give him his mug. Mom swatting at him and telling him he'd burn himself, then setting the cup down to give him a deeper kiss. At the time, Sophie had been thoroughly disgusted. But now—now she realized what a rare thing they'd had. And they'd lost it. Just as she'd lost the rare thing she had with Spencer.

But maybe—

Maybe it wasn't too late.

"Everything's fine." Mom's sarcasm yanked Sophie back to the problem at hand. "If you consider losing possibly the best land on the peninsula as fine."

Dad rolled his eyes. "Don't be so dramatic, Katherine."

"Dramatic?" Mom plunked her coffee cup to the counter. "We could have put a whole villa on the Richardson estate. But your father wasn't willing to go high enough to get it. Now the Pearsons have it, and you know they're going to do something tacky with it. Probably another mini golf course."

"What's wrong with mini golf?" Sophie couldn't help the question.

Mom shot her a glare. "The point is, the market is prime for development, and we lost out on our best shot at it."

"They wanted too much for it." Dad's voice was the calm monotone that always infuriated Mom. "More land will come on the market soon enough."

"And when's soon enough, David? Six months? Nine? A year? Land like that doesn't ever just show up on the market anymore. Most of the big farms have already been pieced out, and the rest have no intention of selling."

"Actually, I might know someone who's selling." The words were out before Sophie could think about them. But as soon as she said it, it hit her—this was a solution that would benefit everyone.

Both of her parents swung their attention to her, and Sophie almost couldn't go on. She couldn't remember the last time she'd felt like the center of their world. What if they hated the idea?

But she had to put it out there. For Spencer's sake, if nothing else.

"I heard that Hidden Blossom Farms might go up for sale. I could probably convince the owner to entertain an exclusive offer."

"Is that the orchard in Silver Bay?" Her father sounded eager. "That's a prime spot. We've made numerous proposals to them, but they've never been interested in selling. Where'd you hear this?"

Sophie shifted in her seat. Was she doing the right thing, telling them? Spencer's father hadn't made his announcement in the hope of securing a buyer. But if she didn't step in, Spencer would let his sense of responsibility get in the way of the smart decision and anchor himself to a failing business. She couldn't let him do that.

There's no way he'd be able to match any price her parents could offer. The land was worth a million and a half, easy, and that would set him and his whole family up for a very long time.

"The owner has had some health problems," she said at last. "He's asked his sons if they want to buy it, but I don't see how they could..."

"We could get it for a pretty good price if they're desperate to sell." Her father pulled out his phone and started typing.

A twinge of conscience pinched at the edges of Sophie's heart. This wasn't what Spencer would want.

But she pushed the worry away.

Maybe it wasn't what he wanted.

But it was what he needed.

Chapter 25

Spencer couldn't take his eyes off Sophie as he approached the spot where she stood at the end of the pier, gazing out over the water. A simple white sundress flowed around her legs, and her hair caught the light from the sunset.

He came up behind her and wrapped his arms around her shoulders, relishing the way she leaned into him, her light, flowery scent, the way her hands came up to rest on his arms.

These moments—the perfect kiss last night, the perfect dinner tonight, this perfect sunset—were only making his decision about the farm harder.

She shouldn't factor into his decision.

Rationally, he knew that.

But all day as he'd worked repairing fences and fixing equipment, he'd wavered back and forth. It seemed so unfair that choosing one thing he loved would mean giving up the other.

But he couldn't see any way around it.

Unless Sophie would be willing to stay here. With him.

Three times already tonight, he'd almost asked her. But every time, he'd chickened out.

He should ask her now, while they were standing wrapped together like this. But if he asked, he might shatter this moment. And it was too perfect to risk that.

Instead, he leaned toward her ear. "What are you thinking about?"

She shivered against him, and he wrapped her tighter.

"I was just thinking about that time we camped with Vi and Cade, do you remember?"

He nodded his head against hers, letting her hair caress his cheek. "I remember." His voice was soft with the memory.

Sophie had insisted she could never sleep in a tent, but she'd proved to be more outdoorsy than any of them had given her credit for. The two of them had sat up around the fire long after Violet and Cade had called it a night, talking softly about the past. And the future.

When they'd started yawning, they'd pulled their sleeping bags out of their tents and laid down next to each other to talk some more. As the fire's embers died, Spencer grabbed her hand, finally working up the courage to tell her the words that had been burning him from the inside out for weeks. "Sophie, I love you."

At first, she didn't move, didn't respond at all, and he thought she was trying to figure out how to let him down easy.

"I just wanted you to know," he added, kicking himself for not waiting to tell her. He knew it was too soon. That he had spooked her.

But then she rolled toward him, and in the firelight, he saw it in her eyes—she felt the same way. She wrapped her arms around him. And that was all he needed.

They stayed like that until she fell asleep. But Spencer laid awake for a long time, watching her. He had never been happier—or more terrified—than when he realized the depths of his feelings for her as she slept curled up next to him.

In the morning, he woke to find her watching him. "I do, too, you know." Her hair was mussed, and she had a groove in her cheek from sleeping on the ground all night, but she'd never looked more beautiful.

He pressed a kiss to her lips, his heart a mess of joy and hope and a knot of fear that he would never be able to give her the life she deserved.

"I'm never going to stop loving you," he'd promised in that moment.

She'd cocked her head to the side, as if trying to work out the meaning of the word *never*.

"Not until forever?" she'd asked.

"Not even then."

It was a promise he'd kept in spite of his best efforts not to over the past five years, he realized now. A promise he couldn't break if he tried.

"Soph." His voice barely worked.

"My parents still think I spent that weekend in Cancun with Vi." She laughed lightly.

She may as well have doused him with lake water. He loosened his grip around her shoulders and walked to the opposite edge of the pier.

Her parents.

She'd never told them about him. Obviously, she'd never been serious about him. About a future together.

"Spencer?" Sophie edged closer. "What's wrong?"

The lights of a small craft slid past the rocky breakwater, the soft chugging of its engine followed by the slap of its wake against the rocks.

He should forget it. Her family life was her family life, and he obviously would never be part of it. "Nothing. We should go."

"What? No." The desperation in her voice froze him. "Please tell me what it is."

He rounded on her. The last flickers of sunlight reflected off her eyes, and he had to look away. "Why didn't you ever tell your parents about me?"

"What?" Her brow wrinkled and her mouth dropped into a confused frown.

"My parents were ready to welcome you into our family when I proposed. And here you had never even mentioned me to yours. You introduced me to them as a classmate the other day. A *classmate*. Is that all I was to you?" He could feel the sneer twisting his lips. "Or are you too ashamed to tell them you dated a farmer? That he wanted to marry you?" He broke off, his breath coming in short gasps.

Sophie's sharp inhale told him he'd hit his mark.

Her hand fell on his arm, but he jerked away and stepped back. She wasn't going to get out of this with a soft touch.

Sophie lowered herself to sit on the pier, her legs dangling over the side, a foot or two above the water that had darkened to ink. Spencer peered into the bruised blue of the sky, trying to figure out how he'd let the night go so wrong. And yet, if this was going to work, she had to be real with him. They both had to be real.

She gestured for him to sit next to her. He watched the spot where her elegant fingers patted the rough boards. He should walk away right now. Protect his heart from any more damage.

But heaven help him, he couldn't bear to leave her looking so vulnerable and . . . unsure. Two words he never would have used to describe the Sophie he used to know.

He sat, kicking his own legs over the side of the pier.

When she was silent for a full five minutes, he finally looked at her. She was twisting the ring on her finger again.

"What is it?" He broke the silence.

She startled as if she'd forgotten he was there and followed the direction of his stare. "An amethyst. Nana gave it to me before . . ."

Three heartbeats of silence.

When she continued, her voice was stronger. "When she gave it to me, she told me that if I ever found love, I should hold on to it. But Spencer—"

She lifted her eyes to his, and he had to catch his breath.

"I was afraid. I *am* afraid." She tore her eyes away and squinted toward the horizon. "I'm not ashamed of you, Spencer." Her sigh floated on the wind. "I'm just—" She pressed her lips together.

Spencer waited, giving her room to gather her thoughts.

"My brother was planning to work with my parents, did you know that?"

Spencer shook his head but slid a fraction closer.

"Mom and Dad were so devastated to lose him that I just sort of tried to fill in for him, you know?"

Spencer lifted his head to watch her. She'd only been ten when her seventeen-year-old brother had died. That was a lot of pressure for a little girl to put on herself.

Her forehead wrinkled. "But my grades were never as good as his, and I was never an athlete, and I was terrible at music. I could tell my parents were disappointed with my efforts all the time."

"Oh, Soph." He slid the rest of the distance between them and wrapped an arm around her. How had she never told him this before?

"Is that why you went into real estate?" He gently turned her to face him.

The creases in her brow deepened. "I never really thought about it, but I guess so." She chewed her lip. "I confess I was hurt when they didn't offer me the job they were planning to give Jordan. Even though I probably wouldn't have taken it if they had. I wanted to show them what I could achieve on my own."

She shook her head. "Which doesn't answer your question about why I never told them about you. About us."

"You don't have to—"

She pressed a finger to his lips, and he couldn't have said anything more even if all the words he'd ever learned hadn't just flocked from his head in a mass exodus.

"I think." She turned the words over slowly. "I was worried that they wouldn't approve of you." Her fingers brushed back and forth over the worn wood of the pier. He tried to ignore the gut punch of her words. He'd been right after all.

But she grabbed his hand in both of hers, and he had to look at her. "I was afraid you wouldn't approve of them. Wouldn't like them." Her gaze dropped to her lap. "And then you would all stop approving of me. Would stop loving me."

His heart opened wide, and he wanted to wrap her in it. Had she really thought anything could make him stop loving her?

"Soph." He lifted her chin until she had no choice but to meet his eyes. "My love for you was never conditional. You never had to earn it." Her eyes closed, and he waited for them to open again. He needed her to know this next part. "You still don't."

He slid his arms around her neck and brought his lips to hers, letting the knowledge that he still loved her wash over them both.

In the distance, a boat's horn sounded a warning, but they ignored it.

Chapter 26

Sophie sat upright in the passenger seat of Spencer's truck as he drove toward her parents' house. It was late—the clock on the dashboard showed well past midnight—but she was anything but sleepy. Every fiber of her being zinged with the awareness of Spencer's nearness. It scared her, her desire to be with him, but it also exhilarated her. His strong hand intertwined with her fingers.

She felt warm, protected.

Loved.

It was a feeling she'd missed. A feeling she'd longed for without realizing it.

She squeezed Spencer's hand, and he offered her that soft smile that made her stomach flip as if caught in a wave. He squeezed back.

For the fifth time, she opened her mouth to tell him she still loved him, too. But the same fear that had held her back the first time seemed to have clamped down on her vocal cords.

"Spencer?"

"Hmm." He lifted her hand to his lips and placed a gentle kiss onto her palm.

She closed her eyes. He was making this so easy for her. So why was it so hard?

"There's something I want to tell you."

He waited, and it took her three tries to swallow. She was going to say it this time.

But instead of the *I love you* she wanted to say, what came out was, "Why didn't you come after me?"

Spencer's head jerked toward her. "What?"

Sophie stared out the windshield. She could feel his gaze swiveling from her to the road and back again.

"That day. When you asked me to marry you. You didn't try to stop me when I left. You never called me. Never came after me." Her voice broke, but she pushed on. "Was I not worth it?"

She knew she wasn't being fair. His father had been sick. He'd had a lot to worry about. And she was the one who had walked away from him.

But still, she'd waited for his call begging her to reconsider. Telling her they didn't have to get married but that he still wanted to be with her. But it had never come.

The truck slowed, and Spencer pulled onto the shoulder, bringing it to a stop.

She shifted to look at him. "What are you doing?"

He slid the gear into park and flipped on the four-way flashers. "I need you to hear me when I say this." He angled in his seat so that he was facing her head-on. She felt the need to press toward him and draw back at the same time, but his eyes locked her in place.

He reached for her hand, and she let him take it. "You don't know how many times I almost called you, almost drove to see you. Not coming after you was the hardest thing I've ever done." His voice was ragged. "But when I got home and looked around at what I had to offer you, I knew it wasn't enough. I knew you deserved more. So I let you go."

His hands slid up her arms, pulling her to him. "It was the biggest mistake I ever made." His voice was muffled by her hair.

Her arms went around him, too.

This was where she belonged.

With him.

Forever.

The word didn't scare her anymore.

She lifted her head and brought her lips to his.

Because she knew now.

Her home wasn't in Hope Springs. Or in Chicago. It was with Spencer. Wherever that took her.

Sophie paced the kitchen, running her fingers along the worn edges of Nana's journal. She'd read it cover to cover twice already, and the words were so precious to her that she couldn't wait to go through them a third time. But she knew someone else who needed them more right now.

She'd been waiting for Mom to appear for her morning cup of coffee for twenty minutes already. Maybe she'd missed her. If Mom was working on a big deal, she might have slipped out early.

Sophie couldn't wait to get on with her day. She'd been so busy cleaning at Nana's house yesterday that she'd only gotten to see Spencer for a few minutes when he stopped by to help her haul some of the bigger furniture to a local women's shelter. But they'd made plans for dinner tonight, and she and Vi were going to try to finish up the work at Nana's before then.

But she couldn't do any of that until she gave this to Mom.

Sophie eyed the counter. Maybe she should leave the journal there for Mom to find. It'd be easier anyway.

But no, there were things she had to say to Mom. Things she'd promised Spencer she'd say. Things she'd promised herself.

She poured herself another cup and set to pacing again. Finally, the click of Mom's heels announced her arrival. Sophie filled a second mug and passed it to Mom the moment she entered the room.

Mom eyed the outstretched mug, then took it from her hand, setting it on the counter to doctor it with the raspberry creamer Sophie had gotten out for her.

"Thanks," Mom finally said after she'd taken her first sip. "To what do I owe such service?"

If Mom noticed that Sophie's laugh was forced and nervous, she didn't let on.

"I just thought—" Sophie moved to the table. "I thought we could talk for a few minutes. Maybe?" She gestured toward the other chair, trying not to seem like a little girl seeking her mother's approval.

Mom's glance flicked to the clock on the stove. "I have about ten minutes before I absolutely have to leave. We're placing an offer this morning."

"That's great." Sophie waved a hand, barely listening. She had to clear her head for what she wanted to say.

Mom sat, sipping her coffee. Sophie stared at her mug, gathering her thoughts. Mom tapped her fingers on the table, and Sophie gritted her teeth.

Here went nothing.

"The thing is, Mom, I've realized lately how much of my life—how much of my energy—I've dedicated to trying to win your approval and Dad's."

Mom's mouth drew into the straight line Sophie had always associated with disapproval, and she quailed.

But she made herself push forward. "I think especially after Jordan—"

Mom sucked in a sharp breath and pushed to her feet.

Sophie slid her chair back and stood, too, blocking the exit. "I know you don't want to talk about Jordan. Or Nana."

Mom's face had gone whiter than the marble countertop.

"But at some point, you're going to have to face your feelings. Trust me, you can only keep them shoved into a corner of your heart and shut yourself off from the world for so long." She held out the journal to Mom. "When you're ready, I think this will help. Nana left it for me, but I think it's really a love letter to you, too."

Mom's lips trembled as she read the cover of the journal. Sophie stepped closer, until Mom had no choice but to take the journal or push Sophie backward.

She took it in a shaky hand.

"And if you ever wanted to talk—about anything—I'm here." Sophie's whisper cut through her ache for Mom to wrap her in her arms.

But Mom didn't move.

Sophie took a step back, blowing out a long breath. She'd said what she'd come to say.

But when she reached the hallway, she realized there was something else she wanted Mom to know.

"I love you, Mom."

Mom's silence followed her down the hall and out the door.

Chapter 27

The diamond was smaller than he remembered, but it still sparkled.

Spencer's hand trembled slightly as he held the tiny box out in front of him, toward the mirror. The ring had been buried in the bottom of his sock drawer for five years. Could he really present it to her again? Risk her rejection again?

But after the last few days, he knew. She was the woman he was meant to be with, and he wasn't going to let his fear—or hers—stop him. He would just have to make her see how much he loved her. How he would spend the rest of his life doing anything for her.

Even if it meant leaving the farm he loved.

If that's what she wanted, he'd give it up in a heartbeat. The farm wasn't his life.

She was.

"Hey, Spence—"

Spencer snapped the case shut and whirled away from the mirror at the sound of his brother's voice. But based on the open-mouthed stare Tyler speared him with, he'd been too slow.

"So." Tyler pushed into the room uninvited and plopped onto Spencer's bed.

"Come in," Spencer muttered, shoving the ring box back into his drawer. But when he turned to confront Tyler's hard glare, he wished he still had something to occupy his hands.

"What?" He didn't mean to snap, but he hated the mix of pity and understanding Tyler was directing at him.

"You're not really going to go down that road again, are you?"

"What road?"

Tyler pointed toward the dresser, and Spencer could swear he was using X-ray vision to see right through the wood to the spot where he'd nestled the ring.

Spencer planted his feet in a defensive stance. "I was thinking about it."

Tyler stood and walked toward the door, then wheeled around and strode toward Spencer. He clapped a brotherly hand on Spencer's shoulder. "Spencer, do you really want to put yourself through that again? Emma told me how hard it was for you to get over that woman the first time and—"

"Her name is Sophie." Spencer's fingers clenched into a fist, and his shoulders tensed.

"Easy." Tyler held up his hands. "I know her name. And I like her, I really do. She's good with the twins. And she's nice and funny."

"Then what's the problem?"

"But that doesn't mean she's worth risking your heart for again. Just because everything seems perfect right now doesn't mean it's going to stay that way. And what about the farm? We should at least talk about that before you get carried away and do something irrational."

But it wasn't irrational. It felt like the most rational thing he'd done in months, years maybe—following his heart instead of his duty.

"Let me ask you something." Spencer pinned Tyler with his stare. They hadn't talked much about Julia since Tyler came back. Spencer had wanted to give his brother the space he needed to deal with everything.

But now, he needed to know.

"Let's say Julia showed up here tomorrow. Or next week. Or three years from now. And she told you she was sorry. That she still loved you. Could you really walk away from that second chance?"

Tyler opened his mouth, then slammed it shut and stalked out of the room.

"That's what I thought," Spencer called after him.

Sophie laid another Christmas decoration from her grandmother's collection into the box of items she wanted to keep. The basement was almost empty, and then she'd be done cleaning out the house. She'd have no more excuses to stay in Hope Springs—except her own desire.

"That nutcracker is too cute." Vi bounced down the steps after a trip upstairs with a box full of items she was going to sell in her store.

Sophie held it out to her. "Better start another box for the store."

"You don't want it?" Vi pushed her wild curls out of her face and snapped a ponytail around them.

"Are you kidding? These things kind of creep me out." She gave an exaggerated shudder. "Anyway, I already have way more stuff than I can fit in my apartment."

Unless she didn't go back to her apartment. If she stayed . . .

"Hey, Soph, can I ask you something?" Violet's voice was quiet, serious, as if she'd sensed the direction of Sophie's thoughts.

Sophie waited, even though she already knew the question.

"What are you doing? With Spencer, I mean."

Sophie grabbed a snow globe off the shelf and examined it. Inside, two figures stood with their arms around each other in the yard of a cozy-looking house. "Honestly? I don't know."

Vi passed her a sheet of newspaper to wrap the snow globe. "I think you need to figure it out. Before you get his hopes up. He doesn't deserve to be hurt again."

Sophie blinked back a sudden wave of emotion. Didn't her friend realize she already knew that? Spencer deserved only good things. Only everything. "The last thing I want is to hurt him."

"I know." Vi plucked a glass ornament off the farthest reaches of the shelving unit. "But if you let him think there's something there, that you—"

"I still love him, Vi."

Vi fumbled the ornament. She caught it just before it smashed to the floor.

"You do?" Vi's smile was genuine, but Sophie felt a pang for her friend. Vi had never doubted her love for Cade, would never have chosen to let him go, but she hadn't been given a choice in the matter.

"I mean—" Vi set the ornament gingerly into the box. "I knew that, but I was afraid you wouldn't realize it until it was too late."

Sophie could only grin at her friend, who'd always been better at reading her than Sophie was at reading herself.

"So does that mean you're staying? You're not going back to Chicago?"

Sophie lifted her arms helplessly. She had no idea what it meant. Only that she was open to the possibility. "Maybe?"

Vi squealed and dove at her for a hug. "I'll take maybe."

Sophie returned the hug, but a new bout of questions assailed her.

"Uh oh." Violet pulled back. "I know that look."

"What look?"

"The one that says you're not sure you're making the right decision."

Sophie gnawed at her bottom lip. "Well, am I? I mean, am I crazy to consider giving up a job a lot of people would kill for, a life in the city I've always dreamed of living in, to come back to the one place I've always wanted to escape? I mean, what if Spencer doesn't want— What if he doesn't feel—?"

Vi laughed gently. "If you can't see how Spencer feels, you're denser than I thought."

"Yeah, but—" Sophie ignored her friend's teasing tone. "I don't deserve a second chance. Not after how I left things last time." She passed a hand over her eyes. "I don't really deserve a second chance with you, either, come to think of it."

Vi shook her head. "You know, Soph, for a smart woman, you sure are slow sometimes."

"Hey." But Sophie waited for her to go on.

"You've always worked so hard to prove yourself, to earn everything, to be the best. But some things you don't have to earn. They're just . . . gifts."

"But—"

Vi raised a hand to silence her. "That's the thing, there are no buts. I forgive you and so does Spencer."

Sophie looked away and wiped at her eyes. What had she done to deserve such amazing people in her life? According to Vi, nothing, apparently. They were a gift. One she treasured.

Vi's arms wrapped her in another hug. "As far as staying, I can't tell you if it's the right move or if it's crazy." She let Sophie go and wrapped another ornament in tissue paper. "Have you prayed about it?"

Sophie stared at her friend. How did she always know what to do? Of course she should pray. Had it really been so long since prayer—since God—had been a regular part of her life that she never thought of it anymore?

"I will," she promised. She grabbed the tape gun and ran it across the last box. "There. Now I have four days free. What should we do?"

Vi ogled her. "*You* should get yourself over to Spencer's and tell him how you feel."

"Oh, but—" In theory, yes, it was what she was dying to do. But now that she faced the possibility of actually doing it—impossible.

Her phone blared, making them both jump.

Sophie set down the box she'd been about to haul upstairs. Her heart accelerated. She had no idea what to say to Spencer, and she didn't want to do it over the phone.

"Tell him," Vi chanted as she grabbed Sophie's abandoned box and started up the stairs.

Sophie tried to take a calming breath, but it was only halfway in when her eyes fell on the name on her screen.

Chase.

She deflated. She should let it go to voice mail. But she'd ignored every single one of his calls since she'd sent him back to Chicago. It was time to face up to him.

"It's a good thing you decided to answer this time." Chase's voice was hard-edged.

Sophie's stomach clenched. She hadn't exactly expected a warm greeting, but his anger threw her.

"I'm sorry, Chase. I've been busy here and—"

"I don't need your apologies. I just called to tell you that you need to be back here tomorrow morning."

"Tomorrow? But—"

"Or don't bother to come back at all."

"What?" Sophie tried to figure out exactly what he was saying. Was he threatening her? "If this is about—"

"It's not about anything, Sophie." Chase's voice softened. "I got the VP position, and my first job as VP is to call to inform you that company policy states that vacations of more than three days must be approved a month in advance, and since yours wasn't—"

Heat flooded Sophie's chest. "If you think burying my grandmother was—"

"As we understand it, the funeral was last week. The extra time off this week is a vacation. And your vacation is done." He hesitated a beat. "So will I see you tomorrow at eight, or should I have Tina pack up your office?"

Sophie pinched the bridge of her nose. This wasn't really happening. Sure, she'd been considering leaving Chicago, but it wasn't a decision she could make this moment, this way. She needed to think it through. Talk to Spencer. Figure out what she really wanted.

"Sophie?" Chase's voice held a trace of impatience.

"I don't— I don't know." She hung up before he could remind her what she'd be giving up if she didn't return.

Her hand shook as she dropped the phone to the makeshift workbench Nana had fashioned out of sawhorses and an old countertop. She braced herself against the counter, but it shifted and toppled to the ground with a crash.

"Everything okay down there?" Vi's voice was followed by her hurried footsteps on the stairs.

"Yeah." Sophie kicked at a disfigured sawhorse as she picked up her shattered phone. "No."

Vi moved closer, concern in the lines around her mouth. "Did Spencer not—?"

"It wasn't Spencer. It was my boss. He said I have to be back by tomorrow or I'm out a job."

"What?" Vi's hands slammed to her hips. "He can't do that. He—"

"Actually, he can." She'd been so excited to get this job that she'd read through the company handbook four times before her first day. Chase was right about the vacation policy.

"Okay, then. Why don't you quit? You said you were thinking about staying anyway, and—"

"*Thinking* about. Not going to do it this very minute." Sophie rubbed at her temples. Why did everything have to get more complicated the minute she thought she had things figured out? "I have a lot to consider. I haven't even talked to Spencer yet, and—"

"So go talk to him." Vi grabbed her arm and dragged her up the basement steps toward the front door.

"I don't have time. If I'm going to be back in the office by tomorrow morning, I have to take off right now."

"Make time." Vi's voice was firm.

"I can call him when I get to Chicago." She glanced at the splintered screen in her hand. "Once I get a new phone."

The thought left a hole in Sophie's heart, but what else was she supposed to do? "I can always come back. It's not like I'll be stuck there forever."

"Sophie Olsen." Vi's dark eyes flashed. "We both know if you run back to Chicago, you won't come home. And sure, you'll save your job. But you might lose everything that really matters."

"I'm sorry, Vi. This isn't how I wanted to leave." She leaned in and gave Vi a quick hug, then pushed out the door and jumped into her car before she could see the look of betrayal she was sure Vi wore.

Chapter 28

Spencer lifted his shirt to wipe at the sweat dripping from his face. He jogged across the yard toward the house. He should have just enough time to shower before Sophie arrived. It'd taken all afternoon, but everything was finally ready. Using the ATV to haul the bench from his workshop to the hidden blossom tree had been a bear, but it was totally worth it. It was the perfect spot to do this—to carry on the family tradition.

He'd pack a picnic, they'd take the ATV to the clearing, enjoy dinner together. And then, on the bench he'd made for her, he'd tell her he wanted forever with her.

"Hey, Spencer." Dad's voice from behind caught him as he was about to open the door.

He turned. Dad was looking so much better it was amazing. Probably thanks in large part to the fact that Mom wouldn't let them say a word to him about how things were going on the farm or about their decision. Not that they'd made one yet.

But Spencer hoped to know more after tonight. If Sophie said yes to him—*please, Lord, let her say yes*—they'd make the decision together. And he'd be willing to do whatever she was comfortable with.

"What's with you?" Dad reached the steps and thrust a plastic dish into his hands. "Here, your mother sent this."

Spencer took the dish, barely glancing at the cookies inside.

"Nothing's with me. What are you doing here?"

His father pushed past him into the house. "I came to talk to you about the farm."

"Yeah, Dad, I haven't made my decision yet. I might know more after tonight, but . . ." Spencer pushed a hand through his hair.

"Well, that's what I came to tell you." His father grabbed the container back out of Spencer's hand and snatched a cookie. "Don't tell your mother." He took a bite of the cookie and closed his eyes. "Oh, that's good."

Spencer checked the time. Sophie would be here in ten minutes. "Look, Dad, can we talk about this another time? I kind of have plans."

Dad sniffed at the air, then moved into the kitchen, like a dog following a scent trail. "Is that fried chicken I smell?"

"Yeah." Spencer followed his father, trying not to let his exasperation show. "Sophie's coming over, so . . ."

"That's great. Maybe I'll hang out. I haven't seen her in a while. She brought me flowers, you know."

Spencer's mouth worked. Having Dad here when Sophie arrived was not part of the plan. "Dad—"

His father laughed and winked. "I'm leaving already." He slugged Spencer on the shoulder. "I just wanted you to know that if you decide not to buy, we'll be okay. We got an offer today."

Spencer blinked at his father. "An offer? I thought you were going to wait to put it on the market until Tyler and I decided."

His father held up a hand. "Before you go getting all offended, I didn't put it on the market. I don't even know how they heard about it. But it's a good offer. Really good."

"How good?" Spencer's eyes narrowed. Was this Dad's way of telling him he'd rather sell outside the family?

"It's good. I'm not going to name numbers right now because I don't want you to feel pressured to meet it if you do decide to buy. But just know that you shouldn't feel obligated to buy just to help me out."

"Who's the offer from?"

His father shrugged. "A development firm. Olsen, I think. They want to develop it into a resort or something. Condos, maybe. I don't remember the exact details."

But Spencer had stopped listening. "Olsen?"

Dad nodded, snatching another cookie. "I'll go so you can get ready for your date." At the door, he turned. "Tyler mentioned that you were planning to ask a certain question tonight. Think he wanted me to stop you. But sometimes you have to let go of the past to have the future you dream of." His sigh was deep. "Just like me and this farm."

But Spencer couldn't think about the past or the future right now. All he could think about was Sophie. He'd been willing to give up everything for her. Only it turned out she'd already made that decision for him. All to make her parents a few bucks.

Chapter 29

Sophie couldn't stop the bouncing of her leg against the car's seat, the drumming of her fingers on the wheel, the slamming of her heart against her rib cage.

It'd taken her all of ten minutes to pack up her stuff at her parents' house. A mix of relief and regret swirled in her gut at the fact that neither had been home. She'd left a note, promising to come back soon. A promise she already doubted she'd keep. Not that her parents would care.

Vi's words hadn't stopped playing through her head since she'd left Nana's. *We both know if you run back to Chicago, you won't come home.* She wanted to deny it, but the past two weeks had felt so much like a dream. Maybe it was best if she kept it that way. Dreams couldn't disappoint the way real life could.

Sophie slowed as she drove through the downtown. A young couple stood arm-in-arm on the pier, two children pressed against their legs. She had to look away to keep the wave of longing from overtaking her.

The clock on the dashboard caught her eye. She was supposed to have been at Spencer's fifteen minutes ago. She hated the thought of him standing there, waiting for her.

Realizing she'd run away from him again.

No.

She couldn't do that to him.

Not this time.

She pressed her foot to the brake, drawing a sharp honk from the car behind her. She lifted a hand in apology, then took a hard left.

Vi was right. She had to talk to Spencer. See where his head was. Where his heart was. If he wanted her to stay, well, then she wouldn't have to worry about whether she had a job to go back to.

And if he didn't—she could drive all night to get back by morning if she needed to.

The thought that he might not want her to stay—that he might tell her to hurry back to Chicago because she was too late here—was almost enough to make her drive right past his house. But she was done running from her feelings. She'd see this through, no matter what that meant for her heart—no matter what kinds of feelings she'd have to deal with as a result.

By the time she pulled into the now-familiar driveway of Hidden Blossom, she felt calmer, more at ease, than she had in months.

She didn't know what she was going to say or how Spencer would respond, but she could almost picture his huge smile, the way he'd wrap his arms around her and kiss her in that slow, sweet way he did. The way he'd ask her to stay.

The second the engine stopped, she sprang out of the car. In her tennis shoes, it was an easy jog across the lawn. The clean air buoyed her as she knocked.

A moment later, the door pulled open.

She squinted against the sun that hovered just above the edge of the house's roofline. She made out his dark shirt and jeans first. "Sorry I'm late. Something came up and—"

Her words died as her gaze fell on his face. His jaw was set, his eyes hard. He pushed out the door. She took a step to the side as his presence filled the whole porch. The loathing in his expression was more than she could bear, and she shifted her gaze to the edge of the porch, where newly opened azaleas bobbed in the gentle breeze.

"Hey." She tried to keep her voice light, but his glare made it hard.

"You told your parents the farm was for sale." It wasn't a question.

Her eyes jumped to his in surprise. "Yeah. Did they make an offer?" Good thing she hadn't quit yet. Maybe he wanted to move to Chicago.

"Why would you do that?" He sounded like a hurt little boy, and Sophie moved closer, but he stepped back.

She pursed her lips. Couldn't he see she'd done him a favor? "I thought it would make things easier for you. I know you have this inflated sense of duty, and I respect you for that. But I didn't want to see you strap yourself to a place that was about to fail."

Spencer folded his arms across his chest, a barrier between them. "You didn't do it for me, Soph." His voice was quiet but sharp. "You did it for you."

Sophie shook her head. How could he not understand this was for him?

"No point in denying it. You've made it clear plenty of times that your parents' approval means more to you than anything else. Than me." He thrust the words at her like knife jabs, and she wanted to hold out a hand like a shield, but he kept going. "You never thought the life of a farmer was good enough. Never thought I was good enough."

Sophie reared back. Is that what he really thought of her?

Her mind went blank. She opened and closed her mouth, then turned away. It had been a mistake to come. One she'd regret for the rest of her life.

"You want to know the ironic thing, Soph?" Spencer gave a sharp, humorless chuckle. "I was going to ask you what you wanted me to do with the farm. I was going to offer to give it up for you. If that's what you wanted. All I wanted was a life with you. But you've made it clear how you feel about a life with me. So I guess I'm free to make this decision for myself."

Sophie bit the inside of her cheeks, hard. She should tell him he was wrong. That she'd done it because she loved him. But what if he was right? What if she'd told her parents about the farm for her own selfish reasons?

She ignored the sting at the back of her throat. "I'm sorry, Spencer. For everything. I actually just came by to tell you that I have to get back to Chicago. My boss expects me in the morning. So I'm going to have to cancel our dinner."

Spencer froze, his eyes locked on her face. She waited, her breath caught in her throat. Even after everything he'd said, some small part of her still hoped he'd ask her to stay.

But when he looked away, she knew.

She stepped to the lawn. "Bye, Spencer."

Somehow, she managed to keep the tears at bay until his farm was out of sight.

Everything in Spencer told him to go after her.

Everything.

But he resisted. She had betrayed him. She had no interest in a life with him. And she'd been planning to leave all along.

He ripped the door open and barreled into the house.

Inside, the smell of the fried chicken taunted him. He pulled it off the counter and dumped it into the trash.

When he sat, something pressed against his thigh.

He shoved his hand into his pocket and ripped out the ring box. He moved to throw it into the trash, too.

But at the last minute, he pulled his hand back.

Instead, he opened the junk drawer and tossed it in there.

That's what his proposal would have been to her, anyway.

Chapter 30

Sophie lifted the hair off the back of her neck, seeking any hint of a cooling breeze. The Chicago summer had been unbearably hot, and the concrete jungle offered little shade. She longed to throw on a pair of shorts and a t-shirt and lounge along the lake, but that wasn't going to happen.

In the two months since she'd returned, she'd been pulling twice her weight, trying to reestablish her loyalty. Earn a shot at the next promotion, since she'd blown the last one. That's what happened when you let your heart get in the way.

The only bright spots in her weeks had been Sunday mornings. She'd found a charming little church where she could let go of all the cares of the world for an hour and just focus on worshipping. Last Sunday, after church, she'd found herself confiding to the white-haired pastor that she felt lost. He'd given her the same encouragement Vi had months ago—pray. Only this time, she had listened. She'd spent hours that afternoon walking along the lake. *I don't know your plans, Lord, and it scares me to give over control of my life, my future. Help me to trust you to lead me to the life you know is right for me.*

The words of Nana's journal still burned in her heart, and she'd prayed about that, too—about finding her worth in God and nowhere else.

The words still had a grip on her as she forced herself to put one foot in front of the other now. All week, it had gotten harder and harder to go to work. Everything she saw, everything she did, seemed to be nudging her toward where she really wanted to be.

Like the leaves that hung limp and listless in the humid air. They made her think of the rows and rows of trees in Spencer's orchard rustling in the cool lake breeze, raining cherry petals around her. When had she been happier?

She pushed through the doors of the office building, shivering in the sudden artificial cold of the air conditioning. As she squeezed onto the nearly full elevator, she pushed down a surge of panic at being in the confined space with so many people. She tried to direct her thoughts to something more pleasant. But they fell on their default: the memories of Spencer that lingered like a kiss.

Stop it. Thinking about Spencer isn't going to help you move on.

Sophie focused on taking deep breaths until the elevator stopped on her floor. By the time she stepped out, she was calm. Focused. Ready to get to work.

Chase accosted her the moment she stepped through the office doors. He pushed a coffee into her hands, along with a folder bulging with papers.

"There's a snag in the Hudson project. I need you on it right away. We can't lose this one."

Sophie took a swig of the coffee, yanking the mug from her mouth as the hot liquid scalded her tongue. She ignored the burn and opened the folder. But the renderings blurred in front of her. The folder seemed to weigh her down, root her to the spot.

A sudden certainty slammed into her. She didn't want this life. She'd made it her dream because she'd thought it was what would make her parents proud, earn their approval. But if she was honest with herself, this had never made her happy.

"I'm done." She said it so softly she wasn't sure anyone had heard. "I'm done." She said it louder this time. Like she meant it.

Chase gave her a bemused smile. "What do you mean, you're done? We've got a few more things to do on this one before we can call it finished."

"No. I mean I'm done. With this. All of it. I quit."

She set her coffee cup on the nearest desk and spun on her heel. She was at the office door before she realized the enormity of what she was doing. But it was the right thing.

Chase grabbed her elbow as she was about to hit the elevator button. "Don't do this, Sophie." She let him lead her to the large bank of windows that overlooked the bustling sidewalk. The crammed street. "You're upset about something. I can see that. But don't ruin your career over it."

Sophie offered a soft smile. She and Chase had worked past the initial awkwardness after her return, and she now considered him not quite a friend—but the closest thing she had to one in the city. She appreciated his concern.

"I'm not upset. I just realized that this"—she gestured around the luxurious office—"it's not right for me."

"That's fine. I get it. But if you walk out like this, you're never going to find a position with another firm. Stay on until you get another job. I'll write you a recommendation."

Sophie shook her head. "You don't understand. I don't want another job. This isn't what I was made to do. I only did it because—" She paused. How did she explain? "Well, it's a long story, but let's just say I'm not passionate about it the way you are."

Chase wrinkled his nose. "So what will you do?"

Sophie bit her lip. The truth was, she wasn't sure. But for some reason that didn't bother her. "Go home for a while. See if there might be something for me there." *Or someone.*

Chase studied her for another minute, as if unsure what to make of her. Then he leaned over and gave her a quick, semi-awkward hug. "Take care of yourself."

Sophie stepped onto the elevator and offered a small wave.

She may not know what she wanted to do with her life.

But she knew who she wanted to share it with.

If it wasn't too late.

Chapter 31

Spencer jiggled little Jeremiah on his lap as he signed his name for the twentieth time.

"Just a few more papers," their banker said. Spencer groaned. He'd also said that forty-five minutes ago. But he was grateful the man had been willing to come out to the house to do the closing paperwork. He couldn't imagine trying to corral these two energy balls in a bank.

He passed the paper to Tyler so his brother could add his signature.

"You're sure about this?" Spencer studied Tyler for any signs of a change of heart.

Tyler snatched the paper out of Jonah's grabbing hand and gave him a clean sheet and a crayon instead. "Would you stop asking me that? I said I was sure."

"Sorry." Spencer tapped his pen against the table. "It's just that you used to be so dead set against this place. I want to make sure you're not doing this out of some sense of obligation or something."

"Have you ever known me to do anything out of a sense of obligation?" Tyler signed his name next to Spencer's on the closing documents. "That's your territory."

Spencer grunted as he signed his name again. But the truth was, he wasn't doing this out of any "inflated sense of duty" as Sophie had accused him. He really did love this land and the legacy it represented. He wanted it to be here to pass on to his children someday. Assuming his heart ever recovered enough from Sophie to meet someone else and start a family. But even if he didn't, at least it would go to his nephews.

"Anyway." Tyler grabbed the next form to sign. "This place has a way of growing on a person."

"Some people, maybe," Spencer muttered.

His brother was watching him, but Spencer concentrated on scanning the forms in front of him.

"Are you just going to make all these veiled references to Sophie for the rest of our lives without ever actually talking about her?"

Spencer shrugged. It seemed to be working for him so far.

"You should call her." Tyler slid another form back to the banker.

Spencer snorted. "Says the guy who told me not to propose again. Learn to quit when you're ahead."

"Yeah, about that." Tyler scrubbed a hand across his buzzed hair. "I may have been wrong. I was projecting my own feelings about Julia onto your situation. And anyway, you were right. If I had another chance, I'd take it." Tyler nudged Spencer's phone closer to him. "Just call. It's clear you're miserable without her."

"I'm not miserable." He scratched his signature across yet another form. Would they never be done with this blasted paperwork? He had other things to do. Namely, escape his brother's interrogation.

Tyler let out a disbelieving *humph*. "Boys, is your uncle Spencer happy?"

Both boys looked at him. Ridiculous. Now he was being psychoanalyzed by three year olds?

Jonah shook his head, his expression somber. "Aunt Sophie gone."

Jeremiah nodded his agreement. "When coming back?"

Tyler cleared his throat. His grip on the pen in his hand tightened. Spencer understood. It was the same question the twins had asked about their mother every day for the first month and a half they'd been here.

The banker coughed lightly. "Last one." As soon as they'd signed, he held out a hand to shake each of theirs. "Congratulations." In spite of their argument, Spencer grinned at Tyler. They were really doing this. Together.

Spencer ushered the banker to the front door, thanking him again for making the process relatively painless. If only he had a series of papers Spencer could sign to guarantee he'd get over Sophie.

He'd been working at it all summer. But with no success. Every time he closed his eyes, he saw her expression when she'd turned away from him that last time. She'd looked so . . . broken. That was the only word for it.

Only days before that, he'd promised his love for her was unconditional. But the moment she'd done something he didn't like—didn't approve of—he'd sent her away. What kind of example of Christ-like love was that?

"Hey, you got any tape?" Tyler called from the kitchen. "Jonah wants to wrap up his picture for grandma and grandpa."

"Yeah, check the junk drawer." Spencer gave the land—their land—one last look before closing the door. If anyone had told him ten years ago he'd be buying the farm with his brother—not to mention living with him—he'd have laughed in their face. He'd all but written Tyler off when he left. But it had only taken two months for his brother and nephews to find a place in his life. Even if his house sometimes felt overcrowded and not so much his own anymore. He couldn't imagine things any other way.

"Ah, Spencer?" Tyler's voice carried to him as he made his way to join them in the kitchen.

"Yeah?" But he froze in the kitchen doorway.

Tyler held a little black box. He'd opened it and was staring at the ring inside.

Spencer snatched the box out of Tyler's hand, opened the cupboard under the sink, and chucked the box in the trash can there.

But Tyler pushed past him and grabbed it out. He held the box toward Spencer, but Spencer refused to take it.

"Look, Spencer." Tyler closed his hand around the ring box. "Maybe it's time to put your pride aside. You clearly still love her. And if you wait, eventually it will be too late."

"It's already too late." Spencer spat the words at his brother. Why couldn't Tyler learn when to butt out? "I've just committed myself to this farm. You think that's the kind of life she can accept?"

"I think—" Tyler set the ring box on the counter. "I think if she's the woman you've made her out to be, then none of this"—he gestured at their surroundings—"will matter to her. I think you've convinced yourself you can't give her the life you think she wants because it means you don't have to put yourself out there. But what if her lifestyle isn't what she cares about? What if all she cares about is you?"

Spencer stared at the box.

Tyler meant well.

But he was wrong about what Sophie wanted.

Wasn't he?

"Hello?" The gruff male voice on the other end of the phone sounded irritated.

And no wonder. This was the third time in a row Spencer had called. He couldn't make himself believe that Sophie had moved on so quickly, that he'd really meant that little to her.

Hearing a man answer her phone just once should have been enough to convince him, but apparently he was a slow learner.

"Sorry, wrong—"

"Look, buddy, who are you looking for?" The dude sounded big, his voice rough and deep. Not at all the smooth, suave voice of the kind of man he'd expect Sophie to be with.

Spencer gritted his teeth. What else did he have to lose at this point? "Sophie Olsen?"

"Never heard of her."

Spencer huffed in disbelief. "This is her number."

"No, this is my number." The guy's voice softened. "It's a new number, so maybe . . ."

She had a new number. Which meant she wasn't with this guy. It might not be too late.

But as Spencer clicked off the phone, his elation dissipated.

If she had a new number, he had no way to contact her.

He rubbed his temples. What now?

He'd spent every moment of the week since Tyler had dug the ring out of the junk drawer praying about what to do. He'd been so sure this was God's answer. Contact her. Tell her he loved her. Ask her to give him another chance.

But now he couldn't even find her.

He picked up his phone and did a search for development firms in Chicago. But there were so many. What had she said the name of it was? Something with a heart in it, he was pretty sure.

He scrolled through the listings until he came to Heartland. Could be right.

Without letting himself think, he dialed the number.

"Heartland," a smoothly professional voice answered. What had he expected? That she'd answer her own phone?

"Yes." He tried to sound official. "Sophie Olsen, please."

A pause on the other end. He could hear papers shuffling and wished he could push himself through the telephone to see what was going on there. To see Sophie in her office.

"I'm sorry. There is no Sophie Olsen at this firm."

Spencer's thoughts spun. Another strike out. "I'm sorry I must have the wrong— I thought—" Why was he explaining himself to a complete stranger?

"A Sophie Olsen used to work here." The secretary's voice was almost conspiratorial. "She quit a few days ago."

Spencer pulled at his hair. He was so close. "Could you tell me how to contact her?"

"I'm sorry, I have no forwarding number. But I didn't get the impression she had another job lined up. I think she said something about moving."

Spencer's heart stopped. "Okay, thank you." He hung up without waiting for a reply. That was the end, then. If she was moving, there was no way he'd ever find her.

Unless—

He picked up his phone and scrolled to Violet's number.

"Hey, Spencer." Violet sounded wary. She'd spent the past two months trying to convince him that Sophie had been ready to stay in Hope Springs if he'd asked. But he hadn't believed her—or hadn't wanted to, not if it meant he'd been the one to ruin their chance of being together.

Last time Violet had brought Sophie up, Spencer had bitten her head off and said not to mention her again.

"Look, Violet, I'm sorry about last week. You were right. I do still want to be with her."

He expected a gasp or a cheer or at least some sort of reaction, but Violet was silent.

"Violet? Do you forgive me?" Had he ruined yet another relationship?

"Nothing to forgive. I knew you'd eventually come to your senses. You should call her."

"That's the thing. I tried, but some guy has her number now, and her firm said she quit and is moving."

There was a sharp inhale on the other end of the phone.

"So you didn't know?" Spencer dropped to the couch and cradled his head in his hands.

But he held on to one last shred of hope. "You said she wanted me to ask her to stay. Do you think there's any chance she's coming back here?" He couldn't take a breath as he waited for Violet to say yes, she thought that was exactly what Sophie was doing.

The silence stretched too long. Finally, Violet sighed. "I hope so, Spencer."

"But you don't think so." The words cut at Spencer's throat.

"No, I don't." Violet's voice was gentle. "I'm sorry."

Spencer almost hung up. But he forced himself to ask one more question.

"Do you have her last address?"

Chapter 32

Sophie sat up straighter in the driver's seat. It was as if she were seeing Hope Springs for the first time. The stores dotting the hillside, the boats dipping up and down in the marina, the lake, bathed in the pinks and oranges of sunset. This was her home. How had she ever doubted it?

A peaceful sensation washed over her. *Thank you for leading me back*, she breathed in silent prayer.

Even the sight of her parents' house didn't leave her with the same tension she'd felt two months ago when she'd come home. She pulled the car to a stop behind the garage and blew out a breath. She hadn't had the nerve to call ahead to let them know she was coming. And now she had to tell them that not only did she want to stay with them indefinitely, but she'd quit at the one thing she'd ever done to make them proud.

Her mother answered the door on the second ring. Her eyes widened at the sight of her daughter on her doorstep, but she took a step back to let Sophie in. "Sophie. This is a surprise." The way she said it, Sophie almost thought she might mean it was a pleasant surprise.

"Sorry to just show up like this." Sophie set her purse on the table in the entryway. She'd left the rest of her stuff in the car for now.

"You're always welcome here. You know that." Sophie stared at her mother. *Did* she know that?

"We were about to eat dinner. Come join us. There's plenty."

We? "Oh, if you have company, I can—"

"What are you talking about? It's just us. Come on, your father will be happy to see you. He thought it was kids selling cookies at the door."

Sophie gaped after her mother's retreating form. Her parents were both home? And eating dinner together? Was she in the right house?

Sophie followed Mom to the kitchen, where she was already pulling out another plate and glass.

"Hey, pumpkin." Sophie's father stood to give her a hug.

It took a moment for her to return it, she was so flabbergasted. "Hi, Dad."

Her mother dished a pile of spaghetti onto her plate and passed it to her. "So to what do we owe this surprise visit?"

Sophie took a big bite, chewing to give herself time to think. But in the end, there was no choice but to tell the truth. "Actually, it's a little more than a visit. I've decided to move back to Hope Springs." They both looked up from their plates in surprise. It was a new sensation, having both of her parents' eyes on her. "I'll find an apartment," she added quickly. "But I was hoping I could stay here until I do."

"What about your job?" Her mother had always been a straight-to-the-point kind of woman.

Sophie swallowed a drink of water. "I quit." She hated how meek her voice was. "I'm sorry. I know you guys are disappointed, but I couldn't—"

"What makes you think we're disappointed?" Her father shoved a bite in his mouth and pointed his fork at her.

"Well, I mean, first— And now I—" She fumbled. Tried again. "But I wasn't happy, and—"

Mom laid down her fork. "If you think being here in Hope Springs will make you happy, then that's what you should do."

Sophie lifted her head, searched Mom's eyes for the judgment she knew would come. But as far as she could tell, Mom was being sincere. Sophie dropped her head and focused on the table, running her fingers over the polished wood.

"Okay, thanks." She couldn't think of anything else to say. She'd been prepared to argue, to defend her choices, to walk away and find somewhere else to stay if she had to. But acceptance—that she wasn't prepared for.

"Do you have any thoughts about what you might do here?" Dad asked.

Sophie shook her head.

"We might have something, if you're interested." With one sentence, Mom offered her what she'd wanted her whole life. What she'd been striving for—their approval.

But she realized now, it wasn't what she needed. "Thanks, but I'm not sure yet what I want to do." Maybe she should tell them about Spencer, too, while they were in an accepting mood, but first she had to see how he felt—if he'd welcome her back as warmly as they had.

Mom got up and rummaged in the fridge, emerging a few seconds later with a cheesecake.

Sophie's mouth watered. "Is that from the Hidden Cafe?"

Her mother nodded. "We actually got it to celebrate."

Sophie looked from one to the other. What was the date? July twentieth. It wasn't either of their birthdays or their anniversary. Not that they usually celebrated that anyway.

"What's the occasion?"

Her parents looked at each other, and Sophie saw something pass between them that she hadn't seen in a long time. Her father laid his hand on top of her mother's, and Sophie fought to keep her mouth from dropping open. "It's been one month since we recommitted to our marriage."

"Recommitted to—?" What did that even mean?

"After you left last time, I read Nana's journal. And I kept thinking about what you said. About shutting the world out." Mom's eyes shone with tears, and Sophie could only stare as Dad tightened his grip on Mom's hand.

Sophie wanted to crawl under the table. She never should have talked to Mom that way. "I'm sorry, I had no right—"

Mom shook her head. "I'm glad you did. It opened my eyes to some things. We've been in counseling together, and it's"—she blew out a breath—"it's going well. We have a long way to go, but we're healing together. In a way we never did before. A way I never let us."

Sophie couldn't wrap her head around what was happening. It seemed impossible this was the same family she'd left two months ago.

"Actually, we wanted to call you, to see if maybe you'd want to talk. If maybe you could forgive us." Mom swiped at a fresh cascade of tears.

Dad cleared his throat. "We realize that a lot of things in our family fell apart after Jordan died." It was the first time Sophie had heard him use her brother's name since the day they'd buried him, and she swallowed against the sudden lump.

"I'm afraid you were the one who suffered a lot of the hurt and anger and confusion I was feeling. Maybe—" The uncertainty in Mom's voice unraveled Sophie, and she had to swipe at her own tears.

"Maybe you'd like to come to counseling with us sometime," Mom finished.

It took a moment before Sophie could answer. "Yeah. I'd like that."

A mixture of nerves and hope swirled in Sophie's belly.

This was what she'd come back to Hope Springs for. She felt wrung out from last night's emotional reunion with her parents, but in a way, it felt as if that was what she'd needed to be able to face this moment. She drove into Spencer's driveway, trying not to think of the last time she had pulled out of it. Trying not to remember how she'd left him. Again.

It was a lot to ask him to forgive her. To expect him to give her another chance.

But she wasn't going to be too proud to ask for it this time.

She frowned as she stopped in front of Spencer's house. His truck wasn't in the driveway. But her parents had assured her that they hadn't bought the property, after all. Which meant he'd have to be back sometime.

So she'd wait for him.

For as long as it took.

This time, she wasn't going anywhere.

Sophie parked and climbed out of the car, inhaling the soothing scents of cut grass and bee balm. She could stand here and just breathe this air all day.

The sound of little-boy giggles from the backyard drew her attention, and her lips lifted into a smile. She followed the sound and found Tyler chasing his sons across the lawn, tickling them whenever he caught them, then pretending to be defeated and let them go.

Jonah spotted her first and came running over, followed two steps behind by Jeremiah.

Sophie crouched to accept their hugs. Their sticky fingers were warm and welcoming on her bare arms.

"Where'd you go?" Jonah asked. "We missed you."

Sophie ruffled his downy hair. "Sorry about that, buddy. I missed you, too. I had to do some stuff in Chicago, but I'm back now."

"Chicago?" Jeremiah tipped his head at her. "What's that?"

"What are you doing here?" Tyler towered over her, frowning, and Sophie pushed to her feet.

"I'm—" Sophie faltered. She'd been sure Tyler would be on her side. "I came back," she finished lamely.

"I see that. But—"

"Wait, Tyler. Before you go telling me not to break your brother's heart again, let me just say I won't. *I won't.*" Her voice was firm. She was sure this time. "This is where I want to be. He's the one I want to be with. I'm not running anymore."

"Actually—" A slow grin tripped across Tyler's face. "I was just going to say that Spencer isn't here. He's in Chicago. Looking for you."

Chapter 33

After driving around the block three times, Spencer finally found a parking spot in front of the address Violet had given him.

Sophie's address. If she hadn't moved yet.

He whispered a quick prayer for guidance, then jumped out of his truck and leaned back, lifting a hand to shield his eyes from the glint of the sun off the skyscraper's glass. The building was exactly the kind of place Sophie would choose—all sleek lines and elegance.

He stopped himself from leaping back into his truck and hightailing it out of there. She might think this was the kind of place she belonged, but he knew better. He'd seen her in his workshop, running her hands over their bench. Watched her opening up to friends at the Hidden Cafe. Laughed with her, mud-covered and adorable, in his orchard. The Sophie he knew belonged with him. Whether she knew it yet or not.

Spencer squared his shoulders and marched to the glass doors at the front of the building.

Inside, he pulled up short in the marble-floored lobby. A large fountain in the middle of the room bubbled cheerfully. He squared his shoulders. He may not be able to offer her marble fountains, but he had a bubbling creek just for her.

"Can I help you, sir?"

Spencer turned toward the voice from the other side of the lobby and approached the reception desk. "I'm looking for Sophie Olsen. Could you direct me to her apartment?"

The burly man behind the desk frowned at him. "Do you know Ms. Olsen?"

"Of course I know her. I'm her— We're—" Spencer stopped. What were he and Sophie? They weren't exactly in a relationship right now. But they weren't nothing to each other, either. Spencer debated saying soul mates, but that would sound a little weird.

"I highly doubt that." The man behind the counter spoke as if he'd read Spencer's mind. "If you're so close to her, you'd know she doesn't live here anymore."

Spencer's shoulders fell and all the hope that had sustained him during the five-hour drive to Chicago slithered out of him. He'd known it was a long shot, but he'd been so sure that this was the Lord's plan for him.

"You wouldn't happen to have her new address?"

The look the man gave him said he wouldn't tell Spencer if he did.

He shuffled toward the fountain and sat down, hard, letting his fingers trail in the icy water. *Now what, Lord?*

The prospect of driving home exhausted him.

His phone pealed, but Spencer ignored it, letting it go to voice mail.

Two minutes later, it rang again.

The man behind the reception desk cleared his throat and shot him a pointed look.

Spencer pulled out his phone. Tyler.

His big brother probably wanted an update. Too bad he'd been wrong to think Sophie was sitting down here just waiting for him.

He answered the phone as he pushed out the building's front door.

The sun glared at him, and he ducked his head. "She's not here, Tyler. I was too late." His bitterness shocked even him.

"Spencer."

He froze. It wasn't Tyler.

"Sophie?" He hardly dared think it, and yet he knew her voice better than he knew his own.

"Hi." She sounded breathless and light and full of laughter. Spencer tipped his face toward the heavens, letting the warmth of the sun wash over him.

"Wait." His head snapped back to earth. "How are you on Tyler's phone? Where are you?"

"I'm in Hope Springs. I'm at your house."

Spencer's head spun. "But why?" She was moving to who knows where. So why was she in Hope Springs? At his house?

Sophie laughed again, and the sound filled him. "I was under the impression you'd be here."

"You were looking for me?" Spencer closed his eyes. Was this really happening?

"I was looking for you, Spencer." Her voice was soft, a gentle caress.

He leaned against the building. The elegant building she'd just moved out of. To go somewhere better, no doubt. "And then where are you going?"

Silence on the other end. So he'd hit the nail on the head then.

"I'm not going anywhere," she said after what felt like forever. "I'm staying right here."

Spencer pushed off the cool wall and strode toward his truck. "Then what am I still doing here?"

Chapter 34

Sophie watched the giant machine wrap its metal arms around the cherry tree. A canvas tarp stretched from the machine to circle the tree trunk like giant bat wings. With a vigorous shake, the cherries toppled from the tree into the tarp. A moment later, the machine's arms had retracted, folding up the tarp and neatly sending the cherries onto a conveyor belt that led to a series of cold-water tanks at the back of the truck. She plucked four cherries off the belt, then handed one each to Jonah and Jeremiah and popped another in her mouth.

"I saw that." Spencer smiled as he climbed down from the cherry picker and walked over.

She held out the last cherry. "It's okay. I held on to one as a bribe."

He took it but didn't eat it. Instead, he leaned down to give her a deep kiss. She wrapped her arms around his neck and pulled him closer. If she lived a hundred years, she'd never get tired of kissing this man.

"All right, enough of that." Tyler's mock-stern voice carried to them. "There are children here."

Sophie laughed as Spencer pulled away.

"Actually—" Tyler gave Spencer a look Sophie couldn't read. "These munchkins need some lunch anyway. How about we take a break?"

"Goodie!" Jonah cried. "Can we have Aunt Sophie mac 'n' cheese again?"

"Hey!" Tyler put on an offended face. "I can cook."

They'd been harvesting together all week, and Sophie had made the boys mac 'n' cheese two days in a row already. Apparently, the gloppy mess she made of it appealed to them more than their dad's burnt noodles.

"Sure." Sophie reached to grab their hands.

Spencer cleared his throat. "Actually, I was hoping we could have a picnic today."

"Yay!" Both boys danced around Spencer, chanting, "Picnic, picnic!"

"Boys!" Tyler had to yell to be heard over them. They both stopped and turned big eyes on him. "I think Uncle Spencer wants to have a picnic with just Aunt Sophie."

The boys directed their pitiful gazes at Spencer. Sophie gave his arm a light shove. There was no way he'd be able to resist them.

But he ruffled their hair and told them to have a good lunch.

"You can come next time," Sophie called after them as they followed their father toward the house, stopping to pick up the cherries that had fallen in the grass along the way.

"That was nice of your brother. To give us some time alone." They hadn't had much of that since Spencer had come rushing home from Chicago and swept her up in his arms. The harvest had kept them all busy. But Sophie had enjoyed every moment of it.

"Yeah, he's a prince," Spencer said wryly. He ducked his head into the cab of the cherry picker and emerged a few seconds later holding a picnic basket. "Actually, he's been a lifesaver. I don't think I could have bought this place without him." His eyes were on her, and she knew he was waiting. She'd already apologized for telling her parents to make an offer on the place. But she needed to say more.

"I'm glad you bought it, Spencer. It's your heritage. And I know how much you love it. Plus—" She plucked another cherry out of the water. "I really think you'll make it successful."

Spencer lashed the picnic basket to the ATV. "Thank you." He held a hand out to her, and she took it. "That means a lot."

They both climbed onto the vehicle.

"So where are we going?"

"You'll see." Spencer turned the ignition and revved the engine, and they were off.

She pressed herself into him, wrapping her arms around his waist and letting her head fall on his back. Never in her wildest dreams had she thought she'd be giving up a prestigious job to ride around a farm clinging to the back of an ATV. But she'd never felt more at home.

The creek was low this time, barely splashing them, and after ten minutes or so, Spencer throttled the vehicle down. The trees were in full leaf now, and she couldn't see through to the clearing. But she knew where they were.

NOT UNTIL FOREVER

They were going to have lunch under the hidden blossom tree. A flutter of nerves tickled her stomach. The location felt significant after all Spencer had told her about his family's history here.

She waited for Spencer to unfasten the picnic basket, then they walked hand-in-hand through the trees.

When they emerged into the clearing, she caught her breath. Red burst from every inch of the hidden blossom tree, and the branches swept low to the ground, heavy with cherries. The ripened fruit was almost more breathtaking than the delicate blossoms had been in spring.

Spencer parted two branches and gestured for her to duck into the tree's shade. Inside, light dappled the ground and fell on—

"The bench!" Sophie gasped and lunged for it, running her fingers over its smooth surface. "How did you—"

But Spencer took her hands and spun her so her back was to the bench, then gently lowered her to sit.

The moment felt familiar all at once, and her hand flew to cover her mouth. Was this really happening?

"Sophie—" Spencer's whisper caressed her. She could feel the love in it—see the love reflected in his eyes.

He reached into the picnic basket and pulled out a small, black box.

Sophie's eyes filled before he'd even dropped to one knee in front of her.

Spencer opened the box.

The ring inside sparkled at her, but Sophie only glanced at it for a moment.

She couldn't take her eyes off Spencer's face.

"Sophie Olsen." Spencer's voice was strong now, sure. "You are everything I have ever wanted. Everything I have ever imagined. Everything I could ever need. Will you let me be the same for you? Will you marry me?"

Sophie remembered the last time he had asked. How her insides had quivered with fear. How she'd felt the need to run. To hide. How she'd known she could never live up to the perfect wife he deserved.

She still knew she couldn't. But this time she knew he'd love her anyway. Just like she'd love him.

"I will."

Spencer laughed out loud and pulled her to the ground next to him, crushing her against his chest.

He leaned back slightly and slipped the ring onto her finger.

"I will never stop loving you." His voice told her it was true.

She watched the light dance off the ring. "Not until forever?"

Spencer lowered his head toward hers.

His words were a breath against her lips. "Not even then."

Not Until This Moment

-Hope Springs Book 2-

"For I know the plans I have for you," declares the Lord, "plans to prosper you and not to harm you, plans to give you hope and a future."

-Jeremiah 29:11

Chapter 1

Peyton wiped her frosting-smudged hands on her apron and eased the kitchen door open to peek into the empty ballroom. Her eyes roamed the elegant table settings, the tall vases filled with amaryllis and orchids, the fairy lights that floated above the room like stars. The bride and groom were at the church, probably exchanging their vows at this very moment, but soon they'd come into this perfect room. Peyton could picture exactly how the bride's face would look. She'd seen that look on every bride's face at every wedding she'd ever been to. It was the look that said this was the happiest day of her life.

Peyton pulled her head back and let the door close, barely suppressing a sigh.

A year ago, she'd thought her own happily ever after was just around the corner. But now it seemed further away than ever.

Leah bustled past with a stack of serving bowls. She shuffled them and reached over to pat Peyton's arm, the same way she had at every wedding they'd worked together in the past year.

Peyton straightened her shoulders and marched to the counter. Standing here dwelling on regrets wouldn't get the cake done.

NOT UNTIL THIS MOMENT

She surveyed the four tiers she'd already stacked and grabbed her bench scraper to smooth the spots where her fingers had left impressions in the buttercream, exposing the red velvet swirl underneath. It was exactly what she would have picked for her own wedding cake—if Jared had ever proposed.

She blinked against the sting behind her eyelids. She had to stop feeling this way every time she set up a wedding cake. It'd been almost a year since he'd told her he never intended to get married. Almost a year since she'd decided she couldn't be with a man who couldn't commit to a future with her. Almost a year since she'd pulverized her own heart when she'd broken up with him.

Time to move on.

With a sudden decisiveness, she grabbed her piping materials and filled them with the buttercream she was becoming famous for. Okay, maybe not famous, but well-known enough around Hope Springs to keep her busy most weekends of the summer and even a few in winter—like this one. She set to work adding the delicate beading the couple had requested for the edges of their cake. She let the noises around her fade as she concentrated on making each tiny circle perfect, just barely connecting it to the next one. The intense focus was soothing.

"You're coming to Tamarack with us next weekend, right?" Leah's voice right next to her made Peyton jump, and she almost yanked the piping tip back from the cake. Fortunately, years of practice had given her a steady hand, even in the face of Leah's enthusiasm. She finished the last four beads, then pulled the tip away and spun the cake to examine her work. Not too bad.

"It's perfect." Leah pretended to swipe a finger toward the frosting, but Peyton batted her hand away.

"Tell me you're coming, or I'll do it." Leah held a finger toward the cake again, her eyebrows waggling as if daring Peyton to tempt her.

Too bad Peyton knew it was an empty threat. Leah didn't have an unkind bone in her body, and she'd never ruin Peyton's work—or a couple's wedding cake.

"I don't think so." Peyton couldn't meet Leah's eyes. She hated to disappoint anyone, least of all the friend who'd come to feel like a sister, but there was no way she could go on the annual skiing trip. Not if Jared was going to be there. And anyway, he was the only reason she'd been invited in the first place. Now that they weren't together, it would be awkward if she tagged along.

"Sawyer specifically told me to make sure you knew you were still invited." Drat Leah's ability to read her mind.

"I'm sure he was only being polite."

Unlike the others who went on the trip every year, Peyton hadn't grown up in Hope Springs. She'd only met Sawyer a few years ago when she'd gone with Jared and his friends to the ski resort Sawyer's family owned.

"Well, if he was, then saying no would be rude." Leah gave her an impish smile, obviously certain she'd won the argument.

But Peyton was tougher than that. "I have another wedding that weekend." Which also happened to be Valentine's Day. Not that she cared about her former favorite holiday anymore.

"I know. I'm catering that one, too. But we'll be back by Wednesday. Try again."

Peyton reviewed her mental calendar. Why couldn't she come up with something else?

"So it's really about Jared." Leah gave her the same half-sympathetic, half-stern look she did every time Jared's name came up.

Peyton snatched her scraper and smoothed a nonexistent dent. Of course it was about Jared. "Don't you have a wedding dinner to get ready?"

Leah planted a hand on her hip. "You said you were over Jared."

She had said that. Multiple times. She'd told it to herself every day, hoping that one of these days it would be true.

"I am over him. I just—"

"Then prove it." Leah crossed her arms in front of her. "If you're over him, you won't have a problem coming skiing with all of us. Maybe you'll meet someone new."

Peyton studied her friend. She should say no. Leah was intentionally pushing her buttons. But her friend knew her well. Knew she was incapable of backing down from a challenge.

"Fine," she huffed. "I'll come. Now let me finish this cake."

Leah gave her a triumphant smile and a quick squeeze. "Gotta run. I have a wedding dinner to prepare." She rushed to the other side of the kitchen, where the rest of her crew worked to unload carts filled with chicken, potatoes, and all kinds of food that made Peyton's mouth water.

Peyton shook her head and tried to force her concentration back to her work. This was one challenge she should have walked away from.

Chapter 2

Jared drove the monstrous conversion van he'd just picked up into the parking lot of the Hidden Cafe.

He'd been waiting for this Friday morning for weeks now. He was ready for this ski trip like he'd been ready for few things in his life. The past year had been rough, and he needed to get out of Hope Springs for a few days. Just enough time to clear his head. To escape the constant fear of running into Peyton. To finally get over her.

As if that will ever happen.

But it had to happen. Peyton had made it clear what she wanted—marriage, a life together, a family. Much as he would do anything to give her the moon and stars, the thing she was asking for—that was the one thing he couldn't give her.

Which didn't stop him from glancing around the parking lot, just in case her car was here.

That sinking feeling in his stomach when he didn't spot it was stupid. He'd known she wouldn't come this year. Or any year, now that they weren't together.

He turned off the vehicle and jumped out. Anyway, it was for the best, he reminded himself as he strode into the Hidden Cafe.

The moment he stepped through the door, he stopped to inhale deeply, just as he did whenever he came here. The scents of home cooking got him every time. His home had never smelled like this growing up.

It had smelled more like . . .

Did fear have a smell?

"Hey, man." Ethan clapped a hand on his shoulder. "Got some muffins for the road." He opened the paper bag in his hand and pulled out a giant muffin, passing it to Jared.

"Thanks." Jared took a big bite of the still-warm pastry, savoring the apple and cinnamon melting on his tongue. "Everyone here?"

"Just about. Ariana's over there." Ethan glowed at the mere mention of his wife's name. "And Leah. Her brother Dan is coming, too. I guess he just moved back to town to serve with his dad at the church."

Jared nodded shortly. He didn't need to know what was going on at the church.

"Emma's on her way. And Sophie and Spencer just called. They'll be here in a few minutes, and they're bringing Spencer's brother Tyler. Vi can't make it this year. She didn't want to close the store."

Jared tallied the group in his head. "So we've got five here, and we're waiting for four."

"Actually—" Ethan cleared his throat and didn't meet Jared's eyes. "We're waiting for five."

Jared did a quick recount. "I only count four."

"That's because you're not counting Peyton."

"Pey—" Jared ran a hand up and down his rough cheek. "Peyton's coming?" His throat went dry. He'd been so sure she wouldn't come. So sure he'd be able to use this time to get over her.

Ethan watched him. "You okay with that?"

Jared gave a tight smile and a quick nod. "Of course."

But Ethan tipped his head to the side. His partner on the volunteer first responder squad knew him better than anyone else. Knew how hard not being with Peyton had been for him. He was the only one who knew why Jared would never marry, too.

"Well, I guess I'm going to have to be, aren't I?" he muttered as the door opened and Peyton stepped inside.

Jared caught his breath as her eyes landed on his for a second, then skipped away. Her mouth was set into a faint scowl as she gazed past him, clearly searching for someone else—probably anyone else.

He shuffled to the side to get out of her way. No reason to make this harder than it had to be.

Her lips curled into a smile, and for half a heartbeat he let himself think it was for him. But she slid past him and let Leah wrap her into a hug.

Jared tried not to think about how long it had been since his arms had been around Peyton. Tried not to notice how they ached to hold her again.

So far so good on being okay with this.

He moved toward the door. "We should get the van loaded." He said it loudly so everyone would hear, but his gaze locked on Peyton and refused to budge. She wore the white ski jacket with pink trim he had helped her pick out the first year they'd gone skiing together. Her pale hair was swept into some kind of messy bun on top of her head, making her look casual and sophisticated at the same time.

And her eyes. Her eyes were what had drawn him to her in the first place. So impossibly light they were almost transparent. But it was more than their color. It was their warmth. Their sincerity. The way they revealed everything she felt.

Which was also what scared him about them.

He held the door as Ethan and Ariana filed past, then waited for the others.

But Leah was introducing Peyton to a dark-haired guy with his back to Jared.

When Peyton smiled at the guy and held out a hand to shake his, Jared's stomach clenched. He'd been waiting for the moment he learned she'd met someone else. But that didn't mean he wanted to witness it.

His eyes flicked to hers again. But all he saw in them was polite interest as she talked to the stranger.

After a second, the three of them moved toward the door. Caught watching them, Jared considered making an escape out to the van. But he couldn't very well close the door in their faces.

He stood his ground as they approached.

Peyton passed through first, barely acknowledging him, though he was pretty sure he heard a mumbled "thanks" before she scooted toward the van. That woman couldn't bear to be impolite, even to him.

"Hey, Jared." He tore his eyes off Peyton's retreating figure and forced them to Leah. "You remember my little brother Dan? He was a couple years behind us in school."

Little brother? The guy easily stood two inches taller than Jared's six feet.

The guy gave Jared a warm smile and held out a hand. "Thanks for letting me tag along."

Jared returned the handshake. "No problem." *As long as you don't steal my girlfriend.*

But that wasn't right. If Dan ended up with Peyton, he wouldn't be stealing her. Jared had already let her go.

Too bad his heart didn't know that yet.

Outside, Sophie, Spencer, Tyler, and Emma were getting out of their cars. Jared opened the back of the van and everyone stashed their bags, exchanging greetings and laughs as they did. Only Peyton seemed quiet.

The moment he opened the doors of the van, she launched herself inside and scooted to the corner of the backseat.

Clearly, she wasn't going to be riding shotgun this year.

Jared waited for the others to load into the vehicle, then jumped in, glancing at Leah, who'd taken the seat next to him.

"We ready for this?" Jared turned the ignition as a resounding chorus of yeses hit his ears.

As he backed out of the spot, his eyes flicked to the rearview mirror. They landed instantly on Peyton, but she was staring out the window, her lips drawn into a thin line.

He was tempted to tell a stupid joke, the way he had a hundred times before to erase that look from her face. But this time he was pretty sure hearing from him would only make the line thinner.

Chapter 3

Trees. Trees. And more trees.

The view never changed.

Not that Peyton didn't like trees. Especially when they glinted with a dusting of snow as these did.

But it was taking a monumental effort to keep her gaze directed out the window. If she let herself peek into the car for even one second, her eyes would seek out Jared. And that electric current she'd felt during the brief second their gazes had collided in the cafe this morning had been enough to warn her away.

She'd never get over him if she couldn't look at him without feeling their connection. So she just wouldn't look at him.

"We're here." Jared's voice reached to the back of the van, a hint of weariness behind the words, and she couldn't help it.

Her eyes tracked to the rearview mirror, and she caught a glimpse of the short stubble on his cheeks and the sharp line of his nose. The color-changing hazel of his eyes. Fortunately, he was peering ahead, not into the mirror.

She shifted her gaze away before he could catch her looking.

Jared steered the van down the long, winding driveway that led to the ski lodge. Peyton focused out the window again, peering toward the massive building. It was chic in a retro-mid-century-modern sort of way, everything chunky and angular and oversized. The first time she'd come here, she'd found it garish, but it'd grown on her. Now she could see how it worked against the backdrop of rolling snow-covered hills and the sharp lines of the trees.

They passed a small stable, with several horses grazing in a paddock beyond it, and Peyton's heart jumped. She could still pick out the two she and Jared had ridden last time they were here. Was that really only a year ago? How had everything gone so wrong since then?

That weekend, she'd been so sure Jared would ask her to marry him. She'd even thought it might be while they were out riding horses. What could be more romantic? Horses. Snowfall. Privacy. It was like God had set everything up for the perfect proposal.

Except it had never come.

Peyton had tried not to be disappointed. Tried to tell herself it didn't mean anything. That Jared was probably waiting for the next weekend—for Valentine's Day, when they'd be back home in Hope Springs. After all, they'd been together three years already, and she knew without a doubt that he loved her. She just wanted to make it official and start their life together.

She had waited until the last possible moment on Valentine's Day, after they'd gone out to dinner, after they'd strolled along the lakefront, after they'd done everything romantic she could think of. But when he'd walked her to her door and said goodnight, when he'd turned and walked down her porch steps, when he'd almost reached his car, she couldn't hold it back any longer.

It had started to rain, a cold, miserable February rain, but she didn't care that she was getting wet. She needed to know.

"Jared." She didn't recognize the way his name came out of her mouth.

He turned so, so slowly, and she could read it in the tension in his shoulders. He knew what she was going to ask. Knew what she wanted. And his answer wasn't going to be what she wanted to hear. But she had to ask anyway.

"Do you think we'll ever get married?"

His mouth opened, but no words came out. He just stood there, blinking at her. Finally, he closed the space between them. Grabbed her hands. Pulled her to him so that her head rested on his chest.

"Peyton, I love you more than anything in this world."

The words should have melted her, should have reassured her, but they didn't. She knew there was a "but" behind them.

"But—"

She tensed, but he didn't let her go. "But I don't plan to ever get married. That's not something—" He swallowed. "That's not something I can do."

"But—" She had to fight for breath. "But why not? If you love me?" She felt like her heart had morphed into an ice sculpture and he was chipping away at it with an ice pick.

He gripped her shoulders, slid her back a little, and waited until she lifted her face toward his. "I *do* love you. No matter what else, you have to know that. But I— I just can't."

"I don't understand. Why can't you?" She was so desperate to understand. To help him see he was wrong, that he could marry. That they *should* marry.

But he simply shook his head and turned around, dragging himself back to his car. "I'm sorry."

"You're sorry?" She was stunned, speechless. She had been so sure he was the one.

As a kid, her mom had told her so many times how she'd known Peyton's dad was the one. He'd made her laugh. He'd made her feel safe and secure and treasured. He'd encouraged her in her faith. And Peyton had felt all those things with Jared. She'd prayed for him as if he were her future husband. So how could he not be the one?

Jared's shoulders slumped as he opened his car door.

"Wait, Jared." Peyton wanted to run to him, to tell him it was okay if he didn't want to marry yet. That they could wait. That if he never decided to marry, she'd be okay with it.

But she knew none of that was true. She wanted a husband, a family. A future.

And if he couldn't be the one to give her that, she had to let him go.

"If you don't—" She stopped to choke down the sob working its way up from her core. "If you don't love me enough to commit to me before God and our friends and family, to want to make a life with me, then you don't love me the way I need to be loved." She gulped at the air to force the next words out. "I don't think we should see each other anymore."

Jared had dropped his head onto the top of his car then, wrapping his arms over it like he was sheltering from a blow. She'd longed to go to him. But she'd kept her feet planted, letting the tears drop down her cheeks faster than the rain. When he'd lifted his head, his face had glistened with moisture. But he'd nodded once, then he'd slid into his car and driven away.

And the ice sculpture that had become her heart had fractured into a million pieces that could never be repaired.

"Going to sit in here all day?"

Peyton's head jerked up at the voice, pulling her out of her memories.

Jared stood at the side door of the van, lips twisted into the tiniest smile. The other seats in the vehicle were all empty, and voices drifted from outside as the others gathered their stuff.

"Yeah." She straightened her stiff legs and hunched over to climb past the empty seats. Jared held out a hand to help her, but she ignored it. If looking at him wasn't safe, touching him would be catastrophic.

Once out of the van, she dashed to the back to grab her threadbare old duffel bag, which was packed so full she'd barely been able to zip it.

It was heavier than she remembered, and she sized up the long walk across the parking lot to the lodge entrance. Jared usually carried her bags for her—teasing her about how many books she packed—but this year she was on her own. Out of the corner of her eye, she noticed Jared watching her, and she could almost see his internal debate about whether to take her bag for her.

NOT UNTIL THIS MOMENT

Well, she'd make that decision for him. She hefted the bag in front of her and wrapped both arms around it.

By the time they made it to the building, her shoulders and back screamed with the strain, but she kept a smile pasted on her face as Jared held the door for them all. The moment they reached the check-in desk, she dropped the bag to the floor with a relieved sigh.

She stretched her arms over her head and gazed around the lobby as Ethan checked the group in. A fire roared in the huge stone fireplace that rose from a sunken area in the middle of the lobby all the way to the top of the building two stories above. A few people lounged on the built-in couches that surrounded it. That's where she planned to hide out most of the trip. Away from the ski hills where Jared would spend his days.

Sawyer popped out from his office in the back to greet them all. When he got to Peyton, he leaned in to give her a quick hug and whispered, "I'm glad you came. Jared is an idiot to have let you go."

"Thanks." Peyton pulled away with a smile she hoped didn't look as awkward as it felt.

A second later, she was again staggering under the weight of her bag as they made their way across the lobby. They always skipped the lodge's slow, clunky elevator in favor of the stairs. Somehow, she got wedged in between Jared and the wall as they began to climb. The subtle, spicy-sweet bergamot cologne she'd have recognized in her sleep washed over her. How could the scent alone be enough to conjure up the feel of his arms around her? She smooshed herself closer to the wall.

Leah handed out keys as they walked. Leah, Emma, Sophie, and Peyton would share one room. Tyler, Spencer, Jared, and Dan would have another, and Ethan and Ariana would have their own. Peyton pushed down a stab of jealousy. Since the first time she'd come here with Jared, she'd looked forward to the day when they could share a room as husband and wife.

"Oh, no." Leah counted the remaining keys in her hand. "We're one key short for the girls' room."

"I'll go grab one." Peyton whirled around before anyone else could offer. She couldn't handle walking next to Jared a second longer. Even if it meant climbing back down and then up the stairs with her ridiculously heavy bag.

"At least let me take your bag for you." Jared's voice was low enough that she doubted any of the others heard.

"I've got it." She ignored the way the muscles in her shoulders knotted as she barreled down the steps and practically ran across the lobby to the check-in desk.

Sawyer was talking to the young clerk there, but he broke off with a huge smile the moment she reached them.

"Peyton. I'm glad you came back down."

"You are?" Peyton dropped her bag again. Her shoulders needed at least a few seconds of rest before she lugged it back up the steps.

"I wanted to give you this." Sawyer reached under the counter and extracted a book. "I know you were reading Dickens last time you were here. I'm sure you already have this one, but I saw it in a bookstore and thought of you, so . . ."

Peyton took the worn copy of *Oliver Twist* he passed her. Her face heated. He'd thought of her? Why? They barely knew each other.

She examined the book. Judging by its cover, it had to be old. She flipped to the copyright page. 1901. And it was in collectible condition. Which made it well beyond anything she could accept.

"Thank you." She held the book out to him. "But I can't take this. It's too much."

"For you, nothing's too much." Something warm lingered in Sawyer's look, and she felt her flush deepen.

"Okay, um." She glanced at the book again. "Thank you."

At his smile, she let herself give in to a smile, too. She couldn't deny that she loved the book.

"So, I was thinking . . . I'm sure things are little awkward with you and Jared. Want to ditch the others and hit the slopes with me tomorrow?"

"Oh." Peyton's heart did a weird, unexpected skip. "I was going to spend the day by the fire reading." She held up the book as if for evidence.

"I don't know if anyone's told you this before, but you're at a ski lodge. You're supposed to ski." His blue eyes glinted, and she couldn't help but laugh.

"Yeah. If you remember, the first time I tried that I ended up with a broken wrist."

"That's because you didn't have the right teacher." He winked at her. "Come on, it'll be fun."

He smiled big enough to show a dimple in one cheek. She'd never noticed the dimple before. Then again, she'd never really looked at him before. She'd had eyes only for Jared.

But Jared was her past.

Maybe Sawyer was her future. Or at least her present.

"Okay." She worked to insert more certainty into her voice. "Yes. Let's do it."

Sawyer's dimple deepened. "Great. Nine o'clock. I'll pick you up at your room."

"Oh, that's okay, I'll meet you down here." A pinch of guilt pricked her stomach at the thought of Jared seeing her with Sawyer. But she pushed it aside. She had no reason to feel guilty.

She was about to grab her bag when she remembered what she'd come down here for in the first place. "Almost forgot. I need one more key for the girls' room."

"You got it." Sawyer's grin made her stomach somersault this time. It felt strange to have that reaction to a man who wasn't Jared. But also nice. Maybe this ski trip was what she needed to get over him after all.

Sawyer passed her the key with one last stomach-flipping smile, and she bent to pick up her bag.

As she yanked up on the strap, there was a loud ripping sound. The bag was suddenly too light as everything she'd packed spilled from the torn bottom to the floor.

She groaned. She'd known the bag wouldn't hold up much longer, but she hadn't had time to buy a new one before the trip. That's what she got for not planning ahead.

Face flaming, she slid her underwear under a pair of jeans as she pushed everything into a pile and tried to get her arms around it.

"I'll get it for you." Jared was striding across the lobby, wearing that same grim expression he'd worn every time they'd run into each other over the past year.

But Sawyer was already at her side, passing her a large canvas bag. "Here, use this."

She took it gratefully and shoved her clothing in first, then her books and makeup on top.

"Thanks." She glanced around to make sure she hadn't missed anything.

When she looked up, Sawyer held a hand out to her. She let him pull her to her feet, then reached for the bag.

But Sawyer got to it first, grabbing it with his left hand while his right still gripped hers. "I'll carry this up for you."

"That won't be necessary." Jared's voice cut in.

Peyton slid her hand out of Sawyer's. But she didn't miss the dark glare Jared shot his old friend.

"I'll take it." Jared reached to grab the bag from Sawyer, who seemed to size him up and then shrugged and held the bag out to him.

Sawyer touched a hand to Peyton's elbow. "I'll see you tomorrow morning, then. Nine o'clock."

He gave Jared a buddy slap on the back, then disappeared through the door behind the counter.

Jared started across the lobby with her stuff, and Peyton double-stepped to keep up. "Didn't you need something from the desk?"

"No." Jared's answer was short, clipped.

"Then why did you come down?" Peyton frowned. Even after they'd spent three years together, she sometimes didn't understand him.

"You'd been down here a long time. I wanted to make sure everything was okay." Jared didn't look at her as he said it.

She stopped in the middle of the stairway, crossing her arms in front of her. "You don't need to check up on me, Jared. I'm perfectly capable of taking care of myself."

"Clearly." Jared's dry tone made her grit her teeth.

He was not going to make her feel guilty for talking to another man. "What's that supposed to mean?"

"Nothing," Jared muttered.

"Fine." She jogged up the rest of the stairs and strode down the hallway ahead of him.

But halfway to her room, she stopped. "Actually, no. It's not fine. You didn't want to share your life with me. So you don't get to make me feel guilty about talking to someone who maybe does."

"Sawyer?" Jared scoffed. "He's only looking for a little fun for himself. He has no intention of sharing his life with you."

"Yeah?" Peyton felt the steam building. What right did he have to try to ruin her shot at happiness before it'd even started? "Is that why he gave me an early edition Dickens?"

Jared blanched at that, and Peyton felt a cold satisfaction pool in her stomach. Followed by a wave of guilt. But she pushed it away. Jared was the one who had brought Sawyer up.

He stopped in front of her. "I'm not trying to make you feel guilty, Peyton." His voice was quiet, almost tender, and she tried to steel herself against it. "Just be careful with Sawyer. He's not—" He cut off and pulled a hand through his hair. "He's not the kind of guy who's looking for a long-term relationship, if you know what I mean."

"Well, you'd know all about that wouldn't you?" Peyton jerked her bag out of Jared's hand. Her anger must have given her superhuman strength because she barely noticed the bag's weight as she ran the rest of the way down the hall and shoved her key into the lock.

She let the door slam behind her.

Chapter 4

Jared's breath fogged in front of him as he stopped at the top of the ski hill, getting ready for another run. He'd been out here two hours already, and still his head wasn't any clearer than it had been yesterday. Seeing Peyton and Sawyer together had hardened the regret that had been swirling in his gut for the past year so that it sat there now, diamond hard and just as sharp.

"Hey. You been out here all morning?" Leah skied up next to him, cheerful as always.

He squinted into the glitter of the snow behind her and shrugged. "Only since the sun came up."

He'd been awake long before that, trying to shove aside the knot of fear that always clustered in his throat when he woke during the night. It'd taken too long to remember where he was. To remember that there hadn't been anything to be afraid of for a long time.

"You up for another run?" Leah peered down the slope. "Thought I was up for this blue trail, but it looks more intimidating than I remembered. They're sure it's intermediate?"

Jared offered a reassuring smile. "I'll go with you. But you'll be fine." Leah had always been pretty solid on her skis. Unlike Peyton, who had to stick to the green beginner slopes.

Jared started to pull his goggles down, but he caught a flash of white and pink jacket near the top of the chair lift. He turned his head to follow the chair as it crested the hill and the couple slid off, the man's hand on the woman's arm. On Peyton's arm.

It was the same way Jared had helped Peyton off the lift the first time they'd come here together. And she gave Sawyer the same smile she'd always given him.

The knot in Jared's gut pulled taut. Sawyer was not the kind of guy Peyton should be with.

Peyton glanced his way once, before her eyes went right back to Sawyer, who was gesturing toward the hill and seemed to be demonstrating the stance she should use. A shot of something hot and sharp that went beyond simple jealousy surged through him. What was Sawyer doing bringing her on this hill? It was way beyond her skill level.

"Ready?" Leah's voice tugged at him, but he couldn't tear his gaze away from Peyton.

"Maybe you should tell her to stick to the greens." He gestured toward Peyton with his chin.

"She's a big girl, Jared. She can make her own decisions about which hill to take."

Except he was sure taking this run hadn't been her decision. Sawyer had certainly goaded her into it.

He didn't know what angered him more: that Sawyer would put her at risk by taking her on a run she wasn't ready for or that she was so eager to impress him that she'd agree to it.

"Come on." This time Leah's command was insistent.

He pulled his eyes away from Peyton and slammed his goggles down. "Let's go."

The wind whipped at his cheeks as he let the swoosh of the snow under his skis take over his senses. For a minute, he let himself forget everything else and focus only on the spray of powdery snow around him, the next turn of his skis, the taste of the cold.

But he reached the runout at the base of the hill too soon, and as he slowed, he automatically turned to squint up the hill, seeking out Peyton.

There.

Halfway down the run, an expression of sheer terror on her face as she flew down the hill—way too fast. Jared scanned the terrain in front of her, on alert for dangers. He recognized Sawyer half a dozen yards ahead of her, looking over his shoulder with a yell of encouragement. What was that maniac doing? Didn't he know he had to watch out for Peyton? Sawyer practically lived on skis, but until four years ago, Peyton had never been on a ski hill in her life. That's why Jared had taken her on the beginner hill and had hung close the whole time, ready to jump in to help at the slightest sign of trouble.

Not that it'd done much good. He'd never forget her tears of pain when she fell and broke her wrist. She'd forgiven him instantly. Said there was nothing he could have done. But her pain had devastated him. He'd promised himself long ago that he'd never let another woman get hurt on his watch. And he'd failed the first woman he'd had the opportunity to keep safe.

Leah skidded to a stop next to him and followed his gaze. "You could just marry her, you know. Then you'd both be happy."

Jared turned away from the hill. "She seems plenty happy to me."

"Is she?" Leah jabbed her ski pole into the ground and gave him a hard stare. "Look, you know I love Peyton like a sister, and I love you, too. Clearly, you two are not over each other. But if you can't marry her and give her the life she deserves, then you need to let her go. Let her start again. It's not fair to her if you don't."

"I can't marry her, Leah." Jared pushed off, making his way toward the lift.

"Then you know what you need to do," Leah called from behind him.

Yeah, he did know what he had to do.

He just didn't know how to do it.

Chapter 5

"Again?" Sawyer shot Peyton the same impish grin he'd given her after every run so far.

Every muscle in her body ached, but she nodded, a return grin stretching her own cheeks. She was having way too much fun to quit.

Skiing with Jared had always been fun, too. But after she'd broken her wrist that first year, he'd hovered so much, always afraid to let her go too fast or get too far in front of him, in case she got hurt. It'd made her feel safe and protected. But it'd also kept her from experiencing the thrill of taking a hill at full speed.

Besides, she'd made more than a dozen runs already this morning, and she hadn't wiped out once. Clearly, Jared had underestimated her abilities. If it weren't for Sawyer, she would still be on the beginner slopes Jared had convinced her to stick to.

Sawyer grabbed Peyton's gloved hand as the chair lift swept under them. Of all the things Peyton missed about being in a relationship, holding hands was near the top of the list. Having her hand in another man's felt odd but not necessarily in a bad way.

"Want to grab some lunch after this?" Sawyer's grip tightened on hers. "We can go to one of the small reception areas that aren't being used. Have some privacy."

NOT UNTIL THIS MOMENT

"Sure." To her surprise, Peyton didn't have to think about the answer. She'd had a nice morning with Sawyer and had even successfully managed to avoid watching Jared most of the time. Lunch with Sawyer—where Jared wouldn't be around to distract her at all—sounded nice.

"Race you down this time." He tugged her hand as they slid off the lift.

"You're on." She had to laugh at herself as she followed him. She never would have expected to enjoy his fun and fast style. But she felt fearless this morning.

Sawyer led her past the head of the blue trail they'd been taking all day to the edge of the hill, where the slope steepened sharply.

Peyton sucked in a breath as she caught a glimpse of the black diamond symbol on the sign off to the side. Was she really up for this advanced trail?

She shoved down the apprehension. If Sawyer thought she could handle it, then she was willing to give it a try. Besides, it was right next to the blue. How much harder could it be?

"Ready?" Sawyer winked at her, then lowered his goggles.

She blew out a quick breath, then pulled hers down and nodded.

"Set."

Peyton's shoulders tensed, and she tightened her grip on her poles, bending her knees so she'd be ready to push off.

"Go!"

At Sawyer's shout, Peyton shoved off, hard. Within seconds, she was flying down the hill, the snow biting at her cheeks. She angled her hips and crouched lower. She needed more speed if she was going to beat Sawyer.

Her heart thundered in her ears, cutting off all other sounds. The speed was exhilarating and terrifying at the same time. She wasn't sure she liked it, but she wasn't about to back off now. She'd started this challenge, and she was going to finish it.

Halfway down, she chanced a glance to the side. Sawyer was a few feet in front of her, but if she went a little faster, she might be able to catch him.

She let out an involuntary scream as she accelerated. She'd never gone this fast before outside of a vehicle. But she was gaining on him.

He looked back and shot her a smile, then started to inch ahead.

Oh, no, you don't.

She pushed her weight forward and concentrated on leaning her knees and ankles to the inside, the way Sawyer had explained. Her heart rate accelerated with the skis, and she let out a wild cackle. She was really doing this.

But just then her right ski caught an edge, and she felt her body jerk off balance.

Instinctively, she shifted her weight, but it was too late. Her feet were no longer under her. Her hip hit the ground first, then an explosion of pain shot through her ankle as her body twisted without her foot.

She laid still, trying to pull in a breath. But her lungs seemed to have frozen in place. She tried not to panic as she waited for them to start functioning again. Finally, she was able to gulp at the air, and she sat up, unable to hold back the moan as she reached for her foot. But before she could free it from her boot, the unmistakable zip of skis on the snow sounded above her. She whipped her head around to see a skier barreling toward her. There was no time to roll out of the way. She lifted her hands to cover her head and braced for the impact.

But only a gentle spray of powder landed on her, accompanied by the swish of skis skidding to a stop.

"Are you okay?"

She should have known it would be Jared. He'd been there to help every time she'd been hurt since they'd met. Including the day they met, when he'd rescued her from a rip current that had dragged her toward the breakwater the first time she'd ventured into Lake Michigan. She'd called him her hero then, and here he was again.

She uncovered her head and laid back in the snow. "It's my ankle."

"I've got it, man," Sawyer called, jogging up the hill in his ski boots.

But Jared was already releasing her foot from the ski and sliding off her boot. She sighed in relief as he lowered her foot to the snow but winced as his hands probed her ankle.

"I know," he soothed. "I need to check how bad it is."

"That was an awesome run." Sawyer dropped into the snow next to her, grinning. "You almost caught me."

Jared aimed a glare at Sawyer. "What were you thinking taking her on a black diamond?"

"What were you doing following us?" Sawyer shot back.

Peyton watched Jared, who didn't look up. Had he been following them?

"I've been on the black diamond for a couple hours now. I happened to see you guys head that way and thought I better keep an eye out. Good thing, too."

Sawyer waved him off. "She's fine. You always were a wimp about this kind of stuff."

Peyton's mouth fell open. The last thing she'd consider Jared was a wimp. Cautious, yes. But the man had run into burning buildings, for crying out loud.

Jared ignored Sawyer and continued to push on her ankle, drawing a sharp hiss when he pressed below it.

"I think it's just a sprain, but we'll keep an eye on it. You should get some ice on it right away."

"Does this count?" She gestured at the snow where her foot rested. She had no desire to get up and go anywhere else right now.

Jared gave her that gentle, easy laugh she used to love. "Afraid not. Come on. I'll help you to the lodge." He squatted at her side and reached to put a hand behind her back.

Sawyer jumped to his feet. "*I'll* help her. We were about to grab some lunch anyway."

Peyton hated the look on Jared's face. Hated that she'd put it there.

But there was nothing she could do about it. He'd chosen this for them.

"Thanks." She gave him a quick smile before accepting the hand Sawyer held out to her.

Jared turned away as Sawyer draped her arm over his shoulder and wrapped his arm firmly around her back.

"Try not to put any pressure on it." Jared called behind them as she hobbled next to Sawyer.

She nodded but resisted the urge to look over her shoulder at him.

By the time they got inside, her ankle was throbbing so hard she could feel her pulse in her whole foot.

"I think I need to sit," she managed to puff to Sawyer.

He steered her to the sunken couches around the fireplace and settled her in, tucking a pillow under her foot.

"I'll go grab you some ice."

Peyton laid back against the couch, closing her eyes. How did she always manage to get herself into these situations? Her mom was the most elegant person she knew, but her dad had always teased that gracefulness skipped a generation. Then he had tweaked her cheek and said her clumsiness was part of what made her so endearing.

She sighed. Maybe it would endear her to Sawyer. It had apparently worked with Jared. He'd come to check on her a few days after he'd saved her life, and they'd gotten to talking. Before they knew it, they were dating seriously.

And look what came of that.

"Here we go."

She opened her eyes as Sawyer passed her an ice pack.

A stab of pain sliced through her foot as she settled the ice onto it, but after a second the throbbing eased.

Sawyer passed her a sandwich and a soda. "Figured I might have to take a rain check on our private lunch. How about dinner instead?"

Peyton ran her hand down the cool side of the soda can. "I don't know." She liked Sawyer, but her insides churned with guilt over the way Jared had looked as she'd walked away with Sawyer's arm around her.

Sawyer settled on the low table in front of the couch. "Come on, it's just dinner." His phone rang, but he clicked it off, leaning forward and bracing his elbows on his knees, as if nothing in the world mattered more to him than her answer.

No was on the tip of her tongue. But the whole point of coming here was to move on. "Okay. Dinner it is."

"Great." Sawyer tucked a loose hair behind her ear.

The move that had felt so familiar whenever Jared did it caused an uncomfortable prickle in her belly. She wasn't quite ready to have Sawyer touching her hair like that.

But he was only being friendly.

She forced a smile as he waved and walked away.

She was still trying to sort out her feelings about the idea of spending time with a new man when Leah charged into the seating area a few minutes later.

"Are you okay?" Her friend's cheeks were pink-tinged, and snow crusted her hat. She must have come straight from the slopes.

"I'm fine." Peyton gestured to her foot. "Aside from a serious lack of grace and a terrible habit of demonstrating my clumsiness in front of a man."

Leah dropped to the couch next to her and leaned over to give her a hug. "I'm sorry I wasn't there. I decided to try the blues on the back side of the hill for a bit. They're a little tamer."

"That's okay. Sawyer was there." She hesitated a second. "And Jared."

"Yeah, he found me and sent me in here. He said it was sprained?"

Peyton tried to ignore the warm glow that came from knowing Jared had been worried enough to send Leah to check on her. And the pang that he hadn't come himself. "He's the expert, so I guess so. He said we'd have to keep an eye on it, but I think the ice is helping already."

"That's a relief. Remember how long the drive to the hospital is?"

Peyton groaned. "That was the longest car ride of my life."

"Your life? I was the one trapped in the car with you and Jared, listening to him apologize a bajillion times and you tell him it wasn't his fault a bajillion and one times." She broke off and covered her mouth with a hand. "I'm sorry. That was a dumb thing to say."

Peyton shook her head. "No, it's okay. Anyway, at least he doesn't blame himself this time. Pretty sure he blames Sawyer, though."

Leah's forehead creased. "Did Sawyer do something to make you fall?"

"No." Peyton leaned forward to pull off the ice, examining her ankle. It had turned an ugly purple-black and was definitely puffy. She hoped Jared was right about it only being a sprain. "He doesn't think I should have been on that hill in the first place. If it was up to him, I'd stay on the bunny hill the rest of my life."

"Well." Leah leaned back against the seat and kicked her feet up onto the table Sawyer had been sitting on a few minutes ago. "There are worse traits in a guy than wanting to keep you safe."

"Yeah. Like not wanting to get married." The bitter words were out before Peyton could hold them back. But she didn't want to talk about Jared anymore. "Anyway, I'm having dinner with Sawyer tonight."

Instead of the triumphant look she expected from her friend, Leah gathered her long hair into a ponytail with her hands, then let it fall.

Peyton knew Leah well enough to recognize that the gesture meant she had something to say but didn't want to say it. "Out with it."

Leah's eyebrows drew together. "I don't know if you should be hanging out with Sawyer."

Peyton stared at her friend. "Why not? Aren't you the one who's been trying to get me to move on?"

"I know." Leah played with the zipper of her jacket. "But Jared doesn't think Sawyer is the best guy when it comes to women."

Peyton snorted. "There's a surprise. He doesn't want to be with me, but he doesn't want anyone else to be with me either."

Leah shook her head. "I know, so I'm trying to take what he said with a grain of salt. But maybe it'd be best if you hung out with Sawyer in a group first."

Peyton couldn't stop the eye roll. "Yeah, because that wouldn't be awkward, trying to talk to Sawyer with Jared hanging over our shoulders."

"I'm sure Jared wouldn't—" Leah stopped. Considered. "Okay, yeah, he would. But that might be better than being alone with Sawyer until you know him better."

"And how am I supposed to get to know him better if I don't get a chance to talk to him alone?"

Why was Leah making such a big deal about this? Sawyer was one of the most charming men Peyton had ever met. It's not like he was going to attack her.

Leah shrugged. "I don't know. I guess in high school Sawyer had kind of a reputation for going through girls pretty quickly."

"High school was a long time ago, Leah. And I don't know that Sawyer. I only know this guy who bought me a book he knew I'd like and who took me out on the slopes and showed me what I was capable of. Now he wants to have a nice quiet dinner with me where we can talk without worrying about my ex being right there. Sounds like a good guy to me."

Leah's forehead was still creased, but she nodded. "I know, Peyton. I just want you to be safe."

Peyton patted Leah's leg. "I know you do, and I love you for it. But I'll be fine."

Better than fine, maybe. If having dinner with Sawyer could help her forget about Jared for even a couple hours, it would be worth it.

So far, nothing else had worked.

Chapter 6

Jared had told himself that the next run would be his last of the day at least five times already. But every time he got to the bottom of the slope, he considered the alternative: go inside and see Sawyer and Peyton together.

No, thank you.

He really did have to make this his last run, though, or he would miss dinner with his friends.

The line for the chair lift was still plenty long, and Jared fiddled with the small chain Peyton had given him for their first Valentine's Day as he waited. At first, he'd thought it was weird. Why would he want to wear a necklace? But now it had become a part of him. So much so that he couldn't bring himself to take it off.

"Excuse me." The woman in front of him turned, long dark hair poking out from under her hat to frame her face. "Do you know what time it is?"

"Sure." Jared dug into his zippered jacket pocket and pulled out his phone. "It's almost six."

"Thanks." She gave him a friendly smile.

"Sure."

"I'm April, by the way." She held out a hand and delivered another smile.

He shook it, letting himself smile back. "Jared."

"That last run of yours was pretty amazing."

Jared lifted his head. She'd been watching him? "Uh, thanks."

He gestured ahead of her, where the line had moved forward, leaving a large gap between her and the group in front of them.

She moved up to fill the gap, then angled back to him. "You want to take the next one together?"

Jared blinked at her. Was she flirting with him? It'd been so long since he'd had to decipher any woman's actions besides Peyton's. And she'd always been so easy to read.

"I was going to— I mean it's my last run, so—" Why was he so tongue-tied all at once?

"So?" She raised an eyebrow. "Make your last run with me. Or are you afraid you can't keep up?"

Jared laughed. She was spirited, that was for sure.

"I'll take that as a yes." She glided ahead again.

Jared followed more slowly. What had he just agreed to?

Dude, it's just skiing. Chill.

He skied up to the lift right behind April. On a whim, he grabbed her hand as they sat. She looked over and smiled.

But the hand in his felt wrong, and he let go as soon as their feet left the ground.

"So where are you from?" April's voice had an easiness to it that Jared wished he could imitate.

"You've probably never heard of it."

"Try me."

"Hope Springs. It's a little town on Lake Michigan, just—"

"You're kidding." April shoved his arm. "My grandma lives there. I love it. That little ice cream shop with the weird name. The Chocolate something. Chocolate Cow?"

"Chocolate Chicken." Jared chuckled. "Don't ask how it got its name. No one knows. Or if they do, they're not telling."

April laughed—probably harder than the comment deserved, but Jared grinned. He couldn't deny that her attention was nice.

They were still talking about Hope Springs when the lift reached the top of the hill. Jared followed April to the start of the black diamond Peyton had gotten hurt on earlier.

"You good for this hill?" he shouted at her back. He hadn't seen her ski yet, and he didn't want another person to get hurt on his watch today.

"Just try to keep up," she called over her shoulder as she pushed off.

Jared shoved off right behind her. After watching her for a second, he relaxed. This obviously wasn't her first time on the slopes. Her technique was flawless as she carved perfect curves down the hill.

By the time he reached the runout, she was standing and watching him, her hat in her hand, a mischievous spark in her eyes.

"Couldn't quite keep up, huh?" She shoved his shoulder playfully.

Jared rubbed his arm, pretending to be hurt. "Hey, let a guy keep some of his pride."

She raised her hands to her sides. "Fine. But I think it's only fair that you buy me dinner since I won."

Jared snickered. "I don't remember there being any wager. Or an official race."

"Okay, then, you can buy me an unofficial dinner."

Jared realized with a start that she was serious. She wanted to have dinner with him.

He should say no. He was supposed to have dinner with the whole group. And he should check on Peyton's ankle. And he shouldn't be having dinner with another woman.

"Come on." She nudged him again. "I want to talk more about Hope Springs. Maybe I'll plan a visit there soon." Her amber eyes were warm and bright, and he found that he didn't want to say no.

"Okay. Let me just go change." He pushed the door to the lodge open and held it for her. "Meet me in the dining area in half an hour?"

"Deal." She grabbed his hand for a quick squeeze, then flounced across the lobby and disappeared down the hallway to the right.

Jared crossed the large room more slowly. What was he thinking?

Peyton would be in the dining room. She'd see him with April. Much as he knew they both needed to move on, he didn't want to hurt her by showing up with another woman.

He stopped at the bottom of the staircase. As soon as he got to his room, he'd call April to cancel dinner.

Except he had no idea what room she was in.

He jogged toward the hallway she'd disappeared down, but it was empty, aside from a middle-aged man who shot him a suspicious glare.

Jared turned around and made his way up the stairs and to his room. When he got to the dining room, he'd just have to tell April he couldn't have dinner. It'd be awkward, but there was nothing that could be done about that.

Decision made, he knocked on the door to the girls' room. Before he did anything else, he needed to check on Peyton's ankle. If it was worse, he wouldn't be going to dinner with anyone. He'd be driving her to the hospital for an x-ray.

Sophie pulled the door open. "Hey, Jared. We were beginning to think you were going to spend the night on the hill."

He grinned. That sounded pretty good, actually. "Nah. Thought I better come in and check on my patient. How's she doing?"

"Better, I think. I actually haven't seen her. Spencer and I spent most of the day in town. We found this cute little antique store that Vi would love—" She broke off. "What's wrong?"

"You haven't seen her? Where is she?"

Sophie bit her lip. "I think Leah said something about dinner."

"With Sawyer?" Jared's jaw clenched. He'd told Leah to warn her about that guy.

Sophie touched a hand to his arm. "I think so."

"I guess I'll check her ankle later then." His voice was stiff, and he made himself gentle his tone. Sophie wasn't the target of his anger. "Thanks, Soph. Glad you and Spencer had a good day."

"You coming to dinner with us?"

NOT UNTIL THIS MOMENT

He shook his head, a sudden decisiveness taking over. "Actually, no. I have other plans."

Chapter 7

"That was the best meal I've ever eaten." Peyton wiped her mouth and set her napkin on her plate.

Sawyer had gone all-out for dinner, ordering them ravioli in a white truffle sauce and a chocolate cherry cheesecake so decadent she was pretty sure it should be illegal. The meal, combined with the intimate reception room, with its widely scattered tables—all empty aside from theirs—and tasteful crystal chandeliers, had her feeling almost like a princess. She'd nearly forgotten about the throbbing in her foot.

"I'm glad you enjoyed it." The two candles that lit their table cast a soft glow on Sawyer's face, and the butterflies Peyton had finally managed to calm as she ate returned with a vengeance.

Being with Jared had become so familiar and comfortable, she wasn't used to this nervousness that kept her constantly off balance.

Sawyer's gaze on her was a little too intense, and she let her eyes travel to the full wall of windows so she'd have a moment to catch her breath. Moonlight glinted off the snow on the trees that covered the hill behind the lodge. Their shadows crisscrossed the ground in an intricate patchwork.

"Stunning, isn't it?" Sawyer's voice drew her eyes back to him. But he wasn't looking out the window. He reached his hands across the table and cupped them around hers.

She felt the heat rise in her cheeks as the butterflies took off at full speed. "It's beautiful here. You live here year-round now, right? What's it like in the summer?"

She was babbling, she knew it. But she needed to slow things down. She liked Sawyer. He seemed to be a nice guy. But she barely knew him. She gently slid her hands out from under his and pretended to adjust the sleeve of her shirt.

A frown puckered Sawyer's face for half a second, but he quickly erased it and gave her an easy smile. "It's even more beautiful, if you can believe it. Wildflowers everywhere. Everything's green and lush. The deer come right up to this window sometimes."

"Wow. That does sound beautiful." This was better. Talking about safe things. Taking it a little slower. Sawyer was the first guy she'd done so much as have a meal with since she and Jared broke up, unless you counted Ethan and Spencer, who were both in happy relationships. She needed to get the feel for this dating thing again before she jumped right in.

"We see deer in winter, too. But they stay closer to the woods. Actually, this is usually about the time they come out. " He swiveled in his chair to peer out the window. "Yep. Two of them. Right over there."

He pointed, and Peyton squinted out the window. "I don't see anything."

"Right at the edge of the tree line."

But all she saw was more trees.

Sawyer pushed his chair back and came to stand behind her. He bent until his face was almost pressed against hers and raised his hand to point again. She tried to follow the line of his finger, but she was too aware of his nearness.

"Where?" Her voice sounded scratchy and unnatural.

He used his hands to turn her head, grazing a thumb across her cheek, then let his arm fall across her shoulders. She tried not to tense as she peered into the darkness. But her heart was beating too fast, and she felt that same mix of exhilaration and terror she'd felt on the ski hill right before she'd crashed.

Finally, she picked out two shapes moving against the silhouette of the trees. "I see them."

The deer were nosing through the snow, seemingly oblivious that they had an audience.

She waited for Sawyer to lift his arm off her and move back to his seat.

But he pressed closer and inhaled deeply. "You smell nice."

"Thanks," she managed to get out. But she needed space.

Right now.

She stood abruptly, and he grabbed the chair to keep from losing his balance.

She limped to the window, pretending to strain for a better look at the deer as she drew in a few calming breaths. Now that she was on her feet, her ankle set to throbbing again, but she ignored the pain.

In the window's reflection, she saw Sawyer move to blow out the candles on the table.

Now she felt bad. She was letting Jared's stupid warning about Sawyer prejudice her feelings about him. He'd done nothing wrong. He just wanted to show her that he liked her.

And she liked him, too.

"I'm sorry." She turned toward him and made herself meet his eyes. "I didn't mean to push you away. I just need to move a little more slowly."

"Of course." His smile was charming and little-boyish at the same time, and she found herself smiling back.

She limped closer, and his expression dropped into a frown. "You shouldn't be on your feet. How about a movie?"

"I don't think there's one playing tonight." She'd checked the schedule for the lodge's small theater when they'd arrived as part of her plan to avoid Jared.

Sawyer winked. "There are some perks to owning the place, you know."

He held out his arm to her, and she took his elbow, letting him support her as they made their way to the theater.

She felt like a kid sneaking in somewhere she didn't belong as he held the door to the dark theater open for her, but she shoved the feeling aside. Sawyer's family owned the place. She wasn't doing anything wrong.

She pushed down the image of Jared glaring at Sawyer on the slopes. Pushed down the warning he'd made Leah deliver to her.

Sawyer was a good guy. She was perfectly safe with him. Jared was just being overbearing, as usual.

"Be right back." Sawyer gave her shoulder a gentle squeeze as he led her to a row of seats on the far side of the theater, then disappeared into the projector room.

Peyton settled in and tried to relax. She wouldn't give Jared another thought tonight.

Chapter 8

Jared held the lodge door open and waited for April to pass through. When he'd met up with her earlier, she'd suggested that they skip the dining room in favor of a pizza place she knew in town, and Jared had jumped at the offer. He couldn't stand the thought of spending another minute in the building where Sawyer was working his charms on Peyton.

"Thanks for dinner." April stopped inside the doors. "Maybe we can do it again tomorrow?"

Jared ran his hand back and forth on his chin. Dinner had been nice enough, but he'd known halfway through that he and April would never work. It wasn't her—she was funny and kind and vivacious. But she wasn't Peyton.

Not that he had any idea how to tell her that. "I'm sorry. I just—"

But she held up a hand to stop him. "I kind of had a feeling. For what it's worth, I hope you patch things up with Peyton."

He chuckled wryly. Had he really talked about Peyton that much? "I'm sorry, I didn't mean to—"

But she dropped a hand onto his arm. "It was sweet, actually. She's a very lucky woman to have someone who loves her so much."

Somehow, he didn't think Peyton would see it that way.

"Anyway, maybe I'll run into you in Hope Springs sometime. My grandma's always bugging me to visit more." She gave that sparkling laugh of hers again, squeezed his forearm, and bounded across the lobby.

Jared shook his head and scrubbed his hands over his face. What was he thinking, letting a woman like that walk away in exchange for something that would never happen?

But he'd realized at dinner that if he couldn't be with Peyton, he didn't really want to be with anyone. At least not right now. Maybe never.

He trudged across the lobby, up the staircase, and through the empty hall toward his room.

He should check on Peyton's ankle, but he had no desire to hear her gushing about Sawyer to the other girls. He could check it in the morning.

But a stab of conscience stopped him as he was about to unlock his own door.

She could be in pain or need more advanced medical attention. She'd trusted him with her care, and he owed it to her to follow up.

With a sigh, he shoved his key into his pocket and crossed the hall to knock on the girls' door.

Leah pulled it open, and her face fell into a frown. "I thought you were Emma. She ran downstairs to grab some ice cream. Want to join us?"

"Where's Peyton?"

Leah shook her head. "You know where she is, Jared."

"She's not back yet?" Jared shoved the door open and looked past Leah. Sophie and Ariana waved from across the room, where they were playing some game at the table.

"Relax." Leah stood aside so he could come in. "She texted a while ago to say they were going to watch a movie."

Jared's hands clenched. "Where?" The theater had been closed when he walked past it downstairs. "If he took her to his room—"

"You know her better than that, Jared." Leah's voice was sharper than he'd ever heard it. "Sawyer opened up the theater for a private screening."

"So she's alone with him?" He clenched his teeth so hard pain shot up his jaw. If that guy laid a hand on her, so help him. "You were supposed to warn her."

"I did." Leah eyed him with a mix of pity and compassion. "But you can understand how she thought your assessment might be a little biased."

Jared blew out a breath. He supposed it might be. But it wasn't jealousy that had motivated him to tell Leah to keep Peyton away from Sawyer. Or at least, not only jealousy. He'd heard Sawyer tell one too many stories to feel comfortable with him being alone with any woman he knew. Especially one as open and trusting as Peyton.

"She has her phone on her, Jared. She'll let me know if anything is wrong."

Jared spun on his heel and stalked down the hall.

"Where are you going?" Footsteps shuffled across the carpet behind him, and the girls' door banged shut as Leah grabbed his elbow. "Don't go after her, Jared. It's not fair. To either of you."

"I just have to see that she's okay."

Leah gathered her hair at the base of her neck. "Jared, she's fine. She said she was having a really good time." She dropped her hair and laid a hand on his arm. "I'm sorry."

Jared pulled both hands through his hair and locked his fingers behind his head, pacing the short width of the hallway. "So I'm supposed to, what— Stand by and watch her go out with him?"

Leah gave him a sad smile. "Yeah. Unless you're going to change your mind and give her the life she wants, that's exactly what you're supposed to do."

Jared dropped his arms, gave Leah one last look, then strode down the hallway.

"Jared, don't." But this time Leah didn't follow him.

"I'm not," he called over his shoulder. "I just need to go for a walk."

"Where? It's late."

He raised his hands to his sides. "Doesn't matter where."

"At least let one of us come with you."

Jared shook his head and kept walking. He knew his friends would do anything for him.

But right now the only thing he needed them to do was leave him alone.

Chapter 9

Peyton tried to make herself relax. Sawyer had chosen *When Harry Met Sally*, one of her all-time favorite movies. But she couldn't concentrate on it with his arm around her. Couldn't get used to the way he was running his hand up and down her shoulder. She shifted on the double seat to put a little more distance between them, but he shifted with her, moving so that his head rested on hers.

He nuzzled his face into her hair. "You smell so good."

"So you said." She tried to keep things light. Maybe Sawyer hadn't understood what she'd meant by taking things slowly.

Then again, he was just smelling her hair.

She forced herself to take a slow breath and unclench her fists.

Sawyer wrapped a hand around hers and lowered his mouth to her neck, dusting a light kiss there.

Peyton reared back, jerking her head away. Her pulse pounded against her temple. She suddenly didn't want to be here anymore.

She half stood, waiting for Sawyer to move so she could get to the aisle. But he grabbed her hand, pulling her down next to him.

Her heart thundered harder, and the impulse to run seized her.

But Sawyer slid a gentle hand along her cheek. "Relax. You don't think I would hurt you, do you?"

She tried to get her heart rate under control. Of course he wouldn't hurt her. She was overreacting.

"Sorry. I'm not used to—"

"I know." His hand slid from her cheek into her hair. "I'm sorry if I'm moving too fast. You're just so beautiful."

He leaned closer, tilting his head down toward hers, and his eyes fell closed.

Peyton closed her eyes, too, telling herself this was what she wanted. She hadn't been kissed in almost a year.

But the moment their lips touched, she knew it wasn't right. His lips were not the ones she wanted to feel.

She pulled back as gently as she could.

Sawyer's eyes remained closed for a second longer, then he straightened. When he opened his eyes, something dark flashed in them for a second, but it was gone so quickly Peyton was sure she'd imagined it.

"I'm sorry." She set a hand on his arm, then drew it back, locking her fingers together in her lap. "I don't think I can—"

"It's okay." Sawyer blew out a breath. "Is this about Jared?"

"No." But if he had even a fragment of skill in reading people, he'd know that was untrue. When Sawyer had kissed her, all she could think was that he wasn't Jared. "I mean, it's complicated—"

"What's complicated?" He gripped her hands. "I like you. I think you like me. Jared has nothing to do with anything anymore."

She nodded. Of course he was right. Jared shouldn't have any bearing on anything she did.

His grip on her hands loosened, and he moved closer, sliding his hands up her arms. "That's better. Now let's try this again."

Before she'd figured out what he meant by "this," he'd wrapped both arms around her back and was pressing his lips to hers.

She gasped in a sharp breath and tried to slide away, but he squeezed her tighter, his mouth moving hungrily against hers. Nothing about it felt sweet or warm or right.

Blood pounded in her ears as she raised her hands to his chest and pushed. But he was bigger than her and had her wrapped too firmly.

"Please," she gasped around his mouth. "Stop."

He pulled his head back and loosened his grip slightly. "What's wrong?"

"I just— I want to go back to my room—" She tried to wriggle free from his grasp, but his arms didn't budge.

He gave her a slow smile. "That sounds nice. But we're alone here. No one's going to disturb us."

Fear clawed at her lungs. That wasn't what she'd meant.

"No, I—" She struggled harder.

But he was already leaning closer, bringing his mouth toward hers.

She gave a hard shove against his chest and screamed the only word she could think of in that moment.

"Jared!"

Chapter 10

Jared jolted upright and swiveled his head to search the lobby. It was empty, aside from an older couple snuggling in front of the fire. But he could have sworn he heard something.

He was probably going crazy from sitting here so long.

After walking the grounds for an hour, he'd been frozen through, but he hadn't been able to face going up to his room, so he'd planted himself in the lobby. He couldn't help it that the comfortable seat he'd chosen happened to be tucked into a nook near the theater. Or that he had a view of the theater doors if he leaned out and craned his neck. Which he'd found himself doing.

Frequently.

He glanced at the oversize clock on the opposite wall. He'd been here for forty minutes already. Surely their movie would be done soon, and they'd come out. He'd see that Peyton was safe, and everything would be fine.

He tried not to imagine what else they might be doing in there besides watching the movie. He knew Peyton intended to wait for marriage.

But that didn't mean she was immune to Sawyer's charms.

Jared jumped to his feet and started toward the theater doors.

But halfway there he drew up short. Leah was right. He had no business interfering. He should go to bed.

He turned toward the steps, but a sound stopped him.

This time he was sure he heard it. A shout of some sort.

He swiveled to search the lobby again. But the couple by the fire were laughing, and the desk clerk was typing on the computer.

Anyway, it had sounded like it came from behind him.

From the theater.

He spun and rushed the door, not letting himself pause to think. He charged inside but drew up short at the sudden darkness.

"Sawyer, please!" That was definitely Peyton's voice.

Jared's heart lurched, and he stumbled forward, not caring when he bashed his leg against the back of a seat.

His pulse drummed in his ears as his eyes swept the empty seats. There.

Sawyer had his arms wrapped around Peyton, his face lowered to hers.

Jared froze. Everything in him went numb. Nothing could have prepared him for seeing Peyton kissing another man.

But she jerked her head back. "Stop!"

Her scream shot him across the room as a boiling rage took over.

In two seconds flat, his grip was locked on Sawyer's shirt, and he yanked him into the aisle.

He pulled his fist back and drove it into Sawyer's cheekbone.

Sawyer staggered to the side, grabbing his face and swearing. "What the— Who do you think you are?"

But Jared ignored him and turned to Peyton. She was white and shaking.

He held a hand out to her. "You okay?" His voice was gruff and barely controlled.

She nodded but then screamed as a hand fell on his shoulder and spun him around. He knew what was coming, and he knew what he had to do.

The punch landed against his eye socket, shooting fireworks through his skull. But he shook off the pain. He'd dealt with worse than that.

He pivoted on his rear leg, putting all his force into the reverse punch that smashed into Sawyer's nose, followed by a swift hook to his jaw.

Sawyer doubled over, lifting a hand to staunch the flow of blood from his nose.

"You will never touch her again." All the rage Jared had ever felt for his father, for any man who would hurt a woman, spiked his words.

He grabbed Peyton's hand and pulled her out of the seats. She clutched at his hand as he led her down the aisle, but she kept stumbling.

He stopped and swept an arm under her knees to pick her up.

She hissed in a breath but didn't protest.

Neither of them said a word as he carried her out of the theater and across the lobby.

"I can walk," she finally said at the base of the staircase.

He set her down. But he couldn't look at her.

NOT UNTIL THIS MOMENT

Now she knew the real him. Knew the anger he was capable of feeling. The hurt he was capable of inflicting.

The silence stretched as they made their way slowly up the stairs. She was limping pretty badly, but she kept climbing, her breaths coming in short puffs.

When they reached their rooms, he made himself look at her. She was studying the key in her hand.

"I should check your ankle."

"It's fine." She shoved her key in the lock.

He started to protest, then closed his mouth.

After seeing that he could use his hands for far more than healing, she probably wanted to get as far away from him as possible.

And he didn't blame her one bit.

Look at the bright side. He stuck his own key into the lock. *At least now she won't want to marry you anymore.*

Some bright side.

Chapter 11

If it was possible, Peyton's eyes were heavier now than they'd been when she'd finally dropped into an uneasy sleep an hour before dawn. She groaned as she pushed the covers off herself. She'd spent most of the night reliving the paralyzing helplessness that had washed over her when Sawyer refused to stop kissing her. The relief she'd felt when Jared burst into the theater looking ready to burn down any obstacle to get to her. The anger she'd felt at herself for not listening to his warning in the first place.

But she'd wanted so badly to believe that Sawyer was the answer to her prayers for a future.

She scowled at herself in the mirror as she limped toward the bathroom. The others had already gone down to breakfast, but she'd pleaded a headache and said she'd meet them in the lobby so they could go to church together. Usually, Sundays were her favorite day of the trip. She loved the little country church they attended, with the friendly locals. Loved the little diner they always went to for lunch. Loved the park next to it where they'd had more than one snowball fight.

But today the thought of all that left a sour feeling in her stomach.

She stepped into the shower, trying to let the hot water wash away her memories. But it only seemed to amplify them.

Not only memories of last night. But memories of all the beautiful moments she'd shared with Jared. Of how he'd always made her feel safe. Of how he'd told her he couldn't marry her.

Why not, Lord? Why isn't the future I want happening for me?

Her tears mingled with the spray from the shower. Didn't God see that she needed some divine intervention here? She was trying so hard to find a husband and a family and the life she'd always wanted. So why wasn't it happening?

By the time she got out of the shower, she had five minutes to finish getting ready before she had to meet the others. She threw on her clothes, swiped on some eye makeup to hide the puffiness and dark circles, then hobbled out the door as quickly as she could, wincing with each step.

Halfway down the staircase, a sudden trembling took over her legs. What if Sawyer was at the desk? What if he approached her?

She tried to ignore the shakiness and keep going, but her legs refused to carry her down another step.

She stood, frozen.

"Peyton." Leah's relieved cry from the bottom of the staircase drew her eyes, and before she could move another inch, her friend had run up the steps and engulfed her in a hug. "Jared told us what happened. Are you okay?"

She nodded even as tears pricked at her eyelids again.

Leah wrapped an arm around her and led her toward the rest of the group, gathered in the sunken area around the fireplace. She started to breathe easier.

Until she caught sight of Jared.

A vicious purple and green bruise surrounded his eye, which was almost swollen shut.

He stood with the others but refused to look at her.

She didn't blame him. What must he think of her after what he had seen last night?

Had she even thanked him for coming to her rescue? Everything was such a blur she couldn't remember.

"I've already let the desk clerk know we'll be checking out today," Ethan said in a low voice. "We'll leave it up to you if we go to church first or just head out right away."

"Oh, we don't have to leave." Peyton was touched, but there was no way she was going to let Sawyer ruin their whole vacation.

"We're leaving." Jared's voice was hard, brooking no arguments.

Leah gave him a look, then turned to her. "Do you still want to go to church?"

"Yeah. I'd like that."

She tried to ignore Jared's grimace. She hadn't seen him in church since they'd broken up, but he'd just have to deal with it. She needed the reassurance of God's love right about now.

They moved as a group toward the door, her friends surrounding her like a human shield. As they crossed the parking lot, Peyton tried to maneuver closer to Jared so she could thank him. But every time she got near him, he skirted away.

Then they were in the van and she was pressed between Leah and Ariana, who seemed determined to keep her distracted.

But once they were seated in church, there was nothing to keep Peyton's mind from wandering to last night. What would have happened if Jared hadn't come in? Would Sawyer have tried to do more?

A shudder passed through her, and Leah reached over to squeeze her hand. Peyton squeezed back gratefully, then bowed her head, trying to pray as she waited for the service to begin.

But she had poured out everything she had in the shower this morning. So she sat quietly and waited for God to calm her spirit as he had so many times in her life.

She didn't understand why she felt more agitated than ever by the time the service started. The calming words of the hymns only stirred her up more, until she felt a restless need to move. She bounced her leg and twisted her hands in her lap. Leah shot her a raised eyebrow. Peyton sat on her hands and tried to still her legs.

But as the pastor stood to deliver his message, she felt the need to move again.

Until he started talking.

"Have you ever felt like God doesn't know what he's doing with your life?" The pastor sounded as if he were having a conversation with a friend.

Peyton fell dead still. Was he talking directly to her?

"Sure," the pastor continued, "you trust that he's in control. But you think he's making a mess of everything."

Peyton leaned forward in her seat, mouth open. That's exactly how she felt. She'd prayed over and over and over again for a husband who would love her the way her parents loved each other. And God had given her that man in Jared. But he wasn't willing to be her husband. And then, yesterday, she'd thought God had sent her another man. Another chance.

Wrong again.

So what was she supposed to do next?

Peyton forced her attention back to the sermon. The pastor was telling a story from his own life. Something about how he'd wanted to be a baseball player. He'd even made it to the minor leagues. And just when he was on the cusp of his big break, he'd been in an accident that had destroyed his shoulder.

"Let me tell you, I railed at God about that. I told him, I said, 'God, next time maybe you should check on what my future is going to be before you go letting me waste my time on something that's never going to pan out.' Can you imagine talking to God that way?"

Peyton dropped her gaze to her lap. She didn't have to imagine it. Hadn't she done the same thing a thousand times? *God, make sure the next one wants to marry me first.*

"And then I was so bold as to tell God what he should do with my life now that he'd messed it up. I said, well, if I can't be a baseball player, I want to be a coach. High school, college, pro, I didn't care. I applied for all these jobs. And each one came back: no, nope, no thank you. And I was devastated. Why was God blocking my plans at every turn?"

The pastor paused, and Peyton held her breath. That's what she wanted to know, too. Why did God keep stopping her plans? When would he start making things happen for her?

"And here's the thing I've finally realized." The pastor paused, looking at each person in turn. When his eyes fell on Peyton, she stilled. She could feel that whatever he said next was going to be the truth.

"I didn't see it at the time," he continued. "I was too busy resenting God. But now, I can see it. It's right there, in Jeremiah 29:11. God says, 'For I know the plans I have for you, plans to prosper you and not to harm you, plans to give you hope and a future.'"

The pastor spread his arms wide. "Do you see it?" He smiled as if he'd just delivered the greatest gift. "I was running after *my* plans. Not God's. And that was about the dumbest thing I could do. Who was I to think that I knew what was best for my future? God's plans are perfect. Why would I want anything less than that?"

Peyton sank back in her seat. Was that what she was doing? Running after her own plans instead of God's? Had she really thought she knew what she needed better than her heavenly father did?

Okay, Lord. The prayer flowed from her heart. *Help me to stop fighting your plans. Whatever they are, I know they are better than any plan I could come up with.*

She shifted in her seat. What if God's plans for her didn't include marriage and a family? What if they looked nothing like what she wanted so badly? *Help me to be content with the hope and the future you give me, even if it means remaining single.*

Simply praying the words pierced her heart, but as she stood to sing the next song, a stillness settled over her. Trusting God with her future was right. No matter where he may lead her.

Chapter 12

Jared exhaled in relief. The church service was finally over. He'd had to force himself to stay in his seat as the pastor had gone on and on about God's plans.

Where were God's plans when he was a kid? Was it God's plan for him to watch his dad beat his mom to within an inch of her life? Was it God's plan for his mom to walk out, leaving him alone with his dad? Was it God's plan to give him a past that guaranteed he couldn't have a future?

Because if those were God's plans, no thank you. He was doing just fine with his own plans.

What plans? To be alone and miserable the rest of your life?

He shoved the thought aside as he filed out of the pew behind the others. Alone and miserable was better than being with someone and constantly fearing he'd hurt them someday.

In the lobby, Peyton was having an enthusiastic conversation with the pastor. At least if she dated him, Jared probably wouldn't have to worry about her safety.

For the millionth time he kicked himself for letting her get into that situation with Sawyer yesterday. He should have done more than tell Leah to warn her. He should have warned her himself. Or barged in there sooner and dragged her away from Sawyer, whether she liked it or not.

Being the object of her fury would be better than being the one who had let her get hurt.

Again.

"I'll be in the van," he muttered to Leah.

He pushed out the church doors before she could answer. The others would catch up when they were ready. He couldn't stay in here a minute longer.

In the van, he leaned his head against the seat and let out a long breath. He couldn't wait to get home. To put this entire weekend behind him. To put Peyton behind him. Now that he knew she'd never look at him without seeing the monster he'd become last night, maybe she'd be easier to let go of.

The passenger door opened, but Jared didn't turn his head.

"Hey." It was Dan's voice. "How's the shiner? Need some ice?"

Jared shook his head. Pastor Boy here could go ahead judge him for hitting Sawyer last night. He'd do it again a hundred times if it meant keeping Peyton safe.

"At least you didn't break anything. I got in a fight once in high school and broke my hand."

Jared turned his head a fraction, eying Dan.

"It was stupid." Dan chuckled lightly. "The kid was like twice my size. But he insulted my dad, and I kind of lost it. I aimed for his face, but he ducked and my hand ended up smashing into a locker."

"At least you had a dad worth defending," Jared muttered.

"Yeah." Dan sounded thoughtful. "I guess I never thought of it that way."

Funny how people who had good parents—parents who loved them—never really thought about it. What would his life have been like if he hadn't had to give his dad a thought?

"Anyway." Dan flipped on the heater. "Just remember that even if your earthly father is less than perfect, you have a heavenly father who loves you perfectly."

Jared nodded tightly. He knew Dan meant well. But for Dan the word father meant safety and love and acceptance. For Jared, it meant terror and loathing. So he didn't need two fathers. One was more than enough.

"Look, I know we don't know each other that well. But if you ever want to talk—"

"Here come the others." Jared jabbed at the buttons to open the back doors, and Dan fell silent.

Jared kept his focus on the steering wheel as the others climbed in so he wouldn't accidentally catch a glimpse of the fear he knew would hover in Peyton's eyes when she looked at him now.

"Let's eat. I'm starved." Leah tapped the back of his seat. "To the diner, driver."

Ten minutes later, Jared pulled the van into the already full diner parking lot.

He swallowed a groan. They'd be waiting here for at least an hour before they were seated.

"Should we skip it?"

But he already expected the variations of "no way" that sounded from the backseat.

"Peyton?" His eyes sought hers in the rearview mirror. Her opinion was the only one he cared about right now. If she wanted to get out of here, he was going to take her home, no matter what the others wanted.

She met his eyes in the mirror for a second. "I think we should stay."

He sighed and ran a hand over his head.

Fine.

They'd eat and then they'd be on the road.

He pushed his door open and waited for the others to clamber out.

Peyton hung back as the rest of the group surged toward the door.

He gestured for her to go ahead of him, but she remained planted.

"Can we talk?" Her brow was furrowed into grooves, and she refused to look him in the eyes.

He'd known this was coming, but his heart shriveled anyway.

"Yeah, okay."

"How about the park?" She pointed to the tracked-up snow at the park next door as if he didn't know exactly where she meant.

He took stock of her leggings and sweater. "Won't you be cold?"

She gave a little laugh. "You worry about me too much."

He supposed he did at that. But he didn't know how not to. Especially after last night.

"At least let me help you walk there." He held out his arm, bracing for her refusal. But she wrapped her hand around his forearm, leaning her weight into him.

He tried not to let himself feel anything at her touch, but it was impossible not to notice the electricity of her hand on his arm.

"I should really check your ankle." If it was broken, she shouldn't be walking anywhere.

"It's a little better today."

He stole a glance at her. "Liar."

She puffed out a breath. "Forgot you could read me. But at least it isn't worse than it was yesterday. That's a good sign, right?"

"I'll feel better after I check it."

"Fine." She tightened her grip on his arm as they moved into the snow-covered grass. "You can check it when we sit down."

He led her to the closest picnic table and waited as she lowered herself onto it, her leg stretched to the side on the bench.

He sat carefully next to her foot, gently sliding the bottom of her legging up just enough to examine her ankle. It was still purple and bruised, but the swelling had gone down a bit. He set a hand lightly to the skin, careful not to apply too much pressure.

Finally, he was satisfied. "I'm going to stick with mild sprain. But you really have to stay off it for the next few days."

She waved a hand in the air. "I'm not going to be doing any more skiing, if that's what you mean. I was stupid to think I could handle that black diamond."

Jared shrugged, gazing toward the swings. "Sawyer should have known better."

The name sent a tension crackling through the air between them. They both fell silent.

Jared chanced a sideways look at her. Her face was turned away from him, and her lips were tipped into a deep frown. Was that how she would always look when she saw him now?

"Peyton, I—"

"Jared, about—"

They both stopped and laughed nervously, then fell silent again.

"You go first," he said after a minute.

"I just wanted to say, what you saw last night—" She stared at her hands in her lap. "I wasn't— I just don't want you to think—"

"I know."

She nodded and blinked quickly. "I should have listened to you. I shouldn't have let him—"

Jared shoved to his feet and moved to crouch in front of her. He grabbed her hands. "Hey. This is not your fault. This is all on Sawyer." Who deserved a lot worse than what he'd gotten.

"Okay?" He waited for her to look at him and nod, then squeezed her hands and returned to his spot at the far end of the bench.

She let out a long sigh, and he watched her. He needed to know she was going to be okay. She offered him a weak smile. But it wasn't enough to hide her shiver.

"See, you are cold. Let's get back to the diner." He stood to help her up, but she refused his hand.

"Not until you go."

"Go where?"

"You were about to say something before."

He wrapped a hand around the back of his neck. He didn't want to say it anymore. Not when things finally felt a little easier between them. But he had to.

He slipped off his jacket and held it out to her. She hesitated a moment, then took it and wrapped it around herself.

The sharp breeze sliced through Jared's dress shirt, but he didn't care.

"I just wanted to apologize for the way I reacted last night. I shouldn't have lost my temper like that. I'm sorry if I scared you." He focused on the spot where his toe was plowing a bare spot in the snow.

"Jared."

He'd thought he knew every tone of her voice, but this one he didn't recognize. It was enough to pull his eyes to hers. That pale blue drew him in. He took an involuntary step forward. She shifted so that her foot was on the ground, then grabbed his hand and tugged him to sit on the bench next to her.

"You didn't scare me. You *saved* me. I don't know what would have happened if—"

She broke off, and Jared's fists clenched. The thought of Peyton being hurt was too much.

"But the way I punched him. You weren't even a little scared to know I was capable of that? You weren't afraid I could do that to you?"

Peyton tilted her head toward her shoulder, studying him. "Jared, you are the person who makes me feel safest in the world. I know you would never hurt me."

Something broke in Jared, and he doubled forward, dropping his head into his hands. How could she trust him? How could she be so sure he would never do that?

But she didn't know how he was raised. Didn't know what his father had been capable of. What he'd passed on to Jared.

A soft hand fell on his back. "Where is this coming from?" Her voice was gentle, concerned. Inviting. But he shook his head. He couldn't tell her. Couldn't let her know about the true monster he was destined to become someday.

"Jared, please. Don't shut me out." Her whisper shot right through him, and he stood abruptly.

She thought she wanted to know?

Fine.

Maybe this was the final severing their relationship needed.

"You know how I don't talk to my dad and I don't see my mom? You want to know why that is?"

Hurt crossed Peyton's face. "You know I do. But you always refused to talk about it."

"That's because I didn't want to see the way you'd look at me. I didn't want you to be afraid of me."

"Afraid of you? Jared, I just told you I could never—"

He held up a hand. If he was going to tell her this, he had to do it now, before he took the coward's way out again.

"My dad beat my mom. Gave her bruises. Sometimes broke her bones. One time almost killed her."

Peyton's eyes widened, and she covered her mouth with both hands. He turned away. He didn't need to see her horror.

"I told my mom so many times to leave him. That we weren't safe. And she finally did." He sucked in a shaky breath. "Only she left me, too."

Peyton's gasp echoed across the empty park and stuck in his heart.

But he wasn't done yet. He hadn't told her the worst of it. "He hit me sometimes. Not as bad as he hit her. By then, I think he knew I was big enough to hit back." He swallowed, blinking back the memories. "Anyway, I moved out the day I graduated high school. And you know what my dad said to me that day? He said—" He made his voice gruff and hoarse, in an impression of his father. "'You think you're too good to turn out like your old man, son. But you wait and see. This is your future. Same as it was mine. Same as it was my father's. It's in our blood.'"

His breath came in short gasps at the memory. He'd been trying to forget it, trying to ignore it, trying to tell himself his dad was wrong his whole life. But deep down, he knew he was his father's son.

At least now Peyton knew. At least now he wouldn't have to be afraid of her finding out. Of what she'd think of him once she knew.

Even if it nearly killed him to realize how she must see him now.

"Oh, Jared." A pair of gentle arms wrapped around him from behind.

Every muscle in his body lost the tension that had been keeping him upright. He sagged and spun toward her, letting his arms go around her and ducking his head until it rested on hers.

A single sob tore lose from his middle, and her arms clutched him closer.

He stood there, just breathing. Slowly, a feeling of safety and peace descended on him. How could someone so small make him feel so protected?

After a few minutes, she pulled back, but she slid her hand into his and led him toward the bench. She pressed close to his side as they sat. After all he'd told her, what was she still doing here?

"You never told me." There was no accusation in her voice. More like . . . understanding.

"At least now you know why I can't marry. I have to break the cycle. I will not become my dad."

Peyton dropped her head to his shoulder, and he ached at the familiar move of trust.

"Whether you marry or not, Jared, you are not your father."

"But he said—"

"He was wrong. I know you. I know your heart. You would never hurt me or any other woman or child. You are a good man, Jared. You've made it your mission in life to help people who are hurt. Do you really think one day you're just going to switch that off and start hurting people?"

Jared shrugged.

"You know." Her voice was soft and sure at the same time. "I realized something in church this morning."

Jared tensed, but he found he wanted to know what she had to say, even if it was about church. "What's that?"

"I realized I thought I had my future all planned out and that God would just work things to match my plans." Her smile was tinged with sadness. "But much as we might want to plan our future, that's not what God calls us to do. And I think, you've been so sure all these years that your future was what your dad said it would be. But it's not, Jared. That is not God's plan for you."

He wanted to believe it. "How can you be so sure?"

"Because—" She locked her fingers with his. "You have another father, too, Jared, and he has made you into the most incredible man I know. He used all those awful, awful things that happened to you because of your father to shape you into a man who serves others without ever thinking about his own safety."

He blinked at her, all his air caught in his throat.

Was that really how she saw him?

But he could tell by the way she looked at him.

It was.

Chapter 13

"Check." Peyton gave a triumphant smile as she sat back in her seat.

"No way." Jared leaned forward to peer at the chess board, and Peyton couldn't stop herself from studying his face. The swelling in his eye had gone down, although the bruise was a sickly greenish blue. But that's not what drew her attention. Instead it was the relaxed set of his jaw, the new light in his eyes. He seemed to have become a different man since they'd talked in the park yesterday. A man more at peace with himself and the world around him. A man more willing to trust and open up.

It'd taken a lot of talking to convince him and the others that they should stay to finish out the trip. They'd only finally agreed to it when she promised she'd make sure she was with at least one of them at all times. So far today, Leah had popped in three times and Dan twice to offer to take a turn sitting around the fireplace with her so Jared could ski. But he refused to leave her side.

She couldn't deny the warmth that filled her with. Even if he was only doing it to keep Sawyer away. Fortunately, it seemed to be working. She hadn't seen Sawyer once all morning.

NOT UNTIL THIS MOMENT

She and Jared had already played four games of chess, two games of Scrabble, and a single round of Pictionary that had them laughing so hard at her terrible drawings that they were gasping for breath. She couldn't deny that the morning had been nice. Comfortable.

Enough to make her want more.

But she pushed the thought aside. She was done trying to force things to happen. For now, it was enough to be talking to each other and having fun together again. She'd missed their friendship more than anything.

"Actually." Jared gave her a stunned smile. "That's checkmate. You beat me."

"I did?" Without thinking, she leaned over and hugged him. He'd taught her to play chess when they started dating, but she'd never beat him at it before.

"Wait a minute." She pulled back, trying to ignore the spicy sweet scent that lingered on her from the contact. "You let me win, didn't you?"

He raised his hands in front of him. "Nope. I promise. I know how much you hate that."

She grinned again. He'd tried to let her win a game of tennis once but had learned pretty quickly that wasn't going to score him any points with her.

Jared stretched his arms over his head, and she looked away so her eyes wouldn't be drawn to the way his t-shirt tightened against his biceps.

"You hungry?" Jared leaned forward to put the chess set away.

"Starved." On cue, her stomach rumbled, and Jared nudged her with a laugh. He'd always teased that he could set his clock by her stomach.

He stood and held out a hand to help her up. As soon as she was on her feet, he wrapped an arm around her back to help her hobble toward the dining room. The familiar feel of his arm around her was almost enough to make her forget that a whole year had gone by since he'd last held her close.

He steered her into the dining room, where a huge buffet had been set out. Peyton's mouth watered as the smell of lasagna wafted to her.

Jared led her to a table and pulled up an extra chair for her to prop her foot on. "I'll be right back with some food."

Her eyes followed him across the room. She wondered, did anyone else watching him see the demons that haunted him? Until yesterday, she'd had no idea. What he'd told her had broken her heart—both for the young boy who'd had to endure such treatment and for the man who carried around the weight of thinking he'd turn out like his father.

How could he believe that?

And how could he have let that keep them from having a life together?

But now that he'd told her, maybe he would rethink things.

She tried to tamp down the hope rising in her chest.

She'd promised she would wait on God's plans. And she had to accept that those plans most likely did not include Jared. They might not include anyone.

Then again, the way Jared was looking at her as he crossed the room carrying two plates stacked with food, maybe she wasn't so crazy to hope he was part of God's plan for her after all.

"They had those breadsticks you love." He passed her a plate as he sat, offering a smile that made her pulse do funny things. "I got you a few."

She glanced at the plate, and a laugh burst out of her. "I'll say." Breadsticks took up at least half of the space. Not that she was complaining.

She folded her hands and bowed her head to give silent thanks for the food.

Heavenly father, thank you—

"Do you mind if I pray with you?" Jared's voice was low, hesitant, but that didn't stop the enormous smile she felt stretching her lips. How had God answered that prayer before she'd even asked?

She reached across the table and gripped Jared's hands in hers. As they both bowed their heads, Jared began to pray. "Lord, we want to thank you for this meal you have provided. And that they had Peyton's favorite breadsticks."

She couldn't help the giggle that bubbled up. Who was this lighthearted man she was praying with?

"And thank you," Jared continued, "for keeping Peyton safe and for making her the strong, resilient, trusting woman she is. Please help her to seek after your plan for her life."

Peyton's smile melted, and she had to blink away the moisture that suddenly clung to her lashes. She'd always been touched when people prayed for her. But to hear Jared praying for her? *That* arrowed right into her heart. In the best way.

"And—" Jared cleared his throat. "Thank you for using her and others to remind me that you are my perfect father."

"Amen," Peyton choked out. She had to keep her head bowed for a second after the prayer ended to get her heart under control.

"Thank you," she whispered as Jared slid his hands gently from hers.

His smile was soft and easy as he scooped a forkful of lasagna.

She started with a breadstick, savoring the garlic butter that coated the airy dough.

"How are things at the bakery?" Jared snatched one of her breadsticks, and she pretended to swat at him. He grinned and took a bite.

"It's going well. I'm getting to be pretty booked solid with weddings." The familiar pang shot through her at the mention of weddings, but it wasn't as sharp as usual. "I have one this weekend, actually. Since it's Valentine's Day, the cake is going to have a trail of fondant hearts all the way up the layers."

She broke off. Valentine's Day was the last thing they should be talking about together.

But he leaned forward, his warm gaze inviting her to continue.

"Anyway, if things keep up like this, I think I'm going to have to hire some help. At least for the summer."

"That's great. I'm proud of you."

She ducked her head and concentrated on cutting through a noodle. "Thanks."

She'd met Jared only days before she was scheduled to open her bakery in the cute little building that had drawn her to Hope Springs. He'd encouraged her when the idea of getting a single customer had been daunting. His support was a large part of what had given her the courage to keep going after her first wedding was a disaster, ending with the top of the cake on the floor.

"I wonder if—" But Jared broke off as the rest of their friends surrounded them. Was she only imagining the flash of disappointment in his eyes?

"Couldn't wait for us?" Ethan gave Jared's shoulder a light bump. Everyone's cheeks were pink, and they'd brought the fresh scent of the cold in with them.

"You know Peyton's stomach." Jared gave her a private smile that made her insides swoop the way they had when she and Jared first started dating.

Hopefully no one else noticed the blush she felt rising to her cheeks.

"You will not believe what happened to me out there." Leah plopped into the seat next to Peyton.

As she turned her attention to her friend, Peyton couldn't help sneaking a glance at Jared.

And if she wasn't mistaken, he was watching her, too.

Chapter 14

Jared couldn't stop smiling as he watched the staircase. He'd promised to sit with Peyton again today while the others skied, and he couldn't wait for her to get down here.

He'd insisted on being the one to stay with her yesterday only because he didn't trust Sawyer to stay away unless he knew Jared was with her. But as the day had gone on, he'd almost forgotten about Sawyer. He'd been so caught up in just being with Peyton again.

All those little things he'd fallen in love with—the things he'd spent the past year trying to forget—were still there. The way she tilted her head to the side when she laughed. The way she lifted a self-conscious hand to her hair whenever someone gazed at her for more than a few seconds. The way she could steal his breath with just a look.

And there were new things to fall in love with, too. Like the way she looked at him with complete trust even now that she knew the truth of his past. The way she smiled whenever he said her name. The way she'd rested her hands in his and let him pray for them.

By the time he'd said goodnight to her last night, he'd known he was a goner. He could tell himself he'd get over her someday. But it wasn't true. And he didn't really want it to be.

Because since yesterday, he'd been rethinking what he wanted for the future. And no matter what he did, he couldn't see that future without Peyton. But he didn't know how that could happen—*if* it could. Because the thought of marriage still terrified him. But if that was the only way he could be with her . . .

He forced his thoughts to a stop. For now, he'd just enjoy this day with her.

At last, he spotted her at the top of the steps with Leah and Emma. She wore a soft white sweater that made her hair and eyes look lighter than ever. Jared noted with satisfaction that she was limping less, though it meant he'd have fewer excuses to wrap his arm around her.

Her smile as she crossed the room toward him could have melted all the snow on the hills. If he had to guess, his probably matched.

"You sure you want to stay inside?" Leah got to him before Peyton did. "There's some pretty nice powder out there. I don't mind sitting with her."

"I'm staying." Jared practically growled at his friend, but she shot him a warning look.

"Jared, it's not—"

He held up a hand. "Don't say it's not fair."

"Well, it's not," Leah muttered as Peyton and Emma reached them.

"Good morning." His eyes locked on Peyton's, and he took a step closer.

"Morning."

But Leah stepped between them, turning to Peyton. "I was just telling Jared I'd sit with you so he could get some time on the slopes since it's our last day here."

"Oh, of course. You should ski." Her lips were still lifted in a smile, but it didn't mask the disappointment in her eyes.

If he hadn't already been decided, he was now. "I'm not skiing."

The light that returned to Peyton's eyes made the small sacrifice worth it.

"Fine." Leah huffed. "We'll be back at lunchtime. Maybe this time you two could wait for us before enjoying your romantic meal."

"We—"

But Peyton laid a gentle hand on his arm as Leah marched for the doors, Emma following with a helpless shrug. "She's just trying to protect me. Just like you are."

Jared nodded. He just wished he wasn't the one Leah was trying to protect Peyton from.

Not that he blamed her. He'd already broken her best friend's heart once. If he wasn't careful, he might do it again.

But he would be careful this time.

Starting with being sure of his own feelings before he talked to her about them.

Chapter 15

"Hey." The soft whisper was followed by the gentle press of lips to her hair, and Peyton snuggled closer.

She wasn't sure where she was, but she knew she was safe and warm, and that was enough. She never wanted to leave this spot.

"Hey." The whisper was more insistent this time, and a hand squeezed her shoulder.

"Mmm?"

"We should get you up to bed. You fell asleep."

She opened her eyes, letting them adjust to the low lights, the dark lobby fireplace. An arm was wrapped protectively around her, and her face was pressed into something solid yet comfortable. She jerked upright as she realized it was Jared's shoulder.

"Sorry, I—"

But he smiled at her. "You were in the middle of telling me about the wedding with the flamingos, and you fell asleep."

"I did?" She rubbed at her eyes, trying to work out the tangles in her thoughts. "Sorry if I was boring you with my stories."

"You never bore me." He brushed a piece of hair off her cheek. The move was gentle and familiar, and she couldn't help leaning into his hand.

"Jared?"

"Yeah?"

She meant to tell him she was sorry she'd crossed the line and fallen asleep on his shoulder, but instead, she leaned closer and pressed her lips to his.

He stiffened and inhaled sharply, but then his arms came around her, and his lips responded softly, gently. This was not at all the hungry kiss Sawyer had tried to force on her. Jared's kiss made her feel cherished and protected.

Loved.

Slowly, she pulled back.

The past two days with Jared had been nothing short of perfect. But it was late, and tomorrow they'd go back to their lives in Hope Springs. And she'd have to face the fact that as much as she wanted a future with him, that didn't seem to be God's plan. Or Jared's.

"I'm sorry." The whisper barely made it past her lips. "I shouldn't have—"

A gentle finger tipped her chin up until she was gazing into Jared's eyes. What she saw there made everything in her warm.

"It's okay." One side of Jared's mouth lifted, but his eyes remained totally serious. "Peyton, I've tried to move on. Tried to pretend I don't still feel something for you. But the truth is—" He slid his hands into hers. "I still love you."

He didn't move after he said it. Just waited, watching her. She wondered vaguely if he was even breathing, he was so still.

Then again, she wasn't absolutely sure she was breathing, either.

"I love you, too." She closed her eyes. These next words were going to be the hardest she'd ever had to say in her life. "But we want different things for the future. And I don't think—"

"No, wait, Peyton." He slid closer, gripping both of her hands in his and bringing them to his lips. The kiss he pressed to them was so tender it made her heart squeeze. "I've been thinking about that. And I can't lose you again. I won't. And if that means I need to marry you, then—" He blew out a quick breath, it's warmth tickling her fingers. "Maybe I could consider marriage. Someday."

Her eyes filled. If he'd said those words to her a year ago, she would have been in a dress shop by morning. But she wasn't going to try to force her future anymore.

"I can't do this again, Jared." The whisper scraped against her vocal cords. "I tried so hard for so long to make God give me a future with you. But I'm giving over the reins to him now."

Jared's shoulders sagged, and he directed his gaze to the empty fireplace. "Is this because—" He drew a labored breath. "Is this because of what I told you the other day?"

"No." She grabbed his arm and waited for him to look at her. "It has nothing to do with that. I'm so grateful you told me. And if anything, it makes me love you more. To know what you grew up with and to see the man you became in spite of it. But I don't want you to marry me just because you think it's the only way to hold onto me. If I do get married, I want it to be to someone who wants to build a life with me. Who's committed to forever together."

"I do want—" He lifted her hands to his heart, but she gently pulled them back.

"I'm sorry, Jared."

He looked away and swallowed hard. When he turned back, his red eyes almost made her take back everything she'd said.

But she had to give this over to God.

Had to trust that he had the best plan for her future.

Jared nodded slowly, pressing his lips together. Then he stood. "Let's get you up to bed."

She pushed to her feet. Her body felt heavier than it had ever been as she followed him.

Upstairs, he stepped into his room without another word. She watched his door close, then leaned on her own and let the silent tears come.

She knew trusting God with her future was the right thing to do.

So why did it feel like she was cutting out her own heart all over again?

Chapter 16

Jared rattled the doors of Hope Church one more time, as if expecting them to magically unlock for him. He didn't know why he'd thought the doors would be open on a Saturday afternoon, anyway. He only knew that he needed to talk to someone, and Dan had offered, but he didn't know how else to get ahold of him.

The drive home from Tamarack Wednesday morning had been torture. Every time he looked into the rearview mirror, he'd caught a glimpse of Peyton's puffy eyes and raw cheeks.

He didn't imagine he looked much better after a sleepless night spent trying to figure out how he'd ever let her go in the first place.

He'd thought being home in Hope Springs would soothe the piercing pain that jolted through him with every heartbeat. But he'd been wrong.

Instead, his thoughts had locked on her.

Peyton had said she needed a man who wanted to build a future with her. Who was committed to her forever. Didn't that describe him exactly?

Except for one thing. He couldn't promise her marriage. Not yet. Maybe not ever.

Still, the thought of marrying her had hovered in his thoughts over the past few days like a tantalizing mirage. One he didn't dare approach. He'd spent all of his life so sure that he was never intended for marriage. That the only way to make sure he didn't turn into his father was to remain alone.

Finally, last night he had dropped to his knees next to his bed. He'd prayed for God to make him content with letting go of Peyton so she could have the future she deserved.

Instead, the longer he prayed, the more at peace he'd felt with the thought of marrying her.

But how did he know that wasn't only his own selfish desire instead of what was best for Peyton?

Because as much as he would give everything to be with her, he wanted even more for her to have the future she prayed for—the future God had planned for her.

He'd been hoping Dan could shed some light on the whole knotted mess, but apparently he was going to have to figure this out on his own and pray he didn't do anything to hurt Peyton's chances for happiness.

He was about to get into his car when someone called his name.

He swiveled in search of the voice.

"Over here."

Jared looked over his shoulder and spotted Dan in the snowy yard of the big brick house next to the church. Dan lifted a hand and jogged over.

"I got a call from Mrs. Reinhold on the other side of the church. She was all worked up that someone was trying to break into the building." He laughed and clapped Jared on the shoulder. "I assume that was you?"

Jared joined in the laughter. Much as he hadn't wanted to like Dan, he had to admit the guy was easy to get along with.

"Guilty as charged."

"That's a relief. So what were you after?"

Jared focused on the asphalt parking lot, stained gray from the layers of salt that had been spread on it during the last snowstorm. "I was looking for you, actually."

If Dan was surprised, he hid it well. "Great. You found me. What's up?"

Jared kicked at an ice chunk that had been left behind by the snowplow. "I was wondering if your offer to talk was still good."

"Of course. Come on in."

Jared followed Dan as he led the way across the lawn and into the front door of the old house.

"Don't mind the boxes. Still getting unpacked." Dan wove through the maze of boxes to a worn couch at the far side of the living room. "Have a seat. I'd offer you something to drink, but all I have is water, and I haven't found the glasses yet."

"That's okay." Jared sat, his leg bouncing against the couch cushion. Now that he was here, he had no idea how to ask the question that had been eating at him all night. So he blurted it out. "How do I know God's plan?"

If Dan found the question abrupt, he didn't let on. "His plan for what?"

"Me, I guess." Jared raised his hands helplessly. He didn't know what he was looking for exactly, so how could he expect Dan to provide it? "I mean, that pastor at Tamarack said God has a plan for each of us, right? But how do we know what that plan is?"

Dan studied him, but Jared didn't feel uncomfortable under the younger man's scrutiny. "Remember the verse the pastor quoted? Jeremiah 29:11? It says that God has plans to prosper us and not to harm us." He lifted his hands in front of him. "That's it. That's God's plan for us."

"But—" Jared spluttered. "That's not a plan. I need something more specific. More detailed. Like a sign, I guess. Or something. Anything." Desperation made his voice go up, but he didn't care. There had to be more.

Dan gave a gentle laugh, but Jared could tell it wasn't at his expense. "You have no idea how many times I've wanted that, too. But the thing is, God's plan is for us to honor and serve him. And there are a lot of ways we can do that—many of them not necessarily better or worse than others." He twirled his thumbs around each other, not looking at Jared. "Do you mind if I ask you something?"

Jared grimaced and braced for Dan's interrogation. For his reprimand that if Jared only prayed harder or went to church more or was a better Christian, he'd know God's will without having to ask such stupid questions.

"Is this about Peyton?" Dan met his eyes as he asked.

Jared startled. How had Dan known?

But he nodded. There was no point in denying it.

"I don't know your story, aside from what Leah told me," Dan said.

"She—"

Dan held up a hand. "All she said was that you two used to date but that you wouldn't marry her, so you broke up."

Dan's eyes drilled into his, but there wasn't any judgment there, and Jared's chest loosened.

"And now you're wondering if you made the right decision."

Well, the guy was good. Jared had to give him that much. "Okay, pastor or mind reader?"

"Definitely pastor. Doesn't take a mind reader to see how you feel about her."

Jared nodded slowly. "But is how I feel about her enough? How do I know God's plan for us? How do I know I'm even fit to be a husband?"

Dan was silent for a moment, seeming to weigh his response, and Jared's heart sank. He'd known it was too much to expect that it would be God's will for him to marry Peyton.

"God's plan is for you to honor and serve him, whether you marry or not," Dan finally said. "And if you do marry, his plan is for you to honor and serve your wife. To build her up in her faith. To be there for her, to protect her, to love her through everything. So I guess the real question is, do you love her?"

"You just said you know I do."

"I know, but I want to hear from you how you feel about her."

"I feel—" Jared cleared his throat. How did he put the depth of his feelings for Peyton into words? "She's the best part of me. She makes me want to be this fantastic man she seems to think I am. This past year, I've felt like I was missing a part of me. Not an arm or a leg, but something inside me that I can't name. Something vital. Something I can't live without."

Dan's eyes gleamed as he stared at him. "I think you just answered your own question."

"I did?"

But he knew it, too.

And he knew what he had to do.

Chapter 17

Peyton hummed as she placed the fondant hearts on the cake she'd just finished stacking. It was one of the most breathtaking cakes she'd ever made, if she did say so herself.

"Aren't you cheerful." Leah snatched an extra fondant heart and took a big bite. "Oh . . . This is so good. What's in it?"

"Vanilla bean paste." Peyton grabbed one of the extra hearts and sneaked her own nibble. The creamy vanilla rolled over her tongue.

"So what's up with the humming?" Leah shoved the rest of the heart into her mouth.

Peyton shrugged. "Just happy, I guess."

She shouldn't be, really. Every time she thought of Jared, she still felt a lingering ache. But she was content with her decision to wait on the Lord's plan. She trusted that one way or another, he'd lead her to it—whatever it might be. She only hoped she'd recognize it when he did.

"There." She placed the last heart. "You want to help me get this to the cake table?" She checked the time. She was cutting this one closer to the start of the reception than she liked, but she'd wanted to get everything perfect for this couple's Valentine's Day wedding.

"I'm happy for you." Leah held the kitchen door open so Peyton could push the cart with the cake through.

Fortunately, the swelling in her foot had gone down almost completely, and she could walk without limping at all.

"Thanks. I am, too." Peyton couldn't help smiling as she gazed around the elegant ballroom. Thin copper hearts wrapped with white lights hung from the ceiling, and delicate red glass tea lights decorated each table. The whole room said *love*.

Instead of the usual pang of jealousy, Peyton felt only a faint wistfulness. Maybe she'd have her own wedding like this someday. But until then, she'd be content with this moment in her life.

She wheeled the cart to the round table that had been set aside, waiting for Leah to take a position on the other end of the tray so they could transfer the six-layer cake. She took a deep breath. This was always the most nerve-wracking part of any wedding. One wobble and all her hard work would be destroyed—not to mention a wedding ruined.

But they managed to transfer the cake without incident. After a few touch-ups with her scraper, Peyton was satisfied with her masterpiece.

She gave Leah a quick hug. "I'll get out of your hair now so you can finish up with the dinner prep."

Her friend studied her. "What are you doing tonight? You want me to come over when I'm done here? We can have an anti-Valentine's Day or something."

But before Peyton could answer, Leah's phone rang. She pulled it out of her pocket and rolled her eyes. "Hold that thought."

Peyton wandered among the tables as she waited for Leah to get off the phone.

She couldn't help smiling as she hummed another verse of her favorite Christian song. She appreciated Leah's offer to keep her distracted tonight. But she didn't need an anti-Valentine's Day party.

A year ago, she'd been sure she'd never be happy again. But surrendering herself to God's will had filled her with a kind of joy she'd never known before.

Not that it was easy or that it meant it didn't hurt to let go of her own dreams.

But it took away the constant pressure of trying to make things happen in her own time. The constant despair when things didn't work out according to her plans.

Leah bustled up behind her. "That was one of my waiters. Who was supposed to be here an hour ago. Calling to say he quit." Leah hesitated. "I hate to ask—"

But Peyton was already rolling up her sleeves. "Where do you need me?"

Peyton stacked her tray with the last plates of cake. Her ankle had started to pulse from rushing around the reception hall all night delivering food and coffee and cake, but it had actually been kind of fun. Usually she was gone long before the cake was served, so she never got to see people's reactions as they ate it. Plenty of people had told her after the fact how much they loved it, of course. But watching them actually savor it brought a whole new level of satisfaction.

She lifted the tray to her shoulder. Miraculously, she'd made it through the night without dropping anything. Maybe some of her mother's grace was finally manifesting in her.

As she started across the ballroom toward the farthest table, she let herself observe the bride and groom at the front of the room. The groom was leaning toward his new wife, a huge smile lighting his face. After a second, she smiled, too, then burst into laughter.

Peyton felt her own lips ease into a grin. She only knew the couple from the meetings they'd had to discuss their cake order, but they seemed sweet. She was glad everything had gone so perfectly for their special day.

"Peyton!" The shout from behind her sounded strangely like Jared.

She jumped and whirled toward it. The quick movement made the tray teeter on her arm. She threw up her other hand to steady it.

But it was too late.

One of the plates slid off. Peyton watched, helpless, as it hit the floor with a crash.

She closed her eyes as every head in the room swiveled toward her.

This was not happening.

She had not just ruined this sweet couple's wedding day.

When she opened her eyes, they landed on Jared, who was barreling across the room, weaving between chairs as he made his way toward her. His face was set into an expression she didn't recognize.

But she didn't have time for this right now. She had to get this mess cleaned up.

"I'm sorry," she mumbled to no one in particular as she stepped around the splattered cake and broken china. She needed a broom or a mop or something. Plus, she still had to deliver the rest of the cake slices on her tray.

But Jared had shoved his way between the tables and blocked her path.

"Peyton, wait."

"I have to clean this up, Jared." She tried to keep her voice low so they wouldn't create any more of a disturbance. "What are you even doing here?" As far as she knew, he didn't know the bride and groom. And he wasn't exactly dressed for a wedding in his jeans and polo shirt.

"I went to your house, but you weren't there, and I remembered you had a wedding, so I called around and . . ." He gestured to the room, his eyes widening as if he'd just noticed they had an audience. "I need to talk to you."

She tried to get past him, but there wasn't enough room to step around him without smacking a guest in the head with her cake tray.

"Jared, whatever it is, it's going to have to wait."

"This has waited too long, Peyton. It can't wait any longer." He took the tray from her and gave it to a guest at the nearest table.

"What are you—" But before she could comprehend what he was doing, he'd grabbed her hands and dropped to one knee in front of her.

"Jared, what's going on?" But then it dawned on her.

Her bottom lip started to tremble. There was no way he was really going to do this.

But he reached into his pocket and withdrew a white gold ring with a marquis cut diamond. The exact ring she'd looked at a thousand times in the jewelry store but had never mentioned to him.

She was suddenly aware of the silence that had fallen in the room. A quick glance showed that everyone had turned toward them. She tried to tug her hand back. She was supposed to be working right now.

But Jared squeezed her hand and slid closer. "Peyton, I didn't think I'd ever ask any woman this question. I thought my past meant I was destined to live my life alone. But you showed me what love is. You showed me who I really am."

Somewhere in the back of her mind, Peyton was aware of all the eyes on them. But she couldn't have walked away now if the building had been on fire. She had to know what he was going to say next.

"I've been searching and searching for some grand plan. For some sign. But it turns out it was right in front of me all along. Because God's plan is for me to honor and serve my wife."

She closed her eyes. She'd never thought she'd hear that word from his mouth.

When she opened them again, his eyes were shimmering.

He lifted her hand to his lips and dropped the lightest kiss there. "Peyton, will you let me honor and serve and love you all my days? Will you be my wife?"

Peyton pressed her lips tight to hold back the flood of emotion. These were the words she'd prayed so long and so hard to hear.

But Jared had been set against marriage his entire life. He might think he was ready to commit to it, but how could she know for certain?

Which was why she had to give him an answer that ripped at her own heart.

"I don't know."

Chapter 18

The whole room seemed to spin, and Jared felt as if he'd floated up out of his body and was looking down on this wedding where some fool was pouring his heart out in front of a room full of strangers who were shifting uncomfortably in their seats.

"You don't know?" he managed to croak. How could this be happening? The one thing he'd been certain of was that Peyton wanted to marry. Now he was offering that, and she was saying no?

Peyton pulled her hand back from his, and this time he let her.

"I'm sorry, Jared," she whispered, then spun toward the kitchen.

He dropped his chin to his chest. He'd been so sure of this.

Was still so sure.

So why was he just sitting here?

He pushed to his feet and ran after her. He was not going to lose her this time.

Just as she was about to push the kitchen door open, he overtook her.

"Peyton."

"Just go, Jared." The tears on her cheeks almost broke him. He could see it in her eyes. She wanted to say yes, but she was afraid.

"Please, Peyton. You have to understand something. The idea of marrying terrifies me."

She closed her eyes, and he rushed on before she could shut him out. "But you want to know what terrifies me more?"

He waited for her to open her eyes again. To look into his. "The thought of not marrying you, of not spending my life as your husband—that terrifies me more than anything. Because I belong to you—heart, body, soul. I've prayed about this, Peyton. I've prayed for your future and for mine. For our future."

Her tears fell faster, and he moved closer, grasping her hands in his. "What is it?" he whispered, these words meant only for her.

"What if you change your mind?"

He lifted a hand to wipe at her tears, giving her a gentle smile. Didn't she see? She had his heart. "The thing that scared me about marriage was making a promise I couldn't keep. A promise to love you and protect you forever. But now I know that I couldn't stop doing those things—ever. And I'm promising you, right here and right now—" He glanced over his shoulder to see that all eyes were still on them, then turned back to her, raising his voice so that everyone in the room would hear. "With all these people as my witnesses, I promise you that I will marry you one year from today. On your favorite day of the year." He swallowed. "If you'll have me."

The smile spread across her lips so slowly, he wasn't sure if it was there at all at first.

But then she laughed, a light laugh full of hope and joy. "Yes, Jared, I'll marry you."

"You will?" He couldn't move at first. He was sure he'd heard wrong. But she was still laughing and crying, and she held out her hand for the ring he still gripped in his.

He stared at her hand, suddenly awestruck that this woman would have him. "Are you sure?"

Behind them, a few people chuckled.

"I'm positive."

He was sure everyone must be able to see the outline of his heart under his shirt because there was no way his chest could contain such joy. He slid the ring onto her finger. She looked at it for a second, then sprang forward and threw her arms around him.

He wrapped his arms around her and leaned to whisper in her ear. "I love you."

She nodded against him. "I love you, too."

Behind them, the wedding guests burst into applause.

"Congratulations," someone said into the microphone. Jared assumed it was the groom, but he didn't look.

He couldn't take his eyes off his future bride.

He lowered his head and brought his lips to hers. The smile on her face when he pulled back strengthened something inside him. He would work every day for the rest of his life to keep that smile there.

Starting with today.

"I think I have a new favorite holiday." He laced his fingers in hers.

"Oh, yeah?" She tugged him into the kitchen and spun in his arms, tilting her face up toward his. "And what holiday would that be?" She was close enough that her breath skated lightly across his lips.

He grinned and kissed her again. "Every day with you."

Not Until You

-Hope Springs Book 3-

*For as high as the heavens are above the earth,
   so great is his love for those who fear him;
as far as the east is from the west,
   so far has he removed our transgressions from us.*

—Psalm 103:11-12

Chapter 1

Nate squinted into the blinding expanse of the parking lot. Had the world always been this bright, or did it only seem that way after seeing it through bars and walls for the past seven years?

His gaze roved the cars scattered throughout the lot. He'd written home to let his parents know today was his release date, but they'd never written back. Not that he'd expected a reply. After seven years without contact, a person kind of gave up.

Still, he'd half hoped, half dreaded that at least one of them would be here to meet him. He had a grand total of ten dollars to his name. Which left him with the options of sleeping on a park bench tonight or hitchhiking the fifty miles back to his hometown.

"Nathan." There was no mistaking his father's stern voice.

Nate turned to find his dad standing several rows away. He probably couldn't bring himself to come any closer to the building that proved his son was the worst kind of screw up. Dad looked older than the last time Nate had seen him, his once salt and pepper hair now all salt, his suit fitting him more loosely than it used to. He stood as stoic and unsmiling as ever, though.

Nate forced himself to breathe as he approached his father. Forced himself to keep his shoulders straight and his chin up, the way Dad had drilled into him.

Two feet in front of Dad, he stopped and held out his right hand. Dad looked at it a moment, then slapped a piece of paper into it.

Nate flipped it over. A slow churn started in his gut.

"A bus ticket?" He swallowed the bile rising at the back of his throat. The only thing that had gotten him through the past seven years was the promise of going home. Of making things right. Of making up for what he'd done.

He'd work the rest of his life to do it if that's what it took.

"Get in the car. Your bus leaves in twenty minutes." Dad disappeared into the driver's door without another glance at Nate.

Nate stood frozen a moment, then moved toward the passenger door. What had he expected? That Dad would welcome him home with open arms like some sort of long-lost son?

The moment Nate closed his door, Dad backed out of the parking spot.

"Can't I at least see Mom first?" He pressed his lips together, trying to push down the emotion building in his chest. "And Kayla?"

"The bus will take you to Hope Springs."

"Where?" Nate had never heard of the place. "Why?"

But before Dad even threw him the dark look, Nate knew. He was being banished.

"We just bought out a property management firm there." Dad's voice, the voice Nate had remembered for its resonance, was flatter than the cornfields that stretched in every direction around them.

"It's in pretty bad shape. You're going to make it profitable. I expect weekly progress reports."

"Dad, I don't want—"

"Card's in the suitcase." Dad plowed on as if Nate hadn't spoken. "There's a law office next door. They have the key. At least one of our buildings has an empty apartment. You can live there."

"Dad—"

"There's a bag in the back."

Nate swiveled to look over his shoulder. A small suitcase rested on the backseat, as if Nate were going on some sort of vacation.

"There are clothes in it. Some money." Dad's head didn't move so much as a centimeter.

"I don't want money. I want—"

"Frankly, Nathan, I don't care what you want. This is what you get. You made your choices. Now you have to deal with the consequences."

Nate stared at Dad. Didn't he think Nate knew that? That he'd spend the rest of his life living with the consequences of his actions?

He wanted to argue. To plead. But he'd learned early on that once Dad's mind was made up, nothing was going to change it.

A sharp silence sliced the air between them. It took Nate two tries before he could open his mouth to tell Dad what he'd needed to say for seven years. "Dad, I know it's not enough, but I want to say I'm sorry. I don't expect you to forgive me. But you have to know, if I could trade places with Kayla, I would. I—"

"But you can't. And all the sorries in the world aren't going to change that." Still that flat voice. Anger would be better. Or sadness. Anything but this stony, emotionless man.

"I know they're not." Nate said it so quietly he wasn't sure Dad heard him. He made himself speak up. "Can you at least tell me how Kayla is?" Seven years with no word on his sister's condition had been the worst part of his punishment.

Dad's jaw tightened. "You ruined her life, Nathan. And mine. Your mother's. You expect me to sit here and chat with you like we're old buddies?"

"No, but—"

"You know, Nathan, when I think about how excited we were when we learned your mother was expecting you— We thought you would be such a blessing." He let out a sharp, humorless laugh. "Some blessing. We'd have been better off if you'd never been born."

Nate turned toward the window and scrunched his eyes shut, pinching the bridge of his nose between his fingers.

He deserved every one of those hateful words. He'd told himself the same thing every day for the past seven years. But hearing them from his dad's mouth—the same man who had read him bedtime stories and played airplane with him and told him he loved him—sliced through every vital organ in his body.

Dad pulled up to the curb outside the bus station. Nate mashed his teeth together and grabbed the door handle. "Please, Dad. Just let me say goodbye to Mom and Kayla."

Dad stared straight out the windshield. "Show me you're not the worst mistake of my life, and maybe someday you can see them again. Until then, I'm not letting you near my family."

Nate wanted to say they were his family, too. That he would do anything for them. But his words would never convince his father. He'd have to make a success of this new job Dad had assigned him. No matter how much he hated it.

If it meant he could see his mother and sister again, it would be worth it.

Chapter 2

Violet eyed the empty boxes she'd spread across the living room floor of her small apartment. She had to do it. She knew that. She'd been putting it off for three years, but it was time.

The Black Forest cuckoo clock on the wall behind her let out a squawk, as if chiding her to get moving, and she jumped.

"Okay, fine."

She picked up the thriller that had sat, unread, on the side table for the past three years. A bookmark stuck out of its pages about halfway through. A stab went through her as she plucked it out of the book. It was a leaf she had pressed for Cade the first year they'd been married. She'd wrapped it in packaging tape to preserve it. But the leaf was faded now, its edges thin and worn.

She put the book in the box she had marked for donations, but she tucked the bookmark into the Bible sitting on the other end of the table.

There. One item done.

Only six hundred and fifty-seven more pieces of Cade's life to sort through.

She moved systematically through the apartment, adding items to the donation box: Cade's jeans and shoes. His books. The collection of baseball cards he'd never been able to bring himself to part with, even though they weren't worth anything. She let herself keep a few of his sweatshirts, the knit cap someone from church had made him, and the ticket stubs to the first movie they'd seen together.

But everything else she put into the boxes. With each item, she felt like she was shoving a needle deeper into her own heart. And yet it wasn't only pain she felt. Somewhere buried under that was a sharp relief. She wasn't sure which was worse, really—the pain or the relief. This was all she had left of her husband. And if she got rid of it, what would she be left with then? Aside from the giant Cade-shaped hole in her heart?

By the time she got to the bathroom, she'd filled six boxes, and she wasn't sure if she could make herself do more.

She glanced at her phone. She had ten minutes before she had to get downstairs and open the antique shop.

Last room, she told herself.

She sorted through Cade's stuff, which had been shoved to the back of the medicine cabinet. She tossed the deodorant and razors in the trash. But when she came to the fresh, slightly sea-smelling cologne he always wore, she pulled the cap off and spritzed it in front of her. She leaned forward into the mist, inhaling deeply. She could almost imagine Cade standing next to her, close enough to put his arms around her. But no arms circled her. No one brushed her curls off her face. No one dropped a kiss onto her forehead.

No one ever would again.

She stuffed the ache deep into a corner of her heart as she tucked the cologne back into the cupboard and closed the box she'd filled.

She moved it to the laundry room with the others. She needed some time to get used to the apartment without Cade's stuff before she took the final step of donating everything.

Eventually, she'd learn to live without it, like she'd learned to live without Cade.

Have you? a voice in her head taunted.

She pushed it aside and reached to turn off the light, but her gaze caught on her finger.

It's time. That same voice.

But this time it was harder to ignore.

Violet had tried to take the wedding ring off before. But her hand had always seemed too heavy without it.

Quickly, before she could change her mind, she slid the ring over her knuckle and dropped it into the palm of her hand. Her breath came in ragged heaves as if she'd just run a marathon.

In a way, maybe she had.

The past three years had been a marathon of grief and anger and regret.

She stared at the ring, lying still and lifeless in her palm, as she walked into the bedroom. Ignoring the trembling in her fingers, she plucked the ring out of her hand, opened her jewelry box, and deposited the ring inside.

Then she fled to the living room.

But without Cade's stuff everywhere, it felt smaller. Incomplete.

Just like her.

Chapter 3

"This is it." Nate's seatmate nudged him as the bus crested a hill.

"Mmm." Nate turned toward the window to appease the woman, who had introduced herself as Linda or Lucy or something like that. In five hours, she hadn't gotten the hint that he had no interest in talking. She'd even gone so far as to show him pictures of her friend's wedding.

The rain that had started an hour or so ago had slowed, and the sun had pierced through the clouds low on the horizon. Shafts of light glared off the choppy waves at the bottom of the hill. That had to be Lake Michigan. The masts of dozens of boats stabbed toward the sky, where seagulls circled and swooped. Nate's gaze swept down the street, lined with colorful shops.

Great. Dad had relegated him to a tourist trap.

"Oh, look, a rainbow." The woman leaned across him and pointed.

Nate obligingly craned his neck and grunted.

The rainbow stretched above the lake, its far end disappearing into the tree line at the edge of the horseshoe-shaped bay.

Once upon a time, Nate might have convinced himself the rainbow was a sign from God that his new life would be better. But he'd stopped believing in such signs right about the time God had stood by and watched his whole life fall apart.

The bus slowed to a stop. The woman stood and stretched. "It was nice talking with you." She gave Nate a smile without a trace of sarcasm behind it.

Nate almost retorted that it'd been nice being talked at, but he bit his tongue. She was only trying to be friendly. He supposed he'd have to get used to that. Not many people had been kind to him in the past seven years. Which had been fine with him. He didn't deserve anyone's kindness.

Nate followed the woman off the bus.

The air was hot and humid, and the ground was wet. In spite of himself, Nate pulled in a deep breath. The fresh, clean scent of the town made something deep inside him twinge.

"Leah." A middle-aged woman rushed forward with her arms outstretched, and his seatmate—Leah, apparently—stepped into the hug as if it were the most natural thing in the world.

Nate looked away. When was the last time he'd been hugged?

He grabbed his suitcase and riffled through the front pocket until his hand fell on a card.

Benson Property Management. 1201 Hope Street.

Wherever that was.

"Bye. Hope you like Hope Springs." Leah and the woman passed him on the sidewalk.

"Thanks," Nate mumbled, stepping out of their way. It wasn't until they were a dozen steps past him that he managed to get his voice to work. "Could you tell me where Hope Street is?"

Leah turned with a smile. "Sure can. It's right there." She pointed across the parking lot to the street that ran parallel to the lakefront.

Nate nodded his thanks. It felt like the first thing that had gone right for him in seven years. Maybe it was the beginning of a streak.

He picked up his suitcase and kept his head down as he directed his footsteps toward the storefronts lining the street. He passed two gift stores, a fudge shop, an antique store, a restaurant, and the post office before he came to 1201. The sleek steel of the building's exterior stood in stark contrast to the old brick storefronts on either side.

The sign on the door indicated that the building held a law office, a dentist, an accountant, and a property management firm. Apparently *his* property management firm.

Welcome to the first day of the rest of your life. Nate's lips twisted into a sneer directed at himself.

This was a far cry from where he thought he'd be at twenty-eight. If things had gone right, he'd be cutting records and touring with his band now.

But things didn't go right.

No, they didn't. And he had only himself to blame for that.

Nate grabbed the sleek metal door handle and stepped inside. The building was cool and had the faintly antiseptic smell of a dentist's office. He wrinkled his nose. This was where he was going to be spending his days.

A door immediately to the right was marked with the name of the dentist's office. Farther down, on the left side of the hall, was the accountant's office. Which meant his office must be upstairs. Nate followed the long hallway to the back of the building, finally finding a staircase there.

At the top, it opened into another hall, identical to the one downstairs, except with an oversize vase of fake flowers on a small table next to one of the doors. Nate shuffled down the hall.

Of course the flowers would be outside the door to his office. Those would have to go.

He continued to the door of the law office on the other side of the hall.

Thankfully, the lights were still on inside, even though it had to be early evening, judging by the low angle of the sun out the window at the end of the hall.

Nate pushed the door open. No one was at the front desk, but the strains of Rachmaninoff's "Prelude in C Sharp Minor" drifted from somewhere in the back. Nate gave himself a second to listen to the haunting melody. How many times had he played it growing up? His fingers itched to move across a piano again.

He shoved them into the pocket of his jeans.

"Hello," he called tentatively.

No response.

He called again, louder.

A few seconds later a youngish man in khakis and a casual shirt jogged to the front. "Sorry. I didn't know anyone was here."

"No problem." Nate sized the guy up. He didn't exactly look like a lawyer. "I'm Nate Benson. I'm taking over the office next door. I was told you had the key."

"Yeah. Of course. I'm Brandon." The guy stuck out a hand, and Nate shook it.

"I think Cynthia left it up here somewhere." Brandon moved a few stacks of papers on the front desk. "No offense, but you have your work cut out for you. You seen that office yet?"

Nate shook his head, careful to keep his expression neutral. "No, why?"

"Oh, man." The guy let out an exaggerated groan. "Let's just say Bernie was not what you would call organized." He looked Nate in the eye. "At all."

Nate shrugged. How bad could it be?

But five minutes later, after Brandon had finally found the key and Nate had opened the door to his office, he knew.

It was *bad* bad.

The office was small. Or at least it looked small. It was hard to tell with the dozens of boxes scattered across the space, most of them with papers spilling from their interiors onto the floor. A large desk stood against the back wall of the office. Aside from a small corner that held a computer monitor, the entire surface of the desk was strewn with a carpet of paper at least three inches thick. And that wasn't to mention the two-foot-high stack of papers on the leather office chair. Two large filing cabinets stood next to the desk. Nate wasn't sure if he should hope that they held a system for organizing this mess or that they were empty.

NOT UNTIL YOU

He shoved a hand through his hair. Dad hadn't sent him here to prove himself.

He'd sent him here to fail.

Nate wove his way gingerly across the paper-strewn floor to the desk. The mess would have to wait for another day. Right now, all he wanted was to find out which building had an empty apartment, get a key for it, lie down, and figure out how his life had gotten so off track.

When he reached the desk, he shoved the chair aside, rolling his eyes at himself as half of the precarious tower of papers crashed to the floor. Ignoring it, he powered on the computer. Hopefully Bernie had kept better electronic records than he did paper records.

It took some clicking around, but he finally found a database titled Occupancy. He clicked on it, holding his breath. If this didn't give him the information he needed, he'd end up having to spend the night here. Not an appealing prospect for his first night of so-called freedom.

Nate scrolled through the master file. There must be a few hundred properties here. Most of them with addresses in towns Nate had never heard of. He vaguely recognized a couple of the names as little blips of towns they'd passed through on the bus ride here. But he had no way to get to any of them. He needed something in Hope Springs.

There. A one-bedroom apartment.

And it looked like this one was just down the road, on Hope Street.

Most of the records looked outdated, but hopefully this apartment really was vacant as Bernie had noted here.

Now he just needed a key.

Nate pulled open the desk drawers but came up empty.

He scanned the room. If the keys to the vacant properties were in one of the boxes, he was sunk. It could be weeks before he found them.

His eyes fell on the filing cabinets again. They had to be in there, didn't they?

Two giant steps over the piles of papers landed him in front of the cabinets. But when he tugged the first drawer handle, it stuck. He tried another and then another.

Nope.

Both cabinets were locked.

And he hadn't seen a key for them in the desk. Who knew where it might be in this mess—if it was here at all? Bernie could have easily taken it with him when he left.

Nate laid his forearm across the top of the closest filing cabinet and rested his head on it. It would be nice if something happened easily for once.

He was pretty sure he'd seen some paper clips scattered across the desk. Not that he had any idea how to pick a lock. But it was worth a shot.

He waded back through the papers and rummaged around the desk until he came up with one. He examined it for a second, then unbent it. It looked nothing like a key.

NOT UNTIL YOU

But he made his way back to the filing cabinet and stuck the end of the paper clip into the keyhole. He wiggled it up and down, then side to side. Nothing.

After ten minutes, he had to face the facts: he was a terrible lock pick.

He glanced around the room. Now what?

There.

In the opposite corner, next to one of the boxes, half buried in papers. It looked like a toolbox.

Nate hurried across the room, almost slipping on a loose sheet of paper. He uncovered the toolbox and surveyed its contents.

A screwdriver, four nails, and a hammer.

Not much, but he could probably work with it.

He scooped up the screwdriver and hammer and recrossed the room.

After studying the first cabinet a minute, he stuck the screwdriver in the keyhole, drew the hammer back with his other hand, and smacked the handle of the screwdriver with a solid blow.

Three more blows and the lock released. Nate yanked open the drawers.

More papers.

But no keys.

He dropped his head but moved to the next filing cabinet. They had to be in here.

He lined up the screwdriver and was about to strike it with the hammer when the door to the office burst open.

"What are you doing?"

Nate spun toward the door. Brandon stood there, looking half startled, half amused.

"I need to get into this to find the keys." Nate turned back to the cabinet.

"Does that actually work?"

"Yep." Nate lined the hammer up again and hit the screwdriver square in the middle of the head.

He didn't stop until the lock released four blows later.

"Nice."

Nate glanced over his shoulder. Brandon was still there, looking mildly impressed.

Nate grunted. The dude might as well learn sooner rather than later that he wasn't here to make friends.

He yanked the drawers open. The top two were more papers.

But the middle drawer held several panels with hooks to hang keys. About a quarter of them were full. Nate squatted alongside the cabinet and scanned the address labels above each key.

But there wasn't one for any property on Hope Street.

His shoulders dropped.

That would have been too easy.

He wrenched open the next drawer, even though it was pretty clear fate or God or whoever was not smiling on him today.

The first key he saw was labeled 612 Hope Street.

"Thank you." He grabbed it and stood, not really sure who he was thanking.

"What is it?" Brandon looked like he was about to take a step into the room but then thought better of navigating the mess and stayed put.

"The key to my new apartment." Nate crunched through the papers to get to the door. He grabbed his suitcase and flipped off the light switch.

Brandon stepped backwards into the hallway, and Nate followed, locking the door behind himself, though it might do him a favor if someone broke in and took everything.

He'd probably be better off starting from scratch. Just like with his life.

Chapter 4

Violet straightened and massaged a kink in her lower back.

She gave the Regency style dresser she'd been polishing a final once over. The finish had been dull and scratched when she'd bought it, with a watermark right in the middle of the top, but the stain was barely visible anymore.

She pulled off the old t-shirt of Cade's she'd worn to protect her clothes and moved to the workshop's sink to wash her hands. Although it was the middle of tourist season, it'd been a slow day. She'd only had a handful of customers. And most had browsed the store without buying anything. The others had made only small purchases—some postcards, an old washboard, and a vintage camera. She needed to make a big sale soon if she was going to pay the bills this month.

She stepped through the double doors leading to the sales floor. After such a slow day, she was thankful it was time to flip the sign to closed. But on her way to the front door, she got sidetracked by the stack of mail she'd never opened. A postcard with a picture of a sunrise over the ocean sat on top of the pile. She smiled as she picked it up and flipped it over to read Sophie's neat handwriting. *I think I may be the most blessed woman in the world.*

Violet sighed as she hung the card on the bulletin board behind her desk. Sophie was definitely blessed. She'd finally found her way back to the man she'd loved for years. And now they were married and off on their honeymoon.

Images of her own honeymoon sprang to mind. Cade's expression of wonder as they swam with dolphins, his insistence that they get ice cream every day, the way he'd looked at her like he'd treasure her forever. Out of habit, Violet rubbed at her wedding ring. But her thumb only met bare skin, and her heart jumped. Her ring was upstairs in her jewelry box, where she'd placed it this morning. Her eyes traveled to the bare white patch of skin in its place.

She forced herself to move on to the rest of the mail. A second notice from the electric company. A water bill. And two credit card bills.

She dropped the stack onto the desk. It was too hard. She was never going to catch up. Sales had been slow the last couple years, but she'd managed to survive on Cade's small life insurance policy. But that was gone now.

Maybe it was time to admit she couldn't keep the store going without Cade. But this place was filled with his presence. The shelves he'd made to display the porcelain dolls. The platforms he'd built in the windows to display items that wouldn't fade in the sunlight.

The music box.

She popped onto her toes to take it down from the shelf above her desk. Settling into her chair, she wound the key under the box, then cradled it in her hands as the couple on top spun in circles. This had been the first piece she and Cade had bought together. The piece that had sparked Cade's plan to open an antique shop. Violet had been unsure, but Cade had convinced her that with his business background and her art education, they could make it work.

And they had—for a while. Violet snapped the music box shut. She refused to let her memories go to their argument that day. How she had suggested it was time to close the shop. How they had fought. How she had refused to go with him to pick up a new piece. How he'd never made it home.

It didn't matter if she had once wanted to close the store. She owed it to Cade to keep it going now, whatever it took.

"What am I going to do now, Cade?" she asked the empty shop.

She knew his answer as clearly as if he were standing right there: "Pray and leave it in God's hands."

But she wasn't sure she had the strength to do that this time.

She dragged herself toward the door, feeling a decade older than she had when she woke up this morning. All she wanted now was a cup of tea, a bath, and her bed.

As she reached for the lock, her eyes fell on a man grabbing the door handle outside.

She jumped and pressed a hand to her heart.

Couldn't the guy read the hours posted on the door? The store had closed twenty minutes ago. That's what she got for letting herself get distracted instead of locking up on time.

But she pasted on a smile and tugged the door open. Her store wasn't known for its hospitality for nothing.

"Hi there. I'm sorry, but I'm closed for the day. I reopen at ten tomorrow morning, though." She winced at the artificial cheerfulness in her voice.

The man took half a step back with a scowl. "I'm not here to shop."

"Oh." Violet closed the door a fraction. She'd had enough salesmen drop by unexpectedly to know the signs. The twitchy movements. The look like he expected her to throw him out at any moment. "I'm sorry, I don't need any—"

"I'm here to move into my new apartment."

Violet studied the man. There was an empty apartment upstairs, right across from hers. But she didn't know anything about anyone new moving in.

"I'm sorry, I think you must be mistaken. This is an antique shop."

The man craned his neck toward the second story and pointed up. "Yes, and those are apartments up there, correct?"

She nodded. There was no point in denying that.

"And one of them is empty?"

Again she had to nod. "Yes, but the building's manager didn't say anything about a new tenant."

He stared at her, and she shifted, glancing past him down the nearly empty street. What would she do if he tried to force his way in?

She moved to close the door again, but the man pressed a hand against the glass. "That's because I'm the new manager."

For a few seconds, it looked like the woman was going to shut the door in his face. Or call the police. With the hand that wasn't holding the door open, Nate reached into his pocket. He handed her the business card Dad had given him.

She looked from the card to him and back again. "This doesn't prove anything."

Apparently she wasn't the trusting type.

He fished for the key he'd gone to so much trouble to procure. He held it out to her. "Does this?"

She tugged on one of the dark curls framing her face. "Do you have some ID?"

Nate stared at her. Was she serious?

But he let go of the door, relieved when she didn't immediately slam and lock it, and slid his wallet out of his pocket. He turned it so she could read his ID.

"See. Nate Benson. As in Benson Property Management." He brandished the business card again.

"Why didn't I get a notice that the building was under new management?"

Nate let out a *pfft*. "You will. I just got here today. I have a few, ah— papers to sort through."

And the award for best understatement of the year goes to Nate Benson.

"Well, what does this mean? Is this going to affect my lease? I haven't—"

Nate held up a hand. "I'm sure it won't. But like I said, I have a lot of paperwork to go through yet. Right now, all I know is that I'm looking for apartment three at six twelve Hope Street. Is that here?"

With one last long look, the woman nodded and let her lips relax into the tiniest smile. It made her look . . . sweet.

Nate shoved the thought back. He had no business thinking anyone looked sweet. Or pretty.

"For future reference, the apartment entrance is at the back of the building. But you can come through here this time." She stepped aside and opened the door all the way.

Nice of her to let him cross through his own building.

He tried to smile as he stepped inside, although he was pretty sure his face got stuck at grimace.

The store was bigger than it looked from the outside, with space for several large dining tables set with fancy china, half a dozen or so dressers, a large desk, and more. Smaller displays held porcelain dolls, old tools, and various knickknacks. Off to the right was a doorway that looked like it led to another, smaller room. Nate supposed the store was cute, if you liked that sort of thing.

Which he most decidedly did not. He didn't understand why people didn't throw all this junk away. All these reminders of pasts they couldn't outrun.

The woman locked the front door, then led him through a set of double doors to a large workshop area filled with what appeared to be projects in various stages of completion. The sharp tang of mineral spirits hung in the air, coating Nate's tongue. He followed the woman around several large pieces to a wooden door that led to a hallway. A narrow staircase ran along the far wall.

She waved toward the steel door at the bottom of the staircase. "The residential entrance." She pointed to the strip of mailboxes. "You'll have to put a new label on this one."

He shrugged. He wasn't exactly expecting a heap of fan mail.

The woman's curls bounced as she started up the steps. He watched his feet as he followed. Halfway up, the smell of mineral spirits faded, replaced by what could only be apple pie. Nate's mouth watered. Someone in the building must bake.

The floor widened out into a large landing at the top of the staircase. There were two apartments to the right, one to the left.

"That's apartment three." The woman pointed to the apartment on the left. A mat that had probably once said welcome lay in front of the door, its letters long since faded into a black smudge.

The woman moved to apartment two, across from his, and stuck her key in the lock. She gave him one last look over her shoulder, then disappeared inside.

Well.

At least he wouldn't have to worry about putting on a friendly act with the new neighbor.

Nate faced his own door. But before he could unlock it, the sound of a door opening behind him made him turn again. Now what did she want? But the apartment door across from his was still closed. A tiny white-haired woman stood on the doorstep of the apartment at the front of the building.

"I thought I heard voices out here." She walked slowly toward him, her back stooped, and her right leg dragging slightly.

Nate wasn't really in the mood to meet anyone else. But watching her walk was painful. He stepped toward her, so she wouldn't have to come as far.

When he stopped in front of her, she held out a hand twisted by arthritis. Her sharp knuckles dug into his fingers as she squeezed his hand. "I'm Mrs. D'Angelo. Do you like pie?"

Nate blinked at her. What kind of question was that? Who didn't like pie?

"Thanks, but I should get my stuff unpacked." He gestured lamely toward the single suitcase parked outside his apartment door. "Maybe next time."

He fought not to squirm under the stare she leveled at him. "I'll hold you to that. It's been too long since we've had a young man around here." She started to shuffle toward her apartment. "I look forward to getting to know you."

Nate grunted in answer. She'd be looking for a long time. He wasn't here to get to know people. He was here to do his work, prove his worth to his father, and—well, that was about it, really. There was nothing else for him anymore.

Mrs. D'Angelo was still in the hall when Nate unlocked his own door and stepped inside, pulling his suitcase behind him.

Once he'd closed the door, it took a moment for his ears to adjust to the silence. It was almost unnerving.

He hadn't known a moment of quiet in the past seven years.

He took in the space. The door led right into a small living room with a worn plaid couch and small TV. To the left, the kitchen was complete with citron appliances and a chipped table. He left his bag at the door as he moved slowly through the apartment, observing the 1980s style bathroom, the small but functional laundry room, and a decent size master bedroom.

The apartment was nice enough, and he supposed he should be grateful Dad had arranged a job for him. But Nate didn't want any of this.

How many times had he told Dad he could make his own life, that he'd find success on his own terms? He swallowed the acid that burned his throat at the knowledge that Dad had been right all along. When it came down to it, Nate was nothing but a giant screw up.

But he was a screw up with a second chance. Even if he didn't deserve it, he had to make the most of it, if only to prove Dad wrong.

Nate strode to the door and retrieved his suitcase as if he had a purpose. He dragged it to the bedroom and lifted it onto the bed.

Should be interesting to see what Dad had thought he'd need to survive in his new life.

He opened the suitcase to find a toothbrush, toothpaste, and deodorant on top of a stack of three dress shirts, two suits, and four ties.

He picked up one of the suit coats, remembering the day Dad had taken him to pick it out for his internship in Dad's office. He'd hated how the coat made him feel—all stuffy and claustrophobic. But Dad said it would grow on him.

It never did.

Nor did the internship, which he'd quit after only a month to focus more intensely on his music.

And now here he was again: wearing a suit and working for Dad.

Nate tried to pull the coat on over his t-shirt. But he'd been a scrawny kid the last time he'd worn it. His shoulders and chest had broadened now, thanks to daily weightlifting. The coat strained at the shoulders, and he could barely lift his arms.

He moved to put the empty suitcase away, but the sound of something sliding inside stopped him. He was sure the main part had been empty.

He tipped the suitcase to the side.

The zip of something sliding against the fabric liner was quiet but unmistakable. He unzipped the small side compartment and slid his hand in, feeling around until his fingers brushed against something hard and smooth.

He pulled it out, and his breath caught.

It was one of the shells he and Kayla had collected on their trip to Florida as kids.

Had the shell been stuck in the suitcase all this time? Or had Kayla put it there as a message to him?

He opened the drawer of the small nightstand next to the bed, sliding the shell into it.

Just because he couldn't forget didn't mean he wanted to remember.

Chapter 5

Violet traced Cade's name on the smooth gray stone, then ran her finger over his favorite Bible verse, inscribed below: "Those who hope in the Lord will renew their strength. They will soar on wings like eagles; they will run and not grow weary, they will walk and not be faint."

She sighed, settling onto the grass in front of the stone. Cade was in heaven, where he would never grow weary or faint again. But she was stuck here. About as weary and faint as a person could get.

All week she'd resisted coming to the cemetery. But one more Sunday of worshiping without Cade had done her in. Christ had always been the center of their relationship, from the time they'd attended Sunday school together as kids.

But now every time she went to church, it felt like one person was missing from the relationship. Not that she needed Cade to have faith. That came from the Holy Spirit alone. She knew that. But Cade had encouraged her and helped her grow in her faith. She missed the deep spiritual conversations they'd had, the feeling that not only their hearts but their souls were connected.

She ran her hand over the daisies she'd planted at the beginning of summer. They'd been scraggly then, but now that it was August, they'd filled in to create a cheerful blanket in front of the gravestone. She leaned forward to smell them, the guilt she'd been trying to push down all week working its way to the front of her thoughts. Guilt over packing Cade's stuff away. Guilt over her inability to keep the store going. Guilt over the way her heart rate had sped up on the few occasions she'd run into her new neighbor over the last couple days. It was only because it still surprised her to see a man living in the building again after three years of only her and Mrs. D'Angelo. She knew that perfectly well. It's not like she and Nate had said more than a muttered "hello." But it still felt like a betrayal of Cade.

She pushed to her feet and peered down to the lake. The day was hot and still, and only the tiniest ripples marred the surface. It reminded her of the day she and Cade had gone snorkeling just off the beach. The water had been flat and smooth, and Cade had been sure they'd find fish and seashells and maybe even some treasure. But the water was so murky that they'd barely been able to see their own hands in front of them. Even so, Cade hadn't been discouraged. He'd said the most disappointing adventure with her was better than any day without her.

Violet wrapped her arms around her middle as a chill wracked her body in spite of the heat. Had she ever told him she felt the same way? Because she knew for a certainty now that the worst day with him had been better than every single day without him.

She kissed her fingertips, then pressed them to the top of the gravestone. She didn't let herself look back as she crossed the cemetery to her car, parked in the church parking lot.

"Violet!"

She lifted her head and turned toward the yard to her left.

"Hey, Dan." She tried to perk up her voice so he wouldn't worry. Leah's younger brother had moved back to Hope Springs only six months or so ago to join his dad as pastor of the church. But he'd quickly become a friend to all of Leah's friends. He'd offered a shoulder for Violet on more than one occasion.

"How are you today?" Dan's creased forehead told her he knew where she'd come from.

"I'm doing okay." It didn't pay to tell him she was good. He would see right through it.

"I haven't talked to you much since Sophie and Spencer's wedding. You doing okay with that?"

She gazed toward the church next door. She couldn't describe the mix of emotions that had swirled through her as Sophie walked down the aisle. Joy for her friend, of course. Wistfulness for her own wedding day. Anger at how short her time as a wife had been. And—she hated to admit it—a shard of jealousy that had worked its way into her heart. Sophie had never wanted to get married and have a family. Whereas Violet—she and Cade had been planning to start their own family since they were fifteen. So how was it fair that Sophie was now living the life Violet had dreamed of? While Violet was stuck in a life that had gone all wrong.

"It was hard, but I'm okay," she finally answered Dan.

He laid a hand on her arm. "It's okay if you're not, you know. We all understand."

Violet nodded and pressed her lips together. Her friends had all been so careful to let her know it was okay if she couldn't be one hundred percent happy at the wedding. But the thing was, none of them could understand. Not really. They were all marrying and moving forward with their lives. Her life on the other hand—the brakes had been put on that the day she buried Cade.

"I got a postcard from them the other day." She didn't have to feign the joy that had brought her. "Looks like they're having a great time."

"I bet. When do they get back?" Dan pulled out his phone to check his calendar.

"Two more weeks. Her parents insisted on getting them this trip, and since the cherry harvest went well this year, Sophie managed to convince Spencer to agree to it." Violet pressed down the flutter of nerves over Sophie's return. Her oldest friend had only come back to Hope Springs—and back into her life—a year ago. Now that she was married, what if she cut Violet out altogether again?

You're being ridiculous. Sophie had been nothing but the perfect best friend in the past year, even as she was busy planning a wedding and helping Spencer open a new farm store on the orchard they owned.

"Let's plan to grill out when they get home. I'll make burgers." Dan's eyes widened as he checked his phone again. "Oh, I'm supposed to be leading Bible study. Like ten minutes ago."

Violet couldn't help the laugh. Dan was quickly becoming notorious around the church for losing track of time. But his love for his flock was so apparent that no one held it against him.

As Dan jogged toward the church, Violet strolled to her car. The guilt and sadness that had pressed so hard at Cade's graveside had eased a little, and for that she was grateful.

By the time she got home, an energy she hadn't felt in a long time pulsed through her. The shop wasn't open today, since it was Sunday, but that didn't mean she didn't have plenty of work to do. Her workshop was way too full of half-finished projects. Projects that couldn't make her money until they were out on the sales floor.

She jumped out of the car and ducked into the workshop, pulling one of Cade's old t-shirts on over her sleeveless top. Its familiar comfort wrapped around her as she set to work. She wasn't sure how long this energy would last. But she as going to make the most of it while it did.

Nate slapped another lease agreement on top of the pile he'd already gone through and pushed back from his kitchen table. It hadn't even been a week, and already he wasn't sure how he was going to survive another day—let alone a lifetime—of working for his father.

He'd spent all week sorting through the mess at the office, and he'd barely gotten through a quarter of the files. But that wasn't the worst of it. The worst was the fact that Dad called every day—always at a different time, which Nate knew was to check up on him.

That was why Nate had spent his entire Saturday in the office yesterday, waiting for Dad's call. It had finally come at six o'clock.

Nate's only satisfaction was the surprise in Dad's voice when he had answered on the first ring. Dad had surely been expecting the phone to go to voice mail so he could leave a blistering message about Nate not living up to his responsibilities.

But Nate had made it clear to Dad that he wouldn't be in the office today. So what if he'd implied it was because Sunday was for church? In the eighteen years he'd lived under his parents' roof, he'd never been allowed to miss one weekend of church, so it was no shock that Dad thought he still attended. As if he wanted anything to do with a God who had failed him.

Instead of worshiping, Nate had spent the day holed up inside his apartment with the files he'd brought home.

It wasn't like he had anything better to do anyway.

But his eyes kept drifting to the window, where sunlight streamed in, casting a sharp line across the living room floor. Maybe he should get some fresh air.

Nate stood and stretched. Ten minutes and then he'd get back to work. When he'd told Dad about the mess in the office, Dad had been less than sympathetic. He'd expected Nate to get it cleaned up and get him a status on all their properties on the peninsula in two weeks.

It was an impossible task. Nate knew that. So did Dad. That's why he'd assigned it, Nate was sure.

But if the only way to see Mom and Kayla again was to kill himself working for Dad, then that's what he'd do.

He stepped out of the apartment and gave his neighbors' doors a quick glance. He'd talked to Mrs. D'Angelo a few more times during the week. She kept pressing him to come in for a piece of pie, but he kept declining. His other neighbor, though—he'd only run into her a couple times. And they'd never said more than "hi" to each other.

Which was perfectly fine with him. He wasn't here to make friends. He was here for a new start. And the only way to ensure that was to keep his life to himself.

Nate jogged down the stairs to the first floor. He paused as a high-pitched whining sound caught his ears. It took a second to place it, but he was pretty sure it was a sander. The sound was coming from behind the back door to the antique shop.

A momentary wave of curiosity swept over him. But he nudged it aside. Keeping his life to himself meant minding his own business.

He pushed the outside door open and stepped into the small parking lot. Beyond it, a grassy hill dropped gradually to the rocky beach below. The weight that had been pressing on his shoulders all week eased a little as the scent of the lake drifted up to him. He let himself take a moment to look around. He had to admit this was a pretty town. It might even be a nice place to live, if he'd been given the opportunity to choose it for himself.

Nate wandered toward the water, glad he'd thought to pick up some shorts when he'd gone shopping for new clothes the other day. The heat clung to him, dampening the skin at the base of his neck.

At the bottom of the hill, the grass gave way to small pebbles and crushed shells, leaving the beach a brilliant white. A couple hundred yards to the south, the beach looked darker, sandier. Towels dotted the ground, and a handful of people swam in the water. To the north, the pebbly beach continued a quarter mile or so, until it was taken over by large boulders, some jutting into the water.

Nate turned north.

The crunch of shells under his feet was satisfying after the stifling silence of his apartment, and he let himself walk farther than he intended. When he reached the boulders, he climbed up on one, then stepped across to another and another, until he was perched on top of one that stood several feet into the lake.

He let himself just breathe. When was the last time he'd been free to do that?

A new feeling settled over him. Not peace, exactly—he was pretty sure he'd never feel that again—but something a little softer than the despair that had hung over him for seven years.

He shouldn't allow himself even this brief reprieve. Not while Kayla had to deal with the consequences of his mistake every day. But if he didn't take just a moment, he would never survive this assignment to see her again.

It wasn't until the sun had shifted to shine directly in his eyes that he realized how low it had sunk in the sky.

He stood reluctantly. Sitting out here all evening wasn't going to win him any points with Dad.

By the time he got back to his building, the sun had dropped to the horizon. Lines of purple and red burst from it, painting the sky and the water in hues Nate wasn't sure were real. He allowed himself one more look, allowed himself a second to feel the awe the sunset had once inspired in him. The awe that had led him to write an entire song about the one who made it.

But that awe was misplaced.

He knew that now.

Because a God who could paint a sunset like that but couldn't protect his sister—that wasn't a God he wanted anything to do with.

He locked the awe away and opened the door.

He was at the foot of the staircase when a loud crash reverberated through the building, followed by a muted cry.

He stopped with his foot on the first step, his heart thrusting against his chest wall, and stared at the door that led to the antique store's workshop. It was probably nothing. He should ignore it.

Even if his neighbor needed help, he wasn't the one to provide it. Hadn't he proved that when he couldn't do anything to help Kayla? He couldn't handle the thought of feeling that helplessness again.

But what if his neighbor was hurt and no one else came?

He jumped off the step and yanked the back door to the antique store open. As he scanned the space, he didn't see anyone. "Hello? Are you okay in here? I thought I heard—"

"Over here." The woman's voice was faint and shaky. "I think I need help."

Chapter 6

Fire surged from Violet's wrist to her shoulder as she lay sprawled on the floor, her arm trapped under the armoire that had crashed on top of her. She wasn't sure how much longer she could fight down the scream.

Footsteps pounded across the floor. "What happened?" The voice sounded familiar.

A second later, a face warbled into view above her. It was her new neighbor. Nate.

She had no idea where he had come from, but this was the first time she could say she was genuinely happy to see him.

He squatted at her side. "I'm going to lift this. Do you think you can move your arm out when I do?"

Violet nodded. Or at least she thought she did.

"Ready?" Nate planted his hands close to the spot where her arm disappeared under the armoire. A second later, the pressure eased. She slid her body away from the armoire, biting her lip to keep from yelling. A small whimper managed to escape.

There was a thud as Nate set the armoire heavily on its back, then crouched at her side. "That looks pretty bad. I think it's probably broken."

She turned her head to examine her arm. Her wrist was bent up and then down at an odd angle, and a huge lump had formed below her elbow.

The room whirled around her, and she slammed her eyes closed again.

"Take a deep breath." Nate was moving next to her, but she didn't open her eyes.

She focused on inhaling and exhaling in a slow rhythm.

"Do you think you can stand?"

"I—" She licked her lips. "I think so."

But the moment she sat up, the room spun, and fireworks exploded behind her lids and through her skull.

The whole world tilted to the side, and she felt strong hands lowering her to the floor.

"Did you hit your head?"

"I'm not—" She swallowed against the nausea. "I might have."

"Okay. It's okay. I'll, uh—" Nate slid his arm under her shoulder blades and lifted. "I'll carry you. Is there someone who can drive you to the hospital?"

Violet tried to think. She was sure there was, but she couldn't for the life of her come up with anyone's name right now aside from Cade's. She wanted him to be here. To take care of her.

"Okay. Don't worry. It's fine. I'll take you." Nate sounded on the edge of panic, and she felt like she should reassure him. But her voice seemed to have disappeared.

"How am I going to take her?" Nate muttered, and Violet wondered vaguely who he was talking to. "I don't have a car."

"My keys." Why did it take so much effort to say two words? "Upstairs. My door's unlocked."

Nate maneuvered them through the door and into the hallway, then lowered her to the steps. She leaned against the wall. Its coolness felt good.

"Will you be okay here for a second?"

She nodded. The dizziness was starting to wane. She opened her eyes in time to see his legs disappear up the staircase.

A few seconds later he thundered down the steps.

He squatted next to her, passing her a bag of frozen corn. "I couldn't find an ice pack."

He reached a hand behind her again, but she waved him off. "I think I can walk now."

He stood, taking half a step back but not moving too far away, as if afraid she might keel over any second.

The poor guy's face was whiter than the paint on the wall.

He hovered next to her as she walked toward the door, then reached in front of her to push it open. She caught a scent of lemon and mint as she passed in front of him. For some reason, it calmed her.

Ten seconds later, he was unlocking the passenger door of her car and holding it open for her.

She sucked in a sharp breath as she lowered herself into the seat. Every tiny movement of her arm felt like someone was taking a hammer directly to her bones.

"Okay." Nate was muttering to himself again. "Good. Okay. We're good."

If she weren't in so much pain, his pep talk to himself might be amusing.

He jogged around the car and dropped into the driver's seat, glancing at her as he lifted the key to the ignition. His hands were shaking so much it took him two tries to start the car.

"You okay?" His brow creased into worry lines as he looked at her.

"Yeah." She felt stronger now, and her voice came out sure. "I could use a little help with the seatbelt, though."

"Oh." He looked over her shoulder to where the seatbelt hung untouched next to the door.

She used her right arm to press her left arm tighter to her body, trying to keep it as still as possible. "I don't think I can grab—"

He leaned across her and tugged on the seatbelt.

There was that lemony-mint scent again. She tried not to notice when his hand accidentally brushed her shoulder as he pulled the seatbelt across her lap. Once it clicked into place, he sat back in his seat, hands clamped on the steering wheel.

She was overcome by a ridiculous need to comfort him. "Relax. I'm fine. It's just a broken arm."

Jaw hard, he nodded, then reached a stiff arm to shift the car into reverse. "I'll need directions to the hospital."

If Nate gripped the steering wheel any tighter, he'd probably rip it off the console. But he couldn't make himself relax.

Not when he hadn't driven in more than seven years. When he wasn't supposed to be driving at all. He wouldn't get his license back for another year.

That was, if he didn't break the law by driving with it revoked.

But this was an emergency. What was he supposed to do? Make her drive herself to the hospital when she couldn't even fasten her own seatbelt? When she could have a concussion?

He allowed himself a split second to glance at her. She clutched her arm to her torso, and her face was drawn in pain. But she didn't look like she was about to pass out anymore. So that was something.

Her eyes slid to his, and he snapped his attention back to the road.

"What happened anyway?" The question was out before he could remind himself that he was driving her to the hospital, not striking up a friendship.

"I was trying to move the armoire—"

"By yourself?" The thing had to weigh at least three times as much as her and was a good two feet taller. What had she been thinking?

"Well, I had to get it out on the sales floor. My friend Spencer usually helps with that kind of thing. But he's on his honeymoon, so—"

"You could have asked me." He didn't know where the offer came from. He most definitely didn't want her asking him for help with anything. But it was better than finding her crushed by some giant piece of furniture.

She gave him a sideways glance.

Okay, fine, he hadn't exactly given off the neighborly vibe. But then again, neither had she.

"Take a left here." She groaned, and when he looked over, her forehead was wrinkled in pain.

That familiar feeling of helplessness rolled over him. "You okay?"

"Yeah." Her features smoothed slightly. "Just tried to point." She gave a half laugh and Nate's jaw relaxed.

Five minutes later, he pulled into the hospital parking lot. His grip on the wheel didn't loosen until he'd shut down the engine. They'd made it. He checked the rearview mirror just to be sure, then let out a long breath.

"You don't have to come in if you don't want to." But the look in her eyes said the opposite. She didn't want to go in there alone.

"Come on." He unclicked her seatbelt, then got out and jogged to open her door. He held out a hand to steady her as she stood, careful not to bump her arm. The wrist and elbow had turned a mottled black and green.

He let his hand hover behind her back as he shepherded her toward the emergency room door, careful not to actually make contact.

There were only a few other people in the waiting room, and Nate dropped into a seat as she went to the desk to register. He didn't want to intrude on her privacy.

But a second later she settled into the chair next to him, passing him a clipboard. "Could you help me with this?"

He eyed the form. "You hurt your left arm."

She shifted so that she was closer to him and peered at the form over his shoulder. "I'm a lefty."

"Oh." He unclipped the pen and picked it up. "Me, too."

He turned his focus to the form, arm poised to write. "Okay. Name?"

She didn't say anything for a second, and he glanced at her to make sure she was okay.

"You know my name."

He shook his head. He really didn't. "Nope."

Her mouth fell open. "That's kind of rude. I told you that first day. When you came barging in the door of my antique store."

"First of all—" Nate tapped the pen on the clipboard. "I did not *barge* into your store. And second of all, you never told me your name."

She opened her mouth, then clamped it shut as realization dawned in her eyes. "Oh. I guess I didn't." She dropped her gaze. "It's Violet. Violet Somers."

"Violet. That's a pretty—" He cut himself off. What was he doing? "That's a good name." He cleared his throat. "Uh, address?"

"Well, that you know."

Duh. He wrote it down, ignoring the flustered swirling in his gut.

After they'd worked through the rest of the form, he brought it to the counter for her.

The few minutes of separation were good. They gave him a chance to push aside the thoughts he'd been having sitting next to her. Thoughts about how pretty her dark eyes were. And how she smelled like a spring day.

Those weren't thoughts he had any business thinking.

When he returned to the seating area, he contemplated taking a seat across from Violet instead of next to her, but fortunately the nurse came out and called Violet's name.

She gave him that half smile again as she passed him to follow the nurse. "I'll be back soon."

Nate nodded. "I'll be here."

Chapter 7

Violet turned off the TV. She was trying to follow the doctor's orders to take it easy, but if she had to watch one more game show, she might go crazy. Fortunately, the store was always closed on Mondays, so she wasn't losing any money right now. But Mondays were usually her days to catch up on paperwork and projects. Which was going to be a lot harder now.

Thankfully, the doctor had been able to set her arm relatively quickly last night. And he was pretty sure she wouldn't need surgery.

For the hundredth time, Violet wondered what would have happened if Nate hadn't heard the crash last night. Would she still be lying on the floor of her workshop right now?

She offered a silent prayer of thanksgiving to God for sending her help right at the moment she needed it.

Even after she'd been so unfriendly and unneighborly with Nate all week. It wasn't like her. She'd been voted friendliest senior in her high school class, for goodness' sake. But that was a long time ago. Back when life was easy and everything was going according to her plans.

So you can only be kind when your life is going well?

Violet shook her head at herself. Hadn't Dan's sermon yesterday been about loving your neighbor? Not that he'd been referring to literal neighbors.

But still . . .

Violet got up. "Fine, Lord, you win. I'll be a good neighbor."

She moved to the kitchen and surveyed her pantry. Cookies seemed like the right way to welcome a new neighbor. But how was she supposed to make them one-handed?

She lifted her left arm the little she could to study the cast. It wrapped from between her thumb and forefinger all the way to the middle of her upper arm.

Well, if she couldn't make him cookies, she could do the next best thing: buy them. Actually, he'd probably appreciate that more anyway. Peyton's chocolate chip cookies were a taste of heaven.

She slipped her sandals on and made the short walk to the bakery at the other end of Hope Street. If possible, it was more humid out here than it had been yesterday. A few people strolled listlessly from shop to shop, but not many people were out today. Mondays were always slow in the tourist town.

By the time she reached the bakery, sweat trickled from her hairline down her forehead. She stepped gratefully into the air-conditioned shop, savoring the mixture of bread dough and fresh-baked cookies that hung in the air.

"Be with you in a second." Peyton's voice carried from the back.

"It's just me. Take your time." Violet moved through the small bistro-style seating area to the display case, her mouth watering at all the treats spread out inside.

"Hey, Violet. What brings— Oh, my goodness, what happened to you?" Peyton rushed out from behind the counter. She wrapped Violet into a one-armed hug on her good side.

"Lost a fight with an armoire last night. It's broken in three spots. My arm, I mean. Not the armoire." At least she prayed the armoire wasn't broken. She hadn't had the courage to check yet. It was one of the most expensive pieces she'd ever purchased. And if she'd busted it . . .

"Jared was on call last night. But he didn't say anything about—"

"It's just a broken arm. I didn't call an ambulance."

"You drove with a broken arm?" Peyton looked ready to scold her, but Violet jumped in.

"My new neighbor drove me. He heard the crash and came to see what happened." A fresh wave of gratitude washed over her.

"Oh, thank goodness." Peyton pressed a hand to her heart. "How long do you have to wear the cast?"

Violet wrinkled her nose. That was the worst part. "Six weeks."

Peyton slipped behind the displays and grabbed one of the red and white striped bags she packed cookies in. "So, this new neighbor. When did he move in?"

Violet shrugged. "Last Tuesday, I think. Maybe it was Wednesday. Anyway, I thought maybe I should get him some cookies. As a thank you."

"Ah." Peyton busied herself selecting cookies and dropping them into the bag. "How old is he?" She kept her voice casual, but Violet heard the suggestion in it. Peyton was thinking what all their friends would think. Maybe this guy would help her finally move on from

Cade. They didn't understand that she didn't want to move on. The only man she wanted was Cade. And since she couldn't have him, she was content being alone. Or at least as content as she could be.

"Around our age, I'd guess." Though she'd never been good at figuring out that sort of thing.

Peyton raised her eyebrows but didn't say anything more. She rolled the top of the bag down and grabbed a sticker to close it. "So is he good looking?" Peyton kept her head down, concentrating harder than necessary on ringing up the sale.

But still, Violet's face warmed. "I don't know. I guess he's okay." Unbidden, Nate's blue eyes popped into her head. They were nearly the same shade as Cade's. And yet where Cade's had been open and inviting, like the lake on a summer day, Nate's were steely and guarded, all churned up like the water during a storm.

"He keeps to himself mostly," she added, as if that had anything to do with his appearance.

"Well, I'm glad he was there when you needed help. And who knows . . ." Peyton passed her the bag of cookies.

Violet started to tell Peyton it wasn't like that. But acknowledging she understood Peyton's insinuation would only add fuel to the fire. So she simply thanked her friend and stepped out into the sticky air.

As she walked home, she worked to direct her thoughts anywhere but to her conversation with Peyton. But she couldn't help rolling Peyton's question about Nate's appearance over in her mind.

Fine, she could admit it. Nate was attractive, with his slightly shaggy brown hair, square jaw, and strong build. But just because he was good looking didn't mean she was interested in a relationship with him. There were plenty of attractive men around Hope Springs, and she'd never felt any desire to date a single one of them.

But your stomach doesn't turn upside down when you see any of them.

Violet silenced the voice in her head. That was neither here nor there.

By the time she got home, she had almost changed her mind about giving Nate the cookies. She didn't want to risk giving him the impression that she was interested in him as anything more than a neighbor.

But then she pictured the concern on his face when he'd found her on the floor, the way he'd carried her, the relief he'd shown when she'd walked out of the ER with only a broken arm and no concussion. The least she could do was give him a few cookies and a heartfelt thank you.

Nate's heart lightened as he reached the back door to the apartment building. He had to admit, he wouldn't mind running into Violet. Just to check how her arm was doing. But the lights in the antique store were off, and her apartment door was closed. He considered knocking, but what would he say?

Throwing her door one last glance, he stepped into his own apartment and immediately fell onto the couch. The springs stabbed into his back as he rubbed his eyes. He hadn't made much more progress on the mess in the office today. At this rate, it'd be next year before he got through everything. Of course, it didn't help that his thoughts had kept drifting to Violet all day.

Where they did not belong.

But he couldn't stop himself from picturing the deep brown of her eyes, a shade darker than black coffee. Or the gratitude in them when he'd brought her home from the hospital last night. He couldn't remember the last time anyone had looked at him with anything approaching gratitude.

He sat abruptly. He had to stop this. He had no business thinking about her—or anyone for that matter—that way. Anyway, the case manager for his extended supervision would be here in twenty minutes. He should probably clean up.

Not that there was much to clean. His eyes swept over his sparse furnishings. The dishes from the microwave dinner he'd had last night and his cold cereal this morning sat on the counter next to the sink.

He dragged himself toward the kitchen. His life felt so small right now. So insignificant compared to the big plans he'd had for his future.

Halfway to the sink, he paused. He thought he'd heard a knock on the door, but it was so quiet he could almost convince himself he'd imagined it.

But as he turned on the water, it sounded again, louder.

His eyes flicked to the clock on the microwave. His supervisor was early.

Well, she'd have to deal with the mess in his sink then.

He smoothed the bottom of his rumpled dress shirt and strode to the door. Might as well get this over with.

The moment he opened the door, he beheld the most beautiful sight he'd ever seen.

A plate of chocolate chip cookies.

He lifted his eyes to Violet's face.

A shy smile played with her lips. "Um. Hi." Her voice had a musical quality to it.

"Hi." Nate's eyes went to her unwieldy cast. "How's the arm?"

She held it at a slight angle away from her body, and Nate wondered how uncomfortable the big cast was. Especially in this heat.

"Oh. It's okay." She dropped her head to stare at the plate, and a long curl fell onto her cheek. His gaze got caught on the shaft of light that spilled from the front window onto the side of her face.

"I just wanted to— Here." She thrust the plate of cookies at him.

He resisted the urge to snatch them from her and eat the entire plate in one bite. "Why?"

Her eyebrows pulled down into a sharp V. "What do you mean why?"

"Why are you giving me cookies?"

The sound that escaped her was a combination of exasperation and something else—amusement maybe. "To thank you for getting me to the hospital last night. And to welcome you to the building. To Hope Springs."

Nate could only look at her. He hadn't done anything to deserve cookies. Even if they did smell divine.

Her cheeks flushed a light shade of pink. "You don't have to take them if you don't want. It's kind of cliché, isn't it? How much more small-town America can you get, right?" She pulled the plate back, and it was all he could do not to lunge for it.

"No." His voice was louder than he intended, and he forced himself to lower the volume. "I mean, thank you. They look delicious." He took the plate. Then he lifted it to his face and inhaled. He didn't care that she was giving him a strange look.

"Sorry." He lowered the plate. "I haven't had anything homemade in a long time."

A soft smile lifted her lips. "Okay, well, enjoy." She took a step back.

Nate moved to close the door, but something stopped him. "Wait. Want to have one with me?"

She hesitated so long he was sure she was going to say no, but she finally gave a slow nod.

He stepped aside and held the door for her to enter the apartment.

They settled at the kitchen table, and he grabbed a jug of milk and two glasses.

As soon as he sat down, he sank his teeth into a cookie. The dough was soft and sweet, the chocolate melting on his tongue. He closed his eyes and savored it. It was the best thing he'd ever tasted.

His eyes snapped open. "Wait. How did you make cookies with a broken arm?"

Violet choked a little on her cookie. "Busted." She took a long drink of milk. "I didn't exactly make them. I mean, I was going to. But then I couldn't figure out how to do it one-handed." When she smiled, her eyes crinkled just the tiniest bit at the corners. "My friend Peyton owns a bakery. She made them." She gave a sheepish grin. "But I did walk there to pick them up."

Nate laughed to cover up how much her admission touched him. She had a broken arm and was supposed to be resting, but she'd taken the time to go out and buy him cookies?

He wasn't worth that kind of effort. And yet it warmed him to know someone had thought of him.

"Well, tell your friend Peyton these are the best cookies I've ever eaten. Seriously." He shoved the rest of the cookie in his mouth and reached for another.

"I will." She popped the last dainty bite of her cookie into her mouth and slid her chair back.

But he didn't want her to go yet.

"You'll have to tell me where else to go in town. Seems I've been missing out."

Her face lit up. "Did you see the fudge shop right next door? My friend Ariana owns it, and she gets orders from people all over the world."

"Do you know everyone in Hope Springs?"

"It's a small town. If you need groceries, Trig's is the best. It's—" She turned as if orienting herself. "About four blocks that way." She pointed to the west. "And then three blocks that way." She pointed south as she rotated her whole body.

Nate couldn't hide his amusement over her method of giving directions. Her cheeks flushed even deeper, but she laughed. "Sorry, my husband always said I give the worst directions. But it's the way that makes sense to me."

Ah, so there was a husband. Nate wondered where he'd been. His eyes went to her hand. No ring. And Mrs. D'Angelo had said there hadn't been a man in the building for a while. Maybe Violet was divorced.

Not that it mattered. He had no business wondering about her marital status.

"Let's see. What else should you know?" She tapped an unpainted nail against her lips, then lowered it and pointed at him. "The Hidden Cafe has the best burgers in town. Oh, and if you're looking for a church—"

"I'm not." The smile inspired by her enthusiasm fell right off his face. Time to shut this conversation down.

She stopped talking, eyes widening. "Not what?"

"Not looking for a church." He checked the time on the microwave. His supervisor would be here any minute. "Thanks again for the cookies, but I actually have an appointment in a few minutes."

"Oh, of course." Hurt and confusion warred in Violet's eyes, and she looked away.

He felt bad about that, but it was for the best. She wouldn't want to get too friendly with someone like him anyway.

She crossed the room as if it were on fire and yanked the door open with her good arm.

"Oh, excuse me." Another woman's surprised voice came from the hallway. "I'm looking for Nate Benson's apartment."

Nate groaned inwardly. His appointment was here. He moved closer to the door, where a tall, light-haired woman he'd guess to be in her early thirties stood blocking Violet's exit.

"You found it." Violet's response rang with false cheerfulness as she neatly stepped around the woman.

"Thanks again for the cookies," Nate called to her back, but she disappeared into her own apartment.

The blond woman glanced over her shoulder at Violet's door, then at him. "Mr. Benson?"

He nodded and shook the hand she held out.

"I'm parole officer Linda Jensen. It's nice to meet you."

Nate supposed he should return the sentiment, but he wasn't terribly excited about meeting the person who was going to be keeping tabs on him for the next two years.

"Come in." He stood aside and let her pass into the apartment.

She marched straight into the kitchen and deposited her briefcase on the table, then started opening his cupboards.

It's not like he'd had any privacy for the past seven years, but it still felt like an invasion. This was supposed to be his new home. His new life.

The woman pulled out a pad of paper and made some notes. "Not a lot of food here."

"Yeah, my neighbor was just telling me where the store is. I've been living off gas station food for the last week." He gave a meager laugh. "Actually, she brought these cookies. If you want one."

The parole officer kept writing. "Not right now, thanks. What happened to her arm?"

Nate regarded her coolly. What was she getting at? Did she think he would hurt his neighbor? That he would hurt anyone?

He took a deep breath. He was overreacting. She was just curious.

"She was working in her antique shop and a big piece of furniture fell on her."

He swallowed. What if she asked how Violet had gotten to the hospital? He didn't want to lie. But if he told her—

Officer Jensen nodded vaguely. "I have a series of standard questions I'll need to ask you each time we meet. You are expected to answer honestly." She didn't give him time to respond before launching into the first question. "Have you had any alcohol since your release?"

Nate stared at her. Was she serious? He'd never touch another drop. One time had been enough to ruin his life forever. "No."

She made a notation on the sheet, then rattled off a slew of questions about his actions over the past week. He wanted to tell her he'd done nothing—had no intention of doing anything aside from getting through the days—but he answered her questions with yes or no. Finally she put the sheet aside.

"And the job?"

"It's fine."

"You're working for your father, correct?"

"Yes, ma'am." The words barely made it past his gritted teeth.

"You're lucky." Officer Jensen rummaged through her briefcase. "A lot of people's parents do nothing for them when they get out."

Nate clamped his mouth tight. She thought what his dad was doing to him was out of kindness? It was simply another form of imprisonment.

"I know mine wrote me off. That's part of why I became a parole officer. Everyone deserves a second chance." She grabbed something out of her bag and held it out to him.

Nate took the small plastic cup.

He knew what it was for, and it didn't exactly scream second chances.

He fought down the shame that tried to swamp him and went to fill it.

Chapter 8

Violet circled the armoire, trying to determine how much damage it had sustained in the fall. It looked okay from the front and sides, but it was still lying on its back, so it was impossible to tell if it had suffered any structural damage. She'd have to wait until Spencer got home to find out. She'd learned her lesson about moving big pieces herself.

She eyed her cast again. She'd spent the whole morning going through bills, pecking numbers on the keyboard with one hand. But as the numbers on the bills had added up, that had quickly become too depressing. So she'd decided to get some projects done back here.

Except she couldn't figure out anything she could do one-handed. She scanned the shelves. She could probably wash the Spode blue Italian china set she'd picked up at an auction a few weeks ago.

The only problem was she'd placed it on a fairly high shelf for storage.

She moved toward the ladder perched next to the back door of the workshop. If she could get up high enough, she could probably hold the box in her right hand and use her left to balance it.

As she approached the door, she glanced out the small window in it. She hadn't seen Nate since he'd disappeared into his apartment with that pretty blond last night.

She didn't know why the sight of the woman had made her stomach sink. It's not like she cared what Nate did one way or another.

She grabbed the ladder and dragged it across the floor, cringing as its foot squealed against the polished concrete.

She wrestled it into place next to the shelf, then looked up to examine the box's position.

This was a bad idea. But she didn't have any other options right now.

She gripped the ladder with her right hand and took a tentative step onto the first rung, holding her left arm as close to her body as she could with the bulky cast.

She slid her grip up a couple inches, then brought her other foot up to the step.

There.

One rung done. Only four more to go.

She pressed her lips together in concentration and worked her way up another step.

On the way to the third rung, the ladder wobbled, and she almost lost her balance, but she grabbed the shelf until she was steady.

Her breath came in short gasps.

She reached for the next rung.

The door behind her banged open and footsteps pounded across the floor. "What are you doing?"

She jumped, almost losing her balance again.

But this time a hand landed on her leg to steady her.

She worked to slow her breathing. It was a second before she could look down. But she already knew who it was.

Nate.

Her heart shouldn't have skipped at his voice.

Which didn't change the fact that it did.

"I need to get this box down." She tried to move her leg to the next rung, but his hand tightened.

"Get down. You're not going up there." Nate's voice was stern, and indignation rose hot in Violet's belly.

"I was under the impression this was my store."

"Yeah. And it's my building." Nate grabbed her right arm and tugged.

She had no choice but to step down or fall.

The moment her feet were on the floor, she rounded on him. "I can't sit around here doing nothing for the next six weeks. My store will fall apart."

Nate studied her for a minute. "You don't have to do nothing. But no ladder climbing with a broken arm, okay? Or moving furniture. If you need something, come knock on my door. I have to be at my office from eight to five. But I'm around any time after that."

She flicked a glance at the clock behind him. "It's only three now."

The slow smile he gave her softened his whole face. "I decided to skip out early today. I wanted to—" He broke off and looked away.

"I wanted to check on you. Make sure you weren't doing anything else that could get you killed. Good thing, too."

He moved to scale the ladder, and she used her right hand to steady it.

She kept her eyes on the floor. But that didn't stop the warmth climbing up from her toes. He had wanted to make sure she was okay?

"Which box is it?"

She looked up to point to the box, but he was gazing down at her, and their eyes locked for a second. The storm she'd seen swirling in his the other day was still there, but it seemed calmer today.

Her throat was suddenly too dry, and she shifted to look past him. She pointed to the box. "That one. Labeled Spode blue Italian."

He reached to grab it, then backed down the ladder, his movements sure. "Where do you want it?"

"By the sink. I need to wash them before I put them out." She followed him as he crossed the room to the oversize sink.

He set it on the long countertop Cade had installed for her.

"So what is Spode blue Italian, if you don't mind my asking?"

She grinned. If she didn't mind him asking? She loved finding new people who wanted to know more about antiques. "It's a kind of china made by Spode, one of the great ceramic manufacturers in England." She opened the box and pulled out a bowl. "See the blue and white designs? They were incredibly popular on ceramics imported from China in the 1700s. But imports couldn't keep up with demand, so Spode started making its own blue and white designs. They're called blue Italian because they show scenes from the Italian countryside." She passed him the bowl. "See? Can't you just picture yourself there?"

Nate wrinkled his nose. "What's wrong with new dishes?"

Violet stared at him. Was he kidding? "Well, they do still make blue Italian, but the new ones have no story yet. No history. Imagine all the people these dishes have seen. All the eras of history they've been through. It's just—" She broke off at the look he was giving her. "What?"

"Nothing." He shook his head and moved away.

"You don't like antiques."

"I have no strong feelings about antiques one way or another." He came to a stop next to the armoire. "It's just—sometimes history is better left buried. For all you know, these plates belonged to a mass murderer."

"Yeah." Violet couldn't hold back the sarcasm. "I hear Ted Bundy ate off blue Italian."

Nate shrugged. "I'm just saying. Not everything about history is good. Sometimes it's better to get rid of everything and start fresh."

Violet considered him. She thought she sensed something deeper under the surface. "Is that what you're doing in Hope Springs? Starting fresh? Is that why you moved in with only a suitcase?"

Nate watched her, and she held completely still. For a second, she thought the storm in his eyes might break.

"I just don't think it's healthy to hold onto the past is all," he finally said. "It can keep you from moving forward."

NOT UNTIL YOU

Violet swallowed hard. The past was all she had to hold onto. Without it, she would come unmoored.

Remembering the past didn't keep her from moving forward. It gave her a reason to get up every day.

Nate turned to the armoire. "I think I can pick this up for you. If it's not too damaged?"

She wanted to ask more about why he'd come to Hope Springs. But he didn't owe her any explanations.

She pushed her curiosity aside and crossed the room to stand next to him. "I've checked it out as much as I could. I think it's okay."

Nate moved to the spot where the top of the armoire rested on the ground. His biceps strained against his sleeves as he lifted. He grunted as he got the wardrobe to waist level and repositioned his hands. Then he maneuvered it the rest of the way upright.

Violet hurried behind the armoire as Nate bent and braced his hands on his knees. "That's heavier than it looks."

"Oh, thank goodness." She set a hand on his shoulder without thinking but yanked it away the moment she felt the warmth of his skin on her fingers. "It's okay."

"That's good." Nate straightened and moved to grab the cart she'd been trying to load the armoire onto the other day.

"What are you doing?"

"If you can hold the cart still, I should be able to get it on there." He spun the cart so that the handle was facing her, and she gripped it with her right hand, bracing it with her hip. Nate moved to the far side of the armoire.

Maybe she'd been too quick to judge him. The first day she'd met him, she'd decided he was rude and standoffish, and so she'd been rude and standoffish in return.

But now she could see he had a generous heart, even if he tried to hide it.

Nate loaded one end of the armoire onto the cart, then braced it with his hand as he moved to the other side.

"Careful." She bit her lip. If that thing fell again . . .

Nate shot her an exasperated look, and she ducked her head. He probably didn't exactly consider her the world's foremost expert on safety at the moment.

With a few more grunts, he managed to maneuver the armoire onto the cart. She stepped aside as he grabbed the handle.

"Where do you want this?"

"I have a spot ready for it in the front corner." She opened the double doors and moved aside so he could steer the cart through.

For someone who didn't like antiques, Nate sure was moving the piece carefully. He stopped every few seconds to check the clearance at the top of the doorframe. The armoire squeaked through with only a centimeter or so to spare.

Violet led the way to the bedroom setup she'd been working on the other day, with a Louis XV style headboard and dresser. The armoire would create the perfect effect of a luxurious eighteenth-century bed chamber.

Nate considered the space, as if mentally sizing it up.

"It will fit." She rolled her eyes. "I measured it."

He gave her a doubtful look.

"You don't think I know how to use a tape measure?" She only used one on a daily basis.

"I'm sure you know how to use a tape measure." Nate's voice held the first trace of amusement she'd ever heard from him. It softened his whole demeanor. "But I think you may have done it wrong this time."

"Okay." She placed her good hand on her hip. "Tell you what. If it doesn't fit there, I'll buy you another plate of cookies. But if it does—" She cocked her head to the side and squinted at him, trying to come up with a good wager. "You have to let me give you a tour of the store and tell you about the antiques." She relished the opportunity. She'd make him come to see their worth.

"You're on." He bent to lift the armoire, and Violet held the cart handle again.

Once it was off the cart, Nate alternated moving each side until it was only inches from the spot she'd cleared for it.

"You sure you want to go through with this bet?" He rested with his arm on the door pull. "I can tell you right now it's not going to fit."

She had to admit the space she'd left looked too small now that the armoire was right next to it. But she was confident in her measurements. "I'm sure."

She chewed her lip as Nate angled the armoire back and forth. "Push it a little to the left."

"No cheating." But he moved it to the left, then wiggled it some more until it slid right into place, a small gap between it and the dresser on one side and the wall on the other.

"Ha."

Nate gave an exaggerated sigh. "Fine. You were right. Happy now?"

She grinned. "Yep. And I'll be even happier once I show you the joys of all the antiques here."

Nate pivoted to look around the large space. "*All* the antiques?" She heard the wariness in his voice.

"Yep. Hope you have some time."

"This clock is one of my favorites."

Nate had to chuckle. She'd said that about nearly every antique she'd shown him so far. And she'd shown him a lot. If the clock she held now was correct, they'd been at this tour for over an hour already.

"See how this window gives you a peek at the gears inside? I love how it gives you a feel for how the clock works without losing that sense of mystery and wonder."

Violet's face was animated, her eyes bright. With every object she showed him, she spoke faster, as if she was afraid he would take off any second.

She shouldn't have worried. He may not share her love of antiques, but her passion for them had completely captivated him.

"How old is it?" He mainly asked to keep her talking.

"This one would be late 1700s, early 1800s."

He let out a low whistle.

"I know. Isn't that amazing? This thing was around when our country was being founded. Just think what it's seen. Sometimes I—" She broke off and set the clock down, turning to grab an old iron from the table next to it. "So this—"

"Wait. Sometimes you what?"

The way her cheeks had turned pink made him curious.

She gave an embarrassed laugh. "Fine. Sometimes I make up stories for the items in here. You know, like this clock." She set down the iron and rested her hand on the clock. "I like to think it sat in the parlor. And when a young lady was waiting for her suitor, she would pace to it to check the time and then go sit down. And then a couple minutes later she'd do the same thing. And then when he came, she'd forget to look at the clock the whole time he was there. But when it was time for him to leave, she'd look at the clock in surprise and wonder how the time had gone by so quickly."

Nate tried to take his eyes off her, but he couldn't. He wished he could see the past like that. Like this place of endless hope and joy. Instead of a string of mistakes and regrets.

She turned her back to him and rearranged a few trinkets. "It's silly, I know. Just something to keep myself amused."

"It's not silly." He cleared his throat. "Well, it's a little silly. But that's what's so—"

A loud chime sounded from the other end of the store, and Violet spun toward the door. A group of older women with cameras around their necks filed into the building.

"Excuse me for a second." Violet hurried toward the women.

"Sure. I should get going anyway." Before he let himself get any more caught up in the feelings that had been tugging at him as she spoke.

He allowed himself one last glimpse of her as he crossed the store. She was talking with the women, who were all laughing at something she had said. She seemed to have a unique gift for bringing joy.

Probably because she'd never known sorrow. At least not the way he had. Some people had charmed lives that way.

Nate looked away. One more reason to leave her alone. He didn't want her to get caught in the trap of his tainted past.

He was nearly to the doors that led into the workshop when he spotted the smaller room to the right. He almost kept walking. But he caught a glimpse of the edge of a piece of furniture. Something about it felt familiar.

He moved closer to take a look.

The moment he reached the entry to the room, he stopped and caught his breath. A Bosendorfer grand piano. He took a few steps forward, until he was standing close enough to touch it. His fingers itched to feel the keys, but he held them back.

The piano pressed on an empty spot deep in his soul. A spot that had once been filled by music. Snatches of the songs he'd written filled his head, and it took all his willpower not to sit down and let the melodies out. He'd promised himself he'd never play again. If it weren't for music, his life would be on track right now.

"It's beautiful isn't it?"

He jumped and took a step back. How long had Violet been standing next to him?

"Yeah." His throat was too dry.

"It's a shame. It's been here forever, and I just can't sell it. It'd be nice if I played, so I could enjoy it for myself at least." She pressed her fingers to the C and D keys, and he winced at the dissonance.

She lifted her hand off the piano. "Yeah. I could use some lessons. You don't happen to play, do you?"

Nate stuffed his hands in his pockets to keep from touching the keys. "I used to. A long time ago."

"Well, it has to be like riding a bike, right?" She nudged him with her cast. "Maybe you can teach me."

He shook his head. "That's not part of my life anymore."

"So this is the perfect chance to make it part of your life again." Her smile was genuine, open.

He had to leave before this went any further. "It will never be part of my life again. Look, I have to go."

He walked away, ignoring the almost overpowering desire to look back.

Chapter 9

The waves rolled over his feet and then retreated. Nate let the cold zip up his legs as he watched the sun rise. Not many people were out at dawn on a Sunday morning. Just the way he preferred it.

So why had the sliver of loneliness worked its way into his heart?

He should be happy. After skipping out of work early Tuesday, he'd put in extra hours at the office the rest of the week and had finally managed to finish sorting through all the scattered paperwork. Now he could start to reconcile it with the electronic records and figure out which properties had expired leases or were in default on their payments. If he kept up the long hours, he might be able to meet Dad's unreasonable deadline for the report.

Plus, he'd be able to avoid seeing Violet.

He'd run into her in the hallway only once since she'd given him the tour of the antique shop, and they'd had some ridiculously mundane conversation about the weather. It was painful.

He could tell she was hurt from the way he'd run out of the antique shop the other day. But he'd had to. Being with her had started to make him want something he couldn't have.

He needed to stay focused on what he was here for. To do his penance. To prove to Dad he wasn't the world's biggest mistake—even if the mistake he'd made had been a colossal one that would define him for the rest of his life. And to earn the chance to see Mom and Kayla again.

Nate took another step but jerked his foot up quickly as something sharp poked into his heel. He bent to pick up the shell fragment that had stabbed him. But it reminded him of the shell sitting in the drawer of his bedside table.

The sliver of loneliness widened into a plank.

He chucked the shell into the water, watching as it floated for a second before being swallowed by the waves. Is that what would happen to him too?

"Duke, come." A guy's angry yell traveled down the beach.

Nate lifted his head in time to spot a big dog barreling at him, water spraying up from his legs. There was no time to get out of the way. The dog sped past, and a wall of water hit Nate square in the face.

"Sorry about that," the guy called as he chased the dog.

But Nate laughed and wiped at the water.

He'd just figured out how to ease his loneliness.

Violet hummed one of the songs from worship this morning as she pulled into the parking spot behind her building. The service today had been lovely. Somehow Dan always knew what she needed to hear. His sermon had been about the loneliness that could only be filled by God.

She had to admit her loneliness had been deeper than usual this week, with Sophie still gone and Nate—whom she'd just started to consider a potential friend—avoiding her as if he feared her love for antiques might rub off on him. But between Dan's reminder that God was the only one who could meet all her needs and a wonderful lunch at the cafe with her friends, her heart was lighter than it had been in days.

Violet gathered up her purse and Bible and was halfway out of the car when something big and powerful slammed into her, knocking her back into her seat.

A slobbery tongue slapped kisses onto her cheek, and she raised her good arm to fend it off. Water dripped from the dog's fur onto her skirt. Violet felt at the dog's neck in search of a collar she could use to get it under control, but it didn't have one.

"Maverick, down."

The dog's ears perked at the distant male voice, but its kisses were relentless.

Violet gave in and held her hand out to the dog, letting it sniff her for a minute. Then she moved her hand to scratch behind its ear. The dog laid its front paws across her lap and leaned into her.

"There we go, buddy. You're not so big and bad, are you?"

The dog responded with a contented groan.

"I'm so sorry." Nate raced up to the car. "I thought a swim would calm him down, but it seems to have riled him up more." Nate's hair was windblown, and a thin sheen of sweat shone on his forehead.

"You got a dog?" Violet hadn't pegged him as a dog lover.

Nate grabbed the dog by the scruff of the neck, pulling him off Violet. "Are you hurt? Is your arm okay?" He groaned. "Oh no, look at your skirt."

Violet straightened her drenched skirt as well as she could, ignoring the muddy paw print in the middle, and stepped out of the car. "I'm fine. I thought this was a strictly no pets building, though."

Nate shrugged. "I changed it. Although I'm kind of regretting that now. They didn't tell me this dog was the devil's child."

Violet considered the animal. He wasn't a beautiful creature, with his splotchy gray and black coat, cropped tail, and ears that hung past his muzzle. But Violet could see the appeal in him. She moved around Nate to the other side of the dog and squatted next to the animal, rubbing his ear again. The dog lowered himself to the ground and rolled over.

"Okay. How'd you do that?" Nate sounded both amused and mystified, and Violet risked a look up at him. His mouth lifted into a smile.

She didn't like the way her heart sped up when he did that. She directed her attention to the dog, busying herself with scratching its belly.

"I always had dogs growing up. I haven't had one in years, though. My husband was allergic. Anyway, this sweet guy just wants some attention."

Nate huffed. "I've given him attention all morning. He repaid me by using my bedroom floor as a bathroom."

Violet couldn't stop the laugh that snorted out. "Sorry. That's not funny." But she couldn't have sounded too sincere around her giggles.

"No, it's not." Nate's voice held a laugh around the edge of the exasperation, and the sound drew her eyes to him again.

"So, do you have any experience with dogs?" She vaguely remembered her mom's frustration with puppy training the first dog she and Jade had convinced her to buy.

She locked the memory away before the ache she always felt when she thought of Mom could rear up again. One constant heartache was enough.

Nate gave a short laugh. "I figured they couldn't be that hard to figure out. Turns out I may have been wrong."

Violet patted the dog one more time and stood, glancing down at the wet skirt plastered to her knees. She must look ridiculous.

The dog sidled from Nate's side to stand in front of Violet, and she bent over to pet him again.

Nate snorted. "Thanks for the loyalty there, Maverick." The dog didn't move.

"Is that really his name? Maverick?"

Nate's forehead creased. "Yeah. Why?"

Violet wrinkled her nose. "It's such a clichéd name. You're a big boy dog so you need to have some big macho name. When clearly he's a sweetheart."

"Well, what would you name him then?" Nate's ocean eyes landed on hers, and hard as she tried to look away, she couldn't.

"Obviously he's a Tony."

Nate laughed out loud this time. "Tony. That's the most ridiculous name I've ever heard for a dog." Nate bent down and patted the dog's head. "Come on, Maverick. I still have to figure out what to do with you while I go spend all my money on the supplies you need."

Nate's hand was perilously close to Violet's on the dog's head, and she straightened, letting her arm drop to her side.

"You mean you got a dog before you had any dog supplies?"

Nate straightened, too. "Um, yeah." He ducked his head. "Not my smartest move ever."

Violet studied the dog, who perked his ears at her. Her plan had been to come home from church and spend the afternoon cleaning, then curl up with a book.

"I could watch him while you go out."

Nate's eyes met Violet's again. Something warred in his, but it passed in a moment. "I couldn't ask you to do that." He patted his leg for the dog to come.

"You didn't ask. I offered."

Nate studied her, as if not sure she was serious. "You're sure you wouldn't mind?"

"Absolutely sure. That's what neighbors are for, right? Anyway, I've missed having a dog around." She squatted and wrapped her arm around the dog. "We'll have fun, won't we, Tony?"

Nate gave her one last appraising look. Then he walked toward the alley, calling over his shoulder, "His name is Maverick."

Violet grinned at his retreating form. "Not if I have anything to do with it."

The sound of Nate's laugh drifting back to her only made her grin wider.

Chapter 10

Violet pulled the back door of the antique shop closed behind her and locked it. She should be happy. It had been a good day for a Friday. She'd managed to sell a couple of big pieces, along with several smaller items. If things kept up like this, she might be able to make her rent payment on time. Not that it meant she'd be caught up on what she owed in back rent, but at least she wouldn't fall further behind.

But for some reason she couldn't put her finger on, her heart felt heavier than it should. She glanced up the staircase, her thoughts tracking to Nate's apartment. Were he and the dog in there? She'd bonded with the dog when she'd watched him last Sunday—she'd even managed to train him to answer only to Tony. Nate had pretended to disapprove, but she'd seen right past his tough act to the laughter hiding in his eyes.

Over the past few days, she'd gotten used to running into them as Nate took the dog out before work. Yesterday, she'd waited with him on the hill as he let Tony out. And after work, he'd stopped by the antique shop to ask if she needed anything else moved. She'd ended up deciding on the spur of the moment that she needed a whole dining setup rearranged, and he'd spent a good hour helping her. But she hadn't seen him at all yet today.

Not that it mattered.

Violet grabbed her mail from the box at the foot of the stairs, then trudged up to her apartment. But once she was in the cozy space, she couldn't figure out what to do. It was such a beautiful evening that it was almost a shame to spend it indoors. She moved to the window in the small dining area and slid the curtain aside. Although it was after five, the sun was still high in the sky, and groups of children splashed in the water. A few couples strolled along the shoreline. Violet's heart tightened. She and Cade used to do that—long walks where they talked about everything or nothing at all.

She hadn't been able to bring herself to walk on the beach since his death.

She let the curtain fall and moved to the couch. Maybe she'd read. But the moment she picked up her book, she set it down. For the first time in a long time, she didn't feel like reading about someone else's life.

She felt like *doing* something with hers.

Maybe she could go for a walk. Not on the beach. She didn't think she could handle that. But the Sugarbush trail was only half a mile away.

She changed into a pair of running shorts and maneuvered her arm into a t-shirt. The tennis shoes were harder to put on one-handed, but she finally managed.

The moment she opened her door, a shaggy creature crashed into her legs. She couldn't help the smile. "Hey there, Tony. I missed you this morning."

She looked up as Nate closed his apartment door. He was dressed in khakis and a gray dress shirt that made his eyes look steelier than usual. But the steel softened as he met her gaze. "I had to get to work early this morning, so we were out before the sun was up."

She wrinkled her nose. Early mornings were not her favorite time. "Too early for me then. Where are you two off to now?"

"I just got home, actually, so I thought I better let him out for a few minutes. Poor guy has been cooped up all day."

"Well, I didn't hear a peep from him, if it makes you feel better." She gave Tony a pat and moved toward the steps. "I thought I'd go for a walk on the Sugarbush. You two want to come?"

The surprise on Nate's face was probably echoed on hers. She hadn't been planning to invite them along. The words had just come out. But now that they had, she was glad. She wouldn't mind some company. It'd keep her thoughts from drifting to Cade the whole time.

"Sure." Nate's answer was quick. "Just one thing—what's the Sugarbush?"

Violet laughed. "It's a hiking trail. The trailhead is down the road. It's really pretty and—"

She stopped. This wasn't a tourism video.

Nate took stock of his dress clothes. "Give me a second to change." He passed her Tony's leash. "I'll meet you two outside."

Nate let his eyes drift to Violet. She'd set a quick pace for their walk, and her face was bright. She pointed to the little restaurant they were passing. "Have you eaten at the Hidden Cafe yet?"

He shook his head. The scent of home cooking wafting from the cafe had almost lured him in more than once, but so far, he'd stuck with frozen dinners. They were good enough for him.

After another five minutes, Tony's tongue was lolling to the side, and Nate was beginning to wonder if a walk was a good idea on such a hot day.

But Violet steered them toward a wooded area to the right. "The Sugarbush."

Nate picked out a narrow packed dirt path that wound between thick stands of trees. About a hundred yards in, he lost sight of the trail as it jogged to the left. It didn't look like much, but he was willing to give it a shot.

As soon as they stepped into the shade of the trees, the temperature felt ten degrees cooler, even though the humidity still clung to him. They walked single file until the trail widened after a few yards. Violet fell into step beside him.

They strolled in comfortable silence, watching Tony, who kept his nose to the ground and made constant snuffling sounds. Every few feet, he stopped for a longer sniff. Nate tried to tug him along, but it quickly became clear Tony was going to be the one to set the pace.

"This is nice," Nate said after a while, then felt his face warm. He hadn't meant to say the words out loud. "I mean, I had no idea this was here."

Violet pointed at a patch of red berries. "Hope Springs has lots of surprises like this."

She plucked a berry and passed it to him. He held it up and examined it. He hadn't been hiking a lot in his life, but he was pretty sure you weren't supposed to eat random berries in the woods.

"Relax, it's a raspberry." Violet popped one in her mouth. It stained her lips a darker red.

Nate forced his eyes off them and stuck his own berry in his mouth. He made a face at the tartness.

Violet picked another. "Yeah, they're not quite ripe yet. That's how my husband always liked them, but I prefer to wait until they're a little darker."

Nate hesitated with a second berry halfway to his mouth. He shouldn't pry, but that was the third or fourth time she'd mentioned a husband since he'd met her. "If you don't mind my asking, where is your husband? I haven't met him."

The flush drained from Violet's cheeks, and he wished he could take the question back. It's not like it was any of his business.

Violet resumed walking. Nate hesitated a second, then took his spot beside her.

"He died. Three years ago." Her voice was quiet, and Nate wanted to kick himself. He'd never considered the possibility. Not when she seemed so joyful all the time.

"I'm so sorry." It wasn't enough, but what else could he say?

He wanted to know more. What had happened? How had he died? How had she picked up the pieces to remain this cheerful person?

But he sensed she didn't want to talk about it.

After a while, she glanced at him. "So what brings you to Hope Springs, anyway? Your girlfriend?"

He nearly choked. "My what?"

"Sorry, fiancée maybe?"

Who on earth was she talking about? "I don't have a girlfriend or a fiancée."

"Oh." She turned to look at a small pond off the right side of the trail. "Sorry. I just assumed that woman the other day—"

Nate ran the last few days through his mind. He couldn't think of a single woman he'd had contact with besides Violet and Mrs. D'Angelo. Unless she meant—

"Oh, that was my—" He hesitated. If he said parole officer, she'd turn around and sprint back the way they'd come. "That was just a business associate."

"Oh." She tucked a wayward curl behind her ear. He had no idea what she was thinking right now. What surprised him was how badly he wanted to know. Did it change anything, her knowing he didn't have a girlfriend?

"So what did bring you to Hope Springs?"

Nate licked his lips. That question opened up way too many land mines. He decided to go with the most immediate reason. "I came to work for my dad."

She tipped her head to the side. "You don't like it, though?"

His head swiveled to her. "How—"

"It's not that hard to tell. Your hands are clenched into fists. Your jaw is clamped tighter than a lockbox. And you always seem kind of down when you have to go to work in the morning."

Nate gaped. He'd have to be more guarded with her. If she'd figured all that out just from looking at him, who knew what else she might discern.

"So why are you working for your dad if you hate it? Why not quit?" She swatted at a mosquito on her neck.

If only he could. "It's not that simple."

She watched him, as if waiting for more of an answer. But he couldn't give one. Not without making her hate him. And right now she was the only friend he had. Besides Tony.

"So, let's say it was simple." Her voice was easy, and he relaxed a little. "What would you do if you could do anything?"

Nate knew the answer to that without thinking about it. But he wasn't about to share it. That part of his life was dead.

"I don't—" But he broke off as Tony's leash jerked out of his hand.

"Tony!" He lunged for the leash, but it was too late. Tony dashed into the trees, a deer sprinting a couple yards ahead of him.

"Tony!" Nate yelled in his strictest voice. But the dog kept running. He was already at least fifty yards into the woods. "Come!"

"Tony!" Violet's yell wasn't as hard as Nate's, but it was nearly as loud.

Within seconds, the dog had disappeared. Nate squinted in the direction he had run, his heart banging against his ribs. Tony was supposed to be the one friend who would never leave him.

"Tony!" Nate called again.

"He went that way." Violet pointed to the east, where a thick clump of trees hid anything else from sight. "Come on."

Nate followed as she set out at a fast clip in the direction Tony had disappeared.

It was starting to get dark in the woods, and Nate fought down the panic. The trees stretched as far as he could see in every direction. "How large is this forest?"

He was half afraid the forest would be so large Tony could be lost forever and half afraid it was so small that Tony would come out at a road on the other side and be hit by a car.

Violet stopped, turning in a slow circle as she squinted into the distance. "It's pretty big. He'll get tired out and rest soon, and then we'll catch up with him." She gave his arm a reassuring pat.

"Over there." Violet pointed into the trees and set off at a jog, her casted arm swinging at her side.

"Tony!" This time, Violet's voice sounded different—a cry of recognition instead of a call into the unknown.

Nate's head popped up in time to see Violet running full-out toward the dog, who was straining to get to her but was held back by something. The dog let out a sharp cry that went straight to Nate's heart. He'd let his dog get away and now he was hurt. Wasn't there anyone in the world he could take care of?

Violet dropped to her knees next to the dog just as Nate reached them.

"His leg's caught in some old barbed wire." Her voice was calm, and Nate concentrated on it to steady himself. Panicking wasn't going to help Tony.

He leaned over Violet, who had her arm wrapped around the dog, and examined the wire. It was wound tight, trickles of blood darkening the fur where the barbs pierced the leg. Nate inhaled sharply.

"Can you untangle it?" Violet asked, in between cooing to the whimpering dog.

Nate tried to find a loose spot in the wire. "I think so. Can you hold him still?"

Violet nodded, whispering "It's okay, boy," over and over as she stroked the dog's ears. Tony leaned against her, and his whimpers slowed.

Nate moved around Violet to kneel at the dog's other side. The barbed wire bit into his hand as he lifted it away from Tony's leg. The dog yelped and tried to pull away, but Violet continued to pat him, and Nate strained at the wire again.

After several minutes, he managed to work the barbs free. Blood stained the dog's gray legs, but the wounds didn't seem too deep.

Nate fell back, rubbing a hand against his forehead to wipe away the sweat that had collected there from their dash through the woods.

"Nice work." Violet looked up, and her eyes widened. "You're bleeding."

Nate waved off her concern. "It's not too bad."

Violet eyed him dubiously, then gave the dog a pat and slid closer to Nate.

He hissed in a breath as she took his bloodied hand in hers.

"Sorry."

He didn't bother to tell her that the breath hadn't been one of pain.

She opened her water bottle and poured it over his hand, washing away the worst of the blood. "These don't look too deep, but that fence is pretty rusty. Are you up to date on your tetanus shot?"

Nate swallowed and nodded. He knew the exact date of his last tetanus shot.

"Good." Violet moved to Tony and poured the remaining water over his leg. Tony whimpered but licked her. "I think he's going to be okay, too. Right, boy?"

The dog gave her a mournful look, and she patted his head. "Come on."

She stood, then held out a hand to help Nate up. He took it, forcing himself to ignore the sparks in his fingertips.

"You too, boy." She patted her leg, and Tony stood. He took a few limping steps, then started to jog ahead of them.

"I don't think so, boy. Come." Nate hooked the leash onto the dog's collar. Tony looked up at him with his big dark eyes. "Don't give me that look. You were very naughty."

"Oh, don't be so hard on him." Violet touched his arm for a fraction of second. "He's sorry." As if to prove her right, Tony let out a deep sigh.

"Sorry isn't always enough. Some things don't deserve to be forgiven." He kept his voice light to hide the truth behind his words. He knew only too well that some things were beyond forgiveness.

Violet stopped walking, as if his words had shocked her. As if she wanted to talk about them.

Nate kept going.

After a few seconds, her footsteps jogged up beside him. "You aren't really going to hold this against him forever are you? I think he learned his lesson, poor guy."

He sighed. "I suppose I'll forgive him eventually. Once he makes it up to me."

"And how's he going to do that?"

Nate shrugged. "A week of dishes duty, maybe."

Violet burst out laughing, the sound rich and bright, filling the woods. "Remind me not to eat at your house for the next week."

Nate laughed, too. He wanted so badly for his heart to feel as light as hers.

But a heavy lump settled in his stomach. Perhaps Tony could be forgiven someday.

After all, his mistake had hurt only himself.

Nate's, on the other hand, had cost his sister everything.

Chapter 11

Nate checked the time again. How was it only two o'clock?

He'd had Officer Jensen meet him here this morning to avoid any more awkward conversations with Violet about her. But their meeting had been done for a few hours now, and still the clock refused to budge.

He contemplated the remaining stack of leases. He should skip out and enjoy his Saturday. He could finish them next week. But Dad hadn't called yet today. And if Nate wasn't here when he called, it'd be one more strike against him.

He turned back to the computer. He'd asked Violet to stop in and check on Tony if she got a second during the day, and she'd assured him that she would.

He trusted her. But maybe he should give her a quick call. Just to ask how Tony was.

Not because he wanted to hear her musical voice.

He did a quick search for the antique store online and dialed the number before he could change his mind.

"Hidden Treasures. How are you today?"

Just hearing her voice should not make him smile like this. He tried to keep his tone casual. "Hey, it's me. Just wanted to see if you've had a chance to check on Tony or if I should—"

"Nate." Her greeting was warm, and he had to remind himself that was how she always sounded. It had nothing to do with him. "I checked on him this morning and once about an hour ago. He almost convinced me to close the store and take him for a walk, but I stayed strong."

Nate relaxed into his seat. "And how'd Tony take the disappointment?"

"Oh, you know—" He could picture her waving a hand through the air. "He didn't. So I brought him down here with me."

Nate sniggered. "And that's staying strong?"

Violet laughed, too. "I know, I know. But he was so insistent, and he gave me that look. You know the one where he tilts his head way to the side and looks at you out of the corner of his eyes?"

Nate did know. It was how Tony had gotten two treats out of him last night when he'd deserved none for the way he'd behaved in the woods.

"Well, if he gives you any trouble, put him back upstairs. I'll be home in a couple hours." He was getting used to the way the word *home* felt on his tongue.

"Sounds great. And Nate?"

"Yeah?"

"I hope you have a good afternoon." The sincerity in her voice touched something in Nate's core. This wasn't the casual "have a good day" that a store clerk threw out a hundred times a day. This was heartfelt, meant just for him.

"Thanks." He swallowed. "You, too."

The moment he hung up, he was readier than ever to go home. But he couldn't pretend it was only Tony he wanted to see anymore.

He turned to the stack of leases, the smile refusing to let go of its hold on his lips. He entered the information for a property in Grace Falls, wherever that was, and moved on to the next.

By the time he'd entered half a dozen leases, his spirits had dampened only a little. They all seemed to be up to date on their leases and payments, which made his job that much easier.

The office phone blared, and his mood instantly soured. He'd hoped he might be able to go at least one day without Dad checking up on him.

He snatched the phone off the cradle. "Benson Properties."

"Nathan."

Nate could practically feel his blood pressure go up, just like it did every time Dad called.

"Do you have the report I requested?"

Nate scrutinized the dozen or so leases stacked on the desk. "I will in about an hour. I'll email it to you then."

"Good. I have an investor waiting to see a list of potential properties in Hope Springs. So make sure you include expired or almost expired leases or any that are in default on their payments."

"Okay." Nate made a note, then rushed on before Dad could hang up. "Do you think I could come visit Mom and Kayla this weekend? After I get you the report, I mean."

Nate let his hope build at the hesitation on the other end. Was Dad really considering it?

"Two and a half weeks is hardly long enough to prove you're a different man, Nathan. Send that report right away."

Nate pulled the phone away as the dial tone blared in his ear.

He slammed the phone down and grabbed the next lease. But his hand froze as his eyes fell on the names at the top of the paper. Violet and Cade Somers.

He flipped the page and skipped over the legalese to find the needed information. The lease expired in two and a half months.

Nate wondered if Violet knew that. After all she'd been through in the past few years, it probably hadn't occurred to her to check into renewing her lease. Technically, according to the terms of the lease, it was already too late for a guaranteed renewal. Meaning Nate could kick her out and get someone else in there if he wanted to. Which he didn't.

He brought up her account on the computer to review her payment records. His heart sank. According to this, she was three months behind.

Nate set the lease aside and finished up the rest. He used the database to compile a list of properties with expired leases or in default, then scanned the list quickly for Violet's name.

When he came to it, he highlighted the row and hit delete.

One less property wasn't going to hurt Dad.

He saved the file and sent it off. Then he locked up and headed for the one place he wanted to be right now.

Home.

Violet threw the tennis ball down the hill and watched Tony chase after it, his ears flopping as he ran.

"Fetch it here, Tony." She used her most commanding voice.

But Tony apparently wasn't buying it. He carried the ball a few feet up the hill, then dropped it and watched as it rolled back down.

"Tony!" Violet bent in half and shook her head, then stood and ran after the ball herself. He'd done the same thing twelve times already, but she had been so sure that this time he would finally get it.

Tony sniffed her as she bent to pick up the ball, and she gave him a quick rub behind the ears. "It's okay, boy. You'll figure it out next time."

She checked the time on her phone again. Hopefully Nate would be home soon. She was supposed to be at Dan's in half an hour for dinner with her friends. She was dying to see Sophie and Spencer, who had finally gotten home late last night.

Tony gave her a lick, and Violet wiped her cheek. "Come on, let's try again." She started to climb the hill.

"Looks like he has you trained well."

She lifted her head, a smile already tugging her lips up at the sound of Nate's voice. He stood at the top of the hill, hands in the pockets of his khakis, grinning down at them.

"What are you talking about?" She grinned right back at him. "This is exactly what I taught him to do." She covered the last few steps up the hill and stood in front of Nate. A light five o'clock shadow dusted his cheeks and chin, making him look rugged.

His stance was relaxed, but she couldn't help noticing the tension in his shoulders.

"Rough day?"

He looked away. "It was fine."

He seemed ready to say more. She waited, but then he seemed to change his mind. "Thanks for watching Tony."

"Of course. I think I enjoyed having him around as much as he enjoyed being around."

Nate squatted to give Tony a scratch behind the ears. "As long as you don't teach him to like you more than he likes me."

"Oh, don't worry." She lowered herself to scratch Tony's neck, and the dog stepped closer to her. "He already likes me better."

Nate gave her shoulder a playful shove. "Yeah. I can't deny that. But then, you're definitely the more likable of the two of us."

Violet's eyes snapped to his, but he was gazing out toward the lake.

She straightened. "I'd love to stay and play, but I have to get going. What're you boys up to tonight?"

"Oh, you know—" Nate stood, too. "We have big plans with a frozen dinner and some mindless TV."

"Sounds fun." Violet had spent her share of nights the same way. "See you later."

With a last scratch of Tony's ears, she headed for her apartment. She needed to grab her keys and the pasta salad she'd managed to wrangle together with one hand last night.

But when she reached the door to the building, she couldn't help looking over her shoulder.

Nate had settled onto the grass, his knees up in front of him, his gaze directed toward the lake. She let herself wonder for a second what he was thinking about. Something almost haunted hovered behind his eyes most of the time, and she couldn't help wanting to ease it. Whatever it was.

But that wasn't her place.

She was his neighbor and maybe almost a friend.

But nothing more.

She slipped through the door and jogged up the steps. If she stood here wondering about her new neighbor any longer, she'd be late for dinner. And she was starving. The store had been so slammed today she hadn't had time for lunch.

Which had been a good problem to have for once.

She opened the door to her apartment, her mouth already watering at the thought of Dan's burgers. But she stopped inside the doorway as a strange sound hit her ears. It was like the constant rush of a waterfall.

But there were no waterfalls in her apartment the last time she'd checked.

Had she left a faucet on this morning? She'd done that once in the weeks right after Cade died. Fortunately, it had only been for a few minutes while she went downstairs to get the mail, and the overflow drain had kept up with the water flow.

She moved into the kitchen. The sink was off, and the dishwasher wasn't running.

So then where . . .

Water sloshed over her sandals as she stepped into the hallway, and she yanked her foot back in alarm.

The hallway had turned into a stream, flowing from the laundry room toward the bedroom. She followed it toward the source.

When she got to the laundry room, she stopped dead, her good hand over her mouth. The utility sink was on the floor, and water was spraying from a broken-off pipe jutting out of the wall.

"What did— How?" She dropped to her knees alongside the sink, ignoring the spray of water against her right arm as she groped behind the washer for a shut-off valve. There had to be one, didn't there?

Finally, her hand landed on what felt like the spigot of an outdoor faucet.

But when she tried to turn it, nothing happened.

"Come on." She twisted harder. But her fingers simply slipped against the metal.

Now what? She couldn't sit here letting her apartment become a lake.

But by the time a plumber got here, that's exactly what would happen.

She didn't stop to think about it. Just jumped up and ran as quickly as she could without falling through the wet hallway, down the stairs, and out the door.

"Nate!"

He wasn't in his spot at the top of the hill anymore, and she jogged across the parking lot, scanning the hillside.

There.

On the beach, watching Tony splash in the waves.

She hesitated. She'd worked so hard not to go down there. But if she didn't now, she might as well bring the lake indoors.

She set off at a run down the hill, calling Nate's name every few seconds. She was halfway to the bottom when he turned around. Even from here, she could make out the smile that took over his face the moment he noticed her.

But she didn't have time to dwell on it.

She drew to a stop and waved him toward her. "I need your help!"

In under three seconds, he'd called Tony out of the water and was running up the beach toward her.

She waited, trying to catch her breath.

"What's going on? What's wrong?" Concern tightened his voice as he reached her.

"A pipe broke. There's water everywhere."

"Where?" Nate started up the hill at a jog, and Violet ran to match the pace of his longer legs.

"Everywhere," she repeated.

"I mean, where in the building?"

Oh, that made more sense. "My apartment. The laundry room. The sink fell off the wall. I tried to turn the shutoff valve, but it was stuck."

He nodded and opened the door, waiting for her to pass through.

She ran up the stairs. Tony's claws clicked on the steps behind her.

"I just put a load of laundry in maybe twenty minutes ago. Right before I took Tony outside—" She looked over her shoulder, but Nate wasn't there anymore.

She swiveled. How had he disappeared?

The door to her store was closed and locked, and he hadn't passed her on the stairs.

"Nate?"

There was no answer. On the step below her, Tony cocked his head, ears perked.

"Nate?" She called louder this time.

A clanging resounded through the entryway. She looked down. She was pretty sure it had come from under the stairs.

She retraced her steps, more than a little baffled. A narrow hallway ran alongside the stairs, separating them from her store, but as far as she knew, there was nothing there but an old storage closet.

But the door to the closet was open, and a light was on inside. She jumped as the banging began again.

"There we go." Nate's voice carried from the closet, and she moved closer.

She was just outside the door when he emerged, almost plowing into her. "Whoa. Sorry about that." He took a quick step back, and so did she.

She peered over his shoulder. Apparently it wasn't a storage closet after all. A large furnace took up most of the room.

"What'd you do?"

"I turned off the building's main water supply. Just until we can get the shutoff valve upstairs working or replaced." He set down the wrench he'd been holding and flipped off the light. "Let's go check it out."

Violet wanted to tell him he didn't have to do that. That she could take it from here. But the truth was, she appreciated the offer too much to turn it down.

She led the way up the stairs.

Nate stopped at the landing. "Let me put Tony in my apartment. Don't want him to get your place all wet."

She gave him an incredulous look, and he burst out laughing. The sound was so unexpected, she couldn't help joining him. It was the first time she'd heard him really laugh. It sounded good on him.

But as she opened the door to her apartment, their laughter cut off.

A trickle of water had worked its way from the hallway into the living room.

"Well that's not good." Nate stepped past her and followed the water to the laundry room. She walked slowly behind him, thinking about how long this was going to take to clean up. She ducked into the bathroom to grab every last towel out of the linen closet.

"Uh, do you need this stuff in the boxes?" Nate called.

"Oh no." She dropped the towels. In her panic to get the water turned off, she hadn't thought about the boxes of Cade's stuff still sitting on the laundry room floor.

She dashed into the room and squeezed past Nate in the small space. The bottoms of the boxes had transformed into an ugly dark brown as water seeped into them.

"Let's get them out of here." Nate held out his arms, and she passed him a box. Then she grabbed one of her own, grateful he didn't ask what was in them. She choked down the sobs threatening to escape. For some reason, the thought of Cade's things being destroyed hurt more than the thought of giving them away.

They deposited the boxes on the kitchen counter, then went back for more.

When they'd moved them all, Violet started pulling items out as Nate disappeared from the room. She was grateful for the moment of privacy as she spread Cade's stuff across the dining table and chairs, the couch, anywhere there was a dry space.

Fortunately, the only thing that seemed to be damaged was the corsage Cade had worn to their senior prom. She laughed as she rubbed its flaking petals.

"At least you still have your sense of humor." Nate stopped at the entrance to the kitchen, glancing around the room.

Violet gestured toward the corsage. "Cade hated wearing that thing. Kept saying it was poking him all night. It's why none of the guys in our wedding wore a corsage."

Nate gave her a gentle smile. "I got the shutoff valve turned off. I'll go turn the main water supply on, then I'll help you clean up this flood."

"Oh, you don't have to—"

But Nate cut her off. "I know I don't have to. I want to. That's what neighbors are for, remember?"

Thirty minutes later, the floor was finally dry. Violet pushed onto her heels and shoved her hair out of her eyes.

"I think that's good."

Nate looked up from where he was crouched by the washer. "Yeah, I think we got it all." He rocked his head from side to side. She knew the feeling. They'd been on their hands and knees way too long sopping up the water. She couldn't imagine how much longer it would have taken without his help.

"Thank you. I really had no idea who to ask for help."

"Well, I'm always right next door." Nate stood, reaching to massage his back. Violet had a sudden flash of rubbing Cade's back after he'd installed the washer years ago. Did Nate have the same firm muscles? Violet shoved the thought aside and pushed past Nate toward the kitchen.

She started sorting through Cade's stuff.

After a minute, Nate's footsteps shuffled behind her, but they stopped at the doorway.

"Thanks for helping me save all this. I should have taken it to the thrift store a long time ago, but—" She didn't trust herself to continue.

"You're welcome." Nate's voice was soft, and she risked a look over her shoulder, letting their eyes meet. Neither looked away for a heartbeat.

"Anyway." Nate cleared his throat. "It shouldn't be too big of a deal to replace that pipe and get you a new sink. I could do it tomorrow if you'd like."

Violet couldn't seem to get a read on this guy. How could the same person be so aloof and yet so open at the same time? She followed him to the laundry room to examine the broken pipe. Not that she had any idea what to look for.

Nate stepped out of her way and bent to scoop up the pile of wet towels.

"Oh, don't, you're going to get all—"

But it was too late. Nate had already hugged the mass to his body.

"Wet," she finished anyway, around a laugh.

"I don't think either of us can really get any wetter at this point." Nate gestured at her own sopping shorts.

"Yeah. Guess I'd better change before I head out for dinner at my friend's house." She passed him a laundry basket, and he dropped the towels into it.

A sudden thought struck her, but the words stuck in her throat. She knew her friends wouldn't mind. But she also knew they'd read way too much into it.

Still, Nate had saved her home. She owed him dinner at least. "Actually, why don't you come with me? As a thank you." She carefully avoided his eyes.

"That's okay. I was going to—"

"Eat a frozen dinner and watch TV with Tony," she finished for him. "Come on. My friend Dan makes these amazing burgers."

His eyes brightened, and she could tell he was wavering.

"Plus, Peyton usually brings something from the bakery."

He raised his arms in surrender. "When you put it that way, how can I resist?"

"That's what I thought." Violet grinned in triumph. "Change into something dry and meet me here in twenty minutes."

She led him to the door and leaned on it for a second after he left. Thank goodness he'd moved in. Eighty-year-old Mrs. D'Angelo would have been absolutely no help in a situation like this, bless her.

Violet pushed off the door and grabbed her phone on her way to change.

Dan answered on the first ring. "The burgers are almost ready. Where are you?"

Violet pulled a flower print skirt and a white sleeveless blouse out of her closet as she talked. "Sorry. Plumbing emergency."

"Oh no. Do you need help?"

Violet laughed. "Like you know anything about plumbing."

"I knew I never should have used my plumbing failure as a sermon illustration." Dan groaned. "I'm never going to hear the end of that, am I?"

"Not likely. But don't worry, your willingness to make a fool of yourself is what people love about you."

"Great." But Dan was laughing, too. "Anyway, I could have provided moral support."

"Thanks. I'm sure moral support would have stopped the water gushing all over my laundry room floor." Violet opened her makeup bag and started putting on a light layer. Normally, she wouldn't care about wearing makeup when she was just having dinner with her friends, but tonight felt different. "Don't worry about it. My new neighbor saved the day."

"The same new neighbor who rescued you when you fell? The guy's turning out to be a real hero." Dan's voice was half teasing.

"Yeah. I know." Violet tried to ignore the implication. "Anyway, I invited him to come tonight. You know, as a thank you. I get the feeling he doesn't get many home-cooked meals."

She broke off. What was she thinking, bringing a man who wasn't Cade to meet her friends? Even though she wasn't bringing him as a man. It was just as a thank you. But that wasn't how her friends would see it.

"Actually, you know what, forget it. I don't want to inconvenience you or—" She dropped her makeup brush into the bag.

"Violet, relax." Dan's gentle voice calmed her frayed nerves. "Of course he's welcome."

Violet let out a long exhale. "Okay." She wasn't sure that was what she wanted anymore. But there was really no way to uninvite him now.

Chapter 12

Nate dug through the half dozen t-shirts he'd bought at the discount store the day after he'd moved in. None of them seemed right for meeting Violet's friends. He wasn't usually a polo shirt type of guy, but he'd bought one for the office. Maybe that would work.

He dragged a hand through his hair.

Why was he standing here wondering what to wear? It was just dinner with a bunch of strangers.

"Ah, Tony, what have I gotten myself into?" He grabbed the polo shirt off the hanger and pulled it over his head.

He wasn't sure why he'd agreed to go in the first place. He hadn't made new friends in years, and the thought of being around others was daunting.

But the thought of staying home with the dog to eat yet another frozen dinner was worse.

"Alright, boy, wish me luck." Nate put Tony in his kennel and passed him a treat. At the dog's mournful look, he passed him another. "I won't be gone long."

He ducked out of his apartment and knocked on Violet's door.

"Come in."

He had to take a calming breath before he opened the door, and he scolded himself. He was acting like a teenager on his first date, not a grown man going to have dinner with his neighbor and her friends.

He glanced around the apartment. Aside from her late husband's things scattered around the open surfaces, you'd never know the place had been a disaster twenty minutes ago.

In the kitchen, Violet had her head buried in her refrigerator. She seemed to be wrestling with something.

"You need some help?"

"Nope." Her voice was muffled. "Just grabbing this." She emerged with one arm wrapped around a large bowl that looked like it was about to plunge to the floor. "Well, maybe a little help."

He dashed across the room and scooped it out of her hand right as she lost her grip.

It smelled divine. "What is it?"

"Pasta salad. I made it last night."

He ogled her. "You made it? With one hand?"

She shrugged. "Once you learn to maneuver a knife right-handed, it's not so hard."

He shook his head. "Have you always been so—"

She watched him expectantly as he broke off. "So . . . ?"

He searched for a word. "Uh, determined?"

She laughed and pointed a finger at him. "That's not what you were going to say."

He let himself be pulled in. "No, but it was the safer thing to say."

She smacked his arm as she walked past him out the door. "Well, to answer your question, yes, I've always been so stubborn."

"Good to know."

He followed her to her car, trying not to notice how her white shirt highlighted her creamy skin and dark hair. Or how her floral scent drifted over him, fitting right into the summery evening.

He shook his head. What was the matter with him?

As she got into the driver's seat, he stowed the pasta salad in the back, then slipped into the passenger side.

"You can relax." Violet raised an eyebrow as she backed out of the parking spot. "Most of my friends don't eat people."

He let himself smile and eased his fisted hands open. "So, this friend of yours makes good hamburgers, huh?"

They kept the banter light as Violet navigated the city streets. Ten minutes later, she drove into the parking lot of a large church. There were three other cars in the lot, although the building itself was dark.

Nate's stomach tightened. What kind of bait and switch was this? "Your friend lives at a church?"

Violet pointed to a two-story brick house next door. "It's easier to park here."

"Ah." The tension in Nate's shoulders eased a little, but he still felt like a shock wave had gone through him. He hadn't been in a church since the night of the accident. And he didn't ever plan to step foot in one again.

Violet twisted to maneuver her arm awkwardly toward the bowl in the backseat, but he grabbed her wrist to stop her. "You really are stubborn, aren't you? I'll get it."

Her eyes moved to the spot where his fingers rested against her skin, and he lifted his hand. He took an extra second to grab the bowl as she stepped out of the car.

But finally he couldn't draw it out any longer, and he had to get out, too.

His stomach lurched as he stood. This was ridiculous. He'd spent the past seven years living with felons, for heaven's sake. How hard could it be to have dinner with a group of normal people, none of whom had probably been convicted of so much as a parking ticket.

And anyway, these people were strangers. To them, he was a blank slate, a person with no history.

Nate avoided looking toward the church as he followed Violet along the side of the house toward the backyard.

An amazing whiff of hamburgers rolled over Nate. He only hoped Violet couldn't hear his stomach rumbling.

As they neared the corner of the house, the sound of music reached his ears.

He recognized the song immediately as "Resurrection Power."

He'd rehearsed it a thousand times. And played it probably a hundred times on stage.

He did his best to tune it out.

The minute he rounded the corner into the backyard, he almost stopped short in his tracks. He'd expected a small group, maybe three or four people. But there had to be at least a dozen people seated around the patio, plates on their laps. A light-haired woman noticed them first, and before Nate knew what was happening, she'd run across the yard and thrown her arms around Violet.

Violet hugged her back, laughing and—was she crying, too? Nate watched in alarm. He had no idea what to do in this situation.

A dark-haired man walked up. "Don't worry about these two. They haven't seen each other in three weeks. There were bound to be some tears." He extended his hand to Nate. "I'm Spencer."

Nate shook the man's outstretched hand. "Nate."

The woman pulled out of Violet's arms and held out a hand to him, too, swiping at a tear under her lash line with her other hand. "I'm Sophie. I hear we have you to thank for keeping our Violet in one piece. And saving her from a flood."

Nate shook her hand but ducked his head.

Violet seemed to sense his discomfort. "Come on, I'll introduce you to everyone. Then we need some food. I don't know about you, but I'm starving."

They walked closer to the patio, where everyone was talking and laughing and eating. It was such a normal scene. Like the family get-togethers his parents used to host for his birthday every year. A quiet longing took up residence behind his eyes, and he looked toward the table to clear it. A spread of food covered every surface.

"Hey, everyone." Violet's back was to him, but Nate could hear the smile in her voice, and it made him smile, too. "This is Nate. My neighbor."

The conversation stopped abruptly as Violet's friends swiveled toward him.

He tried to hold onto the smile, but his mouth had gone dry.

"Hi," he managed to croak, lifting his hand a few inches in a lame imitation of a wave.

The man at the grill set his spatula down and approached Nate, holding out a hand. "I'm Dan. It's nice to meet you." Nate shook his hand, grateful for the ease with which the man accepted a stranger to his house.

"And this is the group." Violet lifted an arm to gesture at the rest of the people there. "Ethan and Ariana." She pointed to a couple seated together on a stone bench, then to another couple seated at a small bistro table. "And Jared and Peyton."

"The cookie maker?"

They all laughed, and Nate relaxed a tad.

"The one and only." Peyton offered a warm smile. "Hope you liked them. It was the least we could do after you rescued Violet like that."

Nate dug his sandal into a crack between two patio stones. "It was no big deal." These people had to stop treating him like some kind of hero.

"And—" Violet turned toward a small group on scattered lounge chairs. "Emma, Tyler, and Leah."

He stared at the last woman. For some reason, she seemed familiar.

"We've met." The woman jumped up from her chair and came to stand next to him as if they were old friends. "Nate was my seatmate on the bus ride back from visiting my friend in Sibley."

Nate winced. Would they make the connection to the state penitentiary in Sibley?

"Actually, I was showing him pictures of your wedding." She turned to Sophie. "I think he said you looked enchanting."

Nate did a double take. He didn't particularly remember saying anything about the wedding one way or another. And if he'd said Sophie looked enchanting, he was probably being sarcastic, since he'd had no interest in hearing about some stranger's wedding. But Leah seemed completely sincere.

"It looked like a lovely wedding," he finally managed to get out. He shuffled awkwardly from foot to foot.

"Well, eat up, you guys." Dan passed him a plate, and Nate spent the next few minutes concentrating on loading it with two hamburgers, Violet's pasta salad, homemade fries, and a pile of fruits and veggies.

Violet surveyed his heaping plate. "I guess it *has* been a while since you've had a decent meal." Her laugh sparkled across the backyard.

Nate grinned back. It didn't matter how awkward this night got. It had been worth coming just for the food. "I'd take more if my plate weren't already overflowing."

He followed Violet to two empty chairs right in the middle of the others. As soon as they were seated, Violet set her plate down and folded her hands in her lap, eyes closed. Nate watched her for a second, then pretended not to notice what she was doing. If she wanted to thank a God who didn't listen, that was her business.

He took a giant bite of hamburger. The flavor popped on his tongue, and he couldn't help the "Mmm" that came out.

Next to him, Violet opened her eyes and laughed, then took her own giant bite. "Thank goodness. I was bragging up your burgers, Dan, and you lived up to the hype. Didn't he?" Her elbow bumped at Nate's side. He just nodded. His mouth was too full of his next bite. He couldn't remember the last time he'd had an actual meal like this.

Nate listened to the conversation jumping around him, simply enjoying the sounds of their interaction. He appreciated that no one was giving him the third degree. They simply let him eat, occasionally including him in their conversation as they told stories about their week but not demanding anything from him.

When his plate was finally empty, Peyton passed him a cookie and offered to take his plate. As she reached for it, she whispered to Violet, "You were right," and winked.

Violet swatted at her, but a light blush crept up her neck to her cheeks, and Nate got the impression that whatever she had been right about had to do with him. It warmed him in a way he hadn't expected.

"So, Nate." Dan settled onto a chair across from him. "You're from Sibley?"

The food in his stomach congealed at the question. He was going to have to step carefully here. "Not originally. I grew up in Wescott, which is about an hour west of Sibley."

"I love the western part of the state. All those bluffs and valleys along the river."

"Yeah." Nate didn't know what else to say. He longed to go home to see his mom and sister, but other than that, the area had no appeal for him anymore. He shoved the last of his cookie into his mouth, hoping Dan didn't have any more questions for him.

"So what brought you to Hope Springs?" Dan's voice was entirely friendly, without a hit of suspicion.

"My father owns a large investment firm. They bought out a property management place here, and he wanted me to get things up and running."

"I work with my dad, too. Just started recently. It's nice, isn't it?" Dan looked thoughtful. "Though it is a bit of an adjustment."

Nate almost snorted, but he managed to force a short nod instead. Adjustment was an understatement.

"How long have you worked with your dad? Got any advice on how to make it easier?"

This time he did snort. "I'm the last person who could give you advice. I've only been working for my dad a couple weeks, and I'm not sure how I'll survive much longer."

Dan nodded, his expression thoughtful. "Well, I'll let you know if I figure anything out."

Nate thought Dan would get up then, but he settled farther into his chair. "So what'd you do before you worked for your dad?"

Nate grabbed his water bottle and took a long swig to buy time. He scrambled to come up with a lie. Any lie. This was why he didn't go out, didn't talk to people. Eventually, people weren't content to let you be a stranger without a history anymore. They wanted to know about your past—and they didn't care if you didn't want to tell about it.

When he couldn't come up with a convincing lie, he settled on a half-truth. "A little bit of everything." He'd taken his rotation in the laundry room, kitchen, and other duties. Not that he'd had a choice.

"Okay, everyone." Sophie stood, and everyone's attention swung to her. "I have honeymoon pictures. Let's go inside, and I'll show them on Dan's TV."

Nate let out a relieved breath. He may not have any desire to see honeymoon pictures from two people he'd just met, but if it got him out of talking about his own past, he was all for it.

They all stood and grabbed platters and dishes off the table. Nate shooed Violet away from the table, taking the bowl of pasta salad out of her hands. Didn't the woman know how to take a break?

The smile she gave him was almost enough to make him wish she'd pick up something else, so he could take that for her, too.

He followed the others inside and set the food on the counter.

Then they all moved into the living room. Nate took a place next to Violet on the worn plaid sofa, careful not to look at her. He couldn't allow himself the luxury of basking in her smiles.

A few seconds later, images of Rome and Venice and Florence were flashing across the TV screen. Sophie and Spencer took turns telling them about the sights and the food and the gondola captain who had misunderstood Sophie's name and called her Soapy the whole ride.

Nate joined the others' laughter. They seemed like a fun group. A kind and welcoming group, when he deserved anything but.

Next to him, Violet shifted. Her face, which had been carefree and animated outside, was now strained and pale. Her cheeks were drawn in, as if she was biting them, and she stared at her hands in her lap as she rubbed at her bare ring finger. Nate wanted to reach over and squeeze her arm, ask her what was wrong. He sat on his hands instead.

"Excuse me." Violet stood and rushed past him, raising a hand to her eyes as she bolted for the hallway.

Chapter 13

Water blasted from the bathroom sink, and Violet cupped her shaking hands under the flow, splashing the water onto her face. The cold felt like a million scalpels slicing at her, but she didn't care.

She splashed herself with another handful.

What was wrong with her? She should be happy for her friends. She *was* happy for them.

They'd had a lovely wedding and a lovely honeymoon, and now they were starting on their lovely life together.

A life that Violet would never know.

She forced herself to take a few deep breaths, to get herself under control.

She repeated the verse that had sustained her through the past three years: "The Lord is my rock, my fortress and my deliverer; my God is my rock, in whom I take refuge." God was her refuge. Her strength was in him, no matter what she lost in this life. She let the reminder wash over her, willed it to seep into her heart.

After a few minutes, she examined the damage she had done to her makeup. Most of it was gone, though she had to wipe away a small smudge of mascara. Then, steeling her shoulders and painting a smile on her lips, she strode to the living room.

Nate half stood as she reappeared, remaining like that until she had taken her place next to him on the couch again. He slid closer to her as he sat, so that his arm brushed against hers. His nearness was nice. She felt like he was offering her some of his strength.

"You okay?" He said it so close to her ear that she could feel the whisper of his breath on her hair. At her nod, the tension in his shoulders eased.

When Spencer and Sophie had reached the end of their photos, Dan stood. "Okay, well, guys' turn to do dishes tonight." The other guys groaned.

Spencer threw a pillow at Dan. "You know they wouldn't have remembered if you didn't say anything."

"You wanted me to lie?" Dan blinked innocently at Spencer.

"Not lie. Conceal the truth." But Spencer was already heading for the kitchen.

"That's the same thing, just for future reference," Sophie called after him.

Oh, that banter. How she missed that with Cade.

Nate pushed to his feet as the other men stood.

Violet grabbed his arm. "You don't have to help them."

Nate smiled down at her. "Well, technically, I'm a guy, so I think I do." He winked and was gone, leaving her suddenly breathless.

Sophie leaned toward her the moment Nate was in the kitchen. "So, he's cute."

"Shh." Violet smacked her friend's arm.

"You should ask him out." Sophie had never been one to mince words.

"What?" Violet waved a hand as if the thought had never occurred to her. "I'm not interested in him like that. He's just my neighbor."

"Okay. Then you ask him out, Leah." She kept her eyes on Violet as she said it.

Violet's chest tightened, but she knew what Sophie was doing. She turned to Leah. "You should." Actually, now that she thought about it, she realized how stupid she'd been not to realize it earlier. Of course her beautiful friend would be a perfect fit for Nate.

Leah shook her head. "Not interested."

The tightness in Violet's chest eased, which made no sense. She didn't want to go out with Nate. So why did the thought of Leah going out with him bother her?

She glanced over her shoulder to see how he was doing with the other guys in the kitchen. Jared was regaling Nate with a story of some crazy incident or another, and Nate looked more relaxed than she had seen him since they'd met. As she stared, he looked up and caught her eye. Before she could think how to respond, she realized her face had been overtaken by a goofy grin. She raised a hand to wave at him, ignoring the way her friends nudged each other.

"So anyway—" It was long past time for a subject change. She turned to Peyton. "Are you and Jared getting excited for your big day?" Next Valentine's Day, she'd watch two more of her friends move on with their lives while hers stayed still.

They talked wedding plans for the next twenty minutes, until a resounding "Done!" echoed from the kitchen. The men stood in a circle, their arms above their heads as if they'd just had a team huddle.

"If dish washing were a sport," Sophie called, "you guys would get the medal for world's slowest washers."

Spencer plopped onto the couch next to his wife. "And here I was going to offer to do the dishes at home for the rest of our life. But if you think I'm too slow . . ." He rubbed a hand absently up and down her back.

Sophie leaned into him. "I don't care how long it takes you. If you actually do that, you will be the best husband the world has ever known."

Spencer raised an eyebrow. "*If* I do it? You know I'd do anything for you."

Violet looked away as he leaned over to drop a kiss on the top of his wife's head. The ache to have that again was growing in monstrous proportions right now.

Dan looked around at the group, then clapped his hands once. "You a Star Wars fan, Nate?"

Everyone else groaned.

Violet better warn Nate before it was too late. "Don't say yes—"

"Of course." Nate shot her a questioning look.

"Oh no, now you're doomed," Leah called from across the room. They'd all been obliged to listen to the minute details of every piece of Dan's Star Wars memorabilia more than once.

"Trust me, man, you don't want to get sucked into that," Spencer called to Nate. "Dan is the epitome of a Star Wars geek."

Nate laughed. "That's okay. I'm a closet Star Wars geek, too." He smiled at Violet. "Unless you wanted to get going?"

Violet shook her head. "Take your time. I'm exactly where I want to be." She settled back on the couch and raised her feet to rest them on the coffee table, watching out of the corner of her eye as Nate disappeared up the stairs behind Dan.

"I like him." Like his wife, Spencer was nothing if not straightforward.

Violet refused to look at either of them. She knew they were both staring at her, waiting for her to say that this was the guy she'd been waiting for and now her heart was healed, and she'd live happily ever after. But that wasn't how it worked.

Nate passed the scale model of the Star Destroyer back to Dan. He had to hand it to the guy, he sure had an extensive collection of Star Wars memorabilia. He was like a walking encyclopedia of the entire Star Wars empire. Not that Nate minded. Dan had a laid-back manner that made him easy to listen to. And he didn't demand that Nate reveal anything about himself.

It wasn't until Dan yawned that Nate realized it must be getting late. The Death Star clock over the door confirmed it was already midnight.

"Oh man, I'm sorry. I've way overstayed my welcome."

Dan gave him an easy smile. "Not at all. Just got up early today for a meeting." He set the TIE Fighter on his shelf, next to a bobble head of Boba Fett. "Violet is probably worried that I've bored you to death by now, though."

Nate followed Dan toward the door of the extra bedroom that served as his Star Wars room.

At the door, Dan stopped, looking thoughtful. "It's probably not my place to say, but Violet's been through a lot the last couple years."

"Yeah, I've gathered that." Nate waited for Dan to step through the doorway, but Dan remained planted, as if he had more to say.

"It's just— She's still fragile." Dan rubbed a hand down his face. "Just be careful with her."

Nate stared at him. Be careful with her? What did Dan think he was going to do, throw her off a roof?

And then he realized.

"Oh—um—no." Heat rose to his cheeks. "It's not like that. We're just neighbors. I think she invited me tonight because she felt sorry for me, to be honest."

Dan bobbed his head up and down slowly and gave him a searching look.

Nate adjusted his stance, trying to find somewhere else to direct his eyes. "Anyway, thanks for dinner and for showing me your collection." He sounded oddly formal, but he had no idea how else to react.

"Yeah, of course. I hope you'll join us again in the future."

Nate followed Dan down the hallway. He'd have to be careful if he'd given Violet's friends the impression he saw her as anything more than a neighbor. He didn't want to give her the idea that he wanted more.

The only problem was, he wasn't sure how to keep from giving himself that impression. Especially when his heart lightened three pounds when he walked into the living room and his eyes fell on her. She was leaning her head back on the couch, eyes closed.

Spencer and Sophie were the only others still there.

Sophie waved at him.

"Is she asleep?" he whispered.

"No, she's not," Violet fake whispered from the couch, a smile tickling her lips.

Nate felt the smile lift his own lips. "Sorry it's so late. Dan's collection is pretty—"

"Extensive?"

"Boring?"

"Lame?"

The other three all chimed in at once.

Dan stuck his tongue out at them.

"I was going to say impressive," Nate said.

"Oh, don't encourage him." Violet groaned and stretched. "Ready to go?"

He held out a hand to help her up, telling himself it was only the neighborly thing to do. Judging by the look on Sophie's face, she wouldn't have bought his excuse.

But, then, neither did he.

He pulled his hand back and shoved it in his pocket before Violet could reach for it.

Dan was right. He had to be careful. Violet was fragile, and he was the last person who deserved a woman like her.

Dan and Spencer held out their hands, and Nate shook them. He was about to move toward the door when Sophie reached out with open arms. Nate hesitated, then leaned in for her hug. He couldn't remember the last time anyone had hugged him, and he blinked away sudden moisture.

Even without really knowing him, these people were offering him their food, their conversation, their friendship.

If they did know him—if they knew what he'd done—would they take it all back? Would they abandon him just like everyone else in his life had?

Nate wasn't sure. He sensed something different about these people and the friendship they offered. But he wasn't about to take any chances by letting himself get close to them.

Violet's eyes slid to Nate for the umpteenth time. They were only a few blocks from home, and he'd barely said three words since they'd gotten in the car, except to say that her friends were nice and she'd been right about Dan's burgers.

He'd seemed so open and relaxed at Dan's, but now his shoulders were stiff, his jaw set. Had she done something to upset him?

But that was ridiculous. They were just neighbors. He didn't know her well enough to be upset with her.

He was probably tired. Goodness knew he wasn't the only one.

She let out an involuntary sigh. She had enjoyed the night with her friends, even if seeing pictures of Sophie and Spencer's honeymoon had dragged her back to memories of her own honeymoon. A honeymoon she had to remember alone.

She felt Nate's gaze slip to her. She swallowed but kept her eyes forward. If he was ready to talk, she didn't want to scare him off.

After a second, he looked away again.

Violet's shoulders sagged. He wasn't going to talk after all.

But his voice reached for her, quiet. "Everything okay?"

Violet turned her head toward him in surprise. His eyes were right on her. She turned back to the road, but not before a surge of something unidentifiable swept through her.

"Of course. Why wouldn't it be?"

"I don't know." Nate drummed his fingers on the car door. "You seem sort of . . ."

"Sort of?" Violet prodded. "Are you going to call me stubborn again?"

Nate laughed—a gentle laugh his heart wasn't really in. "No. I was thinking you seemed wistful, I guess."

"Huh." Now that he put a label to it, Violet realized that wistful was exactly how she felt. But she wasn't sure what she was wistful for. Cade, of course, but she thought it was more than that this time. The life they had—the life she had lost. She hadn't only lost a husband when Cade died; she'd lost their life together. She'd lost a piece of herself.

But a familiar stirring deep in her soul told her it was still there, buried.

Even if she wasn't sure how to get to it.

"Sorry. It's none of my business." Nate clasped his hands in his lap and resumed staring out his window.

"No. It's not that." Violet lifted a hand toward him but pulled it back before making contact. In the confines of the car she was suddenly aware of how close they were to each other. "It's just, I couldn't really put a word to it, and I think you nailed it."

Nate gave her a slow smile. But there was a layer of sadness behind it, too. Violet wanted to know what had caused it, but she was afraid to ask.

He turned away as she pulled into the driveway. They walked up the stairs in silence, then stood on the landing, an unspoken energy pulsing between them.

"You were a hit tonight." She set a hand lightly on his arm. "You're welcome to join us again anytime."

"Thanks."

Violet couldn't take her focus off the way his lip quirked up on one side when he spoke.

She resisted the urge to step closer to him.

Wild barking broke out from behind Nate's door, and that weird energy dissipated. They both laughed.

"I guess Tony knows you're home."

NOT UNTIL YOU

"I guess so." Nate took a step backward. "I had a nice time tonight."

He turned and disappeared into his apartment.

"Me, too," she whispered.

Chapter 14

Violet hummed along to the radio, her window open to soak up the warm breeze on her way home from church. The humidity had finally broken, and the day was actually comfortable. It'd be the perfect day to spend outdoors.

On days like this, she and Cade used to explore the various tourist attractions on the peninsula that locals so often took for granted. Her favorite was always the Old Lighthouse. The combination of the aged logbook, the smell of weathered wood, and the view across the lake to the spot where it disappeared into nothingness had always stirred her soul.

An odd restlessness wrapped around her. She wanted to go to the lighthouse. She wanted to break out of this odd half existence she'd been living in for the past three years.

But she wasn't sure she was completely ready to do that. At least not on her own.

Her mouth pulled into a frown.

Maybe she'd stay home and curl up with a book.

As she turned onto Hope Street, she slowed, trying to figure out what she was seeing.

A man was walking down the sidewalk, holding what appeared to be a large sink.

An incredulous laugh escaped as she realized who it was and what he was doing.

She was still chuckling as she pulled up alongside him and rolled down the passenger side window. "Nate!"

He looked over in surprise, but his face broke into a smile the moment he saw her.

Her heart jumped, and she told herself it was only because he'd surprised her. So what if she'd begun to suspect there was more to it than that? She wasn't brave enough to examine what it might be.

"Why are you carrying that sink down the street?" She tried to stop the laughter, but she couldn't get it under control. He made the most ridiculous sight she had seen in she didn't know how long.

"Well, I tried to get it to walk itself, but it's not quite as obedient as Tony. Which is saying something." His laugh made her heart do another flip.

"Where did you get it?"

He gave her an odd look. "There's more than one place to get a utility sink in Hope Springs?"

He had a point. But the hardware store was almost a mile away. Had he really carried the huge sink that far just for her?

"Get in. I'll give you a ride the rest of the way."

"Oh, sure. The last three blocks are the hardest."

"Have it your way." She eased down on the gas pedal, watching with satisfaction as he jogged to keep up.

"I'm kidding. I'd love a ride the rest of the way."

She pulled over and waited for him to stash the sink in the trunk and jump into the car.

A slight sheen of sweat shone on his arm as it came to rest on the console between them.

He glanced over at her. "You look nice."

She focused on the road, telling herself it was the warm day that made her suddenly hot. "Thanks. I'm just on my way home from church." She bit her lip. She'd only said it to explain why she was more dressed up than usual, but he'd made it perfectly clear how he felt about church.

He brushed over the comment. "I can install this right away. Unless you have other plans?"

"No, that's fine. I was thinking about going to the Old Lighthouse today, but . . ." The thought of going alone still hung heavy on her heart. "Anyway, I'll just stay home."

"I don't want to change your plans. You go. I can do this while you're gone. You won't be much help with a broken arm, anyway."

She faked a huff at that. "That settles it, I'm staying to prove you're wrong."

But he wasn't wrong, she quickly discovered. There wasn't much she could do with one hand, aside from pass him tools every once in a while. And even then, he only asked her to pass them to give her something to do.

Eventually, she wandered into the living room, where Cade's stuff was still scattered. For some reason, the thought of re-boxing it didn't hurt as much this time. She ran downstairs to grab some new boxes, then started repacking everything.

She'd take it all to the thrift store tomorrow, when her store was closed. She wasn't sure she was completely ready yet. But ready or not, it was time.

After she'd finished packing the boxes, she pulled out her phone. She might as well get her weekly call to her sister out of the way. With a sigh, she tapped Jade's number.

She counted the rings. After eight, Jade's voice mail kicked in, just as Violet had known it would. Just as it had every week for the past six years. Ever since Mom had died and Jade had taken off for L.A.

A beep sounded from the other end of the line, and Violet began to leave the same message as always. "Hey, Jade, it's your sister." But then, instead of the usual "give me a call sometime," she let out what she really wanted to tell Jade. "I just called to say that I miss you, and you're the last family I have, and I really don't think it's fair the way you've pushed me out of your life. I know we both said some things after Mom died, but it's been six years. I think it might be time to talk again."

She yanked the phone away from her ear and dropped it on the coffee table. Her hands were shaking, and she sank to the couch. Had she really done that?

What if something happened and those were the last words she ever said to her sister? Angry words. Just like the last words she'd said to Cade.

Violet reached for her phone. She had to call Jade back and apologize.

"I think that should do it." Nate was drying his hands on his shorts as he stepped into the living room, but the moment he saw her, he stopped. "You okay?"

"Yeah. No." She set the phone down. "I don't know."

He moved closer and perched on the arm of the couch. Only a few inches separated the top of his leg and her shoulder. She stared at the scar on his knee. How had she never noticed that before? It was white and cut a jagged line from the outside to the inside of his leg.

"Want to talk about it?"

She shook her head. "It's just my sister. She's been ignoring my phone calls for six years. I'm not sure why I thought today would be any different."

His hand squeezed her shoulder, and she lifted her head. His eyes, normally so guarded, reflected an understanding that shook her. She looked away.

"Anyway, I didn't mean to get angry and leave a message like that."

Nate snorted, and she glared at him. He thought it was funny?

"Sorry. It's just—" He gestured to the phone. "You call that angry? That was about the sweetest message I've ever heard."

Violet chewed her cheek, considering. It's not like she'd yelled at her sister. But still— "I told her I didn't think she was being fair."

"Well, *do* you think she's being unfair?"

Violet nodded. So unfair. She could admit she should have been more supportive when Jade had said she wanted to pursue a career in acting. But they had literally just buried their mother, and Jade's desire to act had come out of nowhere. Violet had wanted her to slow down and deal with what had happened before she made any major life decisions. And, fine, maybe she had been a little selfish, too. She hadn't wanted Jade to leave her.

But Jade hadn't cared about any of that. She'd packed a suitcase, taken her share of Mom's inheritance, and skipped town on the first flight out.

And she hadn't looked back once.

Nate stood, and she tried not to regret the separation. "Telling people the truth isn't the same as lashing out in anger. Your sister will recognize that. Maybe it's what she needed to hear. You never know, she might be getting ready to call you right this second."

Yeah, Violet wouldn't hold her breath.

But she set the phone down. She could always leave another message later.

She blew a stray piece of hair off her face. "Anyway, how's the sink coming?"

"Come see."

But her eyes were locked on the hand he held out to her. Did he really want her to take it? Did she want to?

As if he'd just realized what he was doing, he jerked it back and shoved it into his pocket.

She followed him down the hallway, leaving plenty of space between them. But she couldn't shake the question: what would it have felt like to hold his hand? Was his rough and calloused like Cade's or smooth and unblemished? Would her hand disappear into his, or would it be just the right size?

There was no way to keep her distance in the cramped laundry room, and she caught a whiff of that mint and lemon scent she was beginning to recognize him by.

"Voilà. Good as new." Nate held out his hands to the sink as if he'd performed a magic trick.

Which he may have. You would never know that just yesterday this place was a disaster. And the new sink was nicer than the crusty old one that had been in here before.

"It looks great. Just let me know how much I owe you."

Nate blinked at her. "Owe me?"

She gestured at his handiwork. "You know, for the sink. And for your time."

"You don't owe me anything. I'm the landlord. This is my job."

"Oh." Violet didn't know why that should disappoint her. She should have realized that he would have done the same thing for any of his tenants. It's not like he'd singled her out for special treatment.

"I also noticed a crack in the wall over here, so I patched it up with some joint compound." He slipped past her to move to the spot where a crack used to run from the top corner of the hallway almost to the floor. It had been there when they moved in, and Violet had long since stopped noticing it.

She stepped closer to examine the spot. The wall was smooth now, although slightly discolored from the wet compound.

Violet squinted at it, trying to detect any hint of the crack that had marred it only this morning. Surely no wound could be covered up so completely. But the wall was totally smooth.

If only it were that easy to patch the cracks in her heart. There wasn't enough joint compound in the world. And yet, she had to admit that since Nate had moved in next door, the cracks were getting a little duller around the edges.

"Thank you. That was very kind of you."

He held up a hand. "Oh, I didn't do it for free."

She raised an eyebrow. "I thought you were my landlord and that was your job."

"Well, this was extra."

"And how much will it cost me?" She couldn't fight down the smile that kept creeping to her lips. The glint in his eyes was too inviting.

"It will cost you one trip to the Old Lighthouse."

"Oh." Violet let out a long breath. She hadn't wanted to go to the lighthouse alone. But did she want to go with Nate?

Something in her gut jumped, and she realized—she did.

"It's a deal." She held out her hand and shook his, trying not to notice that hers fit perfectly into it after all.

Chapter 15

The narrow spiraling stairway creaked under his weight, and Nate winced. Violet had told him the lighthouse was more than one hundred and fifty years old, and if he had to guess, the stairs were original to the place.

"You're sure people are supposed to go up here?" Seemed like a lawsuit waiting to happen to him.

But Violet grinned down at him from four steps above. "You're not afraid of heights, are you?"

"No, but—" He kept climbing, until he was on the step below her. They were eye to eye now, and the openness in her dark eyes made him completely forget what he was going to say.

"Come on." She turned to keep climbing. "We're almost to the top."

He made himself keep moving. He had to snap out of it. Obviously she didn't feel whatever it was that jolted him every time he looked at her. He shouldn't have invited himself along in the first place. He'd sensed her hesitation when she'd agreed to bring him. She'd only gone along with it because she thought she owed it to him after he'd worked on her apartment.

NOT UNTIL YOU

"This is it," Violet called over her shoulder as she disappeared on a platform at the top of the steep stairway. A couple seconds later, Nate emerged onto a wide landing. The floor was bare wood, and the walls were aged-looking concrete.

Violet stood in the middle of the space, looking straight up. Nate had to stop a moment to take in the expression of sheer awe on her face.

"Come here." She kept her head tilted back, the gentle curve of her neck bobbing with her words. "Check out this light."

Nate sidled closer, forcing his eyes off her and onto the light fixture. He had to admit it was impressive. Especially when he considered how long it had stood the test of time.

After a few seconds, Violet grabbed his arm and tugged him toward a narrow open door. "You have to see the best part yet."

She let go of him as she stepped through the doorway and moved immediately to the edge of the observation platform, letting her good hand rest lightly on the railing there.

Nate gave the platform a hard stare. If you asked him, it looked ready to collapse any second.

Violet turned toward him. It was windier up here than it had been on the ground, and her hair blew in wild tendrils around her face. But it was her smile that caught him off guard. It was warm and open but also sort of private, as if it were just for him.

"Come on." She held a hand out toward him. "It's beautiful out here."

Yes, it is.

Nate shook himself. He had to stop thinking like that. So what if Violet was beautiful? So what if his heart felt a strange contentment every time he was near her? That didn't mean he had a right to act on his feelings.

He would have to close off his heart. He'd gotten good at doing that over the past seven years anyway. It had been the only way he could survive.

Ignoring her hand, he stepped onto the observation deck. He followed it all the way around the circumference of the lighthouse, as much to get his heart under control as to take in the view.

And the view was spectacular.

The lighthouse was perched on a bluff above the lake, amplifying the building's height. On the inland side, the view stretched out across the surrounding countryside, over the tops of acres and acres of trees.

But it was the lake side that drew his attention. Half a dozen sailboats bobbed on the waves at varying distances from the shore. Farther out, larger ships stacked with cargo containers worked their way toward the port to the south.

Nate squinted toward the horizon, trying to make out the far shore. But the water disappeared into the sky.

Something about the lake pulled at Nate, and he moved closer to the railing, until he was standing next to Violet.

"Pretty amazing, isn't it?" She was staring straight down to the spot where the surf crashed against the rocks that jutted into the water. The boulders had been worn smooth over time. She had that wistful expression again.

"Do you come here often?"

She gripped the railing, lifting her head to peer toward the horizon. "I used to. With Cade. I actually haven't been here since he died."

"Oh, I'm sorry, I shouldn't have presumed . . . If I had known—" What an idiot. He'd invited himself along on a trip to a place that was sacred to her and her husband. No wonder she'd hesitated. "I didn't mean to—"

But she laid a hand on his arm. "I'm glad you did. I don't think I would have had the strength to come alone. And I've missed this place."

She swiveled toward the lake again but kept her hand on his arm. He should move, but he couldn't make himself do it. If being here with him was any comfort to her, then he wasn't going to take that away.

She probably wouldn't be as comforted if she knew the monster you really are.

Nate shoved the thought deep under everything else. Now was not the time to tell her.

"So what's that island?" He pointed to the north, where he could faintly make out an island about a mile off shore.

"That's Strawberry Island. It has a great beach and some shops and stuff. It's a sweet little place. We should go sometime."

Nate froze. Had she said *we*?

But he knew she had. It was why his heart rate had tripled and his mouth had gone dry.

He allowed himself a glance at her out of the corner of his eye. Her head was turned toward him, as if she were studying him. He wondered what she saw when she looked at him.

Whatever it was, it wasn't the real him. Or at least not all of him.

He should put this to a stop before it started.

It's already started.

Well, then, before it went any further.

Getting into a relationship with her would mean having to let her see the real him eventually. And he couldn't handle that.

Neither could she.

He turned toward her. "Violet, I—"

But the look in her eyes stopped him. For the first time since he'd met her, he didn't see that hint of sadness that always lingered there. Instead, her eyes were filled with a new brightness that he couldn't bear to destroy. Not today.

"Yes?"

He swallowed. "I just wanted to say—" His eyes darted to the water and back to hers. "Thanks for bringing me here."

"You're welcome." Her words were a whisper, barely louder than the wind, and she took half a step closer.

Nate couldn't take his eyes off hers.

A bang from behind made them both jump. A young boy emerged onto the lighthouse deck, followed by an even younger boy, an older girl, and two harried looking adults.

"Talon, do not climb the railing," the woman yelled, darting across the deck to pluck the smallest boy off the bottom rung of the railing.

NOT UNTIL YOU

Violet laughed lightly. "I think that might be our cue to leave."

Nate nodded, swallowing his disappointment, and followed her to the door.

Chapter 16

Nate laughed at himself. Was he really whistling on the way to work?

His heart was lighter than it had been in years. And it was all thanks to a certain dark-haired neighbor. In the nearly two weeks since he'd gone with her to the lighthouse, they'd talked almost every day. Sometimes just a word or two on the landing, but more and more often, he stopped by her store after work or they walked Tony together.

Instead of dreading the days now, he woke up looking forward to them because they meant he might get at least a few moments with her.

Nate hated to admit how much he had come to cherish those moments. He wasn't supposed to be allowing himself that pleasure. But he couldn't seem to resist. Every time he told himself it would be the last time, he found himself craving her company again. It wasn't only that she was attractive—though she certainly was.

But it was the way she listened to him, like what he said really mattered, even when they were only talking about the weather.

The way she always took the time to pet Tony.

The way she asked him to help her with things around the store.

For the first time in a long time, his life didn't feel meaningless. Talking to her, helping her, even in these small ways, had given him something he'd been missing for a long time—purpose.

"What's up with you?" Brandon was unlocking the door to the office building when Nate walked up.

"What do you mean what's up with me?"

"I mean you have the most bizarre look on your face."

Nate frowned. He and Brandon had talked a few times, and he liked the guy well enough. But that didn't mean he was about to spill his feelings to him. "Bizarre how?"

Brandon fell into step next to Nate as they climbed the staircase. "I don't know. You actually look . . . happy, I guess. For a change." He led the way up the stairs. "I mean, don't get me wrong. It's good to see. Just different."

"Of course I'm happy. It's Friday." Nate opened the door to his small office.

But Brandon didn't retreat to his own office. "No, it's not that." He slugged Nate's shoulder. "It's a girl, isn't it?"

"It's not—"

"Has to be." Brandon pointed both index fingers at Nate. "It's that blond who's stopped by a couple times, isn't it?"

Nate's mouth opened and then closed. He'd thought having Officer Jensen meet him here instead of at the apartment would lead to fewer awkward questions. Apparently he'd been wrong.

"She's a business associate." Nate stepped through his office door and closed it firmly.

"Ah, a business associate." Brandon's chuckle carried through the closed door.

Nate sighed. It wouldn't hurt anything to let Brandon think Officer Jensen was his girlfriend. It was better than him knowing who she really was.

Nate took a seat at the desk he'd moved in front of the office's small window. He'd just turned his computer on when his phone rang. He groaned. So much for his good mood.

"Benson Properties."

"My investor wants to take a look at one of our properties." Dad didn't bother with saying hello anymore. Apparently, Nate wasn't worth the effort.

"Which one?" Nate had learned that it was best to be just as abrupt as Dad. It hurt less that way.

"Six twelve Hope Street. Which I'm not seeing on this report you sent me. But he assures me it's one of ours."

Nate could have sworn he heard his heart hit the floor. Of course it wasn't on the list. He'd left it off on purpose. His throat went dry. "I'll have to look into that and get back to you. When does he want to see it?"

"Today." Dad's voice was flat, unapologetic about the last-minute assignment.

"Oh, I don't know if I'll be able—"

"This is your job, Nathan. When I tell you to make something happen, you make it happen."

"Well, I don't know if that property is available or—" The small lie would be worth it if it helped Violet.

"For the right price, any property is available. Look it up right now. What's its status?"

Nate turned to the computer, scrambling for a way to buy more time. He needed to talk to Violet. Give her a chance to catch up on her payments and renew her lease before Dad could pull it out from under her.

He pecked in the address, even though he already knew the status.

"I don't have all day, Nathan."

"Yeah. It's here. The lease expires in two months."

"Excellent. And they didn't exercise their option to renew?"

"No, but—"

"What about payments?"

Nate closed his eyes and pinched the top of his nose. "They're a little behind, but I think there might be extenuating circumstances—"

"Does the lease agreement make any allowance for extenuating circumstances?"

Nate wanted to punch the wall. Dad knew it didn't. "No."

"Good. Then we have no problems. My guy will meet you there in an hour. Don't drop the ball on this."

"I really think—"

"Look, Nate—" Dad's voice softened the slightest bit. "I've been happy with the work you've done so far. If you can make this investor happy, I'll think about arranging a time for you to see Mom and Kayla."

Nate opened his mouth. He should respond. But before he could, Dad hung up.

Nate stared at the phone a second, then slammed it down. Dad had no idea what he was asking Nate to do. Didn't Dad know it wasn't just buildings they were dealing with—it was people's lives? And this particular building involved the life of someone very special.

Nate shoved his chair back.

He'd already ruined the life of one person he loved. Why not another?

Not that he loved Violet. At least, he didn't think he did. But he did care about her, much as he'd tried not to. And if he wasn't mistaken, she'd started to care about him, too.

But that would come to an end the moment he told her what he had to do.

But he had to do it. There was no question about that.

He owed his first loyalty to Mom and Kayla.

And if that meant cutting off any future chance of happiness for himself, then he'd have to accept that.

He only wished Violet didn't have to get hurt in the process.

Violet jumped as the chime on the store's front door gave a violent jangle. What on earth? Customers didn't usually barrel into an antique shop so much as mosey in, sometimes lowering their voices as if they were in a library.

She set down the paint brush she'd been using to apply a new coat of varnish to a bookshelf and hurried to the sales floor.

A spontaneous smile lifted her lips the moment her eyes fell on Nate. She couldn't deny that the moments she'd spent with him lately had been some of the best she'd had in the past few weeks—the past few years, if she was being honest.

Violet moved toward him. "Hey, I was just thinking of you." Her face warmed. She shouldn't have said that. Even if it was true.

But at the look on his face, her smile wilted. "Nate? What is it? What's wrong?"

She wove through the Victorian living room setting she'd rearranged yesterday. He looked agitated and angry. She reached for his hand, but he pulled away.

She swallowed, trying not to take the movement personally.

"Do you have a minute?" The question was brusque and businesslike. Somehow between yesterday and today they'd gone from being friends to being just neighbors again.

She nodded stiffly and gestured to the curved-back Victorian loveseat. But Nate shook his head and took a seat on the stiff chair across from it. Violet lowered herself to the loveseat alone.

"My dad just called to tell me he has an investor interested in renting this property." He stared at the coffee table between them as he talked.

"But I'm renting this property." Obviously, he knew that, so why hadn't he just told that to his dad?

"I know. But your lease expires in two months."

Violet rubbed at her forehead. Was that right? Had five years really gone by since she and Cade had signed the lease on this place? "Okay, then I'll renew it."

Nate shook his head. "The guaranteed renewal option is expired. You would have had to sign that four months ago."

"What?" Violet jumped to her feet. What was he telling her? That he was going to kick her out of her own store? "I didn't know that. Isn't there something you can do?"

Nate raised his hands as if he were completely helpless. "I'm sorry. Maybe if you were current on your rent, I could make a case, but . . ."

A wave of shame swept over Violet. She'd never meant to let things get so far behind. But it had been so hard to keep things going these last few months. And her broken arm wasn't helping any.

The betrayal that rolled through her made her shudder. How could Nate have pretended to befriend her, to care about her, and then turn on her like this? Had that been his plan all along?

Tears built behind her eyes, and she turned away so Nate wouldn't see how he'd affected her.

"Hey." His voice was too close, and she took a step away, but his hands landed softly on her shoulders. Gently, he spun her toward him.

She blinked hard, but a traitor of a tear crept out and slipped down her cheek.

"This isn't what I want. You have to understand that." He bent his knees until his face was in her line of sight. She wanted to look away, but she couldn't make her head turn. He looked sincere.

She nodded once and pressed her lips together. It may not be what he wanted, but that didn't change anything.

"I'm going to do what I can to help, okay? But I can't make any promises."

She sniffed and nodded again. He watched her for a second, then took a step closer, sliding his arms around her. She stiffened as he pulled her in to him. But then her good arm lifted to wrap around him. She let herself lean into him, resting her head on his chest.

She'd almost forgotten what it felt like to be held like this.

His arms didn't feel the same as Cade's. They were slightly shorter. Slightly broader.

It should feel wrong to stand here in his embrace. But to her surprise, she didn't want him to let go.

"There's one more thing—" His voice was muffled as he spoke into her hair.

"What's that?" She was afraid to ask, and yet, with his arms around her, she was pretty sure she could handle anything.

"Apparently, the investor—"

But he broke off as the chime above the door clanged.

"Is here," he muttered as he let her go.

Chapter 17

This was the investor Dad had found? The guy was dressed like a used car salesman and wore a smarmy grin Nate wanted to punch off his face. But he put on a neutral expression and held out his hand. If he played this right, he might be able to convince the guy to open his new venture—whatever it was—in another location.

"John Talmadge." The guy's hand was moist as it landed in Nate's.

Nate resisted the urge to wipe his palm on his pants. "I understand you're looking to lease a property from us."

"Not a property." Talmadge's voice was well-oiled. "This property."

Behind him, Nate heard Violet's sniffle, followed by her retreating footsteps. He didn't allow himself to look at her. "With all due respect, I always advise clients to consider all possible properties before settling on one." Not that he'd ever advised any other clients, but Talmadge didn't need to know that. "If I may ask, what kind of business are you planning to open?"

"A bar."

Nate opened his mouth, then slammed it shut. Dad really wanted to support a bar after a bar had taken so much from them?

Then again, it wasn't the bar's fault Nate hadn't stopped that night.

That was on him and only him.

"So can you?" That Talmadge guy was talking, and Nate realized he must have asked him a question.

He had to stop thinking about what he'd done in the past. The mistakes he'd made.

He had to focus on what he could do now. Before he made another mistake. There must be a way he could steer the guy toward a different property. "I think we have a couple other properties that might be a better fit. Let me put some things together for you, and I'll take you to see them next week."

Talmadge's smile hardened into an expression that said he was used to getting what he wanted. "You can show me some other properties. But I'm telling you right here and now that this is the one I want. And your father told me you would get it for me. I understand you have a lot riding on this."

Nate was sure his smile was just as hard and unyielding as Talmadge's. "Just keep an open mind. I'll get you exactly what you need."

"You won't mind if I take a look around as long as I'm here? In the interest of keeping an open mind." Talmadge smirked at him and pushed his way through the shop, shoving an old tricycle to the side.

Nate snatched at the handlebars to stop the tricycle before it crashed into a table of figurines.

He followed Talmadge into the workshop, where Violet had retreated. She was at the far end of the room, facing the shelves, though Nate doubted she was actually looking for anything. She kept her back to them as Talmadge pulled out a tape measure and ordered Nate to hold the end against the wall.

Nate stared at it a second, then grabbed it. No sense antagonizing the man. He had to keep on his good side if he was going to convince him to choose another location.

Talmadge paced to the other side of the room and leered as he read the measurement. "Perfect size for a kitchen."

Nate's eyes darted to Violet. Her good hand gripped the shelf above her head, the knuckles white.

"Let's see the upstairs." Talmadge reeled in the tape measure and started for the door into the hallway.

Nate couldn't help the gasp that escaped, but he quickly covered it with a cough. Talmadge wanted to take over the upstairs as well? That would leave Violet homeless.

Violet's head dropped to her arm. Nate longed to go to her and promise to make all this right. To make this go away.

But he wasn't sure that was a promise he could keep.

Instead, he followed Talmadge out the door and up the steps.

Ten minutes later, he finally ushered Talmadge out of the shop, less sure than ever that he'd be able to convince the guy to consider another location.

As soon as Talmadge was gone, Nate peered warily into the workshop. He couldn't blame Violet if he was the last person she wanted to see right now.

She was sanding a coffee table, her movements jerky and sharp. Her hair fell over her face, but he caught a glimpse of the tight lines around her mouth. He let himself indulge in watching her a moment longer, then cleared his throat.

She looked up. But instead of her usual room-brightening smile or even the hardened anger he expected, her face was completely blank.

He moved cautiously toward her. "I'm sorry about all of this. I really am. I'm going to try to steer him to another property."

Violet set down her sandpaper and marched toward the sink, swerving to make a wide arc around him.

His stomach dropped, but he slid around an old sewing machine table to meet her at the sink.

He touched the top of her hand, but she yanked it back as if he'd shocked her.

"Just don't." Her voice was as carefully flat as her expression. "I heard what that man said. You have a lot riding on this deal. So just do it and get it over with."

"Violet, I'm not—"

"I have work to do. You should go." She watched the floor as she slid past him toward the front of the store.

Nate stood there, torn between following her and doing as she'd asked. The chime above the front door jingled, and a second later, he heard Violet greeting her new customers cheerfully, in the same voice she'd greeted him with when he'd come in.

Maybe he'd been wrong to imagine she'd been glad to see him when he got here, that they'd started to develop a connection over the past couple of weeks. Obviously she showed that same warmth to everyone.

A soft chorus of laughter carried to him.

Nate nodded to himself.

Then he ducked out the back door.

Chapter 18

Violet slammed her laptop screen shut.

What was the point anyway?

Nate was going to pull the store right out from under her, and there was nothing she could do about it.

The worst part was, she had let herself start to feel something for him, when she'd promised Cade that would never happen.

But it had been so nice not to be lonely for a change. She'd let herself get pulled in by Nate, with his brooding eyes and his smile that came easier and easier the more time they spent together.

But that had all been an act. She'd found out yesterday that the real Nate was a ruthless businessman who was willing to sell her out for whatever it was his dad was offering.

The door chimed, and she spun in her chair, pasting on a smile. Who knew when she might be helping the last person to ever walk through the doors of the store?

But her smile cracked the moment she saw him. "What do you want?" She congratulated herself on keeping her voice firm even as her heart pulsed against the restraints she'd put around it.

He crossed the store, not saying anything until he stood right in front of the counter. She kept her eyes on the wind chime that hung from the ceiling behind him.

"Look, I know you're upset—"

She clamped her mouth shut. Much as she wanted to yell and scream at him, ask him how he could betray her like this, she knew she never would.

"You have to believe me, Violet, I'm doing everything I can to make sure you can keep your store. But you're going to have to help me out."

She let her eyes skip to his for a second. The sincerity there shook her.

It was just an act, too. It had to be. So she wouldn't fight back.

Well, he needn't have worried. After three years of fighting to keep this store going, she didn't have much fight left. The weariness that had lightened over the last couple weeks had cloaked her soul again, darker than ever.

She stood. "Do what you have to do Nate. I'm done." She wasn't sure if she meant with the store or with him.

It would have to be both.

"You can't give up." He came around the counter, holding a hand out in front of him as if she were a wild animal and he was afraid he'd spook her.

He stopped a few feet in front of her. "I went through your lease with a lawyer buddy of mine. We both think that if you caught up on your back rent by the time your lease expires, you'd have a case for renewal."

"You said I would have had to renew four months ago." She crossed her arms in front of her.

"I know." He scrubbed his hands over the scruff on his cheeks. "But we spent all night going through the lease line by line, and he found some unclear wording in the guaranteed renewal clause that he thinks a judge would find in your favor."

"You want me to hang the future of my store on 'unclear wording'?" She couldn't keep the sneer out of her voice. That was thin at best. So what if he said he'd spent all night going over her lease? It was just another ruse.

"It's not much to go on, I know. And it's not the only angle I'm working on. But it's something at least."

"And you want me to take your dad to court over this or what?"

"It won't come to that. My dad is a hard man, but he's fair. If we show him what the lease says, he'll uphold it." Nate's voice was stony. He didn't sound at all like an adoring son who wanted to please or impress his father.

"Do you think there's any way you could catch up on your back rent?" He said it gently, without accusation. "It looks like it's two months' worth."

"Plus this month's in a couple days." She knew it wasn't fair to be angry with him for asking. He was the landlord, after all, and she did owe the money. But it was so much. If the only way to keep the store was to pay it off within the next two months, she wasn't sure there was any hope.

He waited, watching her as if he really cared what she answered. Of course he did. He wanted his money before he shoved her out of here.

"Maybe—" He started pacing the small walkway between the counter and the Queen Anne dining set. "What about a loan from the bank?"

She shook her head. "I'm already maxed out on loans."

"Okay." He was still pacing, picking up speed. "What about family? Do you have anyone who might be willing to lend you some money?"

"I don't have any family anymore." She said it flatly. She couldn't afford to let emotion into this right now.

But he stopped pacing and gave her that soft look that usually melted her. "I'm sorry. I didn't know."

"You couldn't have." She worked to keep her hand from shaking as she waved off his sympathy. She couldn't let him touch her heart right now.

He looked hurt for a second, but then his usual shuttered expression fell into place. More pacing.

She wished he'd stop. He was making her dizzy.

After a few minutes, he snapped his fingers. "What if I found a buyer for the piano?"

Right. And why didn't she just start growing money on trees? Didn't he think she'd already scoured every nook and cranny in search of a buyer for that thing? If it ever actually sold, it would bring in enough money to pay her back rent and then some.

"Mint condition Bosendorfers aren't exactly in high demand in the Hope Springs area." She hoped her sarcasm would be enough to make him give up, but he shoved a hand through his hair, apparently thinking.

"I used to have some contacts in the music world. Let me call around and see if anyone knows someone who might be interested."

Violet opened her mouth. She should tell him she didn't need his help. Didn't want his help.

But he seemed sincere. And she didn't really have any other options. Not if she wanted to keep the store going for Cade.

"Okay." She finally managed to drag out an answer.

By the smile he gave her, you'd think she'd said he could buy a pony.

"Thank you for trusting me." He took a tentative step closer, and when she didn't move away, took another. "I can't promise I'll find a buyer, though. Do you have any other big-ticket items we might be able to sell more quickly?"

"We?"

"Yes, *we*. I'm going to help you through this, just like I said I would."

She watched him for another second, but she couldn't pick out anything besides sincerity in his expression. "Okay, then." She opened her laptop and clicked to the email she'd been looking at before he came in. The pictures of the huge mahogany and glass hutch were beautiful, and she knew she could sell it for a tidy profit if she purchased it, since the gentleman who had emailed her was asking for a more than reasonable price. With a little loving care, she could double her investment. But the seller was located more than two hundred miles away, on the other side of the state.

Since Cade's accident, she hadn't been able to convince herself to drive much farther than Sophie's house, a few miles outside the city.

Nate gave a low whistle. "That's a beauty."

Violet threw him a look over her shoulder. Now was not really the time for sarcasm.

But Nate leaned closer to the computer. "Look at those lines." He held up a finger to point to the curved edges of the piece. "And that whatever it's called." He pointed to the elaborate scrollwork at the top. "That takes some skill. Is that a good price?"

"Yeah." Violet scanned the email. "Really good, actually. I could probably sell it for double."

"Wow. Your problems are solved then. That's not nearly as specialized an item as the piano. There have to be plenty of people around here who would be interested."

Off the top of her head, Violet could think of three regular customers who would kill to get their hands on a piece like this. But it didn't matter. There was no way she could go pick it up. And if she arranged for a truck to deliver it, she might as well give it away for free, since shipping costs would eat any profit.

"How soon can you get it?" Nate's voice was lighter than before, as if he thought all her problems were solved.

Violet rubbed her temples. It wouldn't be that tough, would it? Just get in the car and drive. She'd done it a thousand times before Cade died. Why should now be any different?

But she shook her head. "I'm not."

"Why not?" Nate bent closer, his lemony clean scent overtaking her senses. "Is there something wrong with it?"

Again, she shook her head.

Behind her, Nate's scent weakened as she felt him move back and straighten.

Without warning, her chair spun to face him.

"Why not?" His hand was on the back of her chair, next to her shoulder.

"I can't." The words were almost a whisper.

Nate's brow creased. "This guy obviously wants to sell it to you. Look—" He leaned across her to scroll down to the bottom of the email. "See? He says he knows you'll be fair and find a good home for the piece. Your reputation must precede you."

To her chagrin, tears flooded her eyes. She tried to blink them back, but she was too slow.

"Whoa, hey." Nate crouched in front of her, resting his hands on the armrests of her chair.

Instead of feeling caged in, she felt protected, enclosed.

"What's wrong? You don't have to get the piece if you don't want to. I didn't mean to stick my nose in where it doesn't belong."

Violet attempted a laugh and quickly wiped her eyes. "You didn't do anything wrong." A shuddering breath wracked her frame. "Cade died in a car accident on his way back from picking up a piece. I haven't been able to drive more than a few miles out of town since then." To her own surprise, Violet didn't experience the wave of embarrassment that usually accompanied the admission. Even

Sophie thought it was odd that she never left the city. But Nate simply nodded, his eyes registering a sort of kinship.

He let out a breath and stood slowly, giving her space. Instead of relief, Violet was overwhelmed by a sudden emptiness. She was all alone.

"What if I went with you?" Nate's eyes remained steady on hers.

"What?" Violet tried to make sense of his offer.

"I'll go with you." He said it with more certainty this time, not demanding, more like reassuring.

Violet shook her head. "I'd have to go tomorrow afternoon. You don't want to waste your Sunday like that."

"A day with you wouldn't be a waste."

A warmth spread through Violet's insides. She chewed her lip. If she had someone with her, could she handle leaving the city? Could she put the demons behind her and move forward?

She studied the piece on her computer screen again. She did want it. But this decision seemed bigger than whether or not to go pick up an antique. It seemed like a chance to decide whether to move forward with her life.

"Okay." She turned toward Nate and nodded. "Okay." She said it again, with more certainty. "Let's do it."

A slow grin spread across Nate's face, traveling from his lips to his eyes. Seeing it reassured Violet she'd made the right decision.

After so many years stuck in her grief and fear, traveling out of the city would be the first step on her journey forward.

Who knew what would come next.

Chapter 19

There was a light tapping on the door, and Nate gave Tony a last pat on the head and closed his crate.

"Sorry, buddy, not this time." The dog gave Nate his sad puppy look and sighed. Nate passed him a treat. It amazed him how quickly the dog had managed to work his way into Nate's heart.

Another tap on the door. Nate glanced toward it with a smile, even though he couldn't see her yet.

Tony wasn't the only one who had worked their way into his heart.

He grabbed the bag of snacks he'd put together and headed for the door. The moment he opened it, he caught his breath.

She was wearing a pair of denim shorts and a blue tank top, but she managed to make the ordinary clothes look stunning.

He was grateful she finally seemed to believe that he would do whatever he could to make sure she could keep her store.

He only hoped he didn't disappoint her.

"You ready to go? I packed snacks." She held up a canvas bag.

He held up his own plastic bag. "Me, too."

"Ooh. Let me see." She grabbed his bag and peered into it. After a second, she tossed it back at him. "Those aren't road trip foods."

He peeked into his bag. "What's wrong with apples and bananas?"

"Nothing, for everyday food. But road trips are special. You need special food." She opened her own bag and held it out to him.

He burst into laughter. "Exactly how long do you think this drive will take?" She'd packed two packages of chocolate bars and a party size bag of M & Ms.

Violet echoed his laugh. "I guess I went a little overboard, huh? But I'm an M & M fiend. I might even share some if you're nice." She led the way out the door and to the parking lot.

Nate stared at her car. "Um, I don't want to alarm you, but I don't think that hutch is going to fit in here."

She rolled her eyes. "We're going to pick up a trailer when we get there. And then I'm going to figure out how to drive with a trailer hitched to my car." She pulled a set of keys out of her pocket and fidgeted with them, shifting from one foot to the other as she fingered the key chain. "Unless you want to drive?"

Nate kept his head down. "I can't." He only hoped Violet wouldn't ask why. He tried to convince himself he wouldn't lie if she did.

"It's okay, I trust you with my car." Violet held out the keys to him.

If only that were his concern. "No. It's not that."

Violet tilted her head to the side. "I thought guys liked to drive."

Nate forced a laugh. "It's not that either. It's just—" He watched an ant scurrying on the sidewalk. "I don't have my license."

Violet's mouth went slack for a second as if she thought he might be joking. "You drove me to the hospital when I broke my arm."

"That was an emergency."

She studied him, as if she wasn't sure he was serious. "So you really never got your license?"

Nate stood stock still, unable to decide how to answer her question. He hadn't said he'd never gotten his license. Just that he didn't have one now. He wouldn't have one again for another year.

Before he could say anything, Violet was talking again. "Well, I guess that settles it. I'm driving." Her voice shook.

Nate wished he could do more. That he could be the hero she needed him to be.

He took a step closer and cupped her hands between his own. "I'll be right next to you."

She took a shaky breath, looking at their interlocked hands. Nate pulled his away gently and walked around to open the driver's door for her. Just because he couldn't drive her didn't mean he couldn't be a gentleman.

Violet's arm brushed against his as she climbed into the car, and Nate fought off the wave of longing. He had to stop thinking of this as a day to be alone with Violet and remember he was just doing his part to help save her store. End of story.

But the way his heart forgot to beat for a second when she smiled at him told him he was kidding himself.

Hopefully he was doing a better job of kidding her.

Violet tried to keep her hands relaxed on the wheel, but the closer she came to the edge of the city, the tighter her shoulders tensed.

She couldn't do this. Not even with Nate here next to her.

It was too hard.

She opened her mouth to tell him they had to turn around, that she didn't need the piece that badly, but he spoke first.

"So, how did you and Cade end up with an antique store?" He was looking out the window, but Violet suspected he'd noticed her tension and was trying to ease it.

She focused on answering, ignoring the landmarks going by that said she was almost to the edge of town.

"Completely his idea," she said, letting herself remember his excitement as he'd shared his plans with her. He had been so sure this was what they were meant to do—to save other people's history and pass it on to new owners who could add to that history. "I was an art major working at a dead-end office job I hated, and he was a business major waiting tables in a supper club."

"Sounds glamorous."

"Yeah. Not exactly what we thought our future would be when we graduated from college. But we didn't want to wait until we had established careers before we got married, so we settled for the first jobs we found."

"Makes sense."

She nodded. "Anyway, we hadn't even been married a year yet, and we took this trip up north. We stopped at a rinky-dink garage sale, and we were standing there looking at all this stuff. Cade said what a shame it was that most of it would end up in a landfill. And I could see that it broke his heart, but I thought, 'Well, what are you going to do about it?' But that's the thing: instead of wondering what to do about it, Cade solved the problem. He said we should open an antique shop to rescue—that's the word he used, rescue—all these memories. He had some pretty romantic notions for a businessman."

She glanced at Nate, who nodded, encouraging her to continue.

"Anyway, it took him a while to convince me, which was odd, since I was always the more whimsical, impractical one. But I couldn't see how we were going to make it work." She'd been terrified they'd end up homeless, with nothing to show for their efforts.

"But he wrote up a business plan, got approval for a loan, found a storefront." She swallowed past the memory. "He blindfolded me and brought me there. The place was a mess—the last renter had been a pottery studio—but he had a picnic spread out on a blanket and he'd written Hidden Treasures in big, messy letters on a piece of poster board and hung it on the door. He had the worst handwriting, but—" She shook her head. Her husband had been so full of charisma. "How could I say no?"

Violet pulled herself out of her memories, glancing at Nate to see if he was still listening to her ramble. Not that she would blame him if he wasn't.

But he was staring at her as if he'd never heard anything more interesting. "Sounds like he was very persuasive."

"You could say that. He was—" She didn't know what word to fill in next. Cade was so many things. "He was my everything." The words came out as a whisper, but in place of the usual tightness she felt whenever she thought about Cade, the pressure that had constricted her chest for the past three years eased a bit. She never talked about him with her friends—they had all known and loved him, too, which meant they already knew all there was to tell about him.

By instinct, Violet switched on her signal light to turn onto the highway that would carry them across the state. She hadn't noticed when they'd crossed out of the city, which must have been at least twenty miles ago. To her surprise, her hands were loose on the wheel, her shoulders relaxed. Apparently, she could do this after all.

Nate continued to ask her questions about the shop, and she told him about how they had grown, collected new pieces, made their first sale—an antique trash can of all things—speaking into the welcome of his silence.

By the time she needed a break to stretch, she had gotten to the part a few months before Cade's death when they had started to experience financial trouble.

"I thought it was time to close the shop," she confessed as she pulled into a gas station. She'd never told any of her other friends that. It wasn't that she was afraid they'd judge her; more that she feared they'd tell her maybe she'd been right and she should give it up. But she knew she couldn't do that—not now. Not when it'd be a worse betrayal than refusing to go with Cade that day.

"What did Cade think?" Nate hadn't made a move to get out of the car but instead was studying her in that uncanny and yet somehow inviting way of his.

Violet waved a hand in the air. "Cade was the most optimistic guy you could meet. He said everything would be fine. We just had to trust God." The words seared against Violet's heart. She hadn't exactly been doing a good job of trusting God lately. She took a deep breath.

Maybe this trip was the first step on that road.

Nate washed his hands, then ran them through his hair, taking a deep breath. Listening to Violet talk about Cade was both easier and harder than he'd thought it'd be. Easier because the guy sounded so likable. Harder because it was obvious Violet still loved him, and the raw pain in her voice tore at his insides.

He ripped a sheet of paper towel from the dispenser. He was grateful she'd shared so much with him. He could tell she needed the release. He'd almost been able to see the weight lifting from her shoulders as she talked. If that meant the weight on his own shoulders grew heavier, so be it.

Violet was already behind the wheel when he ducked back into the car. She gave him a sheepish grin as he eyed the handful of M & Ms in her casted hand. "Needed a chocolate break." She offered him the bag, and he grabbed a handful, popping them all into his mouth at once.

"Hey, that's not how you do it."

Nate tilted his head at her, unable to open his candy-stuffed mouth.

"Like this." With her good hand, she picked one piece of candy out of her other hand, lifted it to her mouth, and chewed before taking another.

Nate swallowed his own mouthful and grabbed another handful. "But I get more this way." He stuffed the candy into his mouth, letting her laughter wash over him.

"Well, don't come crying to me when you have a tummy ache."

The words sent a jolt through Nate. That was exactly what his mom would have said. Once upon a time anyway. Now she probably didn't care whether he had a tummy ache or even if he was alive.

Nate caught himself. That wasn't fair.

And besides, now was not the time to dwell on his family.

Violet popped another M & M into her mouth with a dainty flourish, then pulled out of the parking space.

Nate waited, wondering whether Violet wanted to talk about Cade again. He was more than willing to listen. But he didn't want to press her if she didn't want to.

She looked over at him and smiled, and he settled into the comfortable silence.

After a few minutes, Violet turned up the radio, which had been only a low, nearly indistinguishable drone in the background. Static blared through the speakers.

She scanned through the stations. "What kind of music do you like?"

He lifted a hand to rub at the back of his neck. "Whatever you like is fine." Seven years ago, he could have talked about the topic of music for hours. But now he did his best to avoid it.

"How about this?" She stopped on an oldies station, grinning at him. She obviously thought he'd protest, but he just shrugged.

Her lips lowered in a frown that was kind of cute on her. "You don't like music?"

"I'm indifferent about music." He hated to lie to her, but he didn't want to get into this discussion right now. The discussion about how music had been his life—until it had ruined everything.

"No one's indifferent to music." She scanned the stations again, stopping at a country song. "How about this one?"

"This is fine." Country had never been his favorite genre, but at least he wouldn't be tempted to sing along.

"Fine isn't good enough." She pressed the button again, bypassing a classical station, three talk stations, and something rather polka-like.

When she finally stopped, she gave him a hesitant look. "Is this okay?"

His chest tightened, but he nodded. If he'd been indifferent about the other radio stations, he'd have to be indifferent about the Christian station, too. He clamped his mouth shut, so he wouldn't start singing out of pure instinct. Even if the tunes still called to the musician in him, he didn't believe the lyrics anymore.

He settled back in his seat and watched the cornfields zipping by out the window. He tried not to picture the last time he was on a stage. Not to recall how he'd thought his whole life was made that night. Not to remember how it had splintered into a thousand irreparable pieces instead.

"Uh, Nate."

"Yeah?" He kept his gaze directed out the window. The corn stalks were taller than him, but every few seconds they bent almost in half in the hot breeze that had kicked up. Nate wondered if they ever bent so far, they broke.

When Violet didn't answer, he turned to look at her.

She flicked her eyes toward his lap, and he glanced down. His fingers were lifting and lowering in time to the music. He had been playing the piano chords along to the song on the radio without thinking about it.

On the one hand, he was fascinated that his muscle memory was still so strong after seven years.

On the other hand, he'd promised never to play music again. And this came a little too close.

He shoved his hands under his legs and turned to the window, but he could feel Violet looking at him.

"Were you playing lap piano?" Her teasing note caught him off guard.

"I guess I was." He let himself laugh a little.

"How do you know this song?"

"My band used to play it." The words were out before he could consider them. He immediately wanted to reel them back in. Talk of his band was leading to dangerous territory.

"You had a band?"

He couldn't help but look over at the incredulity in Violet's voice. It wasn't that far-fetched was it? "Yeah, a long time ago."

"Well, were you any good?"

He gave a stiff nod. "We were almost signed by a record label. But like I said, it was a long time ago." Hopefully she'd get the hint that he didn't want to talk about it anymore.

"Wow. What happened?"

Nate's throat constricted. "It fell through at the last minute."

"Oh." When she didn't say anything else, he started to relax.

But after a second, she broke the silence again. "Was your family supportive of your band?"

He grunted. "Hardly. My dad insisted I study business. For when my music failed." It didn't matter that Dad had ultimately been right. It still stung that he'd never thrown Nate a crumb of support. Not even when they'd been on the cusp of signing with the label.

"I'm sure your dad is glad to have you in business with him now, though."

An ironic snort erupted from him. "Sure. He loves working with the biggest mistake of his life."

Violet's head snapped to him. "I'm sure he doesn't think that."

Nate looked away from the compassion in her eyes. "His words, not mine."

Violet's gasp was only half stifled. "He couldn't mean that." Her voice was firm, as if she didn't believe any parent could ever think that of their child. But then, she didn't know that his dad had plenty of reason to say that about him.

He stared out the window, hoping the conversation was finally over.

"Do you want to talk about it?"

Nate's stomach clenched. Talking about his family was the last thing he wanted to do. "No thanks."

She nodded and looked away. He hated that he had disappointed her, but she'd be even more disappointed if she knew he deserved everything his father had said about him.

"You know, sometimes when I don't want to talk to people about something, I talk to God." Violet didn't look at him as she said it.

Nate tensed. He didn't want to have this conversation, either. "I gave up talking to God a long time ago."

Violet met his eyes for a second. If he wasn't careful, he would let those eyes capture him.

"Why?"

Nate looked away. "Because God gave up on answering."

"Maybe—"

But the GPS on Violet's phone blared out instructions to exit the highway.

Nate allowed himself a relieved breath as she turned her attention to getting them to the trailer rental place. He had a feeling that he'd narrowly avoided a conversation that would have blown their relationship—whatever it was—to bits.

It was a conversation he couldn't avoid forever.

But he was safe for now at least.

Chapter 20

The car whined as Violet pressed the accelerator, nudging it up the steep hill. Driving with the trailer behind her wasn't as nerve-wracking as she had anticipated, not after conquering her fear to drive all the way across the state.

She couldn't have done it without Nate.

She turned to look at him. He was peering past the lush trees that lined the road to examine the house numbers. But his jaw was tight, and his hands were clenched in his lap.

"Hey." Her voice was soft.

When he met her eyes, his were stormier than ever.

"I'm sorry I asked about your family. I shouldn't have pried."

His lips tipped up the smallest fraction. "It's okay."

How could he say it was okay? How could anyone be okay after their father had said the things Nate's father had? No wonder Nate seemed so haunted most of the time.

"There." He pointed to a stately brick house at the top of the hill. Ivy climbed up one wall, and there were gaps in the mortar between the bricks. But the house had obviously been the jewel of the area in its time.

Violet pulled into the driveway and turned off the car. Then she just sat for a second.

She was stiff and tired, but an overwhelming sense of accomplishment washed over her.

"You okay?" Nate touched a hand to her arm.

"I can't believe I just did that." She felt like she'd been freed from a cage she'd stuck herself in three years ago.

"I can," Nate said simply, opening his door.

Violet stared after him a second before opening her own door. Did he really have that kind of faith in her?

"Come on," Nate called from the foot of the porch staircase.

She hurried to join him. The paint on the porch steps was chipped, and its railing tilted precariously, but the boards underneath were solid.

She knocked on the door, and the two of them waited side-by-side, standing close enough that their arms brushed every time one of them moved. She should step away, but she couldn't make herself do it. After everything they'd shared in the car, she felt closer to him. And she was afraid they'd lose that if she moved too far away.

She reached to squeeze his hand. "Thanks for coming with me. It means a lot."

He squeezed back, offering her a smile that went straight to her heart. "You're welcome."

They pulled their hands apart as the door in front of them opened. A stooped, older gentleman stood on the other side, his dark glasses a sharp contrast to his white hair and pale eyes. When he smiled at them, his face disappeared in a mass of wrinkles.

He held out a hand to Violet, then to Nate. "I'm Barney. I'm so glad you decided to come." He stepped to the side, ushering them through the door. Nate let Violet pass ahead of him, giving her another smile that brightened the dim interior.

Barney led them to the dining room, where a petite woman with white curls was packing china from the hutch into a box.

"They're here, Gladys," Barney said loudly. He leaned toward them and muttered, "She doesn't hear so well anymore. But she's eighty-eight, so what do you expect?"

The woman turned. "I heard that." She tossed a ball of crumpled newspaper at him. "And I'm only eighty-seven. You're the one who's eighty-eight."

Gladys crossed the room and held her hand out to them. Her grip was firm yet kind. "I'm so glad to know you'll find a good home for this hutch. It's been through a lot with us."

Barney wrapped his arm around Gladys's shoulders, tucking her against him.

"The stories this old piece could tell." He whistled, long and low.

Bending over to open the hutch's lower cabinets, Violet gave Nate a significant look.

"See?" she mouthed. He stuck his tongue out at her.

To Barney and Gladys, she said, "Won't you tell us some of them? Where did this beauty come from?"

Barney's eyes lit up, and Violet was in heaven as he spent the next hour telling them about how his great-grandmother had the piece shipped to her from Germany when she immigrated to America in the late 1800s.

"She also brought over all her family's china," Gladys chimed in. "But they had to sell it during the Depression." She gestured at the plate she was wrapping. "When Barney's grandmother inherited the hutch, she bought a new set, and it's been in the family ever since."

"My mother got the hutch after my grandmother," Barney said. "But I didn't have any sisters—just us four boys—so I got the hutch and the china. Not sure it was the best deal since my brothers all got cash, but it's what Gladys wanted."

Gladys swatted at him with a box. "And a good thing, too, since your brothers blew all their money gambling before they could spend a penny of it."

"That's a lovely history," Violet said, shooting Nate another pointed look. To her surprise, he seemed equally fascinated with the story they'd heard. Maybe she'd convert him into an antique lover yet. "What made you decide to sell it now?"

Barney rubbed a hand across his nearly hairless scalp. "Well, in case you haven't noticed, we're no spring chickens."

"Speak for yourself," Gladys interrupted, placing the final piece of china in the box.

Barney ducked his head "I stand corrected. I'm no spring chicken. We've decided to move into a retirement community, and we won't have room for it there."

"And you have no children to pass it on to?" Violet asked gently. She was plenty familiar with that ache. She and Cade had decided to start a family only a few months before he died. For the first few weeks after he was gone, she'd prayed she might at least be carrying his child. But God had chosen to answer that prayer with a no. She still struggled with the grief of that answer sometimes.

"We did. A daughter." Gladys offered a gentle smile. "She went to be with the Lord more than fifty years ago."

"I'm so sorry." Violet laid a hand on the old woman's arm.

"Thank you, but she knew her Savior. She's in heaven now. And one of these days, we'll be there with her."

Barney wrapped an arm protectively around his wife, who fixed him with a sweet smile. They were so cute. Is this what she and Cade would have been like when they were older?

But she had to stop thinking like that. There was no point. She and Cade would never look like this. Because Cade would never grow old with her.

She glanced at Nate. What would he be like as an old man?

She pushed the thought away. She had no intention of growing old with anyone who wasn't Cade.

Nate cleared his throat. "I don't mean to rush things along, but we have quite a long drive yet."

"Goodness, yes. If you let us, we'll go on all day." Gladys shook her head, elbowing her husband. She turned to Nate. "Now, what do you think? Do you want the hutch? Or maybe you need a minute to discuss it?"

Nate shook his head. "This is completely her decision." He pointed at Violet, and she stepped forward, ready to say she'd take it.

But Barney jumped in. "Smart man. A good husband knows when to step aside." He gave Nate an exaggerated wink, but Nate stared back blankly.

It took Violet a second to get what Barney was saying. Nate seemed to catch on at the same time.

"Oh, no, we're not—"

"I'm not her—"

They both laughed. Violet's face warmed, and even Nate's cheeks took on a hint of red.

"We're just neighbors," Violet finally said.

Barney and Gladys glanced back and forth between Violet and Nate, then looked at each other and smiled.

"They're just neighbors," Barney said to Gladys.

"So I hear," Gladys replied. Neither could contain their grins, and Violet bit her lip. Did these two strangers sense the energy she'd started to feel every time she was near Nate?

And what was that half smile on Nate's face? Did he feel it, too?

She shook herself. This was supposed to be a business trip. "We'll take it."

Nate shook out his arms, rolled his neck, and squatted at the corner of the hutch one more time. They'd been trying for an hour to get it loaded, but no matter how many different angles they attempted, it was too heavy for him and Violet to move on their own, especially with Violet's arm still in a cast.

"Let me give it a try." Barney stepped forward, and Nate scrutinized him. He didn't appear frail by any stretch, but the man was nearly ninety years old. Nate didn't want to be responsible for breaking him.

"Barnabas Riley, step away from that hutch right this minute." Gladys bustled into the room, pointing a spatula at her husband.

Barney stepped back. "Busted." But he nudged Nate and whispered, "I wasn't really going to do it. Just had to show her I'm still willing."

Nate laughed with him, but Violet gave the hutch a regretful pat. "Looks like it wasn't meant to be."

"Hold on a minute, dear. You're the one we want to have this." Gladys disappeared again.

Nate and Violet both looked at Barney, but he threw his hands into the air. "Even after sixty-five years of marriage, I don't understand everything about that woman." He winked at them again. "Keeps me on my toes."

Three minutes later, Gladys reappeared. "I called Sylvia, and she said her grandson can come over to help us."

"That's great." Violet pulled out a chair to sit down and stifled a yawn. She looked exhausted.

"In the morning," Gladys finished.

Violet dropped the hand that had been covering her yawn. "I'm sorry. I don't think we can come back tomorrow."

"Of course not." Gladys waved her objection away. "You can stay with us. It's getting late anyway. You don't want to drive back yet tonight."

Nate stole a subtle peek at the time. It was already eight o'clock. And Violet looked ready to drop.

She gave him a questioning look, and he shrugged, hoping she would understand that meant it was up to her.

"I guess that would work. The store is always closed on Mondays anyway." Her eyes traveled to Nate. "Unless you need to be in the office."

He should be. He really should be. If Dad called and he didn't answer, he would never hear the end of it. But right now, he cared more about what Violet needed. And she needed this hutch to save her store.

"I don't need to be in the office."

"Oh, but Tony—" Violet clasped his arm.

She had a point there. He couldn't leave his dog uncared for.

"Unless." Violet pulled out her phone. "Just a second." She wandered toward the kitchen with the phone pressed to her ear.

"Looks like I'm not the only one with a mysterious woman." Barney chuckled so hard he broke into a coughing fit.

"Oh, we're—"

"Neighbors." Gladys rested a hand on her husband's back. "We know."

Barney stopped coughing and straightened, shooting Nate a wink.

Nate was about to argue more, but Violet stepped back into the room. Her smile was enough to steal his protest.

"Sophie's going to stop by to take care of Tony tonight and tomorrow morning. I hope you don't mind, but I told her about your super-secret hiding spot for the spare key."

Nate pretended to be shocked. "How do you know about that?"

"I saw you putting it under the mat the other day when you forgot your keys, remember?"

He did remember. He had been especially enchanted by her laugh that day. It was amazing how many of his recent memories involved her.

Including this one.

"That settles it then." Gladys clapped her hands, looking more like an eight-year-old than an eighty-seven-year-old. "I'll get the extra beds made up. Then we'll all have a nice dinner together. The roast I put in earlier is way too big for Barney and me anyway."

Gladys passed close to Nate as she headed for the stairs. "Don't worry, dear. She may just be a neighbor now. But she'll be more soon." She winked, then was gone.

Nate looked from her retreating form to the other side of the room, where Violet was laughing at something Barney had said. His heart leaped, trying to break free of the tight hold he was keeping on it. But it was getting harder every moment.

Then Violet looked at him, and he knew: it was already too late.

Chapter 21

Violet let a contented sigh escape as she eased into the bed. She hadn't been pampered like this in a long time. Gladys had treated them to a delicious meal of pot roast, glazed vegetables, and a rich and gooey chocolate cake.

Even better than the food had been the entertainment. Barney and Gladys had delighted them with stories about how they met at a butcher shop and how he proposed to her on the Ferris wheel at the county fair. Violet had laughed until her side hurt when he confessed he'd dropped the ring, and they'd had to shut down the ride so they could search the ground. It took three hours, but they finally found it.

They talked about more serious memories, too, including their teenage daughter's death after a five-year battle with cancer and the difficult period in their marriage that had followed. It had taken them several years to find their way back to each other.

As she talked about that time, Gladys had said something that made Violet reassess her whole life the past three years: "We finally figured out that holding onto past hurts was keeping us from experiencing future joy. Letting go didn't make the past hurt less; it just allowed us to recognize that it was only one thread in the tapestry of our lives."

Violet examined the stitches in the quilt on her lap. Was that what Cade had been? One thread in her tapestry? She had thought he was the entire picture, top to bottom, beginning to end. But now the whole thing had unraveled. How did she tie off that thread and graft in a new one? And what did that new thread look like?

An image of Nate popped into her head. Violet had found herself studying him as the older couple talked. He had laughed in all the right places, looked sympathetic when they spoke of the tough times, and yet Violet felt like he wasn't really there. He seemed lost in his own head, a haunted look fogging his eyes as if whatever he saw in there was too painful to bear.

But whenever he'd noticed her watching him, his eyes had cleared, and his smile had become genuine, kicking up a flutter deep in her insides.

Violet had felt her soul stir as she observed the love between Barney and Gladys. But it wasn't the same kind of jealousy-inducing stir she'd felt when Sophie and Spencer showed their honeymoon pictures. It was more of a nostalgia for something she'd never had, if that was possible. And a longing to have a future like that with someone, even if it couldn't be Cade.

Violet sucked in a sharp breath. She had never let herself think that before. She'd told herself that her future was as a single woman. That she'd be faithful to Cade until she joined him in heaven. Thinking anything else felt like breaking her marriage vows.

And yet, her vows had said "till death do us part," and death had parted them.

While that didn't change her love for Cade, it did change her situation. It made her alone—more than that, it made her lonely.

She had thought she was fine with that.

But spending so much time with Nate lately had made her less sure.

Had made her want more.

Violet tugged the pillow over her head. What would Cade think if he knew her line of thought? Would he want to punch Nate? Or would he shake Nate's hand and tell him to take care of her?

She wrestled with the question for hours before she fell into an uneasy sleep.

It seemed like only minutes later when her eyes popped open, straining to see in the pitch dark as her blood thundered through her. Where was she? And what had woken her up?

Slowly, her eyes adjusted to the dark, and Violet remembered she was at Gladys and Barney's. But that didn't explain why her heart had turned into a locomotive. She didn't think it had been a nightmare. Her skin was dry, not clammy, and she wasn't all tangled in the sheets like she was every time she dreamed about trying to save Cade.

A string of yells came at her through the wall, from Nate's room next door. Violet cocked her head, listening more closely. After a minute, the yelling picked up again. It sounded panicked.

Violet slid quickly out of bed and tiptoe-ran to the door. She clicked it open silently, then stood in the hallway, pressing her ear to Nate's door.

When the yelling started again, she grabbed the knob and shoved the door open.

Then she froze.

Nate was curled in a ball on his side, the blankets wrapped around him in a tangle.

He threw out an arm, palm outward, as if trying to stop someone. "No!" His voice was hoarse. "No! Not her!"

He pulled his arm back to his core, his whole body going limp for a second before it trembled under the weight of a huge sob. "NO!"

The word unfroze Violet, and she rushed to the bed, dropping to her knees at Nate's side.

"Hey," she whispered, her hand rubbing his bare shoulder. "Nate. Wake up."

Nate moaned. "Please."

Violet rubbed harder, spoke louder. "Nate, I'm here. It's Violet."

Nate's eyes flew open and skittered wildly around the room. Violet moved her hand to his rough cheek, turning his face toward her. His eyes stopped on hers.

It took a moment, but slowly he seemed to register who she was. He heaved a shaky breath. "Violet."

She was suddenly aware that she was still touching him. She scooted back a little but remained on her knees. "Bad dream?"

Nate scrubbed a hand over his face, wiping away a sheen of sweat, and sat up, extracting himself from the blankets. "Yeah. Sorry. Should have warned you I get them sometimes."

"Me too." Violet's eyes fell on Nate's bare chest. It was well-defined, but that's not what her gaze locked on. A long white scar ran from his left shoulder, across his chest, to the outside of his ribs.

He followed the path of her eyes and reached to grab his shirt, yanking it over his head.

Violet pushed to her feet and shuffled to sit next to him on the bed. "Do you want to talk about it? The dream?"

"I can't." His voice was raw, uncensored, and Violet knew he wasn't trying to put her off. He really couldn't talk about it.

"Mine are always about Cade. Except it's never about a car accident. There's always something else, some danger that I see just before it happens—a cliff he's about to fall off, a current that's about to sweep him away. I try to get to him, to warn him, but I'm always too late." Violet's throat burned just talking about it, and she tried to swallow, but her mouth was too dry.

"Sometimes I wake up before he dies. But sometimes I have to watch it. Have to go through the whole funeral, too. Every little detail of it is in place, except it's like it's in slow motion and it's never going to end." She almost choked on the last words, and yet she was grateful for the release of telling him. She'd never even told Sophie about the dreams. But knowing she wasn't the only one with nightmares had given her courage to share, especially if it might help Nate.

A warm hand gripped her fingers and squeezed. Before he could let go, Violet squeezed back. She needed this connection, this moment to tell her she wasn't alone, she wasn't the only one who hurt and didn't know what to do with it.

They sat like that, their breaths slowly matching one another, until Violet's head started to droop. "I'd better get back to bed."

Nate gave one last squeeze and let go of her hand. Violet fought off the wave of emptiness.

When she was to the door, she turned to look at Nate. He had lain down, his breathing now slow and even.

"Thank you," he said, his eyes closed.

Violet nodded. "Thank you," she whispered.

She fell back to sleep within seconds of climbing back into her own bed.

By the time she woke, a bright line of sunlight streamed in through the slight gap in the curtains.

She stretched, her heart lighter than it had been in ages. Something had happened during the night. The weight of memories hadn't been lifted, but it had changed so that she could start to see the light in them instead of only the dark.

She sat up and folded her hands, bowing her head.

Dear Jesus, You are a great and a mighty God, and I thank you for this new day, for a renewed life, for the promise that you know all my hurts and have the ability to take them from me, maybe in ways I haven't seen or planned. Please bring the same healing you've brought me to Nate's heart, whatever his troubles may be. In your name I ask it. Amen.

Violet sat and just breathed for a minute, paying attention to the air going into and out of her lungs. Somewhere along the line she'd forgotten that each day was a gift from the Lord and had started to look at the days as something to simply survive.

But not anymore.

As she got out of bed, she gave herself a cursory glance in the mirror. Her clothes from yesterday were rumpled but not too much worse for the wear. Her hair, on the other hand, stuck out in every direction. She ran a hand across her curls, attempting fruitlessly to tame them, then gave up. If unruly hair was the worst thing she had to worry about today, she'd count herself fortunate.

Homey smells and muted conversation drifted up the stairs, and Violet followed them to the kitchen. Nate was already there, chuckling at something Gladys had said as he scooped a forkful of eggs off his plate. The moment she walked into the room, his eyes went to hers, and he smiled, not that haunted, half-there smile from yesterday, but a genuine, heart-melting smile that Violet couldn't help but return.

"Good morning," she said softly.

He nodded and finished chewing, never taking his eyes from hers. "Good morning." Was it her imagination or did his voice have a new, tender note to it?

Violet scolded herself. Just because she'd had a revelation last night didn't mean he had. To him, she was still just his neighbor.

She slid her gaze to the table. Gladys obviously loved to cook. She'd laid out eggs, bacon, biscuits and gravy, and a pile of pancakes. "Wow, Gladys, you didn't have to do all this for us."

Gladys's smile was both wistful and filled with joy. "I haven't had anyone to cook for in a long time. Barney's diabetic, so no more pancakes for us." She passed Violet a plate. "Cooking's one of the things I'm going to miss most when we move into the new place. We have a meal plan there, so I won't even need to pour Barney his cereal."

Violet observed the older woman as she filled her plate. Somehow it had never occurred to her that she wasn't the only one entering a new chapter of her life—and there would be plenty more new chapters along the way. Perhaps it wasn't the changing of chapters that was so important but more what you did with the pages in them that mattered.

Violet pulled out the chair across from Nate and sat, bowing her head to give thanks for the food. When she lifted her head, Nate was watching her.

"Sorry I woke you last night."

Violet shoveled a forkful of pancake into her mouth, closing her eyes in bliss as the sweet tang of maple syrup and lightly browned pancakes hit her tongue. She waved her hand at Nate. She wanted to tell him that she was glad he had woken her, glad she had been there with him, glad they had shared that moment.

But with Gladys hovering over them, she said simply, "It was no problem."

The doorbell rang, and Gladys clapped as she had yesterday, making Violet grin. Someone had forgotten to tell the woman she was eighty-seven. "That'll be Sylvia's grandson. You finish up, and I'll get the door."

Nate stood and carried his plate to the sink. Violet started to follow, giving a remorseful look at her half-finished pancakes.

Nate waved her back into her seat. "You finish eating. I've got this."

Violet knew she should argue. But the pancakes were too good.

She kept an ear tuned to the other room as she ate. By the time she'd finished and entered the dining room, Nate and Sylvia's grandson were carrying the hutch toward the front door.

"Easy." She heard Nate's voice from the other side of the room.

She considered following him outside but changed her mind. He had this under control.

Instead, she approached Gladys, who was wrapping the last of the china. "Thank you again for allowing us to stay last night. That was more than was necessary. In fact—" She reached into her purse for her checkbook.

Gladys waved the checkbook off. "I did it as much for me as for you, dear. One last chance to entertain before saying goodbye to this house." To Violet's surprise, Gladys swiped at a tear.

Violet rubbed the woman's arm. "I thought you were happy to be moving somewhere more manageable."

"I am, dear, I am." Gladys patted Violet's hand. "But just because we're happy about the next part of our life doesn't mean we're not sad about leaving the last part behind."

Violet blinked hard so she wouldn't have to wipe away her own tears. Somehow Gladys had expressed exactly what she'd been feeling.

"All loaded up."

Violet and Gladys both jumped at the voice behind them.

Nate eyed them with concern. "Everything okay?"

Violet nodded.

"Perfect," Gladys said. "But I wonder if you could do me one more favor?"

Nate patted the older woman on the back. "After a breakfast like that, I'll do anything you ask."

Gladys rested her hand on the box of china she'd so lovingly wrapped. "Could you load this into your car as well, please?"

Violet already had stacks of unsold china in her shop, but she couldn't say no to a woman who had been so generous to them. "How much would you like for it?"

Gladys reached a leathery hand to stroke her hair, then let her arm drop. "I don't want you to buy it, dear. I want to give it to you." She looked at Nate, then at Violet. "To both of you."

"Oh, but—" That was too generous, on top of everything else. Plus, Violet didn't want to assume the older woman was getting forgetful, but they'd already told her they weren't a couple.

"I won't take no for an answer," Gladys cut in. "And before you think I'm senile, I know you aren't together. So you can each take half of the china. Who knows, maybe you'll join the set back together someday. But this way you can each remember the little old couple you brought joy for an evening."

Violet pretended not to know what Gladys meant about putting the set back together. "That's very kind, but—"

"I told you, I won't accept no. You'll be doing me a favor, anyway. Otherwise, I have to haul this to the thrift store, and it's mighty heavy."

"You could sell it."

"It's not worth anything. Just the cheapest set Barney's grandmother could find." She snapped her fingers toward Nate, then pointed to the box. "Now. Load it up."

Nate looked from Gladys to Violet. Violet gave a subtle shake of her head, but apparently Nate decided Gladys was the more formidable of the two because he crossed the room and picked up the box with a grunt.

Gladys winked at him. "That's a good boy."

Nate studiously avoided Violet's eyes as he slid past them and out the front door. Violet let her gaze follow him for a moment, trying to decide whether she should be angry or amused.

She settled on grateful. "Thank you, Gladys, for everything." She leaned down to give the small woman a hug.

"I know your heart's been broken," Gladys whispered as she held her. "But that doesn't mean it will never feel again. And when it does, you make sure that young man out there knows."

Violet scrunched her eyes shut and nodded against the huge lump that had formed in her throat.

"All set?" Nate called from the doorway.

Violet released her hold on Gladys and nodded. She wasn't sure if she was yet. But she would be.

Chapter 22

Nate fastened the last button of his shirt and tucked it into the waist of his jeans. He couldn't figure out exactly how he'd let himself get talked into the concert. It was the last place he wanted to go, the last place he told himself he'd ever go again. But when Violet had asked, the *yes* had come out in a nanosecond. In the few weeks that had passed since their trip to Barney and Gladys's, something had shifted between him and Violet—in a good way. That night, as he'd clutched her hand after his nightmare and she'd shared her own horrifying dreams, they'd forged a connection.

Since then, they'd stopped pretending that they weren't seeking each other out. They spent nearly every evening together, and he'd taken her out for dinner to celebrate when she sold the hutch a week after they picked it up. It was only pizza, but still—it was something. He'd been spending more time with her friends, too. He couldn't deny that it felt good to finally belong somewhere again. The last time he'd had that feeling was with his band.

Nate shoved the memory away. He couldn't let himself dwell on his lost dreams tonight.

Tony followed at Nate's feet as he padded into the kitchen. He gave the dog a scoop of food and waited absently for him to eat it.

His eyes fell on the saucer from Barney and Gladys's china set that Violet had compelled him to take. He had told her to keep the whole set, but she'd insisted that he take at least one piece because Gladys had wanted them to share it.

He hadn't mentioned that Gladys also wanted them to share more—a life together—since she didn't seem to have picked up on that part of Gladys's ploy. Or if she had, she had pretended not to. As had he. In the end, he'd agreed to take one saucer because he'd figured if her set were permanently one tiny plate short, it would be no great loss.

And if they did happen to reunite the set someday—

Tony nudged Nate's hand with his cold nose, pulling Nate out of his daydreams before they could go too far.

"Okay, buddy." Nate locked Tony in his kennel. "I'll probably be home late tonight. So no parties." Nate almost bit his tongue as the words came out. They were exactly the same words his parents had said to him every time they went out. And he had always obeyed. Until that last night. When he hadn't.

Nate shoved a hand through his hair but then immediately tried to smooth it down.

The knock at the door made him jump, and in spite of himself, his heart picked up speed. It shouldn't react this way to a concert with a friend. But apparently no one had told it that.

Nate threw a treat into Tony's kennel and crossed to the door. He took two deep breaths before opening it.

But the sight on the other side stole those breaths right back.

Violet was wearing a flowing blue dress that hung longer on the sides than in the front and back. She'd gotten her cast off a few days ago, and her dark curls cascaded over her shoulders and onto her bare upper arms. Her lips glistened with a wine-colored gloss that made Nate want to touch them.

"Hi," Violet finally said, making Nate realize he'd been staring.

"Hi. Sorry." Nate swallowed. "You look great."

Violet's smile grew, making her lips even more inviting. Nate glanced over his shoulder, pretending to check Tony's kennel, before turning back to Violet.

But that smile was still there.

"Ready to go?" She sounded slightly breathless and excited.

Nate nodded and followed her to her car.

As Violet drove, they fell into the easy conversation that had become so familiar over the past few weeks.

But ten minutes later, Nate threw Violet a quizzical look as they pulled into the parking lot of the church. The place was jammed with cars, and people dressed in everything from ripped jeans and t-shirts to formal dresses were pouring toward the building.

"Are we picking Dan up?" Nate asked as Violet pulled into one of the few remaining parking spots at the far end of the lot, near Dan's house.

Violet looked away and tapped her fingers against the steering wheel.

Not good. She had something to tell him, and he wasn't going to like it.

"No." She looked away and continued in a rush, "The concert is at the church."

All the air disappeared from the car. She had tricked him into coming. She knew how he felt about church, and she had deliberately not told him she was bringing him to one. Well, she could forget it. There was no way he was going in there.

"Don't be mad." Violet gave him a pleading look.

He told himself he wouldn't be swayed by the genuine compassion in her eyes.

"I didn't tell you because I knew you wouldn't come otherwise. And I really think you'll like the music."

Nate tensed. It wasn't a question of if he'd like the music. This kind of music had been his life once. But it had almost been his death, too.

"If you don't like it, we can leave." Violet laid her hand, smooth and soft, on his. "Please. It would mean a lot to me."

Violet's eyes hadn't left his face, and he both dreaded and loved the hope he saw there.

"Okay." The word scraped up against his will.

"Thank you." Violet squeezed his hand, and in spite of himself, he let out a tight-lipped smile. Making her happy always did that to him.

Violet popped her car door open and bounded out, greeting a young couple who had gotten out of the car next to them. She waved to an older man across the parking lot. Nate watched her in wonder. She seemed to genuinely fit in here, to enjoy and care about these people. And they seemed to return the sentiment.

Of course, she hadn't committed any big, public sin to earn their wrath and scorn.

But as far as they knew, neither had he.

Nate fell into step next to Violet, trying to ignore the churning in his stomach that intensified the closer they got to the door, until it felt like he had swallowed a whirlpool.

An older man opened the church door for them, offering a cheerful hello. Nate mumbled a greeting, pushing past as fast as he could. He was in no mood to make small talk.

Inside, groups of people mingled around the spacious lobby, and the sound of laughter filled the space.

"The sanctuary is this way." Violet steered him past the people, and Nate was grateful when she only waved to a few groups but didn't stop to talk.

Inside, the church floor sloped toward the front, where a large open area held an assortment of instruments, from a drum set to half a dozen guitars and a baby grand piano.

Nate's fingers twitched. He could almost feel the smooth keys, feel the vibration of a perfect chord ringing out.

He shoved his hands in his pockets and scanned the crowd with Violet.

The seats were already half filled, but after a second Violet pointed. Sophie, Spencer, Tyler, Ethan, Ariana, Jared, Peyton, and Leah took up almost an entire row halfway to the front of the church, right in the center of the sanctuary.

Nate followed Violet toward them, his feet heavier with every step. He kept his head down, eyes trained on the floor.

When they reached their friends, everyone stood up to greet them. Their warmth helped Nate relax. This was just a night with friends. No one was going to grill him about his band or his failure. When Sophie leaned over to hug him, he hugged back. After a minute, they all settled into their seats. Nate jammed himself into the space between Violet and the end of the row. Their arms were pressed together, and her flowery scent wafted over him.

"Are we going to have room for Dan?" Nate peered down the length of the row, but he was pretty sure they couldn't cram in another person if they tried.

Violet's laugh startled him. "I don't think he's going to sit with us."

Nate felt his brow wrinkle. Clearly, there was some kind of joke going on here, but he wasn't in on it. "Why not?"

"Well, the pastor usually sits up front." Violet was still chuckling.

"The pastor?" Nate felt his mouth dip into a frown. This didn't make any sense. "Dan is a pastor?"

Violet stopped laughing. "I thought you realized. This is his church. He and his dad are co-pastors here."

Which would explain why he lived right next door. And was always talking about his members. Nate had figured he ran some sort of gym or something.

At that moment, the man himself emerged from a hidden door behind the front wall of the sanctuary. He was dressed in simple khaki pants and a button up shirt without a tie. Not Nate's typical image of a pastor. Dan scanned the crowd. When his eyes fell on their row, he made his way toward them.

As Dan held out a hand to him, Nate thought about the conversations he'd had with the other man. He hadn't held back his opinion that church was a waste of time at best and a fraud at worst. He felt suddenly awkward around this man he had come to see as a friend.

But Dan didn't seem to notice. "Hey, Nate, glad you could make it."

Before Nate could come up with a reply, a panicked looking teen ran up to Dan and whispered something. Dan turned to his friends. "Sorry. Problems with the sound system. I'll see you after the concert."

At the front of the church, the band members began to warm up.

The sharp chords pulled Nate back to the life he'd had before. He'd been so full of himself then, thinking he was someone special. That God had big plans for him. That the Big Guy had his back.

Look how wrong he'd been.

The pianist played a short riff, and Nate found himself leaning forward, eyes fixed on the guy's fingers. They were sure on the keys, just as his had once been.

Nate's gaze moved to the guy's face. His eyes were closed, and he seemed to be feeling the music, living it. Nate knew exactly what that was like. Playing was the only time he had really felt alive in those days—like he was doing what he was put on this earth to do.

"Nate?" A soft hand landed on his arm.

Nate ripped his eyes off the pianist and looked toward Violet, who was clearly waiting for him to say something. He gave her a blank stare, his thoughts still on the feel of piano keys beneath his fingers.

"Sorry, what was that?"

"Are you angry that I dragged you here?"

"What?" Nate forced his attention to her.

"You look kind of . . ." Violet trailed off. "Tense."

Nate glanced at his hands, which were fisted in his lap. His clenched jaw ached, too. He concentrated on loosening his muscles. How could he be angry when she looked at him with that soft gaze?

"No." He gave her what he hoped was a gentle smile. "I'm not upset."

Violet's features relaxed. A second later, the lights in the sanctuary dimmed, and the crowd grew silent.

Nate's stomach lurched. He wasn't sure he could handle this after all.

A spotlight flashed onto the band as the first chord rang across the auditorium. The gathered worshipers cheered and rose to their feet as the band broke into a familiar praise song.

Violet leaned toward Nate and pointed to a large screen behind the band, which showed the words of the song so the audience could sing along. But Nate didn't need the words. He'd sung this song more times than he could count, first as a child in church and then as his band grew large enough to tour.

But Nate's throat was too full to sing. He simply gave Violet a tight nod.

She smiled and closed her eyes, swaying as she sang along to the music.

Nate closed his eyes, too.

But instead of being lifted to the heights of worship, he sank into the past.

As song after song rolled by, Nate saw his band playing in venues just like this one, his hands on the piano keys, a microphone at his mouth.

He'd loved the energy of these events, the communion of worshiping together with so many people who believed in the same God, believed that he was all-powerful and the very definition of love. He'd wanted to dedicate his life to that God.

Of course, that was before he'd discovered it was all a lie. Maybe there was a God; he wasn't ready to go so far as to say there wasn't. But that God was not all-powerful. And he certainly wasn't all-loving.

Nate had learned that the hard way.

No matter how much he fought to resist the memories, they forced their way through. That last night, Nate and his band had played to a packed crowd at his hometown church. They had heard rumors that someone from a Christian record label would be in the audience. The added pressure spurred them on, and they played a flawless set. Afterward, the producer approached them and offered to set up a meeting for the next week.

The offer seemed to prove once and for all that Nate was on the right track with his life, that his father had been wrong about business school, and now he could drop out and do what he was really meant to do.

The producer insisted on taking them out to celebrate. Nate almost said no. He rarely partied, and he was exhausted after the grueling schedule they'd been keeping. But finally making it big felt like a milestone that needed to be celebrated. He didn't want to look back at this moment and realize he'd failed to appreciate it as it happened. Plus, he worried that declining would seem ungrateful. This guy had the chance to make or break his career.

The producer took them to an upscale bar and offered them all a round of drinks.

Nate said no at first.

But he was parched. And he'd turned twenty-one two months before. It was no big deal for him to have a drink.

Only there'd been another round after that. And then another.

Being out had felt good. Finally, he could let go of all the pressure and tension that had been building up for the past several years. For his whole life, maybe, with his dad's constant demand for success.

There was no more need for pressure.

He had made it.

The alcohol went down easier and easier the longer the night went on.

Around midnight, his phone rang. It was Kayla, calling from her own party, begging him to drive her home because she was too drunk to drive, and she was going to miss her curfew.

Nate had lectured Kayla a thousand times about not drinking. She was only sixteen. But he was also realistic. He knew his little sister wasn't a saint. So he'd made her promise that she'd never drive drunk. He'd promised he'd always come pick her up.

So he had downed his last drink, shaken the producer's hand, and congratulated his bandmates again.

Then he'd pulled out his keys and gone to pick Kayla up.

He never gave a thought to the fact that maybe he didn't belong behind the wheel of a car.

Nate's thoughts snapped to the present as someone tugged on his arm. He opened his eyes to find Violet pulling him gently down as all around them people sat. The band had stopped playing, and the lead singer was taking a long swig of water as Dan approached the front of the church. He wore a headset microphone and looked totally at ease in front of the packed church. The same way Nate had felt once.

"How's everyone doing tonight?" Dan called out.

The crowd roared its approval.

Nate swiped a hand over his damp forehead, trying to relax. Violet leaned closer to him, and he tried to use the contact to anchor himself to the present.

"You know," Dan was saying from the front of the sanctuary. "I'm not going to talk long because I want to hear some more of this incredible music. But I wanted to take a minute to talk to you about what an awesome God we have. Maybe you know him already, maybe you don't. Or maybe you knew him once, but you've decided you don't want to know him anymore." Dan wasn't looking anywhere near him, and yet Nate felt as if the words had been directed right at him. His shoulders tensed.

"The thing is, whatever you might know or think you know about God, he knows everything about you."

Nate's insides churned. What business did God have knowing everything about him? Some things were too horrible for anyone—even God—to know.

"But—and here's the important thing," Dan went on. "He loves you anyway." A few people clapped at that, and at least one person whistled. "No matter who you are. No matter what you've done. God loves you. He forgives you."

The weight of Dan's words throbbed against Nate's temples.

"Do you hear me?" Dan turned toward the other side of the church, but Nate could still feel the sear of his openness. "There is nothing—nothing—God cannot forgive. Nothing—not one single sin—Jesus did not die for. So whatever you're holding onto tonight, whatever burden you're carrying, leave it at the cross."

Dan directed one more look Nate's way, then walked to his seat at the front of the church as the band broke into another song.

Nate tried to inhale and focus on the music, but the room had gone airless. He stumbled to his feet, tripping over the end of the row, barely seeing what was in front of him. He charged down the aisle, through the sanctuary doors, and across the lobby.

As he slammed his body through the church doors, the clean night air pulled him up short, and he stood heaving, trying not to choke on the memories that swirled around him, an angry current fighting to pull him under, to drag him to where he couldn't breathe. To where he deserved to be.

The too-sweet scent of lilacs in the air when he picked up Kayla.

The too-loud click of his blinker against the pounding that had started in his head.

The too-wavy center line.

The too-bright lights coming straight toward them.

His too-slow reaction.

The too-high screech of metal on metal, followed by the grinding silence.

The empty seat, where Kayla had been. The broken window. The scramble from the car to find her crumpled in the road, blood spreading around her like watercolor paint.

Collapsing next to her as his own injuries overtook him. A final plea to God: "Take me. Please, take me, not her."

The strength of the memory dropped him to his knees.

He didn't want to hear that God was good, that he could forgive anything.

He didn't deserve to be forgiven for this.

Chapter 23

Violet told herself not to follow Nate, to give him some space. She managed to listen to herself for all of ten seconds.

As she walked deliberately toward the doors, she tried to work out what she would say when she got to him, how she would apologize. She had known how he felt about church, and yet she'd roped him into coming—by deceiving him, no less.

It was just that he'd obviously known the love of God once, if he knew those songs on the Christian radio station and had been in a band that played them. She'd wanted so badly for him to know God again that she'd thought it wouldn't matter how she'd gotten him here; she figured once he heard God's word again, his heart would be mended.

She'd been naive. Clearly, his issues with God ran deeper than she'd been willing to see. Which meant that whatever feelings she'd been developing for him—and she had to admit they were there—would have to be reined in. She could never be in a relationship that didn't have God at its center. She knew God was the reason her relationship with Cade had worked; and he was the only way a relationship between her and Nate would work as well.

Not that he'd come out and said he'd like to have a relationship with her. But she couldn't deny the spark between them anymore, the desire to spend every waking moment with him. She'd finally accepted—started to hope, even—that it could be leading to something more.

She pushed down her rising sorrow that it couldn't. That wasn't what this was about right now. It was about apologizing for dragging him here.

When she reached the glass doors that led outside, she stopped short.

Nate was kneeling in the middle of the sidewalk, his head in his hands.

Violet raised a hand to cover her mouth. He was obviously still fighting with whatever it was that had driven him out here. She should leave him. Let him have the space he so obviously craved.

But he'd been there for her so many times. When she'd broken her arm. When she'd needed someone to talk to about Cade. And when she'd needed help saving her store. Without Nate, she wouldn't be halfway to paying off her back rent already.

She owed it to him to help him through this—whatever it was.

Steeling her shoulders, Violet slipped quietly through the door and hurried over to Nate, dropping to the ground next to him. She let her fingers graze his back lightly. He trembled slightly, and she planted her hand more firmly on his back. "Nate?"

He drew in a shuddering breath, then dropped his hands to his knees and pushed himself into a more upright position. She let her hand fall from his back.

"Sorry about that," he rasped, not looking at her.

"No, I'm the one who's sorry." Violet rubbed at the pale spot on her ring finger. "I tricked you into coming here even though I knew how you felt about church. I should have told you the truth."

A muscle in Nate's jaw twitched as he stared out over the parking lot. "I appreciate that. But I think I'll wait out the rest of the concert in the car." He held out his hand, palm up. "Give me the keys and go inside. I don't want to ruin your evening."

Violet shook her head. She was the one who had ruined the evening.

"I'm not going back in there without you, and you're definitely not going back, so how about we call it a night?"

Nate ran a hand through his hair, making the top stick up in funny tufts that Violet had an urge to run her fingers through. Finally, he nodded, and she took his elbow, leading him across the parking lot to her car.

Violet left Nate to his thoughts during the short drive home, but when they reached their building, each standing outside their own apartment doors, she turned to him. "You seemed to enjoy the concert at first. Was it something Dan said?"

Nate's eyes darted around the landing, as if trying to find anywhere to look but at her. "Let's just say I disagree with his assessment that everything can be forgiven."

Violet waited for him to add more. When he didn't, she said, "It might help to talk about it. I could make some coffee." She ached to take whatever this burden was from him. Or at least to help him carry it.

His eyes finally came to rest on hers, filled with an anguish she recognized only too well. "I can't."

"That's what I thought, too, for a long time." What she'd thought until only a few weeks ago, when she'd found herself opening up to Nate. The least she could do was offer him the opportunity to do the same.

For a second, she thought he was going to say yes. She watched the warring desires in his eyes, praying that for once openness would win out.

But the moment passed, and his guarded look fell back into place. The one she thought he had dropped as they'd grown closer.

"It's too much," he said finally, opening his door.

But Violet wasn't going to give up that easily. "Part of friendship is sharing." She took a step closer to his door. She tried to keep her voice steady, but it hurt that he didn't trust her enough to open up. "But I feel like I'm the only one who's sharing all the time. Every time I ask you anything, you put me off with vague half answers. I don't know why you left your band or why you're so angry with God or what you dream about for the future. None of it."

Nate's face contorted, and she took an involuntary step back.

"You want to know about my past?" His voice was laced with a hopelessness she'd never heard from him before. "My past is dead. You want to know what I dream for the future? Fine. I dream of—" He stopped abruptly and clamped his mouth shut.

"You dream of what?" Violet asked softly. In her heart, he said *you*.

But his eyes traveled from her face to her feet, then to the stairway. "I don't dream of anything for the future. My future is dead, too."

He turned and disappeared into his apartment, the click of the door ricocheting around the landing.

Violet stood staring at the closed door, feeling as if her future had somehow died as well.

Chapter 24

Monday morning, Violet rolled over with her eyes clamped shut when the alarm went off. She'd been finding it easier to get out of bed lately, finding herself actually looking forward to the days. But after last night, she had to face the fact that today held no promise.

She scooted closer to what had been Cade's side of the bed and hugged his pillow to her body, inhaling deeply. But only the clean scent of laundry detergent reached her nose. Cade's sea-spray scent had long since faded.

The fabric grew damp under her cheek as the ache that had been starting to fade reared again in all its brutal glory. Her insides burned with it. She needed Cade here. Needed his arms around her. Needed his hand cupped against the back of her head, stroking her hair and telling her it would all be okay. More than anything, she needed to talk to him, needed the closeness of having someone to share everything with.

She'd almost thought she was finding that again.

With Nate.

But it turned out that had been an illusion, wishful thinking.

What she'd had with Cade was a once-in-a-lifetime intimacy.

She wouldn't find it again with anyone else. So she would stop looking. Focus on the store, maybe get more involved in church, and forget she had almost dreamed of more.

As the alarm blared for a second time, Violet groaned but pushed the pillow away from her face and dried her eyes.

After dressing in sweats and pulling her hair into a messy ponytail, she sent Sophie a quick text asking if they could meet for breakfast. She'd been trying to let Sophie and Spencer adjust to married life without too many interruptions, but she really needed her best friend right now.

She tried not to dwell on the irony that she had always been the one to dispense relationship advice, not the one needing it.

Sophie replied with an immediate yes, and twenty minutes later, Violet was seated at their usual table at the Hidden Cafe, nursing a cup of coffee. The restaurant was bustling today, and every few minutes, someone stopped at the table to say hello. Violet thought she'd done a pretty good job of keeping up the happy pretense so far, but if one more person asked her how she was doing, she was going to bolt.

Fortunately, Sophie breezed through the door just as one of the older ladies from church spotted Violet. Violet gave the woman a quick wave, then got up to hug Sophie.

"Sorry it took me so long to get here." Sophie squeezed her lightly. "Spencer wanted my opinion on the gazebo he's building in the garden."

Violet ignored the pang that shot through her middle. It wasn't Sophie's fault that she was living in wedded bliss while Violet was fighting to get through the day.

"What happened to you guys last night? Is Nate okay?" Sophie let go and settled into her seat.

Violet shrugged. "I have no idea if he's okay." Her voice contained a bitterness that she didn't like to hear from herself. But she didn't know how to make it go away.

"What do you mean?" Sophie's face reflected genuine concern, and Violet realized once more how good moving back to Hope Springs had been for her friend. The hardness that used to keep her from opening herself to others had softened into a kindness that came out in everything she did.

"I mean he shut me out. I found him crumpled on the sidewalk, Soph, completely—" She searched for the word. "Broken." There was no other way to describe it. "But he wouldn't tell me what was wrong. I thought maybe it was because I tricked him into coming to the church."

"You tricked him?" Sophie's voice held a reprimand, but she couldn't be more disappointed in Violet than Violet was in herself.

"I know I shouldn't have." She pressed a hand to her heart. "It's just, he used to be in a Christian band and I thought—"

"He was in a band?" Sophie's mouth fell open.

"I know, hard to believe, right? But for some reason, he stopped going to church somewhere along the line. And I thought if I could get him inside a church, he might, I don't know—"

"Come back?"

Violet nodded. "But I don't think that was the only thing, Soph. I think it was—" She broke off in frustration. "I don't know."

"What makes you think it was more?" Sophie took the coffee the waitress handed her and added cream and sugar.

"Have you ever looked into his eyes?"

"I guess. They're blue, aren't they?"

"They're—" Violet stared out the window at the lake. "They're like the lake in a storm, all churned up and conflicted and almost . . . haunted."

She could feel Sophie watching her, but she couldn't return her gaze. Sophie had been close to Cade, too. What must she think about the fact that Violet had noticed another man's eyes?

"And he has scars," she continued. "One on his knee. And one across his chest."

Sophie's coffee cup clanked to the table harder than normal.

"I mean—" Violet's face warmed. "He had a nightmare that night we went to pick up the hutch. I went in to see what was wrong, and he had his shirt off, and he had a scar from here—" She touched her shoulder and drew a line diagonally across her chest. "To here."

"It sounds like—"

"And that's another thing." Now that she had gotten going, Violet couldn't stop. "That nightmare really shook him. But he couldn't tell me about it. Even though I told him about mine."

"You have nightmares?" Hurt flashed in Sophie's eyes for a second but then was replaced by concern.

Violet reached across the table to grab her friend's hand. "Not so much anymore. I wasn't trying to keep them a secret from you. I just didn't want to worry you when you had all the wedding stuff to deal with."

Sophie laid her other hand on top of Violet's. "I always want to know, Vi, no matter what's going on with me."

"I know." She'd been silly to keep the dreams from Sophie. She was still getting used to her best friend being here for her again.

"Anyway." Sophie gave her a gentle smile. "He may not have come out and *told* you a lot about himself. But he's let you learn a lot about him in other ways."

Violet gaped at her friend. What other ways were there?

"Think about it, Vi." Sophie took a long drink of coffee, watching her over the rim.

Violet fidgeted under her scrutiny. Okay, fine, she knew Nate liked cookies and that he claimed not to like antiques, though she was pretty sure she was bringing him around on that one. She knew he was kind and protective and loved his dog. She knew he had a big heart that he kept guarded most of the time. She knew he had problems with his family and with church. But that was the thing—she didn't know why.

"I get your point," she finally said. "But there are so many pieces missing. And he's not willing to fill them in."

Sophie looked thoughtful. "You know his *character*, Vi. That's not something to take lightly. The rest is just details. And maybe those details are too painful right now. Sometimes people's scars run so deep that they can't see the only way to heal them is to share them."

Violet turned that over in her mind. Nate did seem to be deeply scarred—not only physically but emotionally and spiritually.

"Be patient." Sophie's voice had a gentle quality. "If you're still there when he's ready, he'll tell you."

Violet ignored the strange looks from passing tourists as she speed walked toward Nate's office building. After saying goodbye to Sophie, she'd spent the entire morning walking around town. Walking and thinking.

And she'd realized that Sophie was right. It wasn't important for her to know all the details of Nate's life. What was important was that she *knew* him. Knew his heart.

And she'd come to care about him, much as she'd tried not to.

So she'd be patient with him. Wait for him to be ready to talk to her. And in the meantime, she'd give him the cookies she'd stopped at Peyton's bakery to pick up.

Their mouth-watering aroma drifted from the bag. Maybe she'd stay and eat one with him. If he wanted her to.

She paused in the building's entrance and read the small directory sign. Instead of slowing now that she'd stopped walking, her heart rate kicked up a notch. She pressed a hand to her stomach. It was silly to feel so nervous and excited to see Nate when she'd seen him every day for the past few weeks. But seeking him out at work felt like she was taking things a step farther.

A baby step, maybe.

But still a step.

According to the directory, Nate's office was on the second floor. She wandered down the hallway until she came to a staircase. She climbed it slowly to give her heart a second to calm down.

The second-floor hallway was empty, with two doors leading off it. Neither was marked. She passed the first—she couldn't picture Nate decorating with the big vase of fake flowers that stood outside it.

Inside the next office, a young woman sat at a reception desk. Violet startled. Nate had never said anything about having a receptionist, but then, he didn't talk about his work much, aside from the occasional updates on things with her lease. So far Talmadge had rejected every other property Nate had shown him. Which was why she had to figure out a way to make up the rest of the back rent she owed—and soon.

But she could deal with that later. For now, she just wanted to see Nate. To reassure him that his aloofness wasn't going to scare her away.

"Can I help you?" The receptionist was gorgeous, with blond hair that flowed in a sleek line to her shoulders and high cheekbones defined by perfect makeup. Violet ignored a pinprick of jealousy as she glanced at her running shorts and tried to tuck a stray curl into her messy ponytail.

"I'm looking for Nate Benson." She tried to keep her voice professional.

A young guy emerged from behind the wall that separated the reception area from the rest of the office. "His office is down the hall on the left side. The one with the big vase. But you might want to knock first. I think he's in there with his girlfriend."

Violet's heart faltered.

His girlfriend?

She worked to cover the shock she was sure showed on her face. "Thank you."

She slipped out of the room into the hallway, heart thudding dully against her ribs. Nate had a girlfriend?

The guy had to be wrong. Nate wasn't the kind of man who would string two women along.

Or was he? Maybe she knew him less than she thought she did. Which was barely at all.

She should just go.

But before she could take a step, the office down the hall opened, and Nate ushered a woman through it. Violet recognized her as the same woman who'd visited his apartment right after he'd moved in. He'd said she was a business associate.

But she was carrying a pizza box and a water bottle.

They were facing the other direction, and neither of them noticed her.

"You did not seriously do that." The woman's laugh carried down the hallway, and Violet's hand tightened on the bag of cookies.

"I promise you I did." His rich voice was warm and uninhibited. Unlike last night, when it'd taken all her effort to get two words from him.

"I'd better get going." The woman pulled her keys out of her purse. "Lunch was a brilliant idea, by the way. It was nice to have a few minutes to stop and eat for a change."

Nate laughed. "No problem. See you next time."

The woman set off down the hallway, and Violet stood frozen. She'd been stupid to come. Stupid to think anything was developing between her and Nate. She'd let her own loneliness convince her there was something there that wasn't. It wasn't that his past was too painful to share.

It was that he didn't want to share it with her.

So she'd wait until he went into his office and then slink away and enjoy the cookies herself at home. She tried to loosen her grip on the bag, but it slipped from her hands. The fall wasn't far, but the sound of the bag hitting the floor was enough to make Nate turn his head.

A smile lifted his lips, but it didn't reach his eyes, which were still guarded. Or rather, guarded again. She imagined they'd been plenty unguarded when he'd been talking to his "business associate."

"Hey." He strode toward her. "What are you doing here?"

He leaned forward as if he was about to hug her but then pulled back.

Violet tried to mask the hurt lancing her heart. He'd never offered her anything more than friendship. If she'd come to expect more, that was her own fault.

His eyes widened as they fell on the bag. "Are those cookies from Peyton's?"

She passed them to him. "Just my way of apologizing for dragging you to the concert last night."

She moved to step around him, but he laid a hand on her arm. "I'm the one who should be apologizing. I'm sorry for ruining the evening."

She shrugged. The best thing she could do right now was be indifferent. Or at least pretend to be. "It was no big deal."

Confusion and hurt clouded his expression as he studied her. He grabbed a cookie out of the bag and held it out to her.

"No thanks." She pushed past the outstretched cookie and sped down the hallway.

She couldn't stay here one second longer.

Chapter 25

Nate stared after Violet's retreating form. He must have done something wrong. But he had no idea what.

He took a bite of the cookie he still held in his hand, but he barely tasted it.

What did it mean that she'd sought him out like this? After last night, he'd been sure she'd never want to see him again.

He'd shown her his weakness. His most vulnerable side. And he'd noticed the hurt in her eyes when he'd refused to talk to her about it.

He'd left early this morning so he wouldn't have to run into her, wouldn't have to face her questions about why he'd had a minor breakdown over a concert of all things.

He took another bite of cookie, then dropped it into the bag. It was delicious as always, but he was too stuffed from the pizza he'd shared with Officer Jensen.

He drew up short outside his office door.

Was that what this was about? Did Violet think there was something going on between him and Officer Jensen?

That was ridiculous. But also . . . touching.

When was the last time anyone had been jealous for his attention?

Nate stood in the doorway, undecided.

Should he go after her, tell her she'd misunderstood who Officer Jensen was? But the moment he'd decided he should, another thought came crashing in to smash the plan. If he told her that, he'd have to tell her who Officer Jensen really was.

And he wasn't sure he was ready to do that.

He shuffled slowly into his office.

Maybe this was for the best anyway. He'd let his heart get too far into this already.

Worse, he'd let her heart get into it, too. He didn't deserve a woman like her, and he knew it. He should let things end before he risked hurting her more than he already had.

A part of him refused to agree, arguing that he owed it to her to tell her how he felt. To sweep her off her feet and promise he'd care for her forever.

That was the part he wanted to listen to.

But before he could follow her, the office phone gave the shrill ring Nate had come to despise.

He sighed, resigned. If that wasn't a sign that he'd been about to do the wrong thing, he didn't know what was.

He returned to his desk and picked up the receiver. Lately, Dad had only been calling every few days. Could be that he was starting to trust Nate again. Or could be that he was sick of hearing Nate's voice every day. It didn't really matter to Nate. Either way, not having to check in with Dad every day was a plus.

"Did you look at that clause yet?" Might as well get right to the point. Nate had sent Dad Violet's lease weeks ago, with the unclear clause highlighted, but so far Dad hadn't said what he was going to do about it.

"I had my attorneys look into it." Dad did not sound happy. "They agree that according to that clause, if they make up their back rent, they have until the end of this month to renew."

Nate allowed himself a brief fist pump. "Great. I'll take Talmadge out to a few more places, then. He wasn't willing to look at them before, but—"

"Slow up, Nathan." Dad's voice was controlled, as always. "Talmadge still needs to get into that building. Do you think these people—this Cade and Violet Somers—are going to make the back rent?"

"It's just Violet. Her husband Cade died a few years ago."

Dad was silent, and Nate took it as a sign that he didn't care.

"And, yes, I think there's a good chance she'll be able to make the back rent. She's more than halfway there already."

"That can't happen, Nathan." Dad's voice was hard. "Talmadge wants that spot, and he's going to get it, one way or another."

"If she pays the rent, you can't—" Nate forced himself to stop and take a swig from the water bottle on his desk. He needed a second to get control of the anger boiling low in his stomach.

"You're not hearing me, Nathan. Whether she pays the rent or not, whether she wants to leave or not, whether you're sleeping with her or not, she needs to be out of there."

Nate choked on his water. "Sleeping with her?"

"Talmadge told me what's going on. Said he saw you groping her in the middle of her store. I would have thought your family would have meant more to you than a few cheap thrills, but I guess some things never change."

Nate chomped down on his tongue, hard, and counted to ten before answering.

"First of all, we are not sleeping together." How dare his father imply that? "And I was not groping her. We're friends and I was giving her a hug."

"Frankly, Nathan," Dad continued as if Nate hadn't said anything, "I'm surprised you would jeopardize your chance to see your mother and sister like this. All for some—"

"Don't say it." Nate shoved to his feet, his voice hard and firm.

"Don't say what?" Dad feigned innocence.

"Whatever you were about to say, don't say it. Violet is a kind and wonderful woman, and I'm not going to sit here and listen to you drag her name through the mud."

"If you care about her that much, I'd suggest you convince her to find a new location for her store. Because she's going to be out of there one way or another come next month."

"Why?" Nate dropped into his chair and scrubbed a hand down his cheek. "Why does it have to be this spot?"

Dad didn't say anything for a minute, and Nate figured he wasn't going to deign to answer.

"It's the spot Talmadge wants. And he's offering a lot for it. I don't think I have to remind you that we have some pretty large medical bills to pay off. Or had you forgotten?"

Nate dropped his head to the desk. Of course he hadn't forgotten.

"When can I see them?" He didn't know how much longer he could stand not talking to his mom or his sister.

"Stop yanking Talmadge around to all these other properties he doesn't want and get this done. Then we'll talk."

"And if she pays her back rent? You won't be able to cancel the lease then."

"Don't play hardball with me, Nathan. We both know I could plow her under in court. She doesn't have the resources to pay her rent, let alone deal with court fees. You don't want things to get ugly."

Nate shook his head. He was pretty sure they already had. "So you're going to kick her out of there, regardless of what her contract says?"

Dad hesitated, then spoke slowly and deliberately. "I'm not. You are."

Nate's feet dragged across the sidewalk. Even though he'd walked as slowly as he could, he'd arrived at Violet's store way too quickly. He'd debated coming. After the way she'd fled his office earlier, she obviously didn't want anything to do with him. And he didn't come bearing good news.

But she deserved to know that he was running out of ideas to save her store.

He didn't want to tell her to give up. But what else could she do?

He let himself into the back door of the apartment building, taking a second to steel himself. The light was on in her workshop, so he pushed the door open. But she wasn't back there. He continued to the front of the store. His breath got caught halfway to his lungs the moment he saw her. She was sitting on that Victorian couch she loved so much, the one she'd told him she imagined a young couple had spent hours sitting on, just talking, learning everything there was to know about each other. Nate had recoiled from the idea. The thought of someone knowing everything about him was too terrifying.

But at the same time, he'd been filled with a strange sort of longing for that kind of closeness. Not with just anyone.

With her.

He directed a disgusted grunt at himself. She was the last person he deserved to have that kind of relationship with.

And he was the last person she'd want a relationship with. Especially if she knew the truth about him.

He cleared his throat and stepped into the room.

The moment she turned to him, her eyes widened with surprise and something more—like hope. But a second later, they darkened. She looked away. "I thought you were at work."

"I, uh—" Nate's voice had suddenly dried up, like a desert stream that had gone too long without rain. "Could we talk?"

She pressed her lips into a line but nodded.

He moved closer, remaining on his feet and keeping the low coffee table as a barrier between them. "First of all, I wanted to clear things up." He licked his lips.

She was watching him closely, but her expression was nearly blank. She didn't encourage him to go on, but she didn't stop him either.

"I just thought, ah—" Okay, this was going to be harder than he'd thought. "I mean, I wanted to say that the woman you saw at my office— I'm not—" Why was this so difficult? "I'm not seeing her. Or anything. She's a business associate. We had a working lunch."

Violet shrugged and looked away. "There's nothing to clear up. It's none of my business whether she's a business associate or—" She blinked. "Or something else."

Nate's heart shriveled to a dehydrated lump. Much as he knew she was better off without him, he wanted it to be her business. He wanted her to care. He wanted her to want to be the only one he cared about.

Because she was.

But he forced himself to nod. To say, "Good."

She got up and walked toward her desk. "I should get back to work. I'm swamped today."

Nate swiveled to take in the empty store. It was Monday, so she wasn't even open today.

"Actually—" He followed her. "There's something else."

When she turned, her eyes, usually so warm, were shuttered. "What is it?"

He swallowed. He'd do anything not to tell her this. But he didn't see any way around it. "I just spoke to my father. And I think you might need to start looking for a new space."

Her expression crumpled, but she didn't move, didn't make a sound.

"I'm sorry, Violet. I tried. I'm still trying. But this Talmadge guy isn't giving up, and for some reason my dad is determined to give him what he wants. I don't know—"

"It's fine." Her voice was strained but loud.

"I'll keep—"

"I said it's fine. I'll figure something out."

Nate took a tentative step closer, but she retreated. He dragged a hand through his hair. "Let me help, Violet. We have some other properties that might—"

"I said I'll figure something out, Nate. Thank you for letting me know." Her overly polite tone stabbed at him.

"Yeah, of course." He walked to the door.

When he reached it, he allowed himself a glance over his shoulder.

Violet was holding a small music box in her hands and didn't look up.

He let the door close behind him with a soft click.

Chapter 26

In spite of herself, Violet glanced toward the back door of the workshop. It was Friday, and she'd caught herself doing the same thing all week at this time. The time Nate used to come home from the office and stop by to talk.

She'd barely seen him at all since Monday when he'd told her she might as well give up, and she suspected he was avoiding her as much as she was avoiding him. On the few occasions they'd accidentally run into each other, they'd said hello or made a bland comment about the weather.

But nothing more.

Every word between them was stilted and formal now. Too polite.

Violet felt like a part of her—the part that had started to thaw—had frozen over again, more solid than ever.

She told herself it was for the best. If she'd let it keep thawing, it would only have hurt more when she fell through.

She turned her attention to the silver she was polishing. At least she could rub the tarnish off of some things.

A clang from the chimes drew a groan. She should be happy to have a customer, but it wasn't going to do a lot of good at this point.

Nate had as much as told her she was out of here after next month anyway. She didn't know if she had the energy to start her store again in a new location. Maybe it was time to give up Cade's dream. Even if it had become her dream somewhere along the line, too.

She gave the spoon one last rub, then wiped her hands and started for the front of the store.

But the moment she saw her visitor, she wished she'd run away instead.

Talmadge looked up from a display of muskets and gave her the smile that always made her think of a rodent. She held back a shudder. Something about the guy didn't sit right with her, but she nudged the feeling away. Just because he wanted the same property she wanted didn't make him a bad guy.

"Mr. Talmadge." Her voice wasn't exactly welcoming, but she worked hard not to sound rude. "How can I help you?"

Talmadge approached and held out his hand, as if he were greeting an old friend. She shook his reluctantly.

"Came to take some measurements. My designer needs them to draw up plans for my new space." His smile morphed into a leer. "I trust you'll have all this junk out of here by the time I'm ready to start work."

Goosebumps rose on Violet's arms, but she refused to flinch. "To my understanding, no agreement has been finalized. I'll be staying here until I receive word otherwise."

"Look—" Talmadge lowered his voice. "I don't know what your boyfriend has promised you. But let's just say, this space is going to be mine one way or another. You should take a hint and move out. Before anything forces your hand."

Violet drew back. Was that a threat? Something hardened in her gut. She wasn't going to let Cade's dream go to this man. Not if she could help it.

"I wouldn't get too comfortable here, Mr. Talmadge. I have a lease with Benson Properties, and I intend to hold them to it."

Talmadge's barking laugh bit against her ears, but she didn't move. He held up his tape measure. "You and your intentions can do what you want. I'm going to go take some measurements." He swaggered toward the workshop, still chuckling to himself.

Steam boiled through Violet's blood. Who did this guy think he was, marching into her store and treating it as his own? She was tempted to call the police, but she didn't want to let him know he'd gotten to her.

For half a second, she wished Nate would show up to rescue her. But then she reminded herself that Nate wasn't on her side anymore. He'd probably tell her Talmadge was right and she should start packing.

She prayed for the clock to move faster. In ten minutes, the store would be closed, and she could ask Talmadge to leave. She tried to sort through the day's mail, but she had no idea what she was looking at. Every few seconds, her eyes darted toward the workshop. She could hear him shuffling around back there, but she couldn't see him. And she wasn't about to give him the satisfaction of thinking she was curious about what he was doing.

Finally, with one minute to go before closing time, he emerged. "Got everything I need." His voice was jovial.

She gritted her teeth, eyes still on the mail.

But a second later, she had to look up as he invaded the space right next to her. She resisted taking a step back. She couldn't let him think he was intimidating her.

"This is the last time I'm going to say this. Make things easy on yourself and get out now. Believe me when I say you'll regret it if you don't."

"You'll forgive me if I decline." Violet pushed past him toward the front door. "Now, if you'll excuse me. My store is closed for the day, and I'd like to lock up."

"Of course." Talmadge offered an oily smile and followed her. Halfway to the front of the room, he stopped. "Almost forgot my tape measure."

Violet waited at the front door as he disappeared into the workshop again. Her teeth were clamped so tight, she was afraid her jaw would be locked like that forever. Half a minute later, Talmadge emerged, whistling and tossing his tape measure from hand to hand as if it were a baseball.

He winked at her as he passed through the door. "Have a good evening."

The moment his feet cleared the threshold, she slammed the door and twisted the lock. Then she stood for a moment, her breath heaving.

When she finally managed to walk away from the door, it was on shaky legs.

She had no idea what Talmadge thought he was going to do to get her out of the shop. But seeing him in here had convinced her: She wasn't going to give this place up without a fight.

Nate shut down his computer and shuffled toward his office door. He was a coward, and he knew it.

All week he'd been leaving for the office by six in the morning, long before Violet would be up. He'd been coming home after her store closed, too, slinking past her workshop like a kid sneaking in after curfew, just in case she was still there.

Every time he saw her was like a punch to the gut. A reminder of the life he couldn't have. He needed the distance to help him get over his feelings for her.

Not that it was helping.

Behind the scenes, he was still working to find a way to keep her in the store. But Talmadge had refused to look at the last three properties Nate had proposed to him. And he was getting impatient. The other day he'd threatened to hire movers to come and remove the pieces from Violet's store.

Nate had finally talked him out of it.

He was pretty sure.

The sigh that slipped out as he locked up his office building felt like it would never end. The late September nights had started to cool, and a light breeze blew in off the lake. It was a perfect night to share with someone special. Maybe at dinner. Or maybe a walk on the beach. Or just sitting side by side on a couch.

He picked up his pace.

He had to come to grips with the fact that he would never have that. He kept his head down and walked.

A sharp scent caught at his nose as he approached the back door of the apartment building. He inhaled, trying to place the smell.

Was that smoke?

He looked up and down the street but didn't see any signs of fire. Someone nearby could be grilling out. But the scent wasn't quite right for that.

He gave one last look around before opening the door. The odor hit him full force the moment he stepped inside, and panic flooded his system at the haze of smoke that hung over the stairs. Blood roared in his ears as his hand instinctively flew to cover his mouth and nose. His eyes watered as he swiveled, searching out the source of the fire.

There.

The workshop was supposed to have dim security lights, but it was pitch black now, aside from a faint orange glow in the far corner. Nate's heart kicked up another gear. There were all kinds of chemicals in the workshop.

Flammable chemicals.

And Violet's apartment was directly above it.

Not pausing to think, he tore up the stairs three at a time and rushed her door. But it was locked.

He pounded on it—hard. When she didn't come after a few seconds, he pounded again, then ran to Mrs. D'Angelo's door.

No one answered there, either.

"Come on!" Nate ran back to Violet's door, pounding until his hand throbbed.

The prayer came instinctively. *Please, Lord, let her be okay. Let her answer this door and get out of this building. I don't care what happens to me, but please save her.*

He waited a second, as if he actually thought God might answer his prayer this time.

But when the door still didn't move, he decided he'd have to take things into his own hands. He backed up three steps and charged the door.

He was half a step away from it when it opened, and he went careening through, right into Violet.

He managed to get an arm under her to soften the blow before they both hit the ground.

"Oof. Nate, what—"

"There's a fire. Downstairs." He pushed himself upright but had to stop to cough, and she watched him as if she thought he'd lost his mind. He waved her toward the door, but she didn't move.

He swallowed down the rest of his cough so he could talk. "You have to go. Get outside and call the fire department. I'll get Mrs. D'Angelo."

Her eyes widened in fear, and she scrambled to her feet. A slow stream of smoke had started to filter into the room. She reached a hand to help him up.

But he didn't want her help. He wanted her to get out.

He jumped to his feet. "Go, Violet, now." He grabbed her arm and dragged her into the hallway and toward the stairs, then turned to Mrs. D'Angelo's door.

He pounded on it with two hands.

When he stopped, Violet was right there next to him. "Get out, Violet. Now. Some of those chemicals are explosive."

Violet trembled, but she didn't move away. "Give me your keys."

"What?" But he knew what she was asking. And he wasn't going to let her stay here and risk her life for his dog. He'd get Tony in a minute. After he got Mrs. D'Angelo.

"I'm not leaving without you, Nate, so give me the keys so I can get the dog and you can get Mrs. D'Angelo, and we can all get out of here."

"Why do you have to be so stubborn?" But he was already digging the keys out of his pocket. They didn't have time to stand here and argue. The moment the keys hit her hand, Violet flew across the hall.

Nate gave one more pound on Mrs. D'Angelo's door. When she didn't answer, he barreled at it with his shoulder. It didn't budge. But on the second attempt, he got through.

There was more smoke in here than there had been in Violet's apartment, and he pulled his shirt up over his nose.

"Mrs. D'Angelo?" He ran through the apartment and into her bedroom. She was lying in the bed, eyes closed, and Nate's heart lurched. Had she been overcome by the smoke?

"Mrs. D'Angelo?" He shook her shoulder, but she didn't respond.

He slid one arm under her knees and the other behind her shoulders and lifted her, then careened through the apartment to the landing. The smoke was thicker now, and he fought to see through his watering eyes. "Violet? Tony?"

He moved toward his apartment, but a voice called from the bottom of the stairs. "We're down here, Nate. Get out."

He followed the sound down the stairs and into the night.

Chapter 27

Violet had never seen anything more beautiful than Nate emerging from the building carrying Mrs. D'Angelo. She ran to them and wrapped her arm around Nate's back, steering him to the grassy hill.

Nate laid Mrs. D'Angelo on the grass, and she dropped to the older woman's side. Tony hovered close to them.

Next to her, Nate gasped around coughs. "Is she—"

"She's breathing. And she has a pulse." Her heart eased a little as she felt the faint rhythm in Mrs. D'Angelo's wrist. "The fire department is on the way." Already sirens had cut through the quiet of the night, drowning out the crickets and the waves below.

Nate moved closer to kneel at her side, and they both stared toward the building. From out here, everything looked almost normal, aside from the smoke drifting out the back door. "How bad do you think it is?" she whispered.

A hand slid into hers and squeezed, and she leaned into him. Tony pressed up against her other side.

"It will be okay." His voice was hoarse, but its low rumble was reassuring. "Everyone's safe."

Violet nodded against his shoulder.

A second later, the first fire truck rumbled into the parking lot, an ambulance close behind it.

"Stay with her." Nate jogged toward the rig, where firemen were scrambling to roll out hoses and flip switches. With their equipment on, there was no way to tell if any of them were Jared or Ethan. Violet sent up a prayer for the firefighters' protection, whoever they were.

A few seconds later, Nate returned, along with two firefighters carrying a stretcher between them.

"It's going to be okay, Violet." She couldn't make out Ethan's face in the dark, but she recognized his voice, and a wave of reassurance washed over her.

As Ethan dropped to the ground next to Mrs. D'Angelo, Violet scrambled to get out of the way. Nate moved to her side. The arm he wrapped around her was solid and reassuring. She didn't care about anything else that had happened between them. Right now, she was grateful to have him here.

She bowed her head. She wasn't going to stop praying until this whole thing was over and all those firefighters were out of there safely. She'd meant to pray silently, but she couldn't stop the words from reaching her lips in a whisper. She half expected Nate to drop his arm once he realized what she was doing, but he only pulled her in closer.

After a few minutes, Ethan and the other firefighter lifted the stretcher with Mrs. D'Angelo. Her eyes were open now, and she had an oxygen mask over her face.

"Is she going to be okay?" Violet's voice shook. How would she live with herself if a fire that had started in her workshop took the dear old lady's life?

"We'll know more once we get her to the hospital, but I think so. I really should lecture you two about how you're supposed to get out and leave the saving others to us, but if she'd been in there much longer . . ." He grimaced. "What about you two? Did you inhale any smoke?"

Violet shook her head. "I'm fine. Nate inhaled a bunch, though. He was coughing and—"

"I'm fine." Nate cut her off. "Just get Mrs. D'Angelo to the hospital."

Ethan set off toward the ambulance. "I'll send someone over to examine you," he called over his shoulder.

As she watched Mrs. D'Angelo's still form, Violet's knees went weak. If Nate hadn't gotten them out . . .

She sagged against him, and he lowered her gently to the ground. "You okay?"

She tried to nod, but she was shaking all over now.

"You're in shock. Just a second." Nate passed her Tony's leash and jogged toward the fire trucks. Beyond the trucks, firefighters entered the building, hoses unwinding behind them. She prayed harder.

Nate talked with a firefighter standing next to the fire truck, then jogged back to her carrying a blanket. He wrapped it around her shoulders, then sat next to her and curled his arm around her, moving it up and down her back.

"Thank you." The words were way too small, but there was nothing else she could say.

His arm tightened around her, and she risked a look at his face. His teeth were clenched, but a muscle in his jaw jumped.

"I was in the shower. I had no idea there was anything wrong until I heard you pounding on the door. And then it took me a minute to get dressed." She glanced down, realizing for the first time that she was wearing her kitten pajamas.

"I'm sorry I knocked you down up there." Nate's voice was low. "When you didn't answer the door, I just . . ." That muscle in his jaw jumped again. "I was desperate to get to you."

She shuddered as all the emotions of the night washed over her. "How did you know there was a fire? Was there smoke in your apartment?"

"No. I just got home. I thought I smelled smoke when I was outside, but I couldn't place it. And then I opened the door and realized where it was coming from. I was—" His swallow was audible. When he finally finished the sentence, his voice was barely a whisper. "I was scared."

Violet angled so she could see him better. "But you ran into the building instead of out?"

His eyes met hers in surprise. "Of course I ran in. I wasn't scared for me. I was scared for you."

"Oh." Their eyes held, and her heart jumped. He had risked his life for her. Even after the cold way she'd been treating him all week. She'd been unfair. It wasn't his fault his dad was insisting on leasing the space to someone else.

She didn't know how long they sat like that, but she couldn't make herself look away. After a while, a paramedic came over, insisting that they be examined for smoke inhalation. Even as the paramedic listened to her lungs and examined her nose and throat, Violet couldn't take her eyes off Nate.

When they were finally given a clean bill of health, they walked hand-in-hand toward the fire trucks, where the firefighters were wrapping up their hoses.

One of the firefighters pulled off his helmet and approached them. As he got closer, Violet recognized him, and she let go of Nate's hand to run and hug Jared. "Thank you for being here."

He returned her hug. "The fire is out. It's not as bad as it looks. There's a lot of soot damage, but the structural damage is minimal. It looks like something was smoldering for quite a while before it flamed up. I'd say you caught it just in the nick of time."

Violet's heart jumped. If it weren't for Nate, she could be dealing with a whole lot more than soot damage. "What caused it?"

"Hard to say right now. We'll have an inspector check things out in the morning. In the meantime, you two are probably going to need somewhere else to stay tonight. Just until we can get someone in there to make sure everything is safe."

"Yeah, of course. Thank you again. I'm so glad you're all safe." She squeezed his arm, and he went back to help the crew finish cleaning up.

She pulled out her phone and dialed Sophie's number. She hated to intrude on her friends, but she knew Sophie would never forgive her if she sought help anywhere else.

As she lifted the phone to her ear, she turned to Nate. But he wasn't where she'd left him. She scanned the parking lot. He was at the far end, rounding the building into the narrow alley that led to the street, Tony following obediently.

Where on earth was he going? She set off after him at a run.

"Hi, Violet." Just the sound of Sophie's voice brought tears to Violet's eyes. She was so fortunate to have friends she could count on.

"Hey, Soph." She panted as she ran. "Can you hold on a second?"

"Sure. What's going on?"

But Violet lowered the phone as she closed the distance to Nate. He must have heard her footsteps because he turned toward her a few steps before she reached him.

"Where are you going?" The words came out in little gasps.

"Jared said we couldn't stay in the building tonight, so I figured I'd sleep at my office."

She stared at him with her mouth open. Was he kidding? The guy had saved her life, and he thought she was going to let him sleep in his office? "No one's sleeping in an office. You'll come stay at Spencer and Sophie's with me."

"But I—"

She held up a hand, then lifted the phone to her ear. The moment she told Sophie what happened, Sophie insisted that they both stay there.

"Let's go." She hung up the phone and grabbed Nate's hand, tugging him toward her car.

But his feet remained planted. "I couldn't expect them to do that."

Violet rolled her eyes. And he thought she was stubborn? "They want to do it, Nate. They're your friends. They care about you." She almost added, *I care about you.* But she managed to swallow the words at the last second.

There would be plenty of time to sort out her feelings for him later.

For now, they both just needed a place to sleep.

Chapter 28

"How'd you sleep?" Sophie passed Violet a cup of coffee, and Violet took it gratefully.

"Good, thanks." Better than she'd expected, actually.

Before she'd climbed into bed, thoughts about what could have happened and what would happen next had jostled for position of number-one worry. But the moment her head had hit the pillow, she'd been out.

And she'd begun her morning with a deep, long prayer about everything she had to deal with today.

She was as ready as she ever would be to handle whatever this day held.

"Is Nate up yet?" She tried to keep her voice casual, but the moment she looked at her friend, she knew she hadn't succeeded.

But all Sophie said was, "He's out in the shed with Spencer. I don't think he slept much."

Violet nodded and took another sip, but when she put the coffee cup down, Sophie was watching her.

"What?"

"Nothing." But the soft smile on Sophie's lips said it was something.

"Don't go getting any ideas, Soph. There's nothing going on between us."

Sophie laid a hand on her arm. "The man ran into a burning building to save you, Vi. That's not nothing."

Violet's whole body warmed. "He would have done that for anyone." But she couldn't deny that she'd thought the same thing. "Anyway, I can't really think about that right now. I want to get over to the store and see how bad things are."

"We're coming with you." Sophie dumped the last drops of her coffee into the sink and grabbed her keys. "Come on."

Violet didn't want to take her friends away from their day. But she couldn't say no. She was going to need all the support she could get.

As they stepped outside, Violet let herself pull in a breath of the fresh morning air.

The trees had taken on the brilliant hues of fall, and there was a bite to the air this morning, but she relished the feel of it in her lungs.

She should be depressed and scared after what had happened to her store.

But this morning, she felt blessed.

Blessed to be alive.

Blessed to have such amazing friends.

Blessed to have such an amazing . . . whatever Nate was to her.

It didn't mean seeing her store wasn't going to be hard. It didn't mean figuring out what to do next would be easy. But it did mean she knew she'd get through it, whatever happened.

Tony ran to greet them the moment they opened the door of the pole shed Spencer used as a woodworking shop. Violet crouched to pet him, her eyes searching the space until they found Nate.

He was bent in half, his head under a patio table Spencer had built. "That's some great craftsmanship."

The moment he stood, his eyes fell on her, and she could have sworn they brightened a shade. The light played on his face as he crossed the shed to her, accentuating his chiseled jaw, which was lined with stubble this morning.

It was a good look on him.

"Hey." He stopped just far enough away that Tony could stand between them. "How are you doing?" The concern in his eyes made her heart squeeze.

"I'm good." She squatted to pet Tony again, mostly to break the intensity of the gaze they shared.

"Violet." His voice was so quiet it made her look up. "How are you really?" He searched her face.

She stood and touched a hand to his forearm. "I promise. I'm good. When I take stock of what could have happened and what did happen—"

She swallowed past a fresh knot of emotion at the way God had spared them all. "I'm good."

He gave her an uncertain look but nodded.

"Should we go?" Sophie's voice from behind her made Violet jump. She'd almost forgotten that she and Nate weren't alone.

She made herself look away from Nate. "Yeah. I'm ready."

"Everyone else is going to meet us there. We should be able to make a good dent in the cleanup today." Sophie took Spencer's hand as they led the way out of the shed.

"Everyone else?" Violet stopped in her tracks. "I don't expect everyone to give up their day to do that."

Sophie waved off her comment, so she turned to Nate to protest.

But he smiled at her. "They're your friends. They care about you." She read in his eyes the words he left off—the same words she hadn't let herself say last night.

He cared about her, too.

Violet stared at the clothes iron the fire inspector held out toward her.

The initial shock of seeing her workshop covered with soot and partially destroyed hadn't worn off yet. And now he was telling her he thought the iron had started the fire.

"I don't understand how . . ." She spoke loudly to be heard over the industrial vacuum Dan was using to suck up soot particles.

The inspector passed her a piece of charred fabric. "This is all that was left, but I'd guess the iron was left on top of it, and the fabric smoldered for a while until it caught fire and spread." He gestured to the burned-out remains of a table, a bookshelf, two wicker chairs, and a shelving unit.

"But—" She tried to recall what she had ironed last. "I haven't used this iron in at least two weeks." She'd been working on a particularly stubborn set of drapes then, but they were on the sales floor now.

The inspector's brow furrowed. "It couldn't have been smoldering that long. Maybe you accidentally threw some fabric over it yesterday?"

Violet scrunched her face, trying to remember what she'd done yesterday. "I didn't touch any fabric yesterday. Actually—" She rubbed at the fabric in her hand. Through the char, she could make out a faint pattern of stripes. "This was on a roll on a shelf over there." She pointed across the room to where the rest of the fabric she used for reupholstering jobs rested on a shelf, all blackened by soot.

"You're sure?" The inspector's expression hardened.

"Absolutely sure. I haven't reupholstered anything in months."

Nate came over from where he'd been scrubbing soot off the walls with the special cleaning solution they'd picked up at the hardware store. "Is there anything else that could have caused it?" His voice was sure and firm, and Violet felt again the reassurance of having him near.

"Not that I've seen." The inspector grimaced. "I'll do some more digging, though."

Nate turned to Violet. "In the meantime, what do you want to do with these things?" He gestured to the blackened remains of the furniture that had been destroyed. "Is there any reason to save them?"

Violet shook her head. "No, they're not salvageable. But I should probably take some pictures first for insurance."

When they came to the burnt-through table where the inspector said he'd found the iron, Nate gave a low whistle. All that was left was a leg and half of a bottom support beam.

Violet frowned at the table. Why would she have put her iron here? She always used the ironing board Cade had built into the end of one of the shelving units. And she always put the iron away when she was done with it. Cade's tendency to leave out his tools had driven her crazy for that very reason.

An image of Talmadge rummaging around back here yesterday hit her, and she gasped.

"What's wrong?" Nate's head jerked up.

"Talmadge came in yesterday. He said he had to take some measurements back here."

Nate waited, obviously not picking up on where she was going with this.

"He said if I didn't move out of the store, I was going to regret it. I thought he wanted to intimidate me, but—"

"You think he did this?" Nate sounded incredulous.

"I don't know." She didn't particularly like Talmadge, but did she really think he would have burned down her store?

Nate dropped the table leg and moved closer to her, putting a hand on each of her shoulders. "That seems unlikely. Why would he destroy a building he wants to move into?"

Violet bit her lip. She had to admit it didn't make a lot of sense, but something about the way Talmadge had acted yesterday stuck in her gut.

"Or maybe he was trying to destroy some of my inventory. Make me give up. I'm telling you, he was ready to do whatever it took to get in here."

Nate scrubbed a hand over his face. "Okay. We should at least mention this to the fire inspector. And I'll talk to my dad. We'll get to the bottom of this. I promise."

Nate threw the table leg in the back of Spencer's pickup truck, then edged around the building and pulled out his phone. He didn't want Violet to stumble on this conversation. Not until he was sure.

He hated to think his dad was capable of it, but he had to ask.

The phone rang five times, and Nate was starting to contemplate what kind of message to leave, when someone picked up.

"Hello?"

He sucked in a sharp breath at his mother's voice and blinked back the heat behind his eyelids. He pressed his forearm to the building's brick wall and rested his head against it.

He could barely speak through the well of emotion building from his core. "Mom," he managed to croak.

"Nate?" Mom's voice sounded unsure.

He sniffed and cleared his throat. "Yeah, Mom, it's me." He swallowed past the burn. "It's so good to hear your voice."

"Yours, too." He could hear the tears behind her words.

"Mom, I'm so sorry, I never—"

But she was talking over him. "Where are you?"

He paused. What did she mean, where was he?

Before he could answer, he heard his father's voice in the background, followed by a low murmur from his mother.

"Mom?"

"I thought I told you not to call your mother. Do you have that much trouble following simple directions?" Dad's voice was as uninviting as ever.

Nate stiffened. "I wasn't calling to talk to her. I was calling to talk to you." Anger drew him up taller, as if he were face-to-face with his dad instead of hundreds of miles away. "What did you do to Violet's store?"

"First of all, you'd do well not to talk to me like that. And second, what are you talking about? I told you I was going to get her out of there. And that's what I'm doing."

"By having her building set on fire?" Nate was practically yelling, and he lowered his voice so no one would overhear. "She could have died." He could have died, too, for that matter. But he didn't bring that up. It wasn't like Dad would care anyway.

"Why I what?" The shock in Dad's voice was unmistakable, but Nate wasn't convinced.

"Don't play dumb, Dad. Were you after the insurance payout? Or was this all to get Talmadge what he wanted? Because either way, you failed. The fire is out, and Violet still has a store."

"Nathan. Have you been drinking again? You're not making any sense."

Nate closed his eyes and clutched the phone tighter. There was no *again*. He'd only had alcohol one time in his life. "So you're saying you didn't know there was a fire at Violet's store last night? The store she happens to live above. And so does a sweet old woman, who is now in the hospital with smoke inhalation." He broke off but then decided he might as well go for broke. "Oh, and so do I, by the way. In case you care about the fact that you almost killed your son. Whether you still want to call me that or not."

"Nathan, I didn't— I don't know what you're talking about. You're saying there was a fire at the property Talmadge wants?"

"Yes." Nate bit the word off. He could only take so much more of this game.

"But everyone is okay? You're okay?" Was that genuine concern in Dad's voice?

Nate hardened his heart. He wasn't going to fall for that. "Like I said, Mrs. D'Angelo is in the hospital. But she'll be okay. Violet is okay, although the back of her store is pretty damaged. It could have been a lot worse if I hadn't happened to come home when I did. Her apartment is right above where the fire was."

"And you're okay?" Dad repeated.

"I'm fine." Nate clamped his teeth together. He would not convince himself Dad cared. Not this time.

Dad's exhale crackled over the phone. "And you really think I had something to do with this?"

"Did you?"

"Of course not! For Pete's sake, Nathan, I'd think you'd know that without asking. Why would I set fire to my own building?"

"You were pretty adamant the other day that she had to be out of there one way or another."

"I meant that I was sending an eviction letter for you to sign and give to her. Not that I was going to commit a felony. I leave that to you."

There it was.

Nate had known they wouldn't be able to get through a conversation without his past coming up. He forced himself not to react. "Do you think Talmadge could have done it?"

"What makes you think someone *did* it? Couldn't it have been an accident?"

"Maybe." Nate had to concede that. Violet's theory that someone had used an iron to burn down the store seemed pretty far-fetched. "But Violet is sure the iron that caused it was unplugged and put away, so someone had to get it out. And Talmadge was the last person in the store before she closed yesterday."

Dad snorted. "That's thin. She's probably afraid she won't get the insurance payout if she admits it was her fault."

"She's not like that, Dad."

"Everyone's like that for the right price."

Nate shook his head. This was going nowhere. But he needed to ask one more thing before he hung up. "Could I talk to Mom for a few more seconds? Please."

"You already know the answer to that."

NOT UNTIL YOU

"Does she even know where I am? Have you even told them where you've banished me?"

Instead of answering, Dad hung up.

Chapter 29

Nate wrung the sooty water from his sponge and attacked the wall yet again. Violet had sent everyone else home two hours ago, but he'd insisted he wasn't leaving until she did.

She'd wanted to argue. He could see it in her eyes. But he'd picked up his sponge and gotten back to work, and a minute later she had fallen in beside him.

He wished she didn't have to go through any of this, but he had to admit that it was comfortable working together. Neither of them said much, but that was okay. Somehow, they seemed to be sharing something deeper.

"Phew." Violet dropped her sponge into the bucket and swiped the back of her wrist across her forehead. Nate grinned as her efforts to keep her face clean failed. A light stripe of soot crossed her face. He resisted the urge to wipe at the smudge only because his own hands were even dirtier.

"I'm hungry. How about you?" Her smile went right through him.

He didn't understand how someone who'd been through everything she'd been through in the past twenty-four hours could come out of it smiling like that.

"I could eat."

"Hidden Cafe? My treat?"

There was no way he could say no when she looked at him like that.

"We should probably change first." He pointed to her t-shirt, which had been the lightest shade of pink this morning but was now tinged gray.

Fortunately, they'd been given the all-clear to return to their apartments. And it sounded like Mrs. D'Angelo would be able to come home tomorrow.

Twenty minutes later, Nate had showered and changed and was ready to go. Unlike the first time he'd knocked on her door to go to dinner with her friends, he wasn't the least bit nervous this time. Being with Violet felt more natural to him now than being without her ever had.

When she didn't come to the door right away, he opened it a crack. "Violet?"

"I need ten more minutes," she called from the back of the apartment. "Come on in."

Music filtered to the living room as he stepped through the door, and he found himself humming along without the pang he usually felt. He moved to the couch and patted his back pocket. She may think she was treating, but she was wrong about that. Except his wallet wasn't there.

"Hey, I think I left my wallet down in the store. I'm going to grab it. Be right back."

He jogged down the steps and into the workshop. They'd made good progress today. She'd probably be able to reopen the store in a day or two. For the hundredth time, Nate was swamped by the staggering reality of how much worse it could have been. Of what could have happened. He could have lost Violet. Every time he thought about it, his body had a visceral response, his chest tightening, his throat catching.

But he hadn't lost her.

She was still here. Still alive. And still in one piece.

He couldn't pretend he hadn't prayed for that. Couldn't pretend God hadn't heard him. Couldn't pretend God hadn't answered.

But he didn't know what to do with that information. So he pressed it down and pushed it to the back of his mind. He could process it later. Or not. One answered prayer didn't necessarily mean he and God were all good again.

He grabbed his wallet off the workbench where he'd left it this morning and turned to go, but something made him stop. He moved toward the sales floor. He didn't know exactly where he was going until his feet stopped in front of it.

The Bosendorfer.

He stared at it. It was a beautiful piece, rounded in all the right places, the keys gleaming and just crying out for someone to play them.

But it couldn't be him.

He'd promised himself.

Still, he found himself settling onto the bench and resting his fingers on the keys. Their cool smoothness tingled through his fingertips. All he'd have to do was apply the slightest pressure.

Nate closed his eyes, letting the silent war between his fingers and his brain rage.

His fingers won out.

A G minor chord resonated across the shop, and something stirred in his soul.

He tried a few more chords. It felt right and wrong at the same time to be playing again.

But this was the language of his heart. His soul.

He adjusted himself on the bench and brought both hands to the keys, picking out the first notes of a song he'd written years ago. It was the song that had brought his band to the attention of the record producer, but that's not why he played it.

He played it because it was the song that expressed the deepest longing of his heart, a longing to know that he was loved unconditionally, a longing to know that whatever he had done, God had prepared a place for him. He couldn't deny that he'd felt that longing again lately. But he hadn't known how to soothe it.

Now, he closed his eyes and let the words of the song do what nothing else could. As he sang, a slow trickle of relief flowed over him.

He let the chords carry him, let the song lift him until he didn't know where he was anymore.

Violet swiped on a light layer of lip gloss and emerged into the living room, still humming along to the music she'd just turned off. Today had been hard, there was no denying that.

But her friends had made it easier. They'd dropped everything and spent all day getting soot-covered and dirty to help her.

Especially Nate. He could have walked away. He could have said it was her problem. But he'd stayed, long after she'd insisted he leave.

"Okay, I had to wash my hair three times to get rid of the smoke smell, but I'm finally ready." She stopped as she entered the living room. It was empty.

She glanced around the apartment, but unless Nate had decided to play an epic game of hide and seek, he wasn't here. He'd said he was going to run downstairs to grab his wallet, but that had been at least ten minutes ago.

She grabbed a light coat from the hook next to her door and stepped into the hallway. "Nate?" Had he gone back to his apartment to wait? But when she knocked there, all she heard was a faint snuffling from Tony.

She started down the steps. No one had worked harder than him in the workshop today—maybe he'd gone back to it. Though she hoped not, since then he'd have to clean up again, and she was starving.

The moment she opened the workshop door, the lingering smell of smoke hit her nose. But that wasn't what stopped her in her tracks. A rich melody filtered to her from the front of the store.

The song was somehow familiar even though she'd never heard the words before. She stepped into the workshop and followed the music toward the sales floor. She knew exactly where it was coming from.

After a few more chords, a deep male voice joined the lilting music.

Violet's hand lifted to her heart.

She'd never heard Nate sing before, but that was his voice.

She inched closer, afraid if he heard her, he'd stop. Finally, she came to the alcove where the piano had sat for so long.

Nate's eyes were closed, and his face wore an expression she couldn't place. He bowed his head as he began to sing another verse.

Can your love really be so great, so vast
Can you really love me, no matter my past
No matter my future, or who I am right now
Are you the one I need, or are you a dream somehow
An ache in my heart that will never cease
Or the one who can fill me—fill me with peace?

The song drew her closer, but she bumped against a floor lamp that let out a metallic clang.

Nate's eyes snapped open, but his fingers continued to play over the keys.

His eyes latched onto hers and didn't let go.

Violet couldn't look away.

It was as if her soul was being tugged up from all the layers of grief and pain she had cradled it in the past three years.

She felt raw and exposed and yet also alive.

As Nate's voice picked up the song again, she was drawn closer to him, until she stood only steps in front of him. His eyes were still locked on hers.

Every part of her body seemed to sing with the connection between them.

After another minute, Nate's voice grew quiet and dropped out. The piano, too, softened, then faded.

And still their gaze remained locked.

Violet felt the steady in and out of her breath. Felt the slow thump of her heart.

Finally, she dragged her eyes from his, down to the piano. "You wrote that?" The song had been so raw, so open. Not at all how she thought of Nate.

There was something in his smile she couldn't place—longing, maybe?

"A long time ago."

Something in his voice tugged her closer, and he slid over as she moved to sit on the piano bench next to him. She lifted her hands to the keys. "Can you teach me?"

He watched her fingers for a second, then moved his hand slowly to touch hers, shaping her fingers to the keys. The simple connection of their hands made her feel more awake than she had in years. He pressed gently on her thumb until a note rang out. "C," he said.

He moved to the next finger. "D."

After he'd run through a scale, he lifted his hand off of hers. "We should probably get that dinner now."

She swallowed. Nodded. But neither of them moved.

His head tipped closer, and Violet's heart went wild. He was going to kiss her.

She should turn her head, run, move out of the way. But she didn't want to. She wanted to know what his lips would feel like on hers.

She waited, her breath caught in her lungs.

After a second, Nate slid off the bench. "You were starved an hour ago. You must be famished by now."

He threaded his way through the displays toward the back room. By the time Violet caught up, she'd almost managed to convince herself that it was for the best that they hadn't kissed.

Almost—but not quite.

Chapter 30

The wind cut through Nate's coat, but he didn't care. The weather may have darkened as they'd entered October, but his days had brightened. Ever since that night on the piano bench when he and Violet had been within heartbeats of kissing. He'd kicked himself a thousand times for pulling away. Even if he knew it was what was best for Violet.

In the week since then, he'd been looking for another opportunity to bring his lips to hers. But though they spent nearly every second he wasn't at work together, he hadn't found the right moment yet. He wanted it to be perfect. And he was willing to wait to find that.

She'd invited everyone over for dinner tonight, and he'd promised to help get things ready. Not that he had any idea how to cook, but that didn't matter. He wasn't going to pass up any chance to spend time with her. He'd been foolish enough to waste those opportunities before. Not anymore.

He jogged up the stairs and found Mrs. D'Angelo just emerging from her apartment.

"Hey, Mrs. D. Thanks again for the pie." He patted his stomach. "Though I probably shouldn't have eaten it all in one night."

Only a day after she'd returned from the hospital, Mrs. D'Angelo had brought him an apple pie to thank him for saving her. He'd been embarrassed and yet at the same time, filled with a sense of something larger than himself.

"You're welcome, dear." Mrs. D'Angelo gave him her crinkly smile. She reminded him of his own grandma, and the longing for his family that always hovered in the background flared up.

"God sure knew what he was doing when he brought you to Hope Springs." Her voice was scratchy from the smoke she'd inhaled, but her words were clear.

Nate froze. He could admit that perhaps God had answered his prayer to save Violet. But it wasn't God who had brought him to Hope Springs. It was his own mistakes. "Actually, I moved here to work for my father."

Mrs. D'Angelo shook her head. "That might be the circumstance that brought you here. But do you really think God didn't have a bigger purpose in mind? Look what he's done with you since you've been here. Don't think I haven't seen how you've changed in the past two months. You're not the same surly, feeling-sorry-for-himself man you were then."

"I—" But Nate had no response to that. He wasn't sure if he was supposed to take it as an insult or a compliment.

"God has softened your heart, young man." Mrs. D'Angelo stooped to pick up the paper on her welcome mat. "And if I'm not mistaken, he's used your Violet to do it." She winked at him.

Nate opened his mouth to protest, but by the time he'd come up with a response, she'd already disappeared into her apartment.

"She's not my Violet," he finally whispered to the empty hallway.

He moved slowly to Violet's door and knocked, still contemplating Mrs. D'Angelo's words.

Violet opened the door, greeting him with the warm smile he'd come to love.

There she is. He couldn't stop the thought. *My Violet.*

"Hey." Violet resisted the urge to hug Nate the moment he stepped into her apartment. Much as she wanted to feel his arms around her, she'd never greeted him with a hug before, and it'd be weird to start now.

"Hey." Nate's answering smile made her stomach flutter. She could step closer right now and just kiss him. There was no use pretending she hadn't been thinking about doing just that every moment since they'd almost kissed on the piano bench last weekend.

But he clearly hadn't been ready, and she didn't want to scare him off.

"So, you ready to cook?" She wiped her hands on her apron, more to have something to do with them than because they were dirty.

"As long as you tell me exactly what I need to do." He gave her a self-conscious look. "I may have neglected to mention that I'm not exactly a top chef."

"That's okay." Violet led the way to the kitchen, that nervous fluttering in her stomach still in full force. "I'll go easy on you. You can make the graham cracker crust for the cheesecake."

She passed him a package of grahams. "The food processor is over there." She pointed to its spot in the corner of the kitchen counter.

"Um, okay. Do you have a recipe?"

Violet grabbed a spoon from the antique juice pitcher that held her kitchen utensils. "You're kidding right?"

Nate was staring at the package of graham crackers as if they were a grenade that might explode in his hand.

She couldn't hold back a laugh. "Okay, you weren't kidding. Haven't you ever made a graham cracker crust?"

Nate passed her the grahams. "Literally, the extent of my kitchen experience involves pushing buttons on the microwave."

She opened the package. "Didn't you ever help your mom in the kitchen?" It was a dangerous question, she knew. He always shut down when she asked about his family. But she'd found herself wanting to know everything about him lately, from how he preferred his eggs to what his family was like.

"Not really."

Violet looked up at the edge in his voice, trying not to show her surprise that he'd volunteered even that much information about his family.

"Why not?" She dropped the grahams into the food processor, waiting for him to change the subject like he did every time things turned personal.

"My parents were very traditional. He worked. She took care of the house and cooked. I guess she figured I'd get married and have that kind of relationship, too." He rubbed his chin.

Violet stilled as she listened. "And is that what you thought, too?"

Nate looked toward the window. "I suppose at one time it was." He shook himself a little. "Anyway, that was a long time ago. It's about time I learned how to make something other than a frozen dinner. Teach away." He gestured to the food processor.

Violet watched him a moment longer. He'd ended the conversation but not before revealing more about himself and his life than he ever had before. His face wore a trace of the vulnerability he'd allowed himself to show. It made her want to reach up and touch his cheek.

"Now, you process them, until they're fine crumbs." She pointed to the controls on the food processor and stepped aside to let him do it as she picked up the mixer and turned her attention back to the filling.

As she switched the mixer on, she heard the steady whir of the food processor. He'd done it—taken his first steps into the world of cooking.

A second later, a gritty dust of graham spattered Violet's arms and rained down onto her head.

She spun, lifting the beater out of the bowl as she did.

Cheesecake filling joined the graham crumbs cavorting in the air. A glob splattered her cheek, and another landed smack in the middle of Nate's chest.

Violet gasped and quickly switched the mixer off. But graham pieces were still dancing in the sunlight.

"Turn it off," she shouted to Nate over the sound of the food processor.

"How?" Nate looked like a panicked deer.

Violet reached past him and flipped the switch to off.

In the sudden silence, they stood staring at each other.

A dusting of grahams covered Nate's shirt, which had a blob of filling right over the heart. Another, smaller dollop of filling perched on his shoulder like a flat parrot.

Violet could feel the sticky cream cheese slipping down her own cheek. She lifted a hand to wipe it away.

Nate started laughing first, but it was only half a second before Violet gave in, too. Soon, they were both letting out deep belly laughs, holding the counter for support. Every time Violet slowed down, she took another look at Nate and was attacked by another fit of giggles.

Finally, her sides hurt too much to laugh anymore.

She wiped her eyes as Nate's laughter slowed, too.

"How'd I do?" he asked innocently.

"Perfect. That's exactly what was supposed to happen." Violet raised a hand to her hair, shaking out pieces of graham, then grabbed the towel off her shoulder to wipe the rest of the cheesecake away. She passed it to Nate so he could wipe up his shirt as she grabbed the broom.

"How have you survived this long on your own?" Violet teased as she worked. Her face hurt from all the smiling, but it was worth it.

"No one's ever tried to kill me with exploding graham crackers before."

"Yeah, usually we put the cover on the food processor before we turn it on. I haven't seen your technique before."

Violet set the broom aside and surveyed the room. The counter was covered with crumbs, but that would be easy enough to clean up. The bigger problem was that she had no more grahams to make a crust. "Guess we'll have cheesecake filling for dessert. We'll call it a cheesecake mousse."

"Sounds fancy."

"Oh, yeah, totally five-star." Violet returned his grin as her eyes fell on the blob of cheesecake still sitting on his shoulder. She grabbed the towel from his hand and instinctively wiped at the spot.

Only when his shoulder jumped under her touch did Violet realize what she was doing.

But she didn't stop.

She didn't want to.

Under her hand, his shoulder was firm. Solid. Strong.

"Violet." His voice was low, slightly strangled.

She raised her eyes to his.

They were burning with something she couldn't name.

Something she could only feel.

Her hand stilled on his shoulder, but she didn't drop it.

"You have a little . . ." He raised a hand to her cheek. The feel of his fingers against her skin made her forget everything else.

His hand lingered, his thumb trailing back and forth slowly over her skin.

NOT UNTIL YOU

Violet closed her eyes and lifted her chin, leaning toward him.

The air between them grew thick.

Violet's hand tensed on his shoulder.

His thumb stopped moving as he pressed his palm into her cheek, drawing her closer.

Violet sighed as his breath brushed her lips.

Her heart had run away with her, and she didn't care.

She wanted to feel his lips on hers.

Her whole body tingled as time slowed down.

She could feel him millimeters away.

And then there was a knock on the door.

Chapter 31

Nate jumped back, dropping the hand that had been pressed to Violet's smooth cheek.

Violet looked flustered, and she smoothed her shirt as she strode toward the door.

Moving deliberately in an effort to get his still-hurtling heart under control, Nate grabbed a rag and brushed the graham cracker crumbs from the counter into his hand.

He heard voices at the door, and then Sophie was greeting him with a hug. "Violet's been bragging about your excellent cooking skills. Can't wait to try your graham cracker floor pie."

Nate grinned. He loved how this group could make him feel instantly at ease. "Yes, and did she tell you about her course of cheesecake filling a la shirt?" Nate winked, and Sophie burst out laughing.

Violet joined in, too, the joy in it stirring Nate's heart. Her laugh had become one of his favorite sounds.

"All right, fine, you got me. We make quite a team." She smiled at him, and Nate's heart fumbled. They did make a good team.

"At least dinner itself isn't a bust." Violet pulled a pan of lasagna from the oven. "I didn't let Nate help with that."

As everyone filled their plates, Nate just watched. If anyone had asked him two months ago if he planned to make friends and become part of the community here, he'd have slammed the door on them. But this group had welcomed him in, no questions asked, and they made him feel like he was one of them. Like he belonged.

The apartment was too small for the number of people in it, but it didn't feel cramped. It felt warm and inviting. The small kitchen table was full, and people sat on the couch and the lone chair in the living room. Nate waited until Violet was settled, then moved to sit next to her on the floor in front of the coffee table.

He folded his hands as the others prepared to say grace. To his surprise, he looked forward to it.

Violet's inviting voice lifted over them. "Dear Lord, thank you for bringing us together tonight for good food and even better friendships. Thank you for giving us one another, that we may celebrate our joys and share our burdens and that we may serve as reminders to one another of the perfect love you have for us. In Jesus' name. Amen."

"Amen," Nate murmured. Her prayer had made him unexpectedly emotional, and he had to keep his eyes closed for an extra second.

"You okay?" Violet leaned close enough that her shoulder brushed against his. "You seem like you're—" She gestured in that cute way she always did when she was looking for a word. "Somewhere else, I guess."

The smile he gave her was genuine. As hard as he'd tried to keep a lock on his heart, she'd broken right into it. "I'm here." He bit into his lasagna. "And this is delicious."

When he looked up, Sophie caught his eye. She shot him a conspiratorial wink, and his face warmed.

After dinner, the friends ate cheesecake "mousse" by the bowlful before Violet suggested a game of charades. Nate groaned. He didn't understand the appeal of a game in which you had to make a fool of yourself in front of others.

But he ended up having a great time, acting out the game-winning charade of Snow White by pretending to be every one of the seven dwarfs. Violet made the winning guess, sealing the victory for their team, and he scooped her into a hug without thinking. She squeezed back, burying her face in his neck for a moment. He could have stayed like that all night, but he made himself let her go. When she pulled away, her cheeks were flushed, and her eyes sparkled. He almost moved in for a kiss right then and there. But the room full of their friends stopped him.

After a while, Sophie started to yawn. Spencer wrapped a protective arm around her shoulders. "Time to get my wife home to bed. Thanks for everything, Violet."

An attack of longing hit Nate as he watched the newlyweds. He wanted to have that closeness with a woman. To know that she trusted him completely. And that he would never do anything to break that trust.

The rest of the group followed shortly after Spencer and Sophie. Nate knew he should go, too.

He wasn't sure he could trust himself not to do something stupid if he was alone with Violet. Like act on his growing desire to kiss her.

But his eyes fell on the small mountain of dirty dishes in the kitchen. He couldn't leave her to clean everything up alone.

"Do you prefer to wash or dry?" he asked, leading the way to the kitchen.

"Oh, you don't have to—"

"I helped make the mess, didn't I? With my gourmet cooking skills?" He grabbed a dish rag and a towel, holding both up so Violet could choose which she'd rather use.

She weighed the options for a minute before grabbing the dish rag. "This way I get done first and get to watch you slave away while I relax," she explained, drawing an unexpected laugh from him. He loved how she could do that.

They worked side-by-side in silence for a while, the only sound the clanking dishes.

Just as the sounds were starting to lull him toward drowsiness, Violet spoke abruptly. "Nate, are you a Christian?"

Nate studied the plate he'd been drying, then set it on the stack next to him, cringing as it clattered more loudly than he'd intended. He hadn't expected the question, and he wasn't sure how to answer it.

He set the towel down and leaned against the counter.

Violet dropped her rag into the water and turned to face him.

"I used to be," Nate said slowly. "I mean, I grew up Christian, went to a Christian college, was in a Christian band."

He glanced at Violet, then let his gaze flit away at her earnest expression.

"But that was a long time ago," he continued. He couldn't bring himself to look at Violet. He knew how important her faith was to her and that she'd likely be disappointed—maybe even angry—that he didn't feel that way anymore.

"And now?" Violet's voice was low but not judgmental. She simply sounded as if she wanted to know him better.

"If you had asked me a month ago, I would have told you in no uncertain terms that I had no use for God," Nate said. "But in the last few weeks, I've felt this—" He didn't know how to put it into words. "I don't know—this pull."

Like maybe God was trying to call him back—but he wasn't sure how to say that without sounding crazy. "I guess I would say I'm open to the possibility of God again."

Violet nodded, seemingly satisfied. "I don't know what I would have done without my faith after I lost my mom and Cade and everyone important to me," she said softly.

Abandoning the few remaining dishes, she led him to the living room, and they settled on the couch. She angled her body toward him but looked lost in her own thoughts.

He lifted an arm and slid it behind her shoulders. He wanted to pull her close and make everything she'd gone through all better, but he knew only too well that wasn't the way it worked. "Do you mind if I ask what happened? With your family, I mean? You said you don't have one anymore."

Violet tucked a stray curl behind her ear. "I don't mind." Her voice was soft. "My dad left when I was a little girl. I barely even remember him, really, and I never knew his parents. I remember my mom's parents. They were great. They lived down South, but whenever they came to visit, they'd take me to the Chocolate Chicken for ice cream." A slight smile played over her lips. "But they both died when I was in middle school. First my grandma, and then my grandpa a couple months later. And my mom—" She blew out a quick breath. "She died when I was in college—"

"I'm so sorry." Nate rubbed her shoulder. "That must have been awful." He could barely handle not having seen his mom in years, but at least he knew she was still alive.

Violet tilted her head to the side so that it almost rested on his arm. "It was hard. I was the older sister, and I tried to take care of Jade, but I was pretty wrapped up in Cade and our plans for the future at the time. I should have done more. Maybe she would have stayed."

"Where'd she go?" He ached to pull her in closer but resisted. He needed to let her talk about this.

"She decided she wanted to be an actor. Never mind that she'd never been in so much as a school play in her life. I tried to talk her out of it, but she thought I was trying to hold her back. She took off for L.A. the day after her high school graduation." Violet directed her eyes to her lap. "I haven't talked to her since." Her voice was small and nearly broken.

"You've tried. I've seen you." She had to realize that none of this was her fault.

"I know. I just feel like there must have been something more I could have done. But then I got married and we got busy with the antique store and everything was a rush. Until—"

She broke off, and her throat bobbed as she swallowed.

"Until Cade died," he finished for her.

She nodded, blinking rapidly as moisture collected on her lashes. "Sometimes I feel like everyone I've ever cared about has left me. I've spent days—years, really—praying that God would help me understand why he's taken all these people from me."

"And did he answer you?" Nate leaned closer, finding he needed to know the answer more than he wanted to admit.

She managed a wavery smile. "He showed me that he was in control even in all of these losses. That he's bigger than I am and stronger and that he has a plan for me even in this."

"How can you believe that?" Nate wanted to understand. Wanted to believe she was right about God. But how could he place his faith in a God who would allow this amazing, generous woman to suffer like this? "How do you know it's not that he doesn't care about you and what happens to you? About what happened to your mom and Cade and everyone else you love?"

Instead of giving him the flippant answer he expected, Violet considered his words. When she spoke, her voice was firm. "Only the Holy Spirit can give me that kind of faith." She touched her heart. "It's something I know here, in my inmost soul. And some days I have to fight to remember it, but he always brings me back to the truth that his love for me is even greater than my mom's was, than Cade's was, greater than anyone's ever could be. And if he says that he's working for my good in all things, I trust that."

"Easy as that? You just trust?" If that was the case, Nate was doomed. He'd never be able to trust that easily.

Violet blew out a breath that rustled her hair. "It's not easy, believe me. My sinful nature keeps trying to heap the doubt back on me. That's why I spend so much time in prayer and in his Word. It's the only way I get through the day."

Nate had felt that way once, a long time ago. He'd felt like Jesus was his best friend, like he could tell him anything. But those days were long past. Much as he might wish for that kind of closeness again.

"Would you like to pray together?" Violet's voice was tentative, like she wasn't sure if he'd explode at the question.

A few months ago, he would have.

But tonight, he felt a crack in the armor he'd built up to protect himself from ever getting hurt by God again. Tonight he could see that maybe it wasn't God who had hurt him. Maybe he'd hurt himself.

He allowed himself to nod, not trusting his words to carry the depth of his feelings.

Violet wound her fingers through his. "Dear heavenly Father." Her voice was strong and sure, even though Nate's hands shook in hers. "You have promised us that you are all-powerful and all-loving. And yet sometimes it's hard for us to reconcile these two things, especially when we face hurts that we can't imagine a loving God would allow to happen. But you tell us that you work all things for our good. Help us to trust this, even when—especially when—we can't see it through our own pain. Amen."

Nate clutched her hands tighter as the prayer ended, his eyes still closed. He needed a moment to catch his breath.

It was as if Violet had smashed down all his walls and seen right into his heart. Seen exactly what he needed to hear, exactly what had been weighing on his soul for the past seven years.

She knew him without his ever saying a word.

When he at last opened his eyes, she was watching him. "I'm glad you moved in next door," she whispered.

"Me, too. I like being your neighbor." He meant to keep the conversation playful, but she slid closer.

"Is that what we are? Neighbors?" She lifted a hand to his cheek.

It was only by sheer force of will that he didn't close the rest of the space between them. "Well, we live next door to each other, and that's kind of the defining characteristic of neighbors."

She nodded, but her expression was serious as she moved even closer, until they were only inches apart. His eyes went to her lips, and he felt the catch in his breath and in his heart.

Her eyes closed, and she tilted her head toward him. He let his eyes close, too.

He moved a fraction of a centimeter at a time, giving her a chance to stop this if it wasn't what she wanted.

But she moved closer to him, and then their lips were pressed together.

NOT UNTIL YOU

Hers were soft and smooth and felt like they'd been made just for him. He slid his hand from hers and lifted his fingers to tangle in her hair, letting himself fall into whatever this was.

Whatever it could become.

Chapter 32

Violet felt as if she was on one of those rides that slowly hoisted you a hundred feet in the air and then let you hurtle to the ground. It was exhilarating and terrifying. All night, she'd relived that kiss with Nate. The sheer exhilaration of her lips on his, of his hands in her hair. And the terror of not knowing what it meant for her relationship with Nate—and, worse, what it meant about her love for Cade.

She'd waited as long as she could to call Sophie, but by six, she'd been unable to wait any longer.

A groggy Sophie had invited her to come over right away, even though they'd see each other at church in a few hours. But now Violet stood with her hand on her own apartment door, debating. What if she stepped into the hallway and saw Nate? Would things be awkward? Would he regret their kiss? Would he say it had been a mistake?

She drew in a deep breath and opened the door.

But the landing was empty, and the breath she'd been holding seeped from her as disappointment flooded her chest.

Apparently she'd wanted to see him more than she let herself admit.

But this was for the best.

This way, she could let Sophie help her sort out her feelings first.

Before she acted on them and did something she'd regret.

By the time she got to Sophie's house, she'd almost convinced herself that she already knew what to do. She had to stop things with Nate before they went any further. She was half afraid Sophie would confirm her feelings and half afraid she'd say Violet should go for it with Nate.

She pulled her jacket tighter as she crossed the frost-dusted grass to Sophie and Spencer's front door. Not bothering to knock, she slid inside silently.

Sophie and Spencer were sitting at stools in front of their kitchen counter. Each had a muffin in front of them, and Spencer leaned over to pop a bite of his into Sophie's mouth. Then he kissed her forehead before pushing his stool back.

Violet had to stop at the jolt in her heart. She knew everything about Spencer and Sophie. She'd been the one to set them up—twice—but still, it felt as if she'd walked in on an intensely private moment.

"Hey, Violet." Spencer caught sight of her first and gave her his easy smile. "Grab a muffin and some coffee." He dropped another kiss on his wife's head, then disappeared out the front door.

As soon as he was gone, Sophie turned to Violet. "All right, spill. I saw those looks between you and Nate last night, so . . ." Sophie waved a hand in the air, inviting Violet to finish the story.

Violet covered her face with both hands, suddenly afraid to tell her friend what had happened.

Sophie and Cade had been close. She'd be devastated at the thought of Violet kissing another man. Not to mention that she'd likely tell Violet it was a bad idea.

Which it was.

But that didn't mean she wanted to hear someone else say it.

"You know what?" Violet uncovered her face. "I was totally overreacting. It was nothing." She grabbed a muffin and stuffed a big bite into her mouth.

"If you think you're getting off the hook that easily, you obviously haven't been paying very good attention during the last twenty-eight years of our friendship."

Violet dragged out her bite as long as she could, but finally there was no more avoiding Sophie. There was no way she was getting out of here without telling her friend everything.

"Fine." She worked to make her voice nonchalant. "We kissed."

"Obviously. I could have told you that was going to happen. It's about time." Sophie took a bite of her muffin, letting a smile play on her face.

"You knew we were going to kiss? How? I didn't—"

"The point isn't how I knew. It's how was the kiss?"

Violet closed her eyes, trying to figure out how to describe it.

"That good, huh?"

Violet shook her head, opening her eyes. "I mean, it was good." Really good. "But it was like— Remember that time when we were in fifth grade and we saw that tornado go through the cornfields to the west?"

The tornado had been too far away to damage any buildings in town. But even from that distance, she had been in awe of its sheer power and its destructive potential.

Sophie nodded, giving her a puzzled look. "He kisses like a tornado?"

Violet let out a little laugh. "No. It's just, I feel like I could be completely knocked over and spun around by the strength of it, you know?"

"Oooh." Sophie held the word out longer than necessary.

"What?" Violet knew that sound. And she had a feeling she wasn't going to like what Sophie had to say.

"I haven't seen you like this since you first realized you were in love with Cade." Sophie's voice was quiet, as if she was trying not to alarm Violet, but Violet jumped to her feet, agitated.

"I'm not in love with Nate." She stopped. Reexamined her words. Was she in love with Nate?

"I didn't say you are." Sophie's voice was calm, too calm, as she took another bite of muffin.

"No, you didn't say it, but that's what you think. You think I'm betraying Cade and falling in love with another man." Violet pointed an accusing finger at her friend.

Sophie dropped her muffin and pushed to her feet, looking truly shocked. "Violet, betraying Cade and falling in love with another man are not the same thing. Is that what you're upset about?"

Violet stopped pacing. "Upset? I'm not upset." But the crack in her voice gave her away.

Sophie crossed the room and wrapped her in a fierce hug. "Sweetie, having feelings for another man is not a betrayal. Cade is gone. He would want you to move on."

"No he wouldn't. At his funeral, I promised him I'd never love anyone else like I loved him. And now—" She swallowed the sob she felt building. "Every day, I feel the hole in my heart growing a little smaller. And someday, if I let it, it will disappear, and Cade will be really gone. How is that not a betrayal?" She couldn't hold back the tears any longer.

"Honey, I knew Cade. Almost as well as you did, remember? And he would never— Look at me." She waited for Violet to lift her head. Tears shone in her eyes, too, as she continued. "He would never in a million years want you to have a hole in your heart. He'd want you to have a full life. Including someone to love."

A sob tore loose from deep in Violet's soul, rocking her body and sending shudders through her frame. It took a moment for her to calm down.

But in that moment, she felt cleansed, as if she'd been given a new chance at life. A chance to release her hold on the past and move toward the future.

Chapter 33

Violet's hand shook as she reached behind her neck and tried to work the clasp of the white onyx Cade had given her on their first anniversary. He'd put it inside a huge box, laughing as she dug through piles of packing peanuts to get to it. Then they'd had a snowball fight with the peanuts. It had made such a mess. But the joy of sharing that moment was totally worth the time they'd had to spend cleaning up afterward.

She finally succeeded with the clasp and raised a hand to her lips at the memory of the kiss they'd enjoyed after the clean-up.

Lips that for the past week had been kissing another man.

Lips that wanted to kiss him again.

She could finally admit that letting herself feel this way was okay. It was better than okay.

It was a sign that she still had a heart somewhere in there under all the layers and cushions she'd built up around it.

Violet tried to read over the speech she had prepared for the assembly at the high school. But every time she did, the familiar images of Cade morphed into Nate. It felt like her two worlds—her past and her present—were colliding.

Maybe she should call off her visit to the school. She'd agreed to it more than six months ago. When she was in a very different place emotionally.

But she'd been asked to share the story of Cade's death as part of a campaign to prevent drunk driving among teens. And though she felt sick at the thought of sharing her pain publicly, if it could help prevent even one family from going through what she had, it'd be worth it.

Sophie had offered to go with her, but Violet had said she preferred to do this alone. Now she was starting to rethink that. But it was too late. She was supposed to be at the school in fifteen minutes.

She gave herself a last look in the mirror, then grabbed her purse. If she didn't do this now, she never would.

She opened the door but immediately took half a step back. "Nate!" Her heart hammered and she pressed a hand to her chest. "What are you doing here?"

He lowered the hand that had been lifted. "Well, I was about to knock, but I guess you read my mind." He gave her a sneaky smile. "Since it's Monday and you're off, I thought I'd play hooky so we could spend the day together."

"Oh." She pulled out her phone to check the time. "I'm sorry. I have an appointment."

His face fell, but he leaned forward to peer at her more closely. "Hey. Are you feeling okay? You look really pale." He reached for her hand. "And you're shaking."

"I'm fine." She worked to steady her voice. "Just nervous."

Concern clouded his eyes. "Why? What's going on? Did Talmadge threaten you again? Because—"

"No, nothing like that." She tried to slide past him, but he was blocking the doorway.

"Violet." He lifted her chin with his hand. "Tell me what's going on. I want to help."

"I'm supposed to give a talk at the school. But I'm not sure I can." Her voice cracked on the last word, and he pulled her into his arms. She burrowed closer, letting his warmth cloak her.

"Is there anything I can do to help?"

"Would you—" She swallowed. She wasn't sure she could ask it of him. But she also wasn't sure she could do it without him. "Would you come with me?"

"Do you even have to ask?" He took her arm and led her down the stairs.

The chaotic chatter of teenage conversations filled the high school auditorium. Nate shifted in his seat next to a group of giggling teenage girls. He didn't take his eyes off Violet, who was seated in an uncomfortable looking chair on the stage, even paler than when they'd left the apartment.

She'd barely said two words on the drive here, but from what he had gathered, both she and Cade had gone to school here, and they'd asked her to speak about his death. They were probably establishing a scholarship in his name or something.

Nerves twisted in his gut for Violet's sake. It was obvious she wasn't comfortable with the idea of public speaking. But when he'd asked why she'd agreed to do it, she'd simply said it was important and fallen silent again, so he'd left her to her thoughts.

He tried to catch her eye now, but she was reviewing a stack of index cards clutched in her hands.

A balding man in a suit approached the microphone and tapped it, sending a loud crackling through the space. The buzz of conversations slowed and died, although a couple of the girls next to Nate were still giggling.

"Good morning, students. As you know, we are bringing in a series of speakers this year to highlight the consequences of our choices. Our speaker this morning is a Hope Springs graduate, and so was her husband Cade. I hope you'll give Mrs. Somers your full attention as she tells you about how one teenager's choice to drive drunk resulted in her husband's death at the age of twenty-five. Mrs. Somers?"

The room fell entirely silent as Violet walked tentatively toward the microphone, but a low buzzing had filled Nate's head. He fought to control the nausea rising in his throat.

In one horrifying moment, it all clicked into place. Cade hadn't just been in an accident. He'd been killed by a drunk driver.

By someone like Nate.

It took all of his willpower to remain in his seat. He couldn't get out of his row without stumbling over a dozen students. Plus, he wasn't certain his legs would hold him. And there was a part of him—the part that watched a cut bleed for a few seconds before putting on a bandage—that felt compelled to hear what she had to say. To subject himself to the torment he deserved.

Nate held his breath as he waited for her to speak, as if that could change what she was about to say.

"My name is Violet Somers." Violet's voice shook, but she let her gaze sweep the auditorium, making eye contact with each section. Nate glanced around at the students, but they all had their eyes fixed on the stage. When her gaze reached his row, she paused. Nate dropped his eyes to his lap before she could make eye contact with him. He couldn't handle that right now.

"I grew up here in Hope Springs and went to high school here. I even had some of the same teachers you have. Like Mr. Peterson and Mrs. Fox. And Mr. Jessup was still the principal. Although he had more hair then." There was a smattering of laughter from the students. "From almost before I can remember, I hung out with the same group of friends. We climbed trees together, ate ice cream together, pulled pranks together." She leaned away from the microphone and stage whispered, "But if Mr. Jessup asks, I had nothing to do with the cow in the cafeteria." More laughter from the students. In spite of himself, Nate smiled. Violet had forged an instant connection with these students, and he knew whatever she said to them would have an impact.

"We were a group of boys and girls who loved life. Loved being together." Her voice lowered. "Loved each other."

She took an audible breath. "But then something happened. I don't really know when or how. But one of the boys became more than a friend. His name was Cade."

Nate was entranced by the slight smile on her face whenever she said her husband's name, even if it sliced his heart at the same time. He wanted to be the one to bring that look to her face from now on. But he couldn't be. Not after this.

The smile lingered as Violet kept talking. "We never really declared ourselves boyfriend and girlfriend. Not officially. But that's how everyone saw us. And I guess that's technically what you call it when two people only want to spend time with each other. At least that's what my best friend Sophie told me."

The girl next to Nate sighed.

"Our second year of college, Cade proposed. It was—" That smile again. "It was magical. He had no money at the time, of course, but he talked the art director at our school into letting him use one of the galleries where some of my work was displayed. And he blew up two hundred balloons with his own air. By the time I arrived, he was sitting with his head between his knees."

A gentle laugh went up around the auditorium. They all knew how this was going to end. Otherwise, Violet wouldn't be up there.

Nate clenched his teeth, not releasing even when the pain began to morph into a headache.

"I asked if he was okay, and he said, 'No.' And I was worried. He was all pale and sweating, and I thought, you know, we'd better get this guy to the doctor, he's really sick. And then he grabbed my hand." Violet held out her hand. "And he said—" She blew out a short breath.

Nate could almost feel everyone in the room leaning forward.

"He said he wouldn't be okay until I agreed to spend the rest of my life with him."

The whole room seemed to exhale at once, and nearly all the girls in Nate's row lifted a hand to swipe at their eyes. He pressed his lips together and swallowed down the hard lump that had clotted the back of his throat.

"I said yes before he had the ring out of his pocket." Violet ran a finger under her own eye, and Nate had to look away. He wanted to rush the stage and tell her to stop. Tell her not to hurt herself by reliving this story. Not to hurt him.

But she kept talking, building up to the inevitable.

"We got married the day after college graduation. Not long after that we opened an antique shop. It was—" Violet seemed to be searching for the right word. "It was perfect."

She fiddled with her index cards as she stared out over the heads of the students. For a moment Nate thought she wouldn't be able to go on. But then she shook her head and looked at the audience. "Actually, that's not true. It wasn't perfect. No relationship is. We fought sometimes. Sometimes I thought he was a slob. Sometimes he thought I was a control freak." She laughed a little, and so did the audience. "But it was just right for us, you know?" She sniffed. "We had actually just decided to start a family."

Nate's lungs constricted. He hadn't known that.

"But we didn't get a chance." Violet's voice was stronger now, though Nate knew this had to be the hardest part.

"On June twelfth, three years ago, we were supposed to pick up a piece for our antique shop. It was farther than we usually went, and I wasn't sure we should go at all. At the last minute, we had an argument, and I decided not to go."

Violet took a moment to scan every row of students. When her eyes stopped on his, Nate saw her shoulders rise as if she were drawing strength from him.

Still looking at him, she continued, "I was painting when someone knocked on the door that night. I thought maybe Cade had forgotten his keys. He did that all the time. By then, I'd had time to calm down from our argument, and I was ready to meet him at the door with an apology."

She directed her gaze to the other side of the room, and Nate's breath caught. He didn't want to hear this next part. He couldn't handle hearing it. And yet, he needed to hear it. If nothing else could convince him to let Violet go, this would. After all she had been through, she'd never be with someone like him.

"But it wasn't Cade. It was a policeman. And in that moment, I knew. I just stood there, completely numb, my stupid paintbrush still in my hand, until the officer asked if there was anyone he could call. Without thinking, I said he should call Cade." She closed her eyes for a moment, her face ashen under the stage lights. Nate looked away. He couldn't take much more of this.

"The officer led me into the house and sat me down and explained that he couldn't call Cade because Cade was dead. It was a drunk driver. A teenager who had been at a party." Her shaky inhale rattled the microphone. "Because of one person's mistake, Cade was gone."

NOT UNTIL YOU

Nate had known this was where the story was going. And yet, the words were a rock plunging into his gut.

He couldn't sit here any longer.

Couldn't pretend that he belonged here.

He belonged with the guy who had killed Cade.

He shoved his way blindly past the masses of legs and out the auditorium door.

Chapter 34

Violet faltered as the auditorium door slammed. She tried to convince herself Nate had to use the restroom, but the way he'd plowed through the students told her otherwise. She'd obviously said something to upset him. She should have warned him that she'd be dwelling a lot on her past with Cade in her talk. But that didn't mean she didn't want a future with him.

She forced herself to keep talking, to tell the students that every choice they made had the potential to affect not only themselves but also the lives of people they'd never met, people they might never meet.

As she brought her talk to a close, the auditorium was silent, and nearly every student was either looking at her or looking into their laps. Several were wiping their eyes, and tears sprang to hers as well at the thought that maybe she had impacted them, at least in some small way.

Mr. Jessup came up beside her and spoke into the microphone. "Thank you for sharing your story, Violet. I remember Cade very well, and I know I speak for everyone who knew him when I say we all miss him and we're so sorry for your loss." He laid a hand on her arm. "Do you have a few minutes to answer some questions from our students?"

Violet's stomach dropped. Giving her prepared speech had been hard enough. But live questions were another thing altogether—what if she didn't have the answers?

But the whole room was silent, and Violet felt like the students were waiting for her. She nodded mutely.

A few hands went up across the auditorium, and Violet pointed to a young girl near the back.

The girl stood. "What happened to the driver who hit your husband?"

Violet closed her eyes. She'd left that out on purpose. She didn't like to think about it. But these kids deserved to know what could happen. She made herself look at the student who had asked. "Unfortunately, he was killed in the accident as well."

A collective gasp went up from the students.

"Someone said to me afterward that I must be glad about that." Violet's chest tightened at the memory as she scanned the room filled with kids the same age as the boy who had died with Cade. "How could I be glad that alcohol had taken another life? That's not what Cade would have wanted, and it's not what I wanted, either."

She gave the students a second to digest her answer, then pointed to a boy closer to the front.

"If the other guy had survived, would you have been able to forgive him?"

Violet pondered the question. She'd wrestled with the issue of forgiveness so many times. "Just because he died doesn't mean I don't need to forgive him," she finally said. "It took me a long time to see that I was holding onto my resentment and anger toward this kid. I didn't want him dead, but I did sometimes wish I'd have gotten justice for Cade's death. Or at least that the boy was around to apologize to me or show some remorse."

The student who had asked the question sat down, but Violet had more to say.

"The thing is, I couldn't have forgiven him on my own. But God worked on my heart and showed me that this resentment I was holding onto was poisoning me and hurting my relationship with God. Over time, he helped me see that no one is beyond his forgiveness. So no one should be beyond mine either. He helped me forgive that driver. And I pray for his family. Because they suffered a hurt just as deep as mine." She glanced at Mr. Jessup out of the corner of her eye. He'd always been careful not to bring religion into the school, but he gave her an encouraging smile.

He leaned over her to speak into the microphone. "I think we have time for one more question."

Violet gestured to a girl sitting close to Nate's still-empty seat. "Have you started dating again?"

The girl in the seat next to her gasped and hit her arm, but Violet smiled, even as her heart stuttered. "It's okay. I don't mind the question." She tried to gather her thoughts. "For a long time—until very recently, actually—I had no plans of ever dating again. I was sure that all my best days were behind me and I had no hope for a future. I was still living in the past, too busy looking at what had been to see what could be. But now—" She drew in a quick breath.

"I guess I'm saying, I'm open to the possibility of a future again. And to the possibility of love."

The girl nudged her friend, and Violet smiled. They couldn't have failed to notice that Nate was a little old to be a student here.

After the students had applauded to thank her for being there, Mr. Jessup steered her off the stage and into the hallway.

"One of our student journalists was wondering if she could do a quick interview with you for the school paper." Mr. Jessup spoke loudly to be heard over the clamor of students filing past.

"Sure. I just need to find my friend first." Violet peered through the milling students, trying to spot Nate.

"Great. Why don't you meet her in the courtyard in five minutes? You remember the way, right?"

Violet nodded. Of course she remembered the way. On sunny days, she and Cade had always had their lunch out there.

Mr. Jessup got swept along in the tide of students, and Violet offered him a last wave before turning in the other direction, watching for Nate.

She roamed the emptying hallways for a few minutes, but there was no sign of him. Maybe he'd ducked into a bathroom or was waiting by the car. She'd have to find him after the interview, which hopefully she could make quick. Her speech had left her completely wrung out.

The moment she opened the door to the courtyard, her eyes fell on him, hunched at a picnic table in the middle of the open space.

She breathed out a breath she didn't know she'd been holding and moved toward him.

"You did good." He didn't look up.

She took a seat next to him. "You left before I was done."

Nate turned his head, until Violet could see the pain that always lurked under the surface of his gaze. Except today it was right at the top.

"I'm sorry, I—"

But Violet grabbed his hand, lacing her fingers through his. "I understand why it would be hard for you to hear about my past. About my life with Cade. But—" She squeezed his hand. "I'm not stuck in that past anymore. I've realized that I want a future."

"Violet—" Nate's voice was hoarse.

But before he could continue, the courtyard door swung open. A dark-haired girl stepped through and walked toward them.

Violet waved to her and leaned closer to Nate. "Sorry, I said I'd do a quick interview before we go."

Nate slid his hand out of hers and stood. "That's fine. I'll go wait by the car."

"No, wait." She grabbed his arm. "Will you stay with me? I'm not sure I can handle much more of this on my own."

She could see him wrestle with the answer, but finally he sat down.

"Thank you," she whispered as the girl reached them.

"I'm May. Thanks so much for sharing your story." The girl flipped through the screens on her phone. "You don't mind if I record this, do you?"

"Of course not."

"Great." May set the phone on the table between them. "So I think you did a great job covering everything in there, but I have a few questions that you didn't talk about in your speech." She flipped open the notebook she carried with her and scanned a page. "First, I know the boy who hit your husband died, but if he hadn't, do you know what kind of sentence he would have been facing?"

Nate stiffened next to her, but when she looked at him, he was staring at the brick wall of the school, whole body rigid.

"I'm sorry, I really don't. I never looked into it."

"Sure, no problem." The girl jotted a note. "I know you said you forgave him, but what kind of punishment do you think would have been fair if he had lived?"

Nate climbed over the seat of the picnic table. "I'll be over there," he murmured, taking off for the other side of the courtyard. Violet stared after him for a second. She shouldn't have asked him to stay. More talk about her past was the last thing he needed.

Violet turned over May's question in her mind, searching for the right answer. But the truth was she didn't know what would have been fair. She certainly wouldn't have wanted the kid to spend the rest of his life in prison, but she didn't think a couple days would have been enough, either. "I guess just enough to ensure he would never do it again," she said. "Though I don't know how anyone would ever know what that number would be."

"Fair enough." May made another note.

After a few more questions about some of the specifics of her friendship with Cade and their wedding day, May stood. "Thank you so much for your time, Mrs. Somers. I'm sure it's not easy to talk about."

"You're very welcome. I only hope it makes a difference."

"I think it will." May took two steps toward the door, where Nate was hovering, waiting for them to finish.

Gratitude flooded Violet's heart. He had probably been dying to get out of here, but he'd stayed for her sake.

"Oh, one more thing." May turned back to her and lowered her voice. "You said you were open to the possibility of love again. Did you mean with the hot guy that's with you?"

Violet laughed. She certainly found Nate attractive, but she hadn't known high school girls would consider him hot. She toed at the grass. "It's possible."

May smiled. "Is he a lot like your first husband?"

Violet tugged on a strand of hair, thinking. "In some ways yes, but mostly no."

"Any examples?"

"You sure are a thorough journalist." She considered the question a minute. "Okay, well, Cade was kind of larger than life, you know? Loud and playful and always laughing. But Nate is . . ." She gestured toward him. "Well, not. He's quieter, more sensitive. A musician."

"Yeah?" May's eyebrows went up, interested.

"Yeah, he used to be in a band."

May was scribbling furiously. "And how are they the same?"

"I guess . . ." Violet searched for the words to describe it. "Maybe it's not so much that they're the same but that the way they make me feel is the same. Cherished. Protected. Like they'd give up their lives for me."

May's pen flew across the paper.

"Actually—" Now that she was talking about it, Violet found she didn't want to stop. "Nate recently saved my life in a fire."

"Wow." May's pen stopped and she looked over at Nate again. "That's—just wow. Maybe I'll do a story about that, too. What's his last name?"

"Oh, you should." Violet got caught up in her enthusiasm. "His name is Nate Benson. And he's a hero." She felt herself blushing. "I mean, that sounds corny. But he is."

Chapter 35

Three days.

For the past three days, Nate had been pretending everything was fine with Violet. But he knew she could sense that something was off. Every time she asked if anything was wrong, though, he forced a smile and dropped a light kiss on her lips.

But he felt like an imposter every minute they were together.

Today he couldn't pretend anymore. So he'd skipped out of the office early and slipped past the back door to grab Tony and drag him out to the Sugarbush in spite of the cutting temperatures and the sharp wind that gusted from the lake.

They started out at a walk, but soon Nate's feet picked up speed, and he pushed Tony to run harder. The tree branches above them whipped into a frenzy, dropping leaves all around them.

Nate tried to block out the thoughts that had been circling through his head in a constant loop since he'd heard Violet's story.

He had to tell her the truth about himself, he knew that. But the moment he did, any hope he'd started to have for the future would be shattered.

Every time he thought about it, a dull pain pressed against his ribcage.

NOT UNTIL YOU

A fresh, furious gust of wind whipped against him, and Nate pulled to a stop. Tony tugged on the leash for a minute, but when Nate didn't move, he stuck his nose to the ground and sniffed around.

Nate tipped his head toward the sky letting the sharp breaths stab into his lungs, relishing their sting.

He closed his eyes as the roar of the wind filled him.

He couldn't go through life like this anymore.

Couldn't deal with remembering who he was and what he had done.

Couldn't deal with an empty future of paying for his past sins.

Couldn't deal with the burden of getting through each day.

Nate turned, dragging Tony with him as he jogged toward town. He knew what he had to do.

Still gasping from running all the way to Dan's house, Nate lifted his hand to knock. Next to him, Tony panted, his tongue lolling to the side.

The door opened, and Nate found himself straightening.

"Nate?" Dan looked confused to find Nate on his doorstep, but he offered a genuine smile.

"Are you busy?" Nate shifted from one foot to the other. Maybe this had been a bad idea. But he didn't know where else to turn.

"Of course not. Come on in."

"I have the dog. We can do this out here."

"Don't be ridiculous. It's freezing out. Bring the dog in, too."

Nate hesitated another half second, but his hands were stiff with the cold, so he led Tony into the house. He dropped onto the comfortable old couch in the living room, and Tony settled at his feet.

Dan plopped into the chair across from the couch and sat, waiting.

Nate opened his mouth, but he didn't know where to start. Didn't know what to say.

Dan slapped the arm of his chair and jumped up. "How about a game of pool?"

Nate nodded, grateful. He'd let off some steam with a game of pool, then tell Dan the truth about himself.

Dan led him to the basement, where a beat-up looking rec room contained a pool table and a foosball table.

"The table's kind of warped, just to warn you." Dan racked the balls. "We use it for teen nights. They don't seem to mind."

Nate's memories flashed to his own youth group and the pastor who had mentored him and encouraged him to pursue his music. Just one more person he'd let down.

Dan gestured for Nate to break.

But Nate's shot was off, and he ended up without a single ball in the pocket.

"That sounds about right," he muttered, offering a wry smile.

Dan studied him as he chalked his own cue, then bent to take his shot, sinking the five ball in the far corner.

"Nice shot."

"Thanks." Dan moved around the table to line up his next shot. "So, how are things with Violet?"

Nate's stomach turned. Dan apparently wasn't going to waste any time getting to the crux of the matter. "They're good. Everything's great."

Dan glanced up from his pool cue, and Nate looked away.

It was time to drop the pretense.

"Violet is wonderful. She really is. And I care about her." He licked his lips. "A lot, actually."

"But?" Dan prompted.

Nate looked him in the eye. "I'm not who she thinks I am." He refused to look away. "I'm not who any of you think I am."

Dan straightened, ignoring his shot, and leaned against the pool table. "And who do we think you are?"

Nate sighed. "I don't know. A good guy. A nice person."

"And you're not?" The hint of a smile tugged at Dan's lips, and Nate fought the urge to punch it off. Why did Dan insist on remaining so calm when Nate was about to obliterate the image his friend had formed of him?

"No, I'm not." His voice was hard. "I'm a—" He choked on the word but made himself say it. "I'm a felon."

He watched Dan's face closely, waiting for the disgust and revulsion. But aside from a flicker of surprise, Dan's expression didn't change.

"So am I," the pastor said, as if he were remarking on the weather.

That Nate had not expected. Did Dan think this was a joke?

"What? No—"

But Dan cut him off.

"Maybe not in the eyes of the state. But in God's eyes. We all are." Dan set his pool cue down and sat on the edge of the table.

"I'm not talking about God's eyes," Nate huffed. "I'm talking a felon. As in, I spent time in prison for a crime I committed."

"I understand that." Dan's calm was infuriating. "But it doesn't matter. Sin is sin."

Nate chucked his pool cue at the ground, the clatter of its fall dulled by the thin carpeting. "Fine. Sin is sin. How's this for sin: I almost killed my sister?" He spit the words at the preacher. There. Let him deal with that confession.

This time, Dan couldn't mask the shock on his face.

A flash of vindication washed over Nate, followed by a surge of shame.

The man he had come to think of as a friend now knew his terrible secret.

Knew who he truly was.

And would hate him for it.

Nate fell into the vinyl chair next to the pool table and dropped his head into his hands. Tony's tags jangled as the dog padded across the room, then laid his head on Nate's lap. Nate dug his hands into the dog's fur.

The chair next to him creaked as Dan settled into it.

A large hand rested on Nate's shoulder, and he turned his head to look at Dan. Why hadn't he fled the room the moment Nate told him his secret?

"Do you want to tell me about it?" Dan asked quietly.

Nate swallowed. That was the last thing he wanted to do.

And yet he needed to do it.

He started talking, beginning with his band's success, the celebration at the bar, the beers. Through it all, Dan kept his steady gaze on Nate, nodding now and then to encourage him to continue.

When Nate reached the part where he got into the car, Dan closed his eyes momentarily. Nate could see that his friend knew what was coming. That it would devastate him and ruin whatever friendship they might still have after everything else he had confessed.

Nate hauled in a ragged breath and made himself go on.

"I didn't think twice about getting in that car." His voice cracked. "I had never been drunk before, and I didn't think I was then. But I was. I was drunk and I got in a car, and I crossed the center line."

Next to him, Dan let out a swift exhale. Nate waited for Dan to tell him to stop, to tell him he didn't want to hear the rest. But Dan sat silent, waiting.

"We hit another car head-on. There was only one person in that car, fortunately, and he had some injuries, but he was okay. But Kayla, my sister, was thrown from the car. When I got to her, all I could see was blood spreading around her. I begged God to make her okay." A silent sob racked his body, and he couldn't go on.

Dan gave him a minute, then asked quietly, "What happened to her?"

Nate lifted his head and stared at the pool table with its scattered balls. "I don't know." The despair closed off his throat, and he struggled for a moment just to breathe. When he could finally speak again, his voice was a rasp against his throat. "She's alive, that much I know. But my dad hasn't let me have any contact with her since that day. She was in a coma, and I don't know if—" Air rattled in and out of his lungs as he tried to regain control. "I don't know if she's ever woken up and if she has—if she's the same person she used to be."

He slumped forward, and Dan's big hand fell on his shoulder again.

After a few seconds, Nate lifted his head and pinned Dan with his gaze. "So you wanted to know where I was from. Prison. That's where. I came straight here from prison."

Nate sagged against the back of his chair, waiting for Dan's reprimand. Waiting for the man to tell him what he already knew—he'd gotten off too easy and deserved to be in hell.

Dan contemplated him, but Nate couldn't read his friend's expression.

"You're still in prison."

Nate stiffened. That's exactly what he felt like, but how did Dan know?

"You've made this prison for yourself," Dan went on. "You've told yourself you don't deserve to be forgiven. You're so locked into that belief that you don't see the truth right in front of you: you *are* forgiven."

Nate jumped to his feet, a surge of anger and adrenaline propelling him to the other side of the room. When he got to the wall, he pushed off it like a caged animal.

"I don't want to be forgiven," Nate spat. "I want to know what to do to make up for it. How to make it right. I can't erase that night. But there must be something I can do."

Dan's infuriating calm smile was back. "That's the thing, though. There's nothing you can do."

All the adrenaline drained out of Nate, and he fell against the wall. That's what he had feared. He'd have to live with this weight, this guilt, for the rest of his life.

"Listen." Dan leaned forward, bracing his elbows on his knees. "There's nothing *you* can do. But that's because everything's already been done for you. Jesus paid the price for all sin." He held up a hand as Nate started to protest. "Even this sin. He promises he's removed it from you as far as the east is from the west."

"Well, he shouldn't have," Nate snarled.

"No, he shouldn't have. You certainly don't deserve it."

Nate's head snapped up. At least Dan could admit that he didn't deserve forgiveness.

But Dan kept talking. "I don't deserve it, either. No one does. That's what grace is. God's undeserved love."

That word.

Grace.

Nate knew that word. Once upon a time, he had believed in that word. Had believed that God loved him no matter what he'd done.

What had happened to the little boy, the young man who had believed that?

"You know what else is a sin?" Dan went on.

Nate stilled, waiting to hear how else he had failed.

"Holding onto your guilt. You're not bound by these chains anymore. God has released them. So now you need to let them go."

Something in Nate's heart cracked.

"I don't know how." His voice scratched against his throat.

Dan rose to his feet and crossed the room, pulling him into a tight hug.

"Good thing God has that covered for you, too." Dan released him but kept a hand on his shoulder. "Would you like to pray together?"

Nate nodded, not trusting himself to say anything else.

"Heavenly Father." Dan's prayer was strong and sure, as if he talked with God every day. Which he probably did. Nate used to do that, too, and he had an unexpected longing for that old intimacy with his heavenly Father.

"You know our sins. You know our hurts. You know our hearts." Dan squeezed Nate's shoulder. "We ask that you would soothe us when the guilt of our sins threatens to drown us. When we think we have to do something to deserve your love and forgiveness. Take us by the hand and remind us that there is nothing we have to do—nothing we can do—to deserve you. That you love us anyway. That you died for us. And that you forgive us. Unconditionally. Ease our hearts, calm our spirits, and draw us closer to you day by day. In Jesus' name we ask this. Amen."

Nate stood with his eyes closed, letting the peace of the moment wash over him. He felt as if his soul had been cleansed. As if he'd gotten a second chance at life.

Not that his heart didn't still ache. Not that he didn't still hurt for the past.

But in spite of all that, he knew he could go on. He could live as a forgiven child of God.

"Thank you," he finally whispered.

Dan clapped him on the back. "Any time." He bent to pick up Nate's pool cue and passed it to him. "Your shot."

Nate nodded, still feeling stunned by Dan's forgiveness—and by God's. He bent to line up his shot.

Just as he drew the pool cue back, Dan cut in. "I still don't understand what all of this has to do with Violet."

Nate picked up his head, ruining his shot.

"Oh, sorry." But Dan's eyes gleamed.

"You did that on purpose," Nate accused.

Dan didn't blink. "I'm waiting for an answer."

Nate let out a heavy breath that felt like it might pull his soul right out with the air. "I know how her husband died. If Violet knew the truth about me—" He rubbed roughly at a spot on the pool table. "I'm afraid every time she looked at me, she'd see the driver who killed her husband."

Dan nodded thoughtfully, and Nate's heart dipped. He had half hoped Dan would tell him he was wrong.

"I guess there's a risk of that." Dan lined up his shot. "But maybe you should let her be the one to decide. By not telling her, you're not protecting her. You're protecting yourself." Another ball dropped into the corner pocket.

Nate knew Dan was right. And yet— "She deserves better."

Dan leaned down for another shot. "Violet deserves to smile again. To laugh." He paused, seeming to see through Nate with his stare. "To love. If you're the person who can give her that"—Dan pointed his cue at Nate—"then you're exactly the person she deserves."

Nate's mouth went dry. Is that what he wanted? Love?

But he already knew it was. "How do I know she won't run when I tell her the truth?"

"You don't." Dan bent over, barely pausing to sight his shot, and hit the ball. "Just like you didn't know if you would win this game. But you started playing anyway."

Dan sank the rest of the solid balls, then dropped the eight ball in the side pocket, shooting Nate a wicked grin.

"Well, I hope things go better with Violet than they did in this game," Nate muttered.

But he couldn't stop the laugh that burst out of him. He felt lighter than he had since the night of the crash.

He may not deserve a future with Violet.

But by God's grace, he might get one anyway.

He only hoped it wasn't too late to try.

Chapter 36

Violet couldn't shake the heaviness as she locked up the shop for the day. It'd been a good day, money-wise, and she was getting closer to being able to pay everything off.

But Nate hadn't come by this evening. She tried to tell herself he'd probably gotten caught up at work. He'd probably be home any minute, and he'd knock on her door and ask if she wanted to hang out.

But in her heart, she knew that wasn't going to happen. She'd been sensing him pulling away the past few days, ever since he'd heard her talk about Cade at the school. She was trying to respect the fact that maybe he needed more time and space to deal with everything she'd said. But it was hard. Now that she knew she was ready for another relationship, knew who she wanted that relationship to be with, knew how she felt about him, she didn't want to wait.

As she stepped onto the landing at the top of the stairs, her phone rang, and she paused to pull it out of her pocket. She didn't recognize the number. Frowning, she swiped to answer, just as she heard the door downstairs open.

"Hello?" she said into the phone as she spun toward the stairs.

"Hi, Mrs. Somers. This is May. From the high school?"

"Hi, May." Violet's gaze zeroed in on Nate. He had closed the door and was leaning against it, his eyes directed toward her. But he didn't smile. Instead he looked—

She wasn't sure how to describe it, but if she didn't know better, she'd say he looked almost scared. Her eyes went to Tony, panting at his feet as if he'd spent all day running.

"I was just calling with a couple of follow-up questions." May sounded hesitant, but Violet couldn't focus on that. She was too busy trying to figure out how to reach Nate.

"Sure, May. How can I help you?"

"Well, I was writing my article, and I wanted to see if I could get a little more background on that guy that was with you, so I wouldn't have to bother you, and . . ."

"Yes?"

Violet started down the steps. If Nate wouldn't come to her, she would go to him. Maybe he was hesitant because he didn't know how she felt. So she'd show him.

"Well—" May let out a quick breath. "You didn't mention that he had been convicted of drunk driving."

"What?" Violet jerked to a stop as the whole stairway tilted under her. She either had to sit or fall over.

Right now.

She dropped to the step above her with a thud.

Through the fog that closed in around her, she vaguely saw Nate move toward the stairs, his expression changing to concern.

"So I was wondering if you had anything to say about that? You know, given the way your husband died?" May sounded far away, and Violet was no longer sure any of this was real.

"I'm sorry, I can't— I don't— I have to go." Violet pulled the phone away from her ear and quickly hung up, afraid of what other venom might spew out of it if she didn't.

"Violet?" Nate crouched on the step next to her, and Tony sniffed her knees. "Are you okay? What was that about?"

Violet tried to figure out how to speak while she was drowning. "That was May. The girl from the school newspaper. She wanted to follow up on some things."

She looked away. She didn't want to say the rest. Didn't want to hear him say it was true. But she forced the words out. "She wanted to know how I felt about your drunk driving conviction."

Chapter 37

This couldn't be happening. Nate had come home from Dan's fully intending to tell Violet everything. But not like this.

Her eyes refused to leave his, and he hated the hope shining in hers. She was waiting for him to tell her it wasn't true.

He looked away and held out a hand to her. She hesitated for a second, then took it and let him pull her to her feet and lead her into his apartment.

Inside, he steered her toward the couch. She sat, her moves mechanical.

Nate stepped away from the couch to pace in front of the window. He couldn't be next to her when he did this. It would be too hard not to touch her, not to seek her comfort. But he didn't deserve that.

He almost choked on a shaky breath, his stomach roiling at the thought of what he was about to do.

He loved this woman—he couldn't deny it any longer.

And he was about to ruin any chance that she could ever feel the same way about him.

"I'm so sorry, Violet." Nate swallowed against the burn that had already kicked in at the back of his throat. "I had no idea how Cade died until the other day. I never meant to hurt you."

Violet nodded, not looking at him.

But he knew he hadn't said enough. "I should have told you sooner. I just didn't want you to think—" His voice cracked. "I never meant for it to happen. It was the only time I ever drank, and—" He stopped himself. She didn't need to hear his excuses. "I will regret it every day for the rest of my life."

"So that's what your scars are from? On your chest and your knee?"

He nodded and tried to think of anything else he'd kept from her. Now that she knew, she might as well know everything. "It's also why I can't drive. My license was revoked. And it's why I meet with Officer Jensen, the woman you saw me with that day you brought me cookies—" His eyes flicked out the window to watch a boy struggling to get a kite in the air. "She's my parole officer. I'm a felon, Violet. I just got out of prison."

"Did anyone die?" Violet's voice was so quiet he could have pretended not to hear her. But she deserved to know the whole truth.

"No."

He could see her let out a sigh of relief, but he wasn't going to let himself get off that easily.

"My sister almost did. I actually don't know—" He turned away as he felt himself choking up. He didn't deserve her sympathy, and she had such a soft heart, he knew she'd give it if she thought he was hurting. After a minute, he cleared his throat and turned toward her. "I don't know how she is. That's why I've been so desperate to meet my dad's demands. It's the only way he'll let me see her and my mom again."

Violet inhaled like she was about to say something, but he had to finish this or he never would.

"It was selfish of me to let myself get involved with you when I knew I could never be the man you deserved." He gave a wry laugh. "I tried not to, I really did. But you made me feel like someone else when I was with you. Someone who could be more than this huge mistake. And I let myself get wrapped up in that. I just fell so hard for you and your loving spirit and your—" He dragged a hand through his hair. "Anyway, I'm sorry."

He finally looked at her, but she was watching her thumb slide up and down her empty ring finger.

He moved to the kitchen to get himself a glass of water—and to give her the space he was sure she wanted.

After downing two glasses, he stood with his hands braced on the counter, his head tucked between his shoulders. How could he go back out there? How could he face her now that she knew who he really was?

Please give me strength. He whispered the prayer, then straightened.

But before he could return to the living room, he heard the click of a door opening and closing.

Chapter 38

Violet leaned against the inside of her apartment door. She hadn't meant to flee Nate's apartment, but her thoughts had swarmed and knotted until she felt like she was going to split in two.

She just needed some space. Some time to process what Nate had told her.

She'd talk to him in the morning when she was thinking straight. When she'd worked out what she wanted to say. What she wanted to do.

Violet shuffled to her bedroom and climbed into bed, fully clothed. She closed her eyes and tried to sleep. But she could still hear what Nate had said.

He'd driven drunk. He'd almost killed his sister.

But beyond that, she could see the guilt and torture in his eyes. The shame and regret in his voice.

She'd seen his brokenness. He'd let her in.

Yes, he'd made a mistake.

About the biggest one he could have made.

But did that mean he didn't deserve to be forgiven?

Did she really mean what she'd said the other day at the school? That no one was beyond forgiveness?

She folded her hands and prayed for the strength to forgive. Her prayers continued long into the night, until she finally drifted into sleep.

In the morning, she sprang out of bed the moment her alarm went off. Without bothering to change out of the rumpled clothes she'd slept in last night, she sped through her apartment, out the door, and across the landing to Nate's. She had to catch him before he left for the office. She needed to tell him that she forgave him and that nothing he had told her changed the way she felt about him.

When he didn't come to the door, she pounded harder.

A few seconds later, a door opened across the hall.

Violet spun toward Mrs. D'Angelo, apologetic. She'd gotten so caught up in her emotions that she'd been thoughtless. "I'm so sorry, Mrs. D'Angelo, I didn't mean to wake you."

Mrs. D'Angelo tsked at her. "Please, child, I haven't been able to sleep past four in the morning since you were in diapers. Just heard you knocking there and thought you should know that no one's going to answer."

Violet's stomach dropped. "Why not?"

"Your young man left early this morning, before the sun was up. Had a suitcase with him, so I figured he was taking a trip."

"Did he—" Violet worked to control her voice. "Did he say how long he'd be gone?"

Mrs. D'Angelo gave her a gentle look, and Violet almost lost her composure right there. "I didn't get the impression he'd be back, dear. I'm sorry."

Violet pressed her lips together to stop the trembling.

NOT UNTIL YOU

When she turned to her apartment, her eyes fell on a note that had been taped to her door. She pulled it off with a shaking hand.

Violet,

I am sorry for everything. I want you to know how much you mean to me. That's why I need to leave, so that you can have the future you deserve with someone who deserves you. I wish you only all the best.

Love,

Nate

PS Please take care of Tony. The key is in the super-secret hiding spot.

Violet lowered the note, her heart thudding a rhythm of regret against her ribs. How had she let the one man who made her alive again leave without a fight?

Chapter 39

It was better this way.

Nate had repeated the same thing to himself every ten minutes the entire bus ride, but he still hadn't managed to convince himself.

Leaving without saying goodbye to Violet was easier, but it had left him feeling hollowed out inside.

And the feeling only grew as he thought of the look Tony had given him when he'd shut him in his kennel. He'd miss that dog, but there was no way to bring him on the bus. And he trusted that Violet would take good care of him.

Maybe being with Tony would remind her of him from time to time.

The man in the seat next to Nate let out a honking snore, and Nate pressed closer to the window. He never would have guessed he'd miss Leah's bubbling chatter—the same chatter that had annoyed him on his way to Hope Springs.

Had that really only been two and half months ago? Somehow, in that time he'd gone from resenting his move to Hope Springs to falling in love with the place. He hated the thought of all his friends finding out what he'd done. Hated to imagine what they'd all think of him now. But Violet had made it pretty clear when she'd walked out of his apartment. She didn't want anything to do with him anymore.

He didn't know why he'd let a tiny part of himself hope that she'd be able to see past what he'd done. That she'd see the man he could be, the man she made him want to be. He should have known it was too much to ask. He couldn't blame her for not giving it.

Nate let his eyes drift over the now empty cornfields. He probably shouldn't have bought the ticket. There was no way Dad was going to let him in the house.

But when the woman behind the bus station counter had asked where he was going, the name of his hometown had just come out.

They were only twenty minutes or so away now, and Nate's stomach had become one of those rides at the fair that made little kids get off and promptly barf. He tried to come up with a strategy to get past Dad's objections.

But by the time the bus pulled into the station, he was just as empty as he'd been when he left Hope Springs.

He found his way to the Uber he'd ordered from the bus and gave the driver his former home address. He'd have to knock on the door and wing it.

The drive went way too fast, and when the Uber driver pulled into the driveway of his childhood home, Nate just sat. It looked almost the same, although the plum tree in the front yard was larger now, and they'd painted the door a bold blue.

"We're here," the driver pointed out.

"Yeah." But still Nate sat and stared at the house. For the past seven years, he'd dreamed of the moment he'd walk inside again. But now that the time was here, he wasn't sure he could do it.

"Look, I don't mean to rush you or anything, but I have another . . ." The driver circled his hands.

"Oh, sorry." Nate opened his door and forced his feet to the pavement, grabbing his suitcase and wheeling it behind him. "Thanks."

He'd barely slammed the door before the car was gone.

Nate hesitated. This was it. He either walked up to the door or— No.

There was no *or*. He was going to do this. Right here and right now.

His feet carried him across the driveway, along the path in front of the house, and up the porch steps. It felt odd to reach for the doorbell when he'd opened this door a million times in his life.

But this wasn't his home anymore.

He pressed the button and listened as the bell resounded through the house.

He found himself needing to pray as he waited, but the words wouldn't come. He'd have to hope God got the message anyway.

He tried to peer in through the sidelight, but it was privacy glass, and he could only see faint shadows behind it. Was that someone coming toward the door?

Nate's heart pounded in his ears.

This was it.

He took a step back, staring at the fine cracks in the wood of the porch. He couldn't bring himself to lift his head as the door opened.

"Oh my— Nate!"

His head whipped up when he heard his sister's voice. But the moment his eyes fell on her, he dropped his suitcase and sagged against the doorframe.

"Oh no, Kayla. I'm so sorry." The words were strangling him.

How could he have done this to her?

Because of him, his beautiful, vibrant sister, the one who had been an all-state cross-country runner, was in a wheelchair.

Chapter 40

This was a mistake. He shouldn't have come. Dad was right—he didn't deserve to be part of his family's life anymore. Not after what he'd cost his sister.

And yet she'd insisted that he come inside, and now she was maneuvering around the kitchen to get him a cup of coffee. He wanted to tell her to let him do it. It'd be so much easier for him. And yet, as he watched her, he had to acknowledge how capable she was, deftly wheeling her chair around obstacles and reaching into cupboards.

Even more striking was how grown up she looked. She'd been a gangly seventeen-year-old at the time of the accident, which made her twenty-four now. Twenty-five, he corrected himself. Her birthday was last month. Her face had matured in that time, and in place of her old ponytail standby, she wore her auburn hair in a sleek face-framing cut. Even her hands, with their practiced and sure movements as she added sugar to his mug, seemed grown up.

"Here you are." She set the coffee cup on the table. How could she smile at him and serve him coffee after everything?

"Thank you." He managed to rasp out. He didn't know what else to say, so he took a sip of the coffee. It burned his tongue, but he didn't care. He deserved far worse than a burnt tongue after what he'd done to her.

You're forgiven for that. But the reminder rang hollow now that evidence of what he'd done was right in front of him. Maybe Jesus had forgiven him, but how could his family ever?

"Kayla, I'm—"

But he had to stop as she wheeled up next to him and wrapped her arms around his shoulders. He stiffened for a second, then swiveled to bring his arms around her and pull her in as tight as he dared. Which wasn't very tight.

"You won't break me, Nate." Kayla's voice held both a laugh and a reprimand. "Give me a real hug."

He squeezed harder, closing his eyes against the rush of emotion. How could she want to be anywhere near him, let alone hug him?

"I'm so sorry." He whispered the words into her shoulder. "I never meant for you—"

"I know." She rubbed a hand up and down his back, the same way their mother always had when they were sick.

When she finally pulled back, Nate swiped a quick hand across his cheeks.

"Dad wouldn't let me—" He fumbled. This wasn't the time to blame things on someone else. "I didn't know you were—" The word stuck on his tongue.

"Paralyzed?" She said it gently, not an accusation. Just a fact. As if she were saying that she were tall or dark-haired or something that was a part of her.

He winced. "Yeah."

She touched a hand to his arm. "It's okay, Nate. Really. Remember, I've had a long time to get used to it. You've only had a few minutes."

"So, what—you're just okay with this?" Nate shoved to his feet. How could she just accept this? Why wasn't she angry at him? She should yell at him, scream that he was the worst brother in the history of the world, tell him to get lost.

"I wasn't at first." Her eyes followed him as he paced the room. "Not for a couple of years, actually. I was angry." She dropped her eyes. "Really angry."

He deserved her anger, he knew that. But his stomach plunged to hear her say it. "At me."

She raised her eyes and met his. "A little. But mostly at God."

Nate nodded. Don't get him started on being angry with God. He knew that feeling only too well. And though that anger had begun to fade in the past few weeks, it threatened to rear up again now that he was confronted with what had happened to his sister. He reminded himself that what had happened wasn't God's fault; it was his own.

"But," Kayla continued. "Mom and Dad kept bringing me to church, even when I didn't want to go. They kept reminding me of God's love for me. And God worked on my heart. I eventually got involved with a support group for young adults with injuries and disabilities. And now I'm actually working with kids with disabilities." Her eyes came to life. "It's like I've found my purpose, Nate. And it's a purpose I wouldn't have found without all of this." She gestured at her lap, where her legs sat perfectly still.

"You're saying this is a good thing?" Nate couldn't wrap his head around it.

Kayla looked thoughtful. "Would I have chosen for it not to happen, if I had a choice? Of course. But it did happen. And as terrible as it was, God used it to bring about good. We both know I wasn't exactly on a godly path before the accident. That was you, with your worship band and all your churchy stuff."

Nate let out an ironic laugh. Funny how things had changed.

"I didn't want anything to do with God then. But he used this to show me my need for him. And to show me how he could use me for his kingdom."

Nate was stunned into silence.

Was there a chance that God had used all of this for his good, too? Kayla was right that he'd been into all the churchy stuff, but looking back on it now, Nate could admit he'd been doing it more for himself than for God. He'd wanted the record contract not so he'd have a bigger platform to share God but so that he'd have a bigger platform for himself.

"But don't you miss running?" He finally asked the question that had been dragging on him since the moment he'd seen her in that chair.

"Of course." Her answer was immediate, and it sent a stab of guilt through him.

"Then how can you say—"

She held up a hand. "Running was only a small part of who I am. And anyway, I'm training for a race right now."

Nate stared at her. Was he missing something here?

"There's a big wheelchair marathon in Madison in a couple weeks. I finished in the top fifty last year. My goal this year is top twenty."

"Wow, that's amazing." Nate crossed the room to give his sister another hug. She'd always been spunky; he should have known nothing would stop her from competing.

"You can train with me now that you're here." Kayla slugged his shoulder. "If you think you can keep up. You always were a slowpoke."

"Slowpoke? Hey, I beat you that one time—"

"Yeah, because I had a sprained ankle."

"Oh, come on." But Nate's heart eased. He had missed the brother-sister teasing that used to drive their parents crazy. "You know I—"

But the words died on his lips as the door from the garage into the kitchen opened.

His mother stopped halfway through the door, her mouth half open.

He needed to say something, but nothing sounded right in his head. Finally, he got out the only word he could. "Mom."

It was enough. Mom unfroze and lunged toward him, tears spilling down her face. In a second, she had him wrapped in her arms. Nate lifted her off her feet and held her as tight as he could.

"Nathan, put me down." But her voice was full of joy and tears. Nate gave her another good squeeze.

"What's going on?" At the sound of Dad's voice, Nate set her down, and she moved to the side. Nate was left face-to-face with his father.

He tried not to wilt under Dad's hard stare. "What are you doing here?"

Nate swallowed against the dryness in his throat. This is where figuring out what to say ahead of time would have come in handy.

But as if he'd always known what he would say in this situation, the words started flowing. "This is my family. And I couldn't wait any longer to see all of you. To tell you how very sorry I am. How sorry I will be for the rest of my life. And to beg for your forgiveness." He held up a hand as Dad started to talk over him, and to his surprise, Dad fell silent. "Before you say anything, I know I don't deserve your forgiveness. But I'm hoping you'll consider giving it anyway. Out of sheer grace."

The words out, Nate fell silent.

"I forgive you, Nate." Kayla's words were soft, but they fell like a balm on Nate's soul.

He blinked rapidly and reached behind him to grab Kayla's hand. "Thank you." The words were barely a whisper, but it was all he could get out past the surge of gratitude for her unexpected gift.

"I just think," Kayla continued, her voice stronger. "That if Jesus forgives you for this, then we really have no right not to. Right, Dad?"

Nate couldn't bring himself to look Dad full in the face but watched him out of his peripheral vision. Dad's jaw worked, but he remained silent.

A second later, he fled down the hallway.

It was what Nate had expected, and yet he still felt deflated.

"Give him time." Mom's voice was gentle, and she pulled Nate into another hug.

Nate nodded. At least Dad hadn't asked him to leave. He supposed that was something.

He let Mom usher him to the table and pour him yet another cup of coffee. Then he sat with Mom and Kayla as they caught him up on everything he'd missed over the last seven years.

He told them about his life in Hope Springs, too. He meant to leave off the parts about Violet, but she'd become so wrapped up in every aspect of his life that it was impossible not to mention her. He pretended not to notice the glance that passed between his mom and his sister whenever he said Violet's name.

They didn't know that part of his life was over. That whatever thoughts he'd had about a future with Violet had died the moment she'd found out the truth about him.

After a while, their conversation wound down, and Mom sent him to unpack his suitcase in his old room. As he walked down the hallway, Nate's eye caught on the dozens of pictures hanging on the wall. Some were new—a picture of Kayla in her wheelchair at the finish line of a race, one of Kayla and Mom at the beach, and one of Kayla all dressed up next to some guy Nate didn't recognize. But there were old pictures, too. Even, to his surprise, some of him. He moved to the picture on the end, from the trip where he and Kayla had collected all those shells. That was the day they'd both decided they wanted to be marine biologists. He'd be a musician on the side, and she'd be a runner.

Nate slid a finger over Kayla's youthful face in the image. How could her life—their lives—have turned out so differently from what they'd planned?

A noise from behind the closed door to Dad's office across the hall caught his attention.

Without considering what he was doing, Nate lifted his hand to the doorknob. He eased the door open a crack, then immediately wished he hadn't.

Dad's back was to him, his head bowed and shoulders shaking. The sound of muffled sobs stabbed Nate right through the middle.

He'd never seen Dad break down before. Not even when he'd stood behind Nate as he'd pleaded guilty to the drunk driving charges.

Nate hesitated. Maybe he should go to Dad. Try to comfort him.

But he reminded himself he was the one who had caused this.

He closed the door silently and walked away.

Chapter 41

Tony's whines woke Violet early. She winced as her bare feet hit the hardwood floor on the way to the living room, where she'd tucked his kennel next to the window.

The dog turned in wild circles as she approached.

"Ugh. Nate taught you to be a morning person, didn't he?" She shoved down the swoop of regret at Nate's name. She'd spent all day yesterday telling herself it was better that he'd left anyway. She wasn't about to undo that now.

The moment she let Tony out of his kennel, he raced to the door. She glanced at the window. The sun was barely peeking over the horizon. "Seriously? You want to go outside right now?"

But she padded to the bedroom to throw on some sweats. Tony shouldn't have to suffer just because Nate had left him. Had left them both.

Just like her mom. And her sister. And Cade.

She fought to push aside the loneliness and remember that she had lots of friends, lots of people who cared about her.

Her Bible was lying open on her bedside table. She'd been too tired after the emotional day yesterday to read much. On a whim, she grabbed it. Maybe she could read while Tony played outside.

But the mid-October air sliced at her face the moment she stepped out the door. Maybe she'd been too optimistic to consider reading outside this morning.

"Let's make this quick, Tony," she mumbled. She led the dog to the grassy hill behind the apartment, trying to shove away the memories of all the times she'd stood out here with Nate.

She waited for Tony to do his business, but the dog pulled on the leash, dragging her down the hill. She tried to tug back, but Tony was on a mission. She didn't realize where he was taking her until he stepped onto the beach.

Instinctively, she recoiled. She couldn't walk here.

But Tony didn't give her a choice. She either had to follow him onto the beach or have her arm ripped out of the socket.

The dog tugged her to the water's edge. At first she resisted, jerking back on the leash every few seconds to coax the dog to go back. But after a while, she gave up and let herself be pulled along.

Tony finally stopped at a rocky outcrop. Violet considered it. Her fingers had gone numb, and the wet sand had frozen her toes. But the sun was above the horizon now, and the entire sky was layered in shades of pink and red and orange. She couldn't remember the last time she'd seen a sunrise like this. It felt like an invitation.

She climbed onto a low rock, and Tony scrabbled up after her. He settled against her leg as she tilted her head and watched the colors play across the sky.

After a while, she opened her Bible. She'd been reading through the book of Deuteronomy over the past few days, and she picked up where she'd left off, with Moses giving his final instructions to the

Israelites before they entered the promised land. But her heart was only half in the reading. Until she came to Deuteronomy 31:8: *The Lord himself goes before you and will be with you; he will never leave you nor forsake you. Do not be afraid; do not be discouraged.*

Tears filled Violet's eyes, and a soft peace washed over her.

No matter how many people in this world had left her, no matter how many more would leave her, God would never forsake her.

How had she let herself lose sight of that fact?

The cold had seeped through her sweatpants by the time she slid off the rock, but her heart felt warmer than it had in a long time.

God had brought Nate into her life for a reason, Violet knew that. And even if he was no longer part of her life, he'd been one of the threads pulling together her tapestry. He'd helped her realize that she didn't have to live in the past. That she was ready to move on and—if the right person came along—love again.

Next time she felt that pull toward someone, she wouldn't resist. She would tell them how she felt, as soon as she felt it. Like she should have done with Nate.

That was her biggest regret in all of this.

He'd left without knowing how she felt about him. Without knowing she loved him.

She'd thought about calling him. But something held her back. It wasn't that she didn't want to be with him. But she sensed he needed the space to work through things on his own. She only prayed that he'd know she forgave him. And, more importantly, that he would know the peace that could only come from knowing Jesus had died for his sins.

NOT UNTIL YOU

Violet was halfway up the hill to her building when her phone rang. She pulled Tony to a stop, trying to catch her breath. Had Nate sensed that she was thinking about him? Was he thinking about her, too?

But it was much more likely to be Sophie or Peyton. More likely to be anyone, really, than Nate.

Still, she couldn't stop the surge of hope.

She had to stare at the number for a few seconds before she believed it was true.

The she answered quickly, before it could go to voice mail. "Jade?"

There was no reply at first, and Violet held her breath. Was she really going to get to talk to her sister for the first time in six years?

After a second, a small voice said. "Hi, Violet."

Violet closed her eyes and breathed out a prayer of thanks. "It's so good to hear you."

"You too." Jade sounded like she was crying, and Violet laughed as tears ran down her own face, too.

Chapter 42

Nate made himself knock on Dad's office door. In the two days he'd been home, Dad had barely said a full sentence to him.

But he couldn't put this off any longer. It was time for him to stand up for what was right. He owed Violet that much.

"Come in." Dad's voice wasn't exactly inviting, but Nate pushed the door open.

He tried to ignore the way Dad's eyes hardened the moment they fell on him.

"We have to talk."

Dad sat silent. Apparently that was as much of an invitation as Nate was going to get. He crossed the room to stand in front of Dad's desk, feeling suddenly like a naughty schoolboy facing the principal.

"I don't know what Talmadge has over you, but you have to call off the witch hunt for Violet Somers's property. Before she gets hurt."

Dad crossed his arms in front of him.

Nate ignored Dad's look of disapproval and kept talking. "There are plenty of properties in Hope Springs. There's no reason to let Talmadge ruin Violet's life. She doesn't deserve that. Whatever he has over you, she shouldn't have to pay the price."

NOT UNTIL YOU

Dad's frown deepened, until his whole lower face was a map of downward slanting lines. Nate was reminded once again of how much his father had aged.

"You think he has something over me, Nate? That I'm trying to evict your friend for my own gain?"

Nate stuffed his hands in his pockets. "Tell me I'm wrong."

Dad's frown twisted. "It's not what he has over me, Nate. It's what he has over you. You want to blame someone for what's happening to your friend, blame yourself."

Dad's words fell against him like blows, and he grabbed at the edge of Dad's desk. "Me? What could he possibly have over me?"

Dad scrubbed a hand down his cheek, looking weary. "After the accident, when you were in the hospital and then afterward when you were in—" Dad looked away.

"Prison." Nate filled in. He didn't blame Dad for not wanting to say it. No matter how many times he said that word, he'd always hate the taste of it.

Dad kept going as if he hadn't heard. "We worked very hard to keep everything quiet. To keep your name out of the papers. But there were a lot of reporters at the concert that night because everyone knew that producer might be there." Dad's sigh carried a weight Nate wished he could lift. Everything Dad had been through in the past seven years was Nate's fault. "Anyway, Talmadge was the guy I hired to keep things quiet. He pulled some strings, called in some favors. Nothing illegal but definitely things that were distasteful. He managed to do a pretty good job of it."

"Why?" None of this made any sense. Dad hadn't cared what happened to Nate after the accident. He'd made that abundantly clear.

Dad lifted his shoulders. "To protect you. So you could have a decent life when you got out." He looked away for a second. "Anyway, a couple years ago, Talmadge began talking about how I hadn't really paid him enough for what he'd done. He started demanding more. But the more I gave him, the more he demanded."

Nate felt sick to his stomach. He had no idea Dad had done all of that for him.

"Why Violet's property, though? Why wouldn't he consider any of the other places I tried to show him?"

Dad shrugged. "At first, I think it was just the location. But when he realized that you were in a relationship with Violet, he saw targeting her store as a way to hurt you and hurting you as a way to hurt me, especially when I told him he could have any property but that one."

"But why would he want to hurt you?" Never mind the question of why Talmadge would think hurting Nate would hurt Dad in turn. He obviously didn't realize Dad detested Nate now.

Dad dropped his gaze to his desk. "You're not the only person who's done things you're not proud of. I cheated Talmadge out of a deal years ago. A pretty big one. He's never forgiven me. When I went to him about all of this, I knew something like this was a distinct possibility. But he's the best at this sort of thing."

Nate chewed his lip. "I don't care if people know. Let Talmadge tell everyone. Don't protect me at Violet's expense."

NOT UNTIL YOU

Dad studied him as if unsure who Nate was anymore. "Actually, I just got a call from the private investigator I hired to look into your suspicions that Talmadge started that fire."

"And?" Nate's hands clenched. If Talmadge had intentionally endangered Violet—

"He's passed the evidence he collected on to the Hope Springs police department. They should be picking him up any minute now."

Nate dropped into the plush chair behind him. "And in the meantime? What if he tries to hurt her again?" He never should have left her alone.

"He won't. My guy is on him twenty-four, seven."

Nate pushed to his feet. "And her store? You have no reason to evict her now."

Dad shook his head. "There's still the matter of her back rent."

"She's really close on that. I've got calls out to a couple of guys who might be interested in a Bosendorfer piano she has. And if that falls through—" Nate scrambled for something, anything. "If that falls through, I'll pay it off myself."

Dad snorted. "With what money?"

"I'll get a job flipping burgers. Or I'll work for you. Whatever. You can have my salary until her rent is paid off."

"You really want to do that for her?" Dad squinted at him as if suspicious of his intentions.

"Absolutely. I'd do anything for her."

"Why? What's in it for you?"

Violet's dark eyes and gentle smile popped into his head. "Because she's the best person I know. Because she reminded me who I really was when I couldn't see it. Because—"

Dad held up a hand. "I get it. You're in love with her." He rolled his eyes, but something in his features had softened. "I'll take that into consideration."

Chapter 43

"Have a nice day." Violet smiled at the sweet older lady who had bought a Victorian wall sconce. The sale wasn't quite enough to meet her back rent, and she only had a couple days left before the deadline to pay it off and renew her lease.

She hadn't been able to bring herself to hold a going out of business sale. If it came down to it, she could always move her stuff into a storage unit and get a temporary job until she figured out what to do next.

She rearranged a small display case of porcelain dolls. The one with the tiny dimples reminded her of Jade, and she pulled it out of the case. Next time she talked to her sister, she'd ask for her address and send this to her as a surprise.

They'd talked on the phone once more in the past week. Jade told her about the various odd jobs she'd held down while looking for work as an actor. She'd worked as a waitress, a cell phone saleswoman, and even one of those people who dressed up as a hot dog to try to drum up business for a fast-food joint. Along the way, she'd managed to snag a couple of small parts in commercials but nothing like what she'd hoped to land.

She'd seemed thoroughly discouraged, and Violet sensed there was a lot Jade wasn't telling her, but at least it was a start.

Violet had found herself spilling to Jade about Nate as well. Although Jade hadn't offered any advice, just knowing she was listening made Violet feel less lonely.

After setting the doll aside, Violet picked up the day's mail. She shuffled the bills to the bottom of the pile but stopped when she came to a formal-looking envelope from Benson Properties. She frowned at it. She'd been wondering how Nate would tell her that she had to get out. She'd let herself hope he'd call. It'd been more than a week since she'd heard his voice, and she yearned to talk to him again—even if it was only to say goodbye.

But apparently a formal letter was all she was going to get.

She sat on the stool behind the counter and ripped the envelope open. She might as well get this over with.

She withdrew a thick sheaf of papers clipped together. Her heart accelerated as her eyes fell on the note on top. That was definitely Nate's handwriting.

Dear Violet,

After further investigation, my father has uncovered evidence that Talmadge was responsible for the fire. He has contacted the Hope Springs police department, so you shouldn't have any more trouble. Please know how sorry everyone associated with Benson Properties is for this. We hope you'll accept the enclosed check as reimbursement for any expenses incurred in the cleanup and repairs.

NOT UNTIL YOU

Frowning, Violet flipped through the packet. The tone of the letter made everything clear. Nate was contacting her as a corporate representative. Not as a friend. And definitely not as anything more.

When she came to the check, Violet gasped. It more than covered what she'd spent on the repairs. But she shook her head at the check, as if it could see her. She'd never wanted money from him. She wanted him.

She turned back to the letter.

You will find enclosed a lease renewal agreement. We'd like to renew your lease for five years, if you are still interested in staying. Please consider any outstanding debt canceled as well.

It was too much, and Violet knew she should be grateful. But it all felt empty without Nate here to tell her in person, to celebrate with her.

If all this should prove agreeable to you, please sign and date the enclosed agreement and return it to the address below.

She scanned the address. It was in Wescott. Was that where he had gone? Home? She hoped so. And that he'd found the peace he'd longed for.

The letter continued in smaller, messier handwriting, and Violet had to squint to make it out.

I want to say again how sorry I am about how everything turned out. I want you to know that you changed my life. Really. I hope you are well. And Tony, too. Tell him I miss him. ~~And~~

And what? Violet wanted to shake the letter. Did he miss her, too? Is that what he'd been about to write?

But he'd left the letter like that, signing it, *Yours, Nate.*

Violet's hand shook. He'd given her everything she needed to keep her dream alive.

Everything except himself.

Chapter 44

Nate huddled deeper into his jacket as a gust of wind swept through the crowd lining the route of the Madison Wheelchair Marathon. He shifted anxiously from foot to foot. Mom had gone to the starting line with Kayla, and he and Dad had been standing out here for half an hour. So far, neither of them had said a word.

Although Dad seemed to now accept the fact that Nate was going to be part of their life again, the few conversations they'd had in the past week and a half had been strained. Thankfully, Dad hadn't let that get in the way of doing the right thing for Violet.

Still, that didn't mean things between them were easy.

Not by a long shot.

Next to him, Dad took a step away, putting more distance between them. "I'm going to go grab a coffee. You want one?"

It wasn't meant to be a trick question, Nate knew that. And yet he had to be careful not to let Dad think he was taking advantage of them. He was already living in Dad's house and eating his food.

"I'll grab you one." Dad didn't wait for an answer before he disappeared into the crowd.

Nate let out a long breath. He studied the map of the course in his hand. How was his little sister going to wheel herself twenty-six miles? She'd let him try the wheelchair the other day when he'd been watching her train, and it was *hard*.

But that was Kayla. Completely determined.

Nate tried not to think about what she could have done with that determination if she'd never been injured. He had to remind himself that Kayla was right. God had used her injury for good. Who knows where she would have ended up if she had continued her former lifestyle?

Still, some nights the guilt clawed its way back in, worming and twisting until it almost consumed him.

The only thing he could do those nights was to climb out of bed and spend the night on his knees in prayer.

Thankfully, praying was becoming familiar again, and he'd dug out the old Bible tucked into the drawer of his nightstand. As he read it again, he enjoyed revisiting his old notes and highlights. He felt like that young man again, full of all his new discoveries of God's love in Scripture. And at the same time, he felt like a seasoned veteran, someone who had seen that life wasn't always pretty but that God was there through all of it.

"Here."

Nate jumped as Dad thrust a coffee at him. "The race just started. She won't get to this spot for at least fifteen minutes, though."

Nate nodded stiffly and took a swig of the coffee, burning his tongue. He ignored the pain and kept his eyes on the empty road.

"Look, Nate—" Dad cleared his throat.

Nate waited, shoulders tensed. He'd known it was too good to believe that Dad would let him stay indefinitely. He'd probably been waiting to get Nate alone so he could tell him to get lost.

"I wanted to apologize—"

"Wait, Dad, before—" Nate stopped as Dad's words registered. "What?"

"For what I said when I picked you up that day. About wishing you weren't—"

"Born?" Nate said the word without a hint of resentment. "No problem. I've wished it plenty of times myself." He stuffed his left hand in his pocket and took another sip of the scalding coffee.

"I don't wish that." Dad's voice was low. "I was angry and hurt and holding onto that. You have to understand, I felt like I'd lost two children. Thinking about what you were going through in that place and what Kayla was going through out here—it was too much."

Nate kept his eyes on the route, even though no racers had appeared yet.

"I felt like I had failed to protect you. Both of you. Before all of this, I had such visions for the future for you and for Kayla, and in that one moment, they all came crashing down. It took me a long time to get to grips with the new future."

"And have you now?" Nate found that he really wanted to know. Because he wasn't quite sure he'd come to grips with it himself.

Dad's sigh was ragged. "I'm working on it, son." His hand fell on Nate's shoulder, and Nate didn't dare to move for a second. Then he pulled his hand out of his pocket and lifted it to cover Dad's.

A second later, the crowd around them broke into cheers, and Nate leaned to see past the tall guy who'd stepped into his line of sight. A group of wheelchairs rounded the corner. Nate squinted into the sun, trying to make out Kayla.

"There she is." Dad pointed.

With her neon pink helmet decorated with a purple cross, Kayla was easy to pick out leading the pack.

"Go Kayla. Push it." Nate screamed like he used to scream at her cross-country meets. He'd never been prouder of his little sister, not even when she took the state championship.

When the wheelchairs were past, they followed the crowd toward the finish line so they could catch the end of the race as well.

They met up with Mom halfway there, and Nate found himself comfortably walking between his parents for the first time in nearly a decade. He'd expected it to feel strange to be home again. But nothing felt more normal or more right.

They spent the next hour talking comfortably as they waited for the racers to reach them.

"Oh, Nate." Dad dropped the comment casually during a lull in the conversation. "I almost forgot. Your friend sent in her lease renewal yesterday. She included a very nice letter thanking me."

A wave of simultaneous relief and regret washed over Nate. He was glad Violet was going to be able to keep her store. He only wished things could have been different and he could be there with her.

NOT UNTIL YOU

"She sent a note for you, too." Dad pulled a crumpled piece of paper out of his jacket pocket. He gave Nate a look as he passed him the paper but didn't say anything else.

Nate smoothed the paper on his leg, then tried to read it discreetly, painfully aware of both of his parents watching him.

Dear Nate,

I just wanted to say thank you for what you did to save the store. If it weren't for you, I would have given up a long time ago. The thing is, I used to look at the store as a way to hold onto my past. But now I see it as a way to move into the future. And because of you, I'm ready for that future, whatever it brings.

One thing I didn't get to tell you before you left was that I forgive you. I saw how deeply what happened scarred you and how sorry you were for it. So I want you to know that I don't hold your past against you—and neither does Jesus, just in case you were wondering.

Nate closed his eyes and dropped his hand to his side. For her to say that, after everything. He didn't know what to do with it except cherish it.

After a second, he lifted the letter again, greedy for every single word she had to say to him.

I noticed that your letter came from Wescott. I hope that means that you've gone home to your family and that you've found peace with them. If you ever decide to come back to Hope Springs, I'll be here. And if you don't, I wish you every blessing.

Love,

Violet

Nate reread the last two words. *Love?* As in *love?*

"Is this the same Violet you've been telling Kayla about?" Mom leaned her shoulder into him.

So much for secrets between siblings. But he laughed. "Yeah, it is."

Mom looked like she was about to say something else, but the crowd sent up a roar, and cowbells clanged all around them. Nate's heart leaped as his eyes searched the course. Kayla was still in the lead, but a guy with a green helmet was close to pulling ahead of her. He shoved to the front of the crowd, his parents right behind him. All three of them screamed for her. As she pulled even with them, she shot them the same triumphant smile she'd worn before she'd taken the state cross-country championship. Nate's heart lifted. Despite all that had changed, despite the wheelchair, his little sister was the same Kayla. She had this.

Her wheelchair crossed the finish line a fraction of an inch ahead of the other guy's.

Nate jumped up and down and pumped a fist into the air. He spun to hug Mom. After he let her go, he hesitated a second, then hugged Dad, too. Dad clapped him on the back.

The three of them hovered together as Kayla was presented her medal and gave a few interviews. Nate had been the center of attention once, the cameras and interviews directed at him.

But seeing his sister beam in the spotlight, he didn't miss it at all. What he had now was so much more precious than that.

Finally, Kayla made her way over to them.

"Why don't you guys go get the car?" Kayla told their parents. "Nate and I will wait here." She led Nate to a picnic table in the park where the race had ended.

"So—" Kayla pulled up next to the table as Nate sat on top of it. "I see you got Violet's letter." She gestured to the piece of paper he'd pulled in and out of his pocket a dozen times since reading it.

"Good to know some things are private around here." Nate ruffled her hair in the way she'd hated when they were kids.

But she ignored it. "And?"

"And nothing. That's over now. I messed everything up pretty big."

"Doesn't sound over, judging by the letter. It sounds very much like she wants you to come back."

Nate shook his head. That didn't matter. Even if Violet thought she wanted him in her life, she was better off without him. And anyway, he'd already decided what he was going to do with his future.

"I'm going to stay here. With you." Nate folded the letter and tucked it into his back pocket, as if he were putting thoughts of Violet away forever. As if that were possible.

"And do what? Babysit me? In case you haven't noticed, I'm pretty capable." She held up her medal.

"I did notice. And congratulations." Nate shoved her shoulder.

"Well, then don't use me as an excuse to hide out here."

"It wouldn't be right." Nate scanned the street for Mom and Dad's van. He was ready for this conversation to be over.

"Wouldn't be right how?" Now Kayla's persistence was downright annoying.

"I'm not going to leave you here. Like this." He gestured to her wheelchair. "While I go off and have a relationship. A life."

The glare she shot him made him look away. "You don't think I can have a life?"

"No, of course not. That's not what I meant. But—"

"Because I'll have you know I have a very full life. And a relationship, too."

Nate spun toward her, suddenly finding himself in protective-big-brother mode. "What relationship? With that guy in the picture? Why haven't I met him?"

Kayla played with her hands. "Well, *had* a relationship."

Nate's shoulders tightened. When he found the monster who had hurt his sister, he would rip his face off.

"Relax." Kayla smirked at him. "I'm the one who broke it off. Garrett was a good guy, but I wanted to focus more on my racing and my ministry right now. Maybe someday I'll be ready for a serious relationship but not yet."

Nate exhaled.

"You have to stop defining me by my disability, Nate. I can have just as full and rich a life as anyone. I'm not dead. Now you need to stop living like you are."

Nate stared at his little sister. When had she grown so wise?

"Go back to Violet." Kayla gave his leg a double pat, then wheeled her chair away from the table. "Have a life with her. I promise I'll be fine. I'll even come to visit."

Chapter 45

When the bus finally pulled into the Hope Springs station, relief filled Nate.

He was home.

Despite the assurances of Violet's letter, a flurry of nerves worked through him. Did she really want to see him again? Or was that only something she'd written, knowing he was hundreds of miles away? And what about everyone else? Would they welcome him back now that they knew who he really was?

There was only one way to find out.

Nate squared his shoulders, grabbed the two suitcases he'd brought with him this time—his parents had promised to ship the rest of the stuff he'd spent the past two days packing—and set off through the dark to Hope Street.

The moment he walked into the building, all the memories from the past three months bubbled up, and he couldn't wait another second to see her. He charged up the stairs and knocked on her door.

No answer. He tried not to be crushed by the disappointment. It was Saturday night. She was probably at Sophie's or Dan's or whoever had invited everyone over this weekend.

He dragged his suitcases into his own apartment, which looked the same as when he'd left—except the dog kennel was missing. A pang hit him at the realization of all he'd walked away from. He paced the empty apartment for a few minutes, but if he stayed here all night, he'd go crazy.

Without pausing to consider where he'd go, he made his way down the hill toward the beach and the rocky outcrop that had become his favorite thinking spot.

His breath puffed in front of his face in the cool evening air as he crunched across the seashells. The moon was full tonight, casting a white glow on top of the water, and he watched the waves as he walked, letting their monotonous back and forth motion lull him.

He was almost to the rocks when he heard wild footsteps scrabbling over the shells, followed by happy barking.

Nate's head swung toward the sound, and he squatted just in time for Tony to barrel into him. As the dog planted joyful kisses on his cheek, Nate searched the dark.

The moment his eyes fell on her, a tsunami of hope slammed into him. Violet followed Tony, her footsteps barely making a sound. The moonlight bounced off her dark hair and lit the soft smile on her lips. Nate caught his breath as his eyes met hers. There was a trace of uncertainty there but also hope.

He straightened as she reached him.

"Violet?" his voice was barely a whisper, lighter even than the breeze that played with the tendril of hair on her face.

But somehow she heard him. "Nate."

They looked at each other a beat longer.

Then she stepped into his arms.

Without thinking, Nate pulled her tight against his chest. She felt right in his embrace. He never wanted to let go.

He moved his hands to her cheeks, which were red with the cold. "What are you doing out here?" He stepped back to pull off his sweatshirt and passed it to her.

She pressed her face into it for a second, then put it on. Nate's heart almost burst at the familiar movement.

"I've been coming out here to think. And pray." Violet hid her hands in the sleeves of his sweatshirt.

He brushed a curl off her cheek and tucked it behind her ear. "It's a good spot for that."

He couldn't take his eyes off her lips. He wanted more than anything to kiss her right now.

But first he had to say something.

He took a step back so he'd have a clear head. Or at least clearer.

The hope in her eyes dimmed a little, and he almost stepped forward to take her hands again. But he had to do this first. "There's something I have to say. And I don't want you to stop me. Okay?"

She bit her lip but nodded.

"First, I want to say again how sorry I am that I didn't tell you everything sooner. Not telling you was as good as lying to you. And I don't ever want to do that." He swallowed. "Lie to you I mean."

Violet opened her mouth as if she was going to answer, but he raised a hand, pressing on. "I know you already said you forgive me for that, and I believe you. And—" He took half a step closer. "Thank you. You don't know what that means to me."

He gazed out to the lake, where the waves continued to roll in. "And thank you for reminding me of God's forgiveness. I tried to push it away for a long time. But you and Dan—and even my family—have helped me see that I don't get to decide what God forgives. Jesus did that for me."

Violet raised a hand to rub a finger gently under each eye.

Nate wanted to gather her to him, but he had more to say. "And I'm sorry that I ran away from you. I know you feel like so many people in your life have left you, either on purpose or because of circumstances they couldn't control. I never wanted to be one of those people."

She was crying openly now, and Nate moved closer but didn't let himself touch her, no matter how badly he ached to wrap her in his arms. That had to be her choice.

"And I want you to know that I'll never be one of those people again. I'm here to stay." His eyes locked on hers. "If you want me to."

With a choked cry, she stepped forward. And that's all it took. His arms went around her, and he cupped his hand against the back of her head.

She nestled closer, and Nate sighed.

Somehow, through all the horrible things that had happened, through everything he'd been through and put others through, God had brought him to this point. To this perfect place with this perfect woman.

After a few minutes, she lifted her head, and her eyes landed on his.

NOT UNTIL YOU

He brought his head down slowly, watching every change in her expression. Surprise. Joy. Hope. Love.

He felt all of it echo in his own heart.

He let go of everything except this moment and pressed his lips to hers.

When they finally pulled apart, they whispered the words at the same time: "I love you."

Epilogue

Nerves surged through Violet's whole body as the lights in the sanctuary dimmed. Nate stepped to the front of the church with the rest of the worship band. Down the row, all their friends were applauding and cheering. To Violet's left, Kayla was leaning forward in her wheelchair, an expression of sheer glee on her face. Violet knew the feeling. Nate had been playing with the church worship band for six months now, but this was their first concert. Violet was overcome with a mix of awe and joy and amazement at what God had done in Nate's life. And in hers.

If anyone had told her when he moved in across the hall last summer that she'd soon find herself looking forward to every moment with him, she'd have called them crazy. Not only because he wasn't the friendliest new neighbor of all time. But even more so because she hadn't thought she could ever love another man the way she'd loved Cade.

But, then, she didn't love Nate in exactly the same way she'd loved Cade.

Her love for Nate was just as strong, but her relationship with him was different than her relationship with Cade had been. Where she and Cade had grown up together and knew everything about each other, she was still learning new things about Nate every day. And where she and Cade had matching outgoing personalities, Nate was much quieter and more reserved. Where her love for Cade had been youthful and exuberant, her love for Nate was more mature—quieter but no less certain.

Nate's eyes met hers as the opening chords of a praise song rang through the church. Violet kept her eyes on his as she broke into the chorus with the rest of the audience. She wondered if anyone else in the crowd sensed the energy that pulsed between them as they praised their God together—the God who had given them both a second chance.

Halfway through the concert, Kayla leaned over to give her a hug. Violet squeezed back. Nate's little sister had only arrived for a visit the day before, but already Violet loved her.

"He's always been good," Kayla said into her ear. "But there's something different about him now. It's like he's—" She gestured as if searching for the right word. "Real now, I guess."

Violet nodded. She could feel it. In everything he did, Nate made it clear that he'd experienced God's grace firsthand. And he wasn't going to hide that from anyone.

When the concert came to a close, Violet was exhausted but in a good way, as if she'd poured everything she had into worshiping her Creator. The band waved to the cheering crowd and then exited the church.

All except Nate.

A lone spotlight picked him out on the piano bench.

The audience fell silent again as soft chords floated up from the Bosendorfer Nate's father had purchased from her, then turned around and donated to the church.

Nate's voice picked up the melody of a song she'd never heard.

I thought my life was over,
Thought that I was done
Planned to live out my days
Never knowing the warmth, the warmth of the Son.

But then you opened up my eyes
Told me I was blind but now could see
That you had more in store
That you had plans, that you had plans for me.

Violet closed her eyes, swallowing against the lump in her throat. She knew Nate had written the song based on his own experiences, but it seemed he'd taken the words right from her soul. When Cade died, she'd thought her life was over. But God had used Nate to show her that he wasn't done with her yet.

And so today I thank you
For the life you've given me
It's a life I don't deserve.
It's a life that makes me, a life that makes me free.

Violet swiped at the tears on her cheeks, noticing that most of their friends were doing so as well.

A few minutes later, Nate was at her side, pulling her into a hug.

"Hey, it wasn't that bad, was it?" He dropped a kiss on her forehead.

She shook her head. "That good, actually. These are good tears."

He smiled as he wiped away a teardrop she'd missed. "They're cute on you. I'll have to try to make you cry some more of those sometime."

As if that was some sort of cue, all their friends gathered up their coats and bags.

"Anyone want to grab a bite at the Hidden Cafe?" Sophie slipped her arm into her jacket.

"We'll be there in a little bit." Nate pressed another kiss to Violet's head. "I just have to clean up first, or it's going to be a mess for worship tomorrow morning."

"We can give Kayla a ride over there." Sophie rested a hand on the back of Kayla's wheelchair. Kayla giggled, and Violet could have sworn the younger woman winked at Sophie.

Nate gave his sister a stern look, and she tried to straighten her lips for a second before they tipped into a smile again.

"Yeah, get out of here." Nate shooed her away.

"Maybe I should go along." Violet started to follow. She didn't want Kayla to be uncomfortable sitting at the restaurant with a group of people she'd only met a couple of hours ago.

Nate grabbed her hand and tugged her toward him. "One thing about my little sister. She can handle things just fine on her own."

He lifted Violet's hand to his lips and brushed a light kiss onto her knuckles. "Anyway, I'll get lonely here if you go without me."

She laughed at him. "You'll have the rest of the band." Except the front of the church was empty. She swiveled to search the sanctuary, but that had cleared out, too. Even their friends had disappeared. "Where'd everyone go?"

"It's just us." Nate tugged her toward the piano, which gleamed in the single spotlight that still shone on it. "Come here."

She tilted her head but let him pull her onto the piano bench with him.

"Do you remember when you asked if I'd teach you to play?"

She nodded. Why was he bringing this up now? When they had a whole church to clean up, all by themselves apparently?

"I thought this could be the first song I teach you." He positioned his hands on the keys and started to play. After a couple of notes, Violet recognized the melody as "Canon in D."

Nate played a little more of the song, and then his hands stilled, and he turned to her with a soft smile she couldn't quite read.

She did want to learn the piano, and she was sure he was a good teacher, but—

"That sounded kind of complicated. Shouldn't I start with 'Hot Cross Buns' or something?"

Nate smiled gently and swept up both of her hands in his, holding them to his heart. "Maybe. But I think that would be an odd song to play at our wedding."

"Our—" The electricity of the word traveled through her whole body.

Nate took one of his hands away from hers and reached behind a piece of sheet music, pulling out the saucer she'd given him from Barney and Gladys's set. A small black box sat in the center of it.

His face swam in her vision as her eyes filled, but she was pretty sure he was smiling.

"Are those good tears?" He lifted his hand to wipe one that had fallen onto her cheek.

She sniffed and half laughed. "Very good."

"In that case—" He slid off the piano bench, pulling her to the edge of the seat. Then he bent slowly to one knee, releasing her hands so he could open the ring box and hold it out to her.

"Violet, you helped me find my life again. And now I know that it won't be complete without you. Will you marry me?"

Violet's eyes traveled from the simple solitaire to her finger, where the white band that had once stood out so starkly had faded. Was she ready to put a new ring in that spot?

But she already knew.

She held out her hand to him and let him slip the ring onto it.

Before she could admire it, Nate had gathered her in his arms, almost crushing her with the force of his hug. "You are an amazing woman, Violet. Do you know that?"

Violet shook her head, raising her eyes to meet his. "You said I helped you find your life. But the truth is, you gave me mine back. I was holding onto a past that could never be again. I didn't think I had a future."

She lifted a hand to his face, ran it over the rough stubble on his cheek. "I didn't think my heart would ever be whole again."

Nate dropped his forehead to hers, his breath a whisper on her lips.

"Neither did I," he said. "Not until you."

Thanks for reading books 1-3 in the Hope Spring series! I hope you loved meeting Sophie and Spencer, Jared and Peyton, and Nate and Vi! Catch up with them and the rest of your Hope Springs friends in the HOPE SPRINGS BOOKS 4-6 BOX SET.

Not Until Us: Everyone knows former bad girl Jade and local pastor Dan don't belong together. Jade knows. That's why she left eight years ago. Dan knows. That's why he tries to protect his heart by avoiding her now that she's back. But when what they know and what they feel are two different things, can they trust God to give them a second chance?

Not Until Christmas Morning: Leah is a fixer. It's why she's fostering a troubled teen. And why she wants to help her wounded warrior neighbor, Austin. But what if Austin is too broken for her to fix? Can they turn to God for healing and hope—and maybe a chance at love—this Christmas?

NOT UNTIL YOU

Not Until This Day: Isabel has three simple rules: Keep moving. No friends. No men. It's the only way to keep herself and her daughter safe. But when she moves to Hope Springs, she suddenly wants to break all the rules. Especially when it comes to sweet single dad Tyler... Can she let go of her fears and trust God to give them a future?

Continue reading the HOPE SPRINGS SERIES today!

And be sure to sign up for my newsletter, where we chat about life, faith, and of course books! You'll also get Ethan and Ariana's story (available exclusively to subscribers) FREE.

Visit www.valeriembodden.com/gift to join!

If you enjoyed the HOPE SPRINGS BOOKS 1–3 BOX SET, would you let others know by posting a short review? Your review is a blessing to me as it helps other readers find the book. And it lets me know what you love and want to see more of. Thanks so much!

Read on for an excerpt of the next Hope Springs story, Not Until Us...

A preview of Not Until Us

How had she messed up again?

Jade swiped at her cheeks as she slid the key into the lock of her apartment door. If the God her roommate Keira kept telling her about had any decency, Keira would still be in bed. She wasn't in the mood to be reprimanded by her squeaky clean friend right now. She already knew last night had been a mistake.

One she'd made far too many times.

She inched the door open slowly but let out a frustrated breath as her eyes fell on her roommate, perky as ever, sitting on the couch with some kind of kale-soy-banana-protein drink in hand.

Apparently God didn't have any decency. Or he had one wicked sense of humor.

"Good morning." Keira eyed Jade's clothes—the same ones she'd been wearing when she'd left for work last night.

Jade held up a hand. "Don't say it."

"Say what?" Keira took a long sip of her drink, still watching Jade.

"Fine. I screwed up. Again." She tried to sound defiant, but even as the words came out, a bone-crushing weariness descended on her. She was trying to be a better person. She really was. But old habits were hard to break. Last night had been just one more name to add to her list of lifelong mistakes. Or it would be if she knew his name.

She buried her face in her hands. She was an awful person. "I don't know why I keep doing this." When the guy had walked into the bar, she'd told herself to ignore him. But she'd been bored. And he'd had nice eyes and witty banter. Plus, he was only passing through town on business. There was no chance things would get messy or complicated. He'd go on his way, she'd go on hers, and neither of them would worry about it again.

Besides, he'd practically challenged her to go back to his hotel room with him. What was she supposed to do?

Walk away. The voice in her head sounded an awful lot like her big sister Violet. Not that Violet had any idea what Jade's life was like, aside from the sanitized version Jade fed her on their weekly phone calls.

Keira crossed the small space and pulled Jade's hands away from her face, holding the protein drink out to her. Jade wrinkled her nose and pushed it away. After eight years in Los Angeles, she still had no interest in the stuff that passed for breakfast around here. Give her a donut and a strong cup of coffee any day.

"Change is hard." Keira wrapped an arm over her shoulder and steered her to the couch. "You should pray about it."

Jade shook her head. If there was anything she was less interested in than protein shakes, it was prayer. "I need to pack. My plane leaves in a couple hours."

She still wasn't sure what had compelled her to give in to her sister's pleas that she spend the summer in Hope Springs. But maybe it would do her some good to get away from this town of broken dreams for a while.

Besides, the way Violet talked about Hope Springs made Jade almost homesick for it.

Almost.

Mostly, though, she was going because she owed it to Vi. After six years of completely cutting her sister out of her life, Jade didn't deserve the second chance Vi had given her. The phone calls they'd been exchanging for the past couple years weren't enough. The least she could do was spend the summer helping her sister finalize plans for her wedding.

"Well, look at it this way." Keira sucked down the last of her shake. "Maybe you'll meet a nice, wholesome man in Hope Springs, and you'll get married and live happily ever after."

Jade snickered. "You read too many small town romances. Trust me, there's no one in Hope Springs I'd consider dating, let alone marrying. Besides—" She flopped onto the couch. "I'm not really the happily ever after kind of girl."

Keira tipped her head to the side, studying Jade. "Everyone's a happily ever after kind of girl. It just takes some of us longer to get there than others." She moved to the cramped kitchen to rinse out her glass.

Jade stared after her. Keira could dream about happily ever after all she wanted. But Jade knew the truth. There was no such thing. She'd learned that lesson early, and she wasn't going to forget it anytime soon.

More Hope Springs Books

While the books in the Hope Springs series are linked, each is a complete romance featuring a different couple and can be read in any order. Wondering whose story is whose? Here's a helpful list:

Not Until Christmas (Ethan & Ariana)

Not Until Forever (Sophie & Spencer)

Not Until This Moment (Jared & Peyton)

Not Until You (Nate & Violet)

Not Until Us (Dan & Jade)

Not Until Christmas Morning (Leah & Austin)

Not Until This Day (Tyler & Isabel)

Not Until Someday (Grace & Levi)

Not Until Now (Cam & Kayla)

VALERIE M. BODDEN

And Don't Miss the River Falls Series

Pieces of Forever (Joseph & Ava)

Want to know when my next book releases?

You can follow me on Amazon to be the first to know when my next book releases! Just visit amazon.com/author/valeriembodden and click the follow button.

Acknowledgements

What a blessing that I never run out of people to thank in the acknowledgements section of my books. First, of course, thank you to my perfect heavenly Father, the source of all love. As his Word tell us, "We love because he first loved us" (1 John 4:19).

And speaking of love, I thank the love of my life, my husband Josh, for his continued support and love. If it weren't for him, I might still be dreaming about writing and publishing novels instead of taking the leap into doing it. I'm so grateful for the life God has given us together—and for the four children he has blessed us with. This mama is so thankful to have kiddos who cheer her on and support her. And thanks to my parents, in-laws, and extended family, who support my books by asking about them, reading them, and spreading the word.

A heartfelt thank you also goes out to my amazing Advance Reader Team. If I named all the people who have contributed their thoughts and feedback on the three books in this volume, the list would go on for another two pages! So let me just say that I'm so grateful for all of you. It's been wonderful to get to know you and to consider you friends. Thank you for sharing your honest thoughts on my books, brainstorming with me when needed, and giving so generously of yourselves to encourage me.

VALERIE M. BODDEN

My acknowledgements wouldn't be complete if I didn't say thank you to you as well, my wonderful reader friends! Thanks for coming along with me on this journey. I pray that you may be blessed through this book and encouraged in your walk of faith.

God's richest blessings to you!

About the Author

Valerie M. Bodden has three great loves: Jesus, her family, and books. And chocolate (okay, four great loves). She is living out her happily ever after with her high-school-sweetheart-turned-husband and their four children. Her life wouldn't make a terribly exciting book, as it has a happy beginning and middle, and someday when she goes to her heavenly home, it will have a happy end.

She was born and raised in Wisconsin, and aside from a short stint in Minnesota while her husband trained for the pastoral ministry, has lived there her entire life, in spite of an aversion to all things cold and snowy (except Christmas—a snowy Christmas is good). She periodically tries to coax her snow-loving husband and children to pack up and move to a warmer climate with her but so far has had no luck. So she tolerates the snow for them. That's some kind of love, if you ask her.

Valerie writes emotion-filled Christian fiction that weaves real-life problems, real-life people, and real-life faith. Her characters may (okay, will) experience some heartache along the way, but true to her tendencies as a hopeless romantic, she will always give them a happy ending.

Feel free to stop by www.valeriembodden.com to say hi. She loves visitors! And while you're there, you can sign up for your free short story.